MURPHY'S LAW

# UNFORGETTABLE

## GRACE TURNER

Cover Art: Mayhem Cover Creations

# CONTENTS

*I honestly think Halestorm said it best:*

*"Two is better than one, three is better than two"*

*Do Not Disturb, Halestorm*

# CONTENT NOTE

This book is intended for adults and contains sexual situations. This book also contains some violence and drug-related content.

Otherwise, it's mostly really entertaining, steamy good times. I also recommend first reading book one, *Unexpected*, if you haven't already. Not only because I think you will enjoy it, but also because there will be spoilers.

But you do you!

# ONE

Amanda

Apparently, dealing with stupidity was something akin to a superpower.

Before the rehearsal dinner began, my best friend, Hazel, her sister, and her mom all praised my ability to deal with Hazel's wedding planner, which renewed my determination to bear with her relentless questions and ridiculous tasks. If it was such a superpower, I at least deserved a fucking cape.

I reminded myself, as I recounted the printed menus for the umpteenth time, that Hazel's happiness—well, and Luke's—was most important. As long as their wedding went off without a hitch, then I could stand Bridget and her madness.

"I swear I counted one hundred and sixty-five. How many did you get this time? There should be one hundred and eighty," she asked, then laid the sixth stack of thirty navy-blue menus down on the table. Hazel had designed them herself—navy-blue cardstock with gold calligraphy that listed the dinner options. They were beautiful, but I was sick of counting them.

"Actually, Bridget, they've multiplied. There are now two hundred of them. They're like gremlins, but instead of eating after midnight making them multiply, they multiply every time I touch them."

Bridget whipped her head toward me. Her perfectly styled and colored deep-brown hair flung over her shoulder, and her brows furrowed in the center as her mouth gaped.

"That's not even possible. You're kidding, right?"

I shrugged, straightened the stacks of menus for the last damn time, and brushed past her. "I thought a stupid question deserved a stupid answer. Now, I'm getting a drink and enjoying the party," I said, my sharp tongue getting the better of me, but I could see the finish line, and my patience with the wedding planner was completely gone. So much for dealing with stupid.

I'd still work with her to ensure the wedding day went flawlessly, as was my job as maid of honor, but I couldn't continue to hold my tongue.

I stepped out of the storage room and into the rehearsal space that was crowded with Hazel and Luke's closest friends and family. The actual dinner portion of the rehearsal was over, but the party had only just begun.

We hadn't found it necessary to hire a DJ for both the rehearsal dinner and the wedding day, so I'd curated a playlist for the dinner. The music played at a decent volume on the speakers positioned throughout the space. My phone was plugged into the main sound system behind the bar, and I squeezed past one of the bartenders to check the playlist.

There were still plenty of songs that hadn't yet played, so I set my phone back on the shelf.

"Could I have a double gin and tonic, please? With two limes," I asked one of the bartenders, not even attempting to go around the bar like all the other guests. The maid of honor should get at least a few perks anyway.

While the bartender pulled the gin from below the counter, I spotted Hazel beelining for me. Her ethereal white dress flowed behind her and fluttered around her shoeless feet. She was a glowing bride, and I don't think the smile on her face had fallen for even a minute in the past few days.

Delilah, her sister and matron of honor, and I had done our best to make sure there wasn't a reason for Hazel to be unhappy.

"I think it's going well, right? And this music is perfect, Amanda. Everything is amazing," Hazel said as she pressed up to the bar.

"Everything's perfect. We still have a little over an hour and a half until we officially have to get the hell out, so mingle and dance and drink and whatever else you wanna do," I instructed.

She bounced lightly on her feet and leaned over the bar top, gripped my face, and kissed my cheek.

"You, too!" she shouted over the music. "You've done enough work, so it's time to enjoy it."

I didn't argue because arguing with the bride was explicitly off-limits the day before her wedding. So, I just nodded and watched as Luke wrapped his arms around his bride's waist and pressed a kiss to her neck.

He smiled at me, winked, and then pulled her back into the crowd of people.

They were hopelessly in love and perfect for each other, which was all I could have ever wanted for two of my best friends and two of the best people I had ever known. After all they'd been through with their terrible past relationships and near-death experiences, they deserved a happily ever after.

But I couldn't help the twinge of jealousy at watching them live their fairy tale. Maybe it was more than just a twinge because when the bartender finally handed me my drink, I chugged it like a frat guy trying to impress a half-dressed sorority girl.

The bartender watched me with wide eyes, but I smiled at him sweetly as I pushed the empty glass back to him and requested another.

He only shook his head a little before he began making me another, and that was when a shot of hope zipped through me. I wasn't completely alone—I had brought a date. But I hadn't seen him since Bridget frantically told me that menus had gone missing and requested my immediate help.

I stood on my toes—which was all the more difficult in my heels—and scanned the crowd of people for the tall man with messy brown hair.

Technically, we had only been on a few dates, but it seemed like our connection was growing, which was promising and, honestly, something I had all but given up on.

Since my ex-boyfriend, Tyler, and I had broken up for the last time—because there had been several prior breakups that didn't stick—only once had I found any sort of connection with anyone. But that time had just so happened to be during a threesome with two of my best friends and was a time we hadn't necessarily discussed afterward. I couldn't lie and pretend that it wasn't placed securely in the top three best nights of my life, but it was a line that shouldn't have been crossed in the first place. Which meant I tried to keep it as far from my thoughts as I could, and that took more self-control than I would have liked to admit.

And even given my best attempts to leave it in the past and forget the entire hot summer night, I had been chasing a similar connection at every turn. But everyone, and I seriously meant everyone, had come up not just short but miles from what I'd felt that one drunken and chaotic night.

But when I met Justin, there was more than nothing, which was better than what I'd become accustomed to.

The bartender slid the new drink to me and watched me carefully for a moment, probably curious if he'd have to make the same drink three times in a row. But I knew better, and if I downed another double, I'd be feeling rough in the morning. So, I pulled a few bucks out of my bra stash and put it in the tip jar, much to the bartender's delight, before I continued my search for my date by weaving in and out through the crowd.

Everyone appeared more than content with the food, drinks,

and music, which made me smile since I'd put in so much time and effort to ensure the evening went smoothly.

"Amanda!" I heard my name shouted over the music by an out-of-breath voice and immediately knew who it was. I turned to my right and, sure enough, spotted a heavily pregnant Delilah waddling toward me. She gave one of Luke's old friends a death glare when he almost ran her over, so I met her halfway in a quieter corner of the room.

"Bridget's looking for you," she said, leaning against the white shiplap wall and rubbing her swollen stomach. She was nearly eight months pregnant but wasn't going to miss her sister's wedding for anything.

My mood immediately soured at the mention of Bridget, and my face dropped. "Are you serious? I was just with her counting those damn menus for the millionth time. I swear she has—"

A cruel, delightful smile crossed Delilah's face, and I muttered a few choice words under my breath. "You're kidding, aren't you?"

She smiled wider and threw her head back, laughing. "Yeah, I'm kidding."

I playfully slapped her arm and scoffed before taking a long sip of my drink, enjoying the way the liquor burned the back of my throat.

"That's seriously not anything to joke about. You better be glad you're pregnant. If I never have to speak to that woman again, it would be too soon."

"You're right, I'm a little sorry. But I can't drink, so I need some form of entertainment. Anyway, who were you looking for?" she asked but then sucked in a deep breath because that was a lot of words all in a row for someone who could hardly breathe anyway.

"I was looking for my date."

"Oh, I saw him walk into the main hallway through those doors. Probably looking for the bathroom?"

The hallway she was referring to led out into the larger

wedding venue. If you followed it all the way to the end, then you'd run into the grand room Hazel and Luke had chosen for their wedding reception the following day. And even farther beyond that room and out several pairs of French doors was the outdoor space that overlooked a lake where they'd have their sunset ceremony.

It was all very elegant but had touches of each of their personalities, and it was obvious that Hazel's parents spared no expense. As Hazel's mom had explained, they were over the moon about the love their youngest daughter had found and wanted to celebrate it.

It was a sweet sentiment, while it also made me want to gag.

"Okay, thanks. Now, sit down, and I'll see you later."

Begrudgingly, Delilah allowed me to lead her to a table nearby where our friends, James and Devon, were talking with Hazel's previous coworker. "Watch the pregnant woman, please," I asked them, and they both welcomed her into their conversation. I knew if Delilah didn't sit as much as she could during the dinner and the following morning, there was no way she was going to stand the entire ceremony.

With Delilah left in the best possible hands, I followed the perimeter of the room and slipped out of the side door without anyone spotting me.

The hallway was dark and quiet, but the music beating behind the door echoed through the large space. The dark wood floors that ran the length of the hallway and the white-painted wainscotting didn't do much to absorb the sound. Without the liquor warming my insides, the silent and faintly lit corridor may have been slightly eerie.

If Justin had been looking for the bathroom as Delilah suggested, it wasn't that hard to find, only two doors down from the room we'd been using and with a large sign just above the door. I headed in that direction, taking another long swig of my drink and contemplating whether I should push the door open to see if he was actually in there or be patient and wait for him to come out.

I decided on the latter until a thought crossed my mind, which involved pushing the door open and jumping his very tall bones for a quickie before we had to get back. We'd slept together once on our third date, and while it was... decent, there were still things that could be improved upon with a little practice. Hopefully. Actually, he'd likely need an intensive boot camp to get up to par.

I knew what I liked in the bedroom, and after doing a lot of exploring, I craved someone who could keep up. But finding a partner that met most, if not all, of my needs was a tiresome task.

Without my consent, a memory of Josh beneath me and Reed at my back overwhelmed me. It was one of my favorite positions my two best friends had put me in that night, and the desire I'd felt only seconds before was suddenly roaring through me.

I quickened my steps, hoping like hell that Justin was in the bathroom, when a door closing farther down the hall caught my attention. My brain said it was nothing, just someone who worked at the venue, maybe, but my gut told me to follow the sound.

I decided to investigate further and stop back by the bathroom if it turned out to be nothing.

My heels clicked loudly on the wood floor and echoed off the walls as I hurried down the hallway and farther from the thumping music I'd left behind. The grand doors leading into the reception space with its exquisite chandeliers and already perfectly decorated tables were directly in front of me, but around the corner and to my right, through a door that led to a smaller room, were hushed voices and the faint sounds of laughter.

For such a beautifully built building, the walls were oddly thin, and the wooden door didn't do much to muffle the sounds either.

I stopped before I rounded the corner, so if anyone were to appear from around it, I could feign surprise. There was more laughing and then the sound of something large—likely a table —being moved. I inched a hair closer to the corner and strained to hear any further sounds.

"What are you doing?" a hushed voice whispered directly in my ear. So close to me that their breath tickled my neck, and I all but screamed.

With a loud gasp that nearly turned into a yelp, I turned on my heels as a good portion of my drink sloshed over the top of my glass and splattered onto the floor.

My heart thundered, and my pulse raced, but I looked up to find Reed looking down at me with a smug grin on his face. His ridiculously handsome face.

It took me a few seconds of deep, focused breaths to lower my heart rate and prepare to berate him. All the while, he stood in the dimly lit hallway, his hands casually tucked into the front pockets of his dark jeans and his fitted black jacket open to show off the crisp lines of his tailored white shirt that hugged his defined muscles.

His sharp jawline was dusted with dark stubble, and he'd styled his hair to look like he'd woken up with it perfectly tousled. His honey-colored eyes were alight with a playful spark which immediately pulled me from my unintentional examination.

"Did you have to scare the shit out of me, Reed? And you made me spill my drink," I angrily whispered to him.

He shrugged and opened his mouth to say something until a very loud moan interrupted us. Both of our eyebrows shot up as we peered around the corner in unison.

"Who the fuck is fucking?" Reed asked, and I shushed him quickly as we approached the door where I believed the sounds were emanating from. I leaned my ear against the wooden door, and the telltale sounds of slapping skin greeted me.

I sighed and rolled my shoulders back. "I think it's my date."

Like I knew it would, the revelation made Reed laugh, but I was thankful he at least pressed his hand against his mouth to muffle the sound. I backed away from the door as he stepped forward, resuming the same position with his ear against the wood. He nodded and turned to me as I finished the rest of my drink and hoped it helped. Of course it would be my luck that I would bring a date and he would end up fucking someone else.

"You know for sure it's him?"

I shook my head. "Not necessarily, but he was missing from the rehearsal. So I'm assuming…"

"Amanda, you know what happens when you assume—"

I threw daggers at him with my eyes, but he didn't flinch. "Don't test me right now, Gregory," I said, using his last name as I did when I was pissed. "You scared the shit out of me, made me spill my drink, and laughed when I said I think my date is screwing someone else. You're on thin ice, bud."

He scrubbed a hand over his mouth and down over his jaw to hide the smile I knew was there. He knew just what buttons to press to get a rise out of me, and like he always had, he seized every opportunity to do so. Quickly, he glanced between me and the door, and I saw the moment the idea fully formed in his head.

"You think he is, but you're not sure. So, let's find out."

And without another word, the shithead opened the damn door.

# TWO

### Amanda

My reaction was too late, and once I fully understood what Reed intended to do, the door was open, and my fear was realized.

Only a few feet from the door, and not hidden in any way, was my date with his pants around his ankles and his dick buried inside a cute brunette who had her legs draped over his shoulders. Her dress was only pushed up around her waist, but it was still a compromising position for both of them. I vaguely recognized the woman, but she wasn't who I was focused on either.

All motion and sound stopped when Reed flung the door open, and in an instant, their eyes went wide.

For a second, we all stood there. Justin was still inside the brunette, the brunette still gripped the edge of the table, Reed cocked his head to the side, and I let out a frustrated groan.

"Fuck, Amanda. I'm sor—"

"I swear to God, Justin, if you tell me you're sorry, I'm going to go full *Kill Bill* on your ass. Uma Thurman will have nothing on me," I seethed as I stepped into the room that was only lit by the emergency lights every several feet. "Why don't you remove yourself from that woman and just get the hell out?"

"Amanda, do you want to give them a minute to get dressed and then—" Reed started from behind me, still standing in the doorway.

"No," I said firmly, crossing my arms over my chest. "They didn't have a problem fucking in a public place. They shouldn't have a problem getting dressed in front of an audience."

"Fair enough," Reed said as he stepped into the room and propped the door open with the attached doorstop.

For a fleeting second, I was saddened knowing another one bit the dust. But it didn't last long as I watched him extract his dick from the woman, and then the two of them scrambled to right themselves. I knew I was lying to myself—there wasn't a future between us, and the loss wasn't enough to worry about. What hit me hardest was the fact that I had again invested time into a person that wasn't invested in me. More time wasted and with little to show for my efforts.

"Can I please explain, Amanda? I promise I have an explanation."

The alcohol in my system seemed to be on Justin's side because I was curious to know what bullshit he was going to throw my way. "Fine, you have a minute starting... now," I said, peering down at my wrist and my nonexistent watch.

The bored expression I was intentionally wearing quickly morphed into disbelief as Justin told his side of the story. "I promise this was not planned; I came here with you because I really liked you. But then I saw Christie. We actually dated in college and then decided to go our separate ways after graduation, and when I saw her here, it felt like fate had led us back to each other. I couldn't just dismiss the fact that we both ended up being invited to the same wedding of people neither of us knew. And then one thing led to another, and here we are..." He took a step forward, his arms outstretched and pleading, as I reflexively took a step back. "I didn't mean to hurt you. It was… it was fate."

His voice was sincere, but my give-a-shit meter was broken. "Fate is a fucker. Just leave."

"Amanda, could you—"

Reed stepped up beside me, and out of the corner of my eye, I watched him shake his head. "Anything you say is just going to make it worse, man. I'd leave now before she tears into you for real." Justin's eyes jumped between Reed and me for a moment before he sighed and asked the woman, Christie, if she was ready.

She nodded, threw Reed an apologetic look, and only when I heard her heels clicking against the wood in the hallway did I finally turn back around.

Christie was Reed's date. How fitting.

I opened my mouth, but Reed held up a finger, silencing me. He tapped the pointer finger of his other hand against his ear, and I listened to Christie's receding footsteps. When we could no longer hear her, Reed lowered his finger and waved at me to continue as he closed the door behind him.

"How in the world could this happen? Our dates knew each other from college and then proceeded to steal away to a quiet place to fuck? I swear, my life is a joke, and God has a twisted fucking sense of humor. This, right here, is proof God is a man because a woman would give me at least one win."

Reed stood in the near darkness, hands back in his pockets, and listened to me rant.

"How are you not more upset about this? Your date was a part of this, too, but you don't look like you care at all."

He shrugged and closed part of the distance between us as I leaned back against one of the other tables that they had not just been screwing on. The combination of alcohol, adrenaline, and anger made my hands shake and my heart beat mercilessly in my chest.

"She was only my date, a person to bring so I didn't have to come alone. It wasn't going to ever turn into anything serious, so there's no point in getting upset."

He had a point which irritated me even more.

"Did you see yourself having something long term with *him*?" The way he said it made it clear he didn't believe anything was going to come of it.

"Maybe," I said as my brain shouted, "*No!*" as loudly as it could.

Justin, along with everyone else I had dated recently, failed to measure up to my expectations, which I didn't think were unrealistically high. Justin's downfall, however, was mostly his lack of enthusiasm. His speech about fate was the most passionate he'd been since we'd begun hanging out. Which was unfortunate.

"You're lying," Reed said, taking another step closer.

Still annoyed that he could read me so well, I argued, "No, I'm not. You never know what the future holds. He could have been the one."

He laughed and took another step as my entire body tensed. The playful light I saw in his eyes before he ripped that damn door open was back, but behind it was something more. "You can't lie to me, Amanda. I know you too well for that shit."

I scoffed and tried to pretend like his proximity wasn't having any effect on my body. That it was only the combination —alcohol, anger, adrenaline—making my breath stutter and my skin prick with awareness. It was why I couldn't help but take a deep breath of his clean, manly scent. Like he had showered in the woods in a spring rainstorm.

That had to be the reason I found myself licking my lips and not hurrying away as he finally stepped close enough that I could reach out and touch him if I wanted to. Based on the look in his eyes, that's exactly what he wanted me to do, too.

"I watched you with him tonight, before, during, and after dinner, and there wasn't a lick of chemistry between the two of you. And see, I would have known." His voice had dropped into a deeper register, and as I had become familiar with when around the man in front of me, my body reacted to his voice without my say so. The deep timbre of it made me swallow against my suddenly dry mouth and tense as I prepared for him to continue.

"How would you have known?" I said in a small voice that clearly told him he was having his desired effect on me.

A smile crawled across his lips as he wet them with his tongue. "Because I know what you look like when there's chemistry. When someone's really getting to you, Amanda, your breathing becomes shallow, and the rise and fall of your chest quickens as it happens. Then, you bite your lip to keep the smile from crossing your face, and you adjust yourself in your chair because there's a pulsing between your legs. It's a needy pulse that you have no control over. And you can't maintain eye contact because the person looking at you intently and showing you how much they want you just with their eyes is too much for you. So, you avert your eyes, and if the person really knows you, then that's when they touch you." And so he does. Letting his fingers brush softly against the inside of my thigh, starting at my knee and trailing up my warm skin to the very short hem of my fitted, red dress.

"Which draws your attention back to them and keeps you there as goose bumps follow. Then a shiver makes its way down your spine, sending another jolt of desire where you wish someone would touch you most. But not just touch you, you want them to touch you like you crave to be touched."

It had been so long since I'd felt Reed's hands on me, and it was so overwhelming in the best possible way. His touch stoked a fire he had created inside of me, and I wanted his hands to burn me alive if it meant it never stopped.

"You've been watching me?" I commented for no other reason than I wanted something to say and wanted to continue pushing him. Even with more than a decade of friendship between us, the things he knew about me—like the way I reacted to pleasure or the way I liked to be touched—weren't something only friends knew.

"Of course I do. Don't act like you're surprised. You know what you've done to both me and Josh."

My eyes fluttered shut as Reed spread my legs apart and positioned himself between them, but at the mention of our one-time third, my eyes opened. There was nothing in Reed's eyes besides desire as a possessive hand clasped my face, and he pulled at my lower lip with his thumb. Eyeing it like he couldn't wait to devour it.

If I were stronger, I would have stopped his advances, but I was weak with him. Both he and Josh held some power over me that thankfully, neither of them had acted on since that one night.

"I know you've thought about it. Does it make you wet to know that we've thought about it, too? Sharing you was amazing, but I can't help but wonder what it would be like to have you all to myself."

I was lost to him, and the anticipation that had built over the past year and a half was nuclear.

There was no hesitation between either of us as Reed's mouth slammed over mine. Like the dam had broken, over a year's worth of pent-up desire wrapped in stolen glances and brief touches spilled over and culminated in that moment.

In seconds we were a mess of teeth and tongues and lips as my nails clawed at his soft hair and then shoved his jacket from his shoulders. As his jacket fell forgotten on the floor, I also let all hesitation be forgotten for at least that one moment. I wasn't going to think about the repercussions of sleeping with one of my best friends for a second time because it all felt too good.

His hands tangled in the waves of my blonde hair and tugged just enough to mix the pleasure of our kiss with the slight bite of pain at my scalp. It beckoned me to move quicker and get him closer.

With one hand still gripping my hair, his other pushed my

legs apart even farther as he dipped his hand beneath my dress. His fingers only lightly grazed my wet panties, but the careful touch combined with the intensity of his kiss made my hips lurch forward into his hand.

"*Fuck*, yes. I knew you'd be soaked." Before I registered what he was doing, he ripped my very expensive panties from my body and shoved them into his pocket. But I couldn't be upset because the entire thing was too damn hot and left me without a barrier between my wet heat and his fingers.

I had every intention of getting laid that night, hence the expensive lace panties Reed had decimated and the daringly short red dress. Except it wasn't Reed that I thought would be kissing me breathless and making me grind closer for some sort of relief. I thought I would have been coaxing Justin to grip me tighter and fuck me harder because I wouldn't break. And I was anything but mad about the change—it was like going to a car dealership expecting to buy a used Toyota Camry, but a billion-aire shows up before you sign the papers to buy you the fully loaded, top-of-the-line Maserati instead.

I had nothing against a Camry, but once you sat your ass on the luxurious leather seats of the high-end car and felt the purr of the engine, nothing would ever be the same.

Just as I remembered, his expert fingers circled my clit as I bit into his lower lip. With a growl, Reed wasted no time shoving two fingers inside of me and curling them to rub against my inner wall, finding the perfect spot on the first try.

He had some of the best fingers—long and perfectly thick. But there was something I wanted more, and I made my inten-tions known by fumbling with his belt and unbuttoning his jeans. In seconds, I had his pants tugged down just far enough that I could palm his hard length.

I pumped him up and down, spreading the bit of precum that was already dripping from the large head with my thumb. He was warm and heavy in my hand. My mouth watered as we both broke our kiss to watch my hand wrap around him while his fingers pumped in and out of me.

"Please tell me you have a condom," I pleaded, feeling my orgasm make itself known at the base of my spine.

Reed grinned and untwisted his fingers from my hair to fish out his wallet from his back pocket. With one hand, he flipped it open and grabbed one of the two condoms shoved inside.

A fleeting thought crossed my mind that he likely didn't put those condoms in his wallet thinking about me, and it deflated my mood for a moment until he did this thing with his fingers that had me panting for more. His thumb continued circling my clit as he handed the condom to me.

There was no way I wanted him to stop what he was doing for even a second, so I ripped the corner with my teeth and stretched the latex over the soft skin and thick veins of his impressive length.

With the condom on, Reed let go. He shoved his tongue inside my mouth, claiming me and devouring my eager sounds of pleasure that I forgot I was capable of, before pulling me from the table and flipping me over. My chest hit the cool table as Reed's hand twisted back into my hair and trapped me there. Behind me, he kicked my legs wider and pushed my dress higher. I could feel the denim of his jeans brush against my thighs as he positioned himself between them.

I expected him to immediately slam inside me when I was in position, with the need between us only intensifying each second. But instead, he smoothed his free hand over my ass in an almost adoring touch before he pushed my dress even higher to run his hand up the side of my hip and my stomach until he fingered the bottom of my black lace bra. His fingers traced the outline of my spine, trailing back down and the touch felt like he was memorizing the planes of my body and elicited goose bumps everywhere.

My hot breath fogged up the laminate table Reed was holding me captive against, but I wasn't complaining. I could feel his cock poised at my entrance and when I tried to push back, he tightened his hold on my hair, pushing me into the table even harder.

On the opposite side of my body, his fingers followed the same path, and when his hand traveled back down to my ass, I thought for a moment he'd start all over again. But I was pleasantly surprised by the sound of his hand cracking against my ass. I heard the sound only a split second before I felt the sting burn across my skin and the entirety of his cock slamming into me in one thrust.

The pleasure combined with the pain was overwhelming, and my eyes rolled shut as I moaned out my approval. He responded with his own gasp and subsequent groan. I was by no means a virgin, and I'd had plenty of sex, even recently, but the way Reed filled me was unique.

My body took a moment to adjust to his size, and while I did, his hand slapped against my skin again. He smoothed his hand over my already raw cheek and gripped my hip as he began thrusting into me at a relentless pace.

The room was filled with the sounds of skin slapping and our pleasure-filled moans and there wasn't anything besides the two of us together once again. I wanted to make it last and really be in the moment, but my head was already drowning in a pleasure-induced fog that wasn't helped by the alcohol from earlier.

Reed's palm flattened over my ass again and again, and each time, the walls of my pussy involuntarily clamped down around him, eliciting deep groans from him that radiated throughout my body. I knew he'd picked the position not just for ease of standing sex, given that we were in an empty banquet room, but for the fact that he had easy access to my ass. He was right—he knew me very well as a friend, but after only one night together in which he shared me with his best friend, he also knew what I wanted in bed better than nearly anyone.

"Yes, clench around me just like that. God, you take it so well." The low growl of his voice was like an accelerant to my flames. Reed's grip on my hair had loosened just enough that I could push against the table and find the balance I needed to be able to rock back against him.

A string of mumbled expletives tumbled from his lips as I met him thrust for thrust, impaling myself as hard as I could on his cock. Doggy style was one of my favorite positions, but I wanted to see Reed's face contorted in pleasure. Knowing he was a slave to the way I made him feel pushed me closer and closer to the edge that I was already tumbling toward.

His hands held my hips in a punishing grip that was sure to leave marks as he guided me back at the perfect pace. His hips ground upward into me, and each time he pressed deeper, grazing a part of me I knew would culminate in a powerful release. I was right there, too, just on the cusp of overwhelming pleasure.

While one of my hands kept me in position, braced against the table, my other found my sensitive clit and rubbed vigorously. My body's response was immediate, but only a second later, Reed's fingers moved from my hip to close around my neck. He pulled me up, my back pressed against his front and kept us locked together with his hand around my throat. His grip was tight enough to keep me in place without completely cutting off my air supply.

In heels, my head landed at his shoulder and underneath his chin. He pressed me into him, and I wished we were naked so I could feel his warm skin slick with sweat against my own.

With his thumb, he pushed my head to the side and growled into my ear. His hand that wasn't wrapped around my throat batted away my fingers on my clit. I whimpered at the loss, but my whimper quickly turned into a gasp as his fingers resumed what mine had started.

"I want it to be my fingers teasing your needy little clit when you fall apart all over my cock. Your pleasure is mine. This orgasm is mine, and I want to feel your sweet cunt tighten around me just like I remember. You think you can do that?"

He bit the outside of my ear, then soothed the pain with his tongue as I whimpered at his words.

Words seemed so hard when I was so close to the edge, but Reed needed them and he told me as much by slapping my clit. I cried out at the pain, but the sting easily morphed into pleasure as his cock pumped into me in quick, measured movements.

"Yes," I gasped. "Please, don't stop, Reed. *Please*."

I wasn't above begging, and similar to how Reed knew me, I knew him. And I knew without a shadow of a doubt that he enjoyed hearing me beg. And if I was going to come apart, I was sure as hell taking him with me.

His fingers resumed circling my clit, and his hand tightened around my throat. I reached behind me, tangled my fingers into his short, brown hair and tilted my head back, searching for his lips. He quickly obliged, slamming his mouth down onto mine in a bruising kiss, and when he slipped his tongue against mine, it was all over.

Locked together, he swallowed my cries of ecstasy as the intense orgasm whipped through me with an unrelenting force. I felt my inner walls clamp down around his thick cock and felt him grow even harder before his face contorted as he emptied himself into the condom. His brows furrowed, eyes closing at the overwhelming sensation as his mouth popped open, hovering over my own.

"Yes, fuck. Amanda, *yes*," he cried, resting his forehead against my own as we both fell from our twin highs. For a long second, we stood there, him still inside of me, slowly softening, listening to the sound of each other's quick breaths. With his fingers still around my neck, I knew he could feel the thudding of my pulse, and it didn't slow down for a long while afterward.

"You're amazing," he whispered into my ear. He kissed my neck, where there was most definitely a thin layer of sweat, before he carefully pulled out of me.

My body was spent. Any energy I had before was completely gone, and I leaned forward onto the table for extra support. My dress fell back down around me, and the fabric irritated the tender skin of my backside.

I hadn't had a full-body orgasm like that since... well, since that one night with Josh and Reed so long ago. That was the last time I had remembered feeling so thoroughly sated as well as so thoroughly fucking confused.

Through the thick orgasm fog, I heard what sounded like a trash can lid swinging which I assumed meant Reed had disposed of the used condom. Then seconds later, I heard the sound of a zipper and between my legs and on the floor behind me, I saw him stoop to pick up his jacket that I had carelessly shoved off of him.

I stood on wobbly legs and tugged my dress down farther. The gravity of what happened in the dark room was heavy on my shoulders.

My body and my brain were obviously not very good at communicating because my body thought fucking my best friend was a good idea before, during, and after it happened. However, my brain was too easily swayed by the introduction of gin, and although I didn't give a flying fuck about the repercussion before or during the act, after was another story.

Friendships like ours were hard to come by. And we made it through the first time with only minimal awkwardness and if our other friends had noticed, they hadn't outright said it. So, I considered that a win, but was it worth it to chance it a second time? Especially when we were what? Fuck buddies every once in a while?

"You're thinking too loud," Reed said, smoothing his hands down my sides and twisting me to face him. "Stop worrying about it, Amanda."

I rubbed my temples and peered up at him with my best death glare. "How on earth am I supposed to not worry about it? We got lucky the first time around that the three of us didn't cause issues or become insanely awkward around one another," I said breathlessly, the word catching in my throat ever so slightly. It was only the second time I'd spoken about that night out loud in over a year and a half. "Now, it's like we're tempting fate. Friends don't just fuck without consequences. Especially not in our friend group."

"What if it's not just fucking?" he said in such a soft whisper I thought I misheard him for a moment, but the intensity in his eyes and his overall optimistic expression told me I had heard him right.

I laughed because the idea was ludicrous. We were *us*. "I don't think you know what you're saying. Reed, we can't do this. If it goes south, which in all likelihood it would, then we've messed everything up. Also, when was the last time you were in a relationship? You are one of the most anti-relationship men I've ever met."

"That's not fair. So, you saw the possibility of something more with that jackass, but not with me? I guess cynical Amanda is back, huh?" His voice was flat, which made his words hit me even harder. Not because he was wrong but because he was absolutely right.

My eternal optimism about my recent dating life had been an overcorrection to try to undo my cynical outlook on life. It hadn't worked, and Reed saw right through me as he usually did. He had this uncanny ability to identify my bullshit and call me out on it. Much to my dismay, Josh also had that ability but was usually a little more graceful with the delivery.

Whether or not he was right about me, I was also correct about Reed's anti-relationship past—he had no problem sleeping with women or even dating casually, but when it came time for *"the talk,"* he'd gracefully tell them he wasn't ready for something serious. I'd been witness to a few of the conversations, including one where I hid in his dorm room closet after the girl came over unannounced. It ended with her throwing his chemistry book at his head.

He couldn't call me cynical if I had a legitimate reason to question his motivations.

"What about this..." Reed began, changing tactics as he sensed my hesitation and uneasiness. He scrubbed a hand over his stubble and through his tousled hair. "Let me take you to dinner. Just one date, and we can talk about the possibility that maybe there could eventually be something more between us. No strings attached, and if it goes horribly, I'll even let you pay for half, so it doesn't really count as a date."

"You're giving me a choice?" I asked, dumbfounded because that was unlike Reed. As evidenced by our fucking in the middle of our friend's rehearsal dinner, he usually just took what he wanted (within reason). Not that I wasn't an active and eager participant as well.

One side of his mouth raised in a sly grin as he stepped toward me and placed his hand back around my throat. His lips hovered just above my own, and I wet them without thinking about it, subconsciously preparing for the kiss I knew he was about to deliver. Teasingly, he ran his tongue across my barely parted lips, and I stopped breathing altogether as his warm breath heated my skin.

"No, I'm not giving you a choice because I know we will be incredible together."

I opened my mouth to respond with a laundry list of very valid, logical arguments about why all of it was a bad idea, but my thoughts were interrupted by the sound of laughter and the door opening behind Reed.

"Well, well, well, what the fuck do we have here?" A loud voice we both knew all too well boomed from the opposite side of the room.

"Shit," I groaned, watching Reed's eyes close and his head shaking ever so slightly. Caught red-fucking-handed, and although we were in a less compromising position than we had been in only a minute earlier, we were still pressed against each other. Whether they could only see Reed's back or not, it didn't help that I was hidden behind him.

Reed released his hold on my neck and I let my hands fall

from where I had pressed them against his chest as he spun around to greet our lovely bride and groom.

"We were just discussing the fact that we caught our dates having sex in this very room, actually," Reed said smoothly, and I was impressed by the ease with which he flipped from taunting me to appear nonchalant.

Luke sniggered and Hazel slapped his arm. I was still tucked behind Reed, only watching through the small space between his arm and jacket. He returned to his casual stance, shoving his hands into his jeans pockets and rolling his shoulders back.

"I didn't realize talking with Amanda meant her lipstick smeared all over your mouth. You must have been talking awful close. Digging the red though, man," Luke joked, and I sagged on the table behind me in pure embarrassment. So much for keeping quiet about what had happened.

"Luke, I swear, if you don't leave them alone, you're not getting any."

Even through my embarrassment, I couldn't help but chuckle at the fact that they had also found the room in search of a place for a quickie.

"Okay, fine, I'm done," Luke conceded, not taking kindly to his soon-to-be wife's threat. "Let's find a room that doesn't smell like other people's sex."

He sniffed the air sarcastically and I groaned. They already knew, and I was tired of being there, too, so I shoved aside my mortification and stepped out from behind Reed. Hoping I looked at least semi-decent, I strutted to the door, swinging my ass slightly for Reed's benefit, and only glanced at Hazel for a second before I stepped between the two of them.

In that second our eyes met, Hazel told me all I needed to know: I wasn't off the hook, and we'd be discussing it all later. She had a million questions, and I, sadly, did not have one single answer.

# THREE

## Amanda

"Is everyone decent?" I asked, shielding my eyes as I backed into the room. The groom's quarters were on the opposite side of the grounds from the bride's house, and I had walked the half mile to give Josh Luke's gift from Hazel and retrieve Hazel's gift from Luke. The slight chill in the January air was a much-needed reprieve from the bride's house. With more people than should actually be able to fit into the little house flitting around to finish hair, makeup, and last-minute dress repairs, it had grown so hot I had cheerfully volunteered to do the gift exchange early.

"I come bearing gifts!" I proclaimed while stepping into the wood-paneled room and hoping that if anyone wasn't decent that they would have spoken up. "I'm like Santa Claus except without the red suit and the reindeer likely wouldn't come near me because I'm not usually great with animals besides dogs…"

My words trailed off as I rounded the corner to see the groom and all of his groomsmen already dressed. They were standing around drinking what I assumed was some fancy scotch and laughing. Each of them was wearing a black suit, a fitted white shirt, and a maroon bow tie.

I was impressed that they'd each trimmed their beards, or shaved completely, styled their hair, and much to my surprise, each of their matching maroon pocket squares was perfectly folded and in place.

"Shit, I'm impressed. You look…"

"Wow, we've rendered Amanda speechless. I didn't think it was possible," Reed quipped, a devilishly handsome grin creeping across his face as he made his way to me from across the room. I held my breath while simultaneously getting an eyeful of him. He hadn't shaved completely but had trimmed the stubble along his jaw and styled his dark-brown hair similar to how he had the day before—purposefully tousled and slightly messy.

He looked like sin in his perfectly tailored suit, and I felt like I was in serious need of confession based on the thoughts running through my head. Even if I wasn't Catholic or really religious.

He twirled the amber liquor in his tumbler as he stepped up to me with a similarly devilish look gleaming in his eye. He slid his free hand around my waist as he leaned forward and placed a friendly kiss on my cheek.

*God*, he smelled delicious, and he lingered, his lips against my cheek, for a second.

"You're breathtaking," he whispered against my skin, and I finally breathed out.

Hazel had done well with choosing our bridesmaid dresses. Thankfully, there weren't any bows or poofy skirts in sight. She'd allowed us each to choose our own style of dress as long as it was black. Mine was a one-shoulder formfitting dress with a deep plunge in the back and something I could rewear if the occasion ever arose. And to show off the back, the hair stylist had swept my long blonde hair into a low, messy bun at the back of my head.

"Ditto," I managed to say without giving away everything I

was thinking and feeling. But I knew Reed would know like he always did.

I had managed to keep my attraction to Reed at bay, but after having slept with him the night before, my feelings no longer cared. After spending so much time concealing emotions and forcing my behavior to coincide with the nonchalance I was trying to display, I had become at least decent at hiding my inner turmoil that sparked to life every time he or Josh came close. Or every time I caught one of them staring with a look in their eyes that told me they were thinking of it.

I had done well, but it only took one night with Reed for all of that effort to go to waste. For all of it to completely fall apart.

James and Devon both complimented my dress, effectively pulling me out of Reed's trance as well before they set off in search of some pre-ceremony food.

"You look beautiful, Amanda," Luke said, stepping forward and also kissing my cheek. Sadly, I was still getting used to seeing Luke so outwardly happy. Between his abusive father killing his mother and his mother killing his father, along with his ex-wife, Valerie, who kidnapped his wife-to-be, he'd been through more than most people. He and Josh both had. Even before Valerie kidnapped Hazel, she'd put Luke through hell along with the rest of us.

So it was a miracle to see him relaxed and smiling.

"Okay, so here's your gift from your gorgeous bride. And the only thing is that you *have to* open it by yourself. Make sure none of your groomsmen are lurking in the background."

I placed the heavy black box wrapped in a red ribbon in his outstretched hands as he gave me a confused look.

"That's fine, but why?" Luke asked, shaking the box and trying to guess what was inside.

"Well, probably because you'd likely kill them if they saw what was inside."

Still trying to understand why, Luke shrugged. "Whatever you say. Josh has my gift for Hazel. She can open it with an audience if she wants to," he said before slipping through a door at the back of the room to open his gift.

"Is it something dirty?" Reed asked from beside me, and I gave him a knowing smile.

"Just wait," I said, tilting my head toward the closed door Luke had just walked through. I knew it wouldn't take long for him to tear into the box and find the book inside.

Sure enough, it wasn't more than ten seconds before Luke shouted, "Oh, fuck yes!"

It was exactly the reaction I expected from him, seeing photos of his bride dressed in minimal white lingerie and posed in many suggestive positions. Hazel had brought me along for the photo shoot as her hype woman, so I got to see it all—I think the ones with the halo were my favorite, based on his preferred term of endearment for her, "*Angel*."

"I'm going to take that as a yes." Reed chuckled.

A throat clearing at the opposite side of the room grabbed both of our attention. And just as it did when I spotted Reed, my breath hitched in my throat seeing Josh leaning against the wall, a goldwrapped box in his hands.

Josh, Luke's brother, was the best man. And the third person in our threesome so long ago. He was dressed just as the rest of them were—black suit, white shirt, maroon bow tie—but there was something different about seeing Josh so dressed up. He'd always had a certain boyish charm which included his lack of thought when it came to the clothes he wore, so I guess it was odd because it was a significant contradiction to his usual jeans and a T-shirt.

Similar to Reed, Josh had opted not to shave, but the brown-and-dark-blond stubble across his jaw was neatly trimmed. He'd also mostly tamed his dirty-blond hair and pushed it toward one side. And even from across the room, I could see the vibrance of his bright blue-green eyes.

These men were going to send me to an early grave.

Josh walked toward me with measured steps and as he

approached, I saw a look in his eye that I'd only really seen a time or two before. It was a look that he'd tried to hide since our one and only time together, but that randomly appeared anyway. And when I'd noticed before, he'd shut it down as quickly as it began. But he wasn't hiding it that time as he stopped directly in front of me, the gold box between us. His lack of hiding, and the obvious outward expression of his thoughts, caused a nervous thrill to run through me.

It was a hungry look that didn't just say, "*I want you naked,*" but also said, "*I've seen you naked and know what you taste like.*" And damn, that was a hard look to not pay attention to.

I hadn't given myself the luxury of thinking about it for a long time for the same reasons I described to Reed the night before—it would simply fuck up everything. And I didn't have the time or the energy for that.

But being with Reed, it seemed, had not only stirred up feelings for him that I'd long since suppressed but also feelings for Josh that I'd put in a tiny box some time ago. No matter how hard I tried, I couldn't keep the butterflies from dancing in my stomach or suppress the urge to swallow around the emotion in my throat and my suddenly dry mouth.

"You're devastating," Josh said smoothly and in a husky voice that made me want to clench my thighs together.

The tension was thick between us and was only magnified by Reed's presence that I could still feel to my right. Quietly, he was watching our entire interaction. He was just as invested in it as me and Josh.

Finally, under the weight of both of their attention, I cleared my throat. "You don't look so bad yourself." The words themselves were casual, but the way I said them—all breathy and slightly aroused—said all of the things I didn't actually say.

It wouldn't have taken a rocket scientist to conclude that I was affected by Josh. I was only a middle school science teacher, yet I could have figured that one out. It also didn't help my case that both of them were sex on legs.

"Reed, you think you could give us a minute?" Josh asked, shifting his attention over my shoulder to Reed. I glanced back, following Josh's eyes and noticed the tension in Reed's jaw.

"No, actually, I think I'm good right here, Sunshine," he said, taking a long sip of his drink and ever so slightly inching closer to me.

"If you say so, Amanda," Josh said, turning back to me and setting the gift on the table next to us. "There's something I wanted to talk to you about. I—"

The aggressive ringing of my phone—which I had forced just beneath my armpit in my dress—interrupted Josh midsentence. And based on the fact that the song was "Shut Up" by Christina Aguilera meant it was Bridget, my favorite wedding planner, calling me.

I huffed as both men looked at each other and then looked back at me as I pulled my phone out of my dress and held it to my ear.

"Yes?"

"You know how to sew, right?" Bridget asked in a high-pitched, panicked voice.

"Yes…"

"Okay, get back here now. Delilah just ripped her dress, and apparently no one else knows how to sew."

I groaned and told her I was on my way before I stomped like a petulant child and grabbed Hazel's gift from the table. "I'm sorry, we have bridesmaid dress emergencies that I have to attend to. Can we talk later?"

Josh seemed dejected but nodded. I swiftly kissed them both on the cheek and feeling my face flush at our proximity and the sudden closeness of the act—although it was something I'd done numerous times before—I hurried back to the bride's house and in the direction of the emergency.

# FOUR

## Amanda

WATCHING TWO OF MY BEST FRIENDS GET MARRIED, WHILE EXCITING and beautiful, also made me reassess my own loneliness and lack of a partner.

The ceremony was elegant, beautiful and understated. Everything went perfectly, meaning no one tripped, no one objected to the union, and Luke cried when he saw Hazel appear at the end of the aisle on her father's arm. The sky was painted in deep pinks and purples as the sun set. The diminishing light cast a warm glow on the sea of all-white flowers and thick greenery.

They each wrote their own vows, although Hazel's were far more advanced, just as they should have been, given she was the published author and had a way with words. But there wasn't a dry eye among any of the almost two hundred guests.

From where I stood behind Delilah—who was struggling to stay standing for the short twenty-minute ceremony—I had a perfect view of Luke, who looked at Hazel with all of the love in the world. Like she was his light, his beginning and his end and everything he could ever want.

I wanted someone to look at me like that.

And as I watched the ceremony, diligently holding my bouquet in front of me and dabbing at my eyes with the tissue I'd snuck in, I caught both Josh and Reed stealing glances at me. Each time our eyes would meet, I'd shuffle uncomfortably on my feet, imprisoned under their heavy gazes. From behind me, Stephanie, Hazel's friend and coworker, nudged me to tell me to stop moving once or maybe three times.

The officiant pronounced them husband and wife. I dabbed my tears one last time and nearly lost my voice from screaming. Then I was sandwiched between the two men. I knew it was Hazel's doing, pairing me with both Reed and Josh to exit the ceremony and enter the reception. She was the only person—aside from the three of us that were involved—that knew about our threesome. She was nice enough to only bring it up when she caught one of us staring too long or had drunk too much during one of our many margarita nights.

If her plan was to make me uncomfortable, she had more than succeeded. The last time I had felt the heat of the two of them against me, they were both buried inside of me, and that memory pushed itself front and center as we flawlessly executed our ceremony exit and subsequent reception entrance.

After dinner and speeches, Hazel pulled me out onto the dance floor, where we danced to all the songs we used to grind to in our high school cafeterias. That was until Luke came to steal his bride, and I was looped into a less than thrilling conversation with a few of Hazel's extended family members about the quality of the school systems in Tennessee versus those in Texas.

Each time I tried to politely excuse myself, the man—whose name I couldn't remember—would pull me back into the conversation with another question about our teaching curriculum and standardized testing requirements. Even in the middle of a wedding reception, I was about to fall asleep in my empty martini glass.

"Excuse me, everyone, but I have to steal Amanda. We have some maid of honor and best man things to take care of," Josh said, smoothly inserting himself in the conversation and gripping my arm to haul me away. Eagerly, I stood and followed him. His hand slid down my arm until his fingers intertwined with my own.

"Ugh, thank you! I was dying of boredom."

"I could tell. Your eyes kept darting around like you were hoping someone would save you."

"My knight in a black suit. Don't tell Hazel, but some of her family is *boring*." I laughed as we approached the bar.

"Dirty gin martini for her, and I'll have a whiskey neat. Thanks," Josh ordered for us both. As we waited for our drinks, we watched the party continue around us.

"Dad, Daddy!" Zach, Josh's six-year-old son, ran up to us, waving his tie in the air like a lasso. He was Josh's twin in almost every way, although Josh would argue all day that his son was twice as smart and creative as he was at that same age.

Zach, along with Miles, Hazel's nephew, had been the ring bearers for the ceremony and had become glued at the hip through the entire weekend.

"Aunt Delilah said that I could go home with them and spend the night with Miles if it's okay with you. Please tell me it's okay with you, Dad. *Pleaseee*. They leave in two days, then who knows when I'm going to see him again," Zach pleaded while jumping up and down, his hands clasped in front of him.

"Well, I need to talk to Aunt Delilah and Uncle Tony, and if they tell me that's okay, then that's fine with me."

Zach stopped bouncing and perched his hands on his hips. "Daddy, do you really think I'd lie to you about something this serious?"

Josh laughed and grabbed his drink from the bartender. "No, I don't think you're lying, bud. I just want to make sure it's okay with her."

"Okay, here she comes." Zach pointed behind us as Delilah waddled over.

"You're okay with this?" Josh asked.

"Yeah, it's fine. They can entertain each other. Tony can watch them while I sleep. I'm actually leaving now, though. You can come by Hazel's whenever and come pick him up."

"Sounds good. Zach." Josh stooped down until he was at his son's height and leveled him with a serious look. "What are the rules?"

Zach huffed but obliged his dad's request. "Use my manners, pick up after myself, and treat others the way I want to be treated," he recited.

"What about the last one?"

"But, Dad, I don't have my toothbrush with me!"

I laughed, my martini almost coming out of my nose.

"We have one you can use," Miles chimed in, coming to stand next to his friend.

Josh suppressed a laugh, scrubbing a hand over his jaw, but nodded. "Okay, go. I love you."

"I love you, too!" Zach squealed as he sprinted out of the reception hall, with Miles and Amber following close behind while Delilah struggled to keep up. I wished I had that much energy still or was that excited about a sleepover.

"He's so much like you it's scary."

Josh didn't seem to appreciate the comment the way I meant it—they both loved life and were enthusiastic and outgoing. Josh exuded happiness and a sense of calm.

"He's better than me."

"What does that mean?" I said. I was prepared to tear down each of his arguments and prove his statement incorrect, but he waved me off.

"Let's go talk," he said, placing a hand on the small of my back and leading me to one of the side doors of the ballroom.

"Right now?" I asked but let him lead me into the corridor. The door swung swiftly closed behind us, shutting out the party and the loud music. Although he didn't leave me much of a choice, I wasn't going to argue. Our interaction from that morning stayed with me even through all of the wedding excitement—my curiosity was killing me.

I wasn't sure if Josh had any idea where he was going, but we took a right and then another right until we ended up in a room similar to the one Reed and I had found ourselves in the night before. It was slightly smaller, with fewer tables and less ornate decor on the walls, but it was just as dark and private.

I stepped inside, nervous energy coursing through me as Josh closed the door, plunging us into further darkness. Luckily, it was light enough to navigate the web of tables, and I set my drink down on one closer to the center of the room after taking a long sip.

It wasn't until I set my glass down that I noticed my hands shaking slightly, and it wasn't because the temperature in the room was colder than the rest of the building. I was terrified of what Josh wanted to talk about. What he might have wanted to tell me.

And my nerves weren't calmed at all when I turned to find Josh standing in the middle of the room, hands in his pockets, gazing at the floor. The muted light of the room cast shadows across his body. There was something to it—the way he was holding himself—that made my feet move of their own volition.

I stopped in front of him, the short train of my fitted black dress flowing behind me. My feet landed right where he was staring a hole into the carpet, and his eyes trailed up my body appreciatively until he looked me in the eyes. In the dark room, they appeared more green than blue, and I had the overwhelming urge to inspect them closer.

"I can't decide if it was God or the devil himself who made you this tempting and undeniably gorgeous."

I didn't know what I expected him to say, but it wasn't that. Especially not in his low, husky voice that somehow sounded even better in the near darkness. Then he stepped forward and brushed a stray curl out of my eyes that had likely fallen when my mouth dropped open.

"Because," he continued. "On the one hand, you're an angel. But on the other hand, you're a siren. I feel like you're luring me in, and I have no control over your pull, even if I know it likely won't end well."

My breath caught as Josh's hand slid from my face down my neck. He ran his thumb down the center of my throat, feeling as I swallowed nervously.

"Is that what you wanted to tell me?" I asked in a shaky voice when he hadn't continued speaking and only stared at where his thumb stilled on my pulse point.

"No." He smiled, shifting his focus from my chest to my face. Josh was only slightly taller—maybe an inch or two—than Reed, but I felt like he was a million feet tall as he looked down at me through hooded eyes. "I wanted to tell you that this isn't working."

"What isn't working?" And the award for the most confusing conversation went to…

"Trying to stay away from you."

"We see each other at least weekly, if not every other day, Josh. I'm not sure I understand—"

He shook his head. "I mean, trying to stay away from you the way I want to be around you." My brow was furrowed in confusion, and Josh smoothed it with his thumb, chuckling to himself. "Obviously, I'm not making any sense based on your facial expression. Let me try this another way."

He reached up with both of his hands and cupped my face, not hesitating for a moment as his lips found mine. His kiss was urgent and forceful and perfectly communicated the words he couldn't find.

I felt it throughout my entire body. Each time his tongue brushed against my own, I wanted more. It had been so long since I experienced his skillful lips, and the urgency was propelled by the time we'd spent holding ourselves back.

My intention was to wrap my arms around his midsection and pull him closer, but my hands brushed against his toned stomach, and I couldn't resist raking my nails up and down the shallow indentations of his abs through his white shirt. He sucked in a quick breath, followed by a deep moan that emerged from the back of his throat.

I pushed his jacket off his shoulders and the light brush it made when it hit the ground reminded me of the previous night and before I could control my thoughts, I was thinking about Reed fucking me from behind, slapping my ass and whispering dirty words in my ear. But the thoughts didn't deter me; I wanted to experience Josh again by himself.

And there was no way in hell I would deny the insane connection between us that I knew would explode into abundant amounts of pleasure, likely near ecstasy.

The ache between my legs grew as Josh's hands explored my body—cupping my breasts, flicking my hard nipples through the material of my dress, running down my hips, fondling my ass. When his hands moved toward the front of me, his fingers found the high slit of my dress and he smiled against my lips. He pushed the fabric to the side as he pressed me back into the table, my ass landing on the top.

Josh's fingers were steady as he quickly ripped my panties from my body in one swift motion. I pulled my lips from his, only long enough to see him stuff them in his pocket with a hungry grin on his wet lips. I was about to argue—I was tired of these men taking my expensive underwear—but my protests vanished when Josh dropped to his knees in front of me. Similar to our kiss, there wasn't an ounce of hesitation in his movements. He forced me back farther onto the table, pushed my legs open wider, and suctioned his mouth around my clit.

It was throbbing against his tongue, and my orgasm was already making itself known as he gripped my thighs and yanked me closer to him.

"Fuck, Josh. Yes," I moaned into the quiet surrounding us. He expertly ran his tongue, wet with my arousal and his saliva, up and down my slit, pushing into me as far as he could before doing it all over again. He didn't leave an inch of me untouched, even dropping low enough to lap at my other hole. I bucked against him and the sensation that I hadn't felt in over a year.

When he added his fingers, I swore I saw stars against the black ceiling. He pushed them inside of me, curling them and pressing against my inner wall as his mouth latched back onto my clit.

"Yes, fuck my face. Just like that, sweet girl, take what you need," Josh urged me on, and I was happy to oblige, gripping his soft hair between my fingers and riding his face.

I wasn't sure how we'd lasted more than a year without touching one another when the chemistry between us was atomic. The combination of his tongue and fingers was mesmerizing as he coaxed me to the edge of bliss with his expert touch. He knew exactly what to do, pushing his fingers deeper inside of me and letting them stroke my inner wall as he pulled them out and did it all over again. I thought I was impossibly close to the edge, ready to be sent over, until his teeth grazed my clit and he bit down, sending a jolt of pain and desire to every part of my body.

But in a cruel, cruel joke, Josh removed his fingers and stood from his crouched position in front of me. I cried out at the loss, but my stomach clenched as I watched him undo his fancy black belt while he slipped the fingers he'd been fucking me with into his mouth. He wrapped his lips around them and sucked the taste of me off of them. His eyes stayed on mine the entire time, flaring with unencumbered desire.

"The first time you come, I want it to be all over my cock," he said matter-of-factly. And I whimpered my approval.

In a flash, his hard length was released from behind his dress pants, and he fished a condom out of one of his pockets. I squirmed on the table, legs still spread, watching Josh pump himself a few times before slipping on the condom.

In one sure movement, he positioned himself over top of me, his lips clamped down on my own, and he sheathed himself inside of me in one mind-blowing thrust. I cried out into his mouth, and I was already so close, I nearly came just from him entering me.

Josh's groan was muted against my lips, but I could feel the vibration against my skin. And when he began moving inside of me, there was little I could do besides let it all wash over me and let him fuck me.

I gripped his face in both of my hands, forcing our kiss to deepen and reveling in the scrape of his facial hair against my skin. It was sure to leave a mark—my face would likely be red and irritated—but I couldn't care.

We weren't too terribly far away from the reception, and the low thumping of the music could still be heard behind the closed door. But Josh kept his own rhythm—driving into me at a punishing rate. I lifted my hips, meeting him thrust for thrust and deepening our connection.

Then without warning, he stood up, taking the warmth of his body that was blanketed over me with him, and began a slow, sensual rhythm that made my eyes roll back. He pushed deeper with each measured thrust, making sure the tip of his engorged cock brushed every inch inside of me.

The table beneath me rattled with the force of his thrusts as he fucked me harder. And my moans pierced the silence around us when I could no longer contain them.

"I know, baby girl. I know," Josh groaned. The sound of his rough, desire-filled voice only drove me closer to the orgasm that was teasingly close. Wanting him even closer, I circled my legs around his waist and locked my ankles, the points of my heels digging into his back. Just like me, Josh enjoyed a little pain with his pleasure, too, and his lips parted as I pressed my heels in harder.

His thrusts became more chaotic, and watching the pleasure twist his expression, I knew he was just as close as I was. And although I wanted to make it last—to keep him inside of me as long as possible—our chosen location, along with the urgency clawing through me, made that nearly impossible. The same thought appeared to cross his mind, too, and with nimble fingers, he reached between us and pinched my clit while his other hand gripped the side of my neck.

It was all I could do not to scream as my orgasm powered through me. Each part of my body filled with overwhelming pleasure that I could feel bone deep. And as I clenched around Josh, who stilled as he buried himself deep inside of me, I felt the pulsing of his cock as he emptied himself into the condom and inside of me.

He came with a low growl and a few expletives as we wrung each other dry. Riding each wave with our eyes locked on each other's, connected in more than one way.

"*Fuck,*" he groaned through a few final thrusts as the aftershocks subsided a minute or two later. "I've thought about this since the last time we were together. I wanted to take my time with you, but there was no way that was happening the first time."

He pressed his lips to mine in a soft kiss before he pulled out of me slowly. He brushed his hands down my legs, still spread in front of him, and removed the condom. As he turned to throw it in the trash bin to his right, I took the opportunity to right myself. Pushing up on the table, I slipped onto the floor, my legs wobbling slightly underneath me. I straightened my dress, pushed a few stray hairs out of my face, and used the cocktail napkin of Josh's drink to dab at the sweat that had collected on my hairline and the back of my neck.

I knew I looked like I'd been fucked.

"Next time, I want you in my bed, so I can take my time," Josh said, zipping himself back into his dress pants and retucking his shirt. Apart from his slightly more disheveled hair and maybe a faint blush on his cheeks, he looked the same as he did before we walked into the room.

"Next time?"

"Yes, next time," he said, walking to me with unhindered

confidence in each of his steps and in his voice. He pushed a few additional strands of hair back into my updo and let his fingers fall down my neck and over my exposed shoulder.

The way he was looking at me—with longing and conviction —filled me with unease. I'd seen the same things in Reed's eyes before he demanded to take me on a date. And each of the reasons I conveyed to Reed still stood for Josh.

It would royally fuck up everything when it went south. Josh also had Zach and Zach's mom, Sam, to worry about. And along with Reed, Josh had taken well to the bachelor lifestyle, especially since he'd moved in with Reed. Their apartment had been a revolving door of women since they moved in together six months before.

I wasn't going to be another one of the many when it meant it would jeopardize friendships. Even if the sex was mind blowing with both of them. My time with both men had been one-time slipups. That's all they could be.

"Josh—" I began, but he silenced me by pressing his lips to mine. His method was efficient, and my argument was quickly lost behind the feeling of his smooth lips and his silky tongue.

"Just don't tell me no before we can actually talk about it. We can discuss it when we aren't at my brother's wedding. Can you at least give me that?"

That was the issue with these men—when they were close, it was only them I felt. They overwhelmed all my senses and rid me of my sense. They were eager and excited and seemed like they wanted me so much; whether it was sex or more than that, I wasn't sure. But it made it so hard to tell either of them no.

Josh took my silence for confirmation and a smile pulled at one corner of his mouth, displaying one of his twin dimples that I often found myself struggling to keep my eyes off of.

With one final kiss and no arguments from me, he took my hand and led me out of the room. I had ample time during our walk back to the reception to tell him no and to give my reasons, but when he said we'd discuss it soon, I found that I couldn't speak up. I only nodded in agreement, fully confused over the turn the past two days had taken.

When we stepped into the reception, the party was still in full swing. Josh's hand lingered on the small of my back for a moment before he was pulled into a conversation by Devon and Luke.

I beelined to the bar and ordered another gin martini. From across the room—and while I was trying to ignore the satisfying ache between my legs—Hazel spotted me and waved as her dad grabbed her hand and led her out onto the dance floor. A slower country song filled the space and I watched Luke lead Hazel's mom out onto the floor, finding an open space next to his bride and father-in-law. Everyone else coupled up, too, and I tried to dull the ache in my chest with the fresh drink that appeared in front of me.

Midsip, the glass was tragically pulled from my mouth before I could finish it off. The person behind me set the half-empty glass back on the bar as another warm hand landed on my hip. It only took half a second for the person's scent and presence to wrap around me.

"Reed," I pleaded, eager to finish the rest of my drink.

"Dance with me," he whispered into my ear from behind me, ushering me out onto the dance floor and into the crowd of other guests. In the middle of the floor, he spun me around to face him, keeping a hand on my lower back—barely above my ass— as the other wrapped around my right hand.

With practiced ease, his feet began to guide us around the floor in a slow two-step. His eyes were on me, boring into the side of my face, but my eyes were on anything besides him—I couldn't look at him. I knew I'd see something there that would likely make me feel bad about having just been with Josh, and I didn't need that. I shouldn't have felt bad since Reed and I weren't anything besides friends. We were friends who'd had sex, yes, but that wasn't anything to cause a scene over.

"Dirty girl," Reed whispered into my ear, tightening his grip around my waist and pushing me closer to him without missing a step.

His words and warm breath over my exposed skin made my own breath catch in my throat.

"I don't know—"

"I can smell him on you," he said in a low voice that I could barely make out over the music. And with his words, he swept away the denial that was ready on my tongue.

My eyes widened, and I took a deep breath—trying to smell what he did—but was unsuccessful. The only thing I smelled was Reed's intoxicating scent. I knew there was likely other evidence, including the messed-up makeup around my mouth and my overall disheveled appearance, but it was Josh's smell that Reed pointed out.

"Was it good? Was it everything you remember it being?" he asked on our second lap around the floor.

The joking in his voice caught me by surprise, and without knowing what I was doing, I looked up at him. There was a hint of jealousy in his eyes along with the hunger I'd witnessed the day before, but the playful smirk on his lips matched his tone. He was getting a kick out of ambushing me but still couldn't hide his desire. Two could play that game.

"It was better than good, Reed. I can't believe you didn't hear me screaming his name from here."

His face didn't falter, but when he leaned in, acting like he was going to kiss me, my steps stuttered. I didn't think it was possible, but he pulled me closer. My entire body—chest, hips, legs—pressed up against him, and as we swayed, I could feel his hard length against my lower stomach. I wish I hadn't felt it, but the desire that pulsed between my legs wouldn't be stopped. Whether my brain knew it was a bad idea didn't matter when my body so desperately wanted him again.

My skin flushed thinking about the way we fit together and how much I wanted to feel it all again... and again.

Reed's lips hovered just above my own. They were so close I

could almost taste the whiskey on his breath as we shared the same air. I was immediately thankful for the crowd around us and hoped that no one saw us so intimately close.

With our eyes locked and the song coming to an end, Reed said, in a voice full of promise, "This is going to be fun."

# FIVE

Josh

"And then Sadie ran through the mud and splashed it all over us. And then Aunt Delilah made us take showers, but you were almost there, so I got to use Uncle Luke's new big shower, which was really cool because they have this sprayer that comes off the wall. But I couldn't reach it, so I climbed on the seat in their shower, and then I fell, but I'm okay. And then..."

Zach hadn't stopped talking since we left Luke and Hazel's house twenty minutes earlier. The three of them, including Miles and Amber, got up to more trouble in a short amount of time than I knew was possible. When an exhausted Delilah walked out of the house following Zach carrying a bagful of his muddy clothes, I knew it had to have been bad. Zach also was wearing some of Miles's clothes that were slightly too big for him.

He had recounted the entire night and morning to me as I drove across the city to his mom and my ex-girlfriend Samantha's house. His constant chatter was something I had gotten used to and loved, but my hangover was making it harder than usual to listen.

I also thought that my son's incessant talking was cosmic

karma for the fact that, as a child, I also didn't shut the hell up. Although my dad was always passed out drunk when I was speaking—as was his default—so he never had to listen to me. It was my mom and Luke who got the brunt of my nonstop talking.

Zach was like me in more than one way, though. We both had similar dirty-blond hair, and he was tall for his age, just as I had been. His outgoing personality and athleticism were also from me, however, his eyes were ice blue like his mom's. But I liked to think he was the better version of me—he'd get the childhood I wished I'd had, at least.

Whether Sam and I were together or not, I promised when he was born to do right by him, no matter what. And although Sam and I butted heads, we weren't actually too bad at the whole co-parenting thing.

Our custody agreement meant Zach was with me every Wednesday evening and every other weekend, except in the summer when he stayed with me for a few weeks. It wasn't what I had hoped for when Sam and I renegotiated our agreement based on Zach beginning kindergarten the previous year. Before he really began school and was only attending preschool, our agreement was much more flexible, and although we maintained a decent schedule, I saw him more often.

But we both agreed that it would make more sense for Zach to have a schedule that reflected that change. So, he spent most of his time at Sam's. Luckily, Sam agreed that I could come by on Sundays when it technically wasn't my weekend to spend time with him, and I took him to all of his baseball practices and games.

It was a compromise I could handle, at least in the interim.

"Can we go to Nashville and visit Miles soon, Dad? Aunt Delilah said we could stay with them."

I chuckled as we pulled into Sam's neighborhood. "We'll see, bud."

Zach grunted and crossed his arms over his chest. "That

always means you're gonna say no." He wasn't wrong, that's usually what it meant, but sadly, co-parenting meant decisions like that weren't fully my own to make.

"What else do I usually say when you ask me something like that?" I asked, peeking into the rearview mirror to see him relax and roll his eyes.

"That we have to ask Mama," he answered correctly.

I pulled into the driveway and noticed Sam seated on their porch step. It was odd that she was waiting outside, and I immediately began to grow concerned. Usually, she only waved a "hello" from farther into the house when I dropped Zach off; more often than not, I had to search her out to make sure she was even home.

Seeing her was immediately unsettling, and she looked nervous as her leg bounced on the concrete step.

Zach was out of my truck and sprinting toward the house before I even opened my door. He threw his arms around Sam and kissed her cheek like he hadn't seen her in forever.

"Me and Daddy are gonna go to Nashville, Mama," Zach said, smiling back at me. The kid knew exactly what he was doing.

"I said we had to ask Mom. Don't go getting me in trouble, dude," I said as I set his overnight bag, including the muddy clothes, on the step next to Sam.

He huffed again but mumbled his agreement. Both Sam and I laughed, and he gave me a quick hug before he sprinted into the house, yelling about Legos.

"I'll be by on Tuesday to pick him up for practice," I said to Sam, who hadn't yet made eye contact with me or even acknowledged my presence.

"No, we're going out of town this week. We won't be back until Sunday," Sam said.

"Shit, you're right. To see Travis's family, right?"

Travis was Sam's boyfriend I had met a handful of times. He wasn't my favorite person—he laughed too loud at his own jokes and worried too much about his appearance. But he seemed to care about Sam and, in turn, cared about Zach.

"Yes, we're going up to Michigan to meet his family. It'll be the first time Zach's meeting all of them." That all appeared normal, but I could tell there was something else in her voice. A hesitance that wasn't usually there.

"What's up, Sam? Just tell me."

She sighed and twirled her long ice-blonde hair in her fingers like she always did when she got nervous. It usually ended in her telling me something that I didn't want to hear.

"I think he's going to propose when we're up there, and I just wanted you to know that if he does, I'm going to say yes."

Her confession was like a shot to the gut, and not because I still had feelings for her or imagined that we'd one day be together. But because I knew the carefully constructed relationship and agreement we had precariously built would undoubtedly change with the entrance of a new stepparent. All of our lives would change.

It shouldn't have come as a surprise. They'd been together for two years and, as far as I knew, spent every waking hour together.

"Well, congratulations," I said with as much enthusiasm as I could muster.

"Thanks… that's all you have to say?"

"I'm not sure what else to say. You seem happy, and he's a… good guy."

She studied me for a moment, likely waiting for a bigger, more dramatic reaction, but it wasn't going to happen. After several seconds, she seemed to believe that I had nothing else to add and retrieved Zach's bag from the stairs. I didn't miss her eye roll.

"Will you let me know when y'all get back? I'd like to come by and see him."

She nodded. "Yes, fine. I'll let you know when we're back."

And without another word, I turned and headed back to the truck.

Back across town, I pulled into the parking lot of RG Fitness just after ten in the morning. After years of planning, Reed finally pulled the trigger and opened his own gym. Although he'd only been open for a year, the gym was a decent size with all of the usual equipment, along with personal trainers and several fitness classes. As far as I knew, he was pulling a nice profit already and had recently added a few new classes and two new trainers.

New people were signing up daily, but I had been a client from the start. Reed was my personal trainer, although he also used the time to get in his own daily workout. Luke, Devon, and James also joined us for workouts when their schedules allowed it.

I was late. I was supposed to meet Reed at ten, but it took longer than expected to retrieve Zach after his muddy incident and drive across town.

I also, for likely the first time in our friendship, did not want to see Reed. For several minutes after I turned off my truck, I sat there in silence, contemplating if I really wanted to even go inside.

But when my phone rang and his name appeared, I sighed and decided to just get it over with. Not facing him was only going to prolong the inevitable. I only hoped, as I pushed through the glass door and scanned my card, that I would be able to keep my anger under control.

But that went right out the window when I saw him across the gym, racking weights on a squat rack. His headphones were in his ears, so he didn't hear me approach until the last second when I gripped the back of his shirt and shoved him into his office, which I knew was right around the corner at the back of the building.

"Dude, what the fuck is wrong with you?"

I laughed, but it was hollow and bitter. "What's wrong with me? Better question is, what the fuck is wrong with you?"

Reed sighed and scrubbed a hand down his face before he crossed his arms in front of him and leaned against the back wall of his office. Which, might I add, was in complete disarray and badly needed to be organized.

"Why don't you tell me what's wrong with me then? Since you seem to know."

"What's wrong with you is you're a fucking selfish, competitive asshole!" I yelled directly into his face. Reed didn't flinch, only watched me with expectant eyes as I nearly combusted. "I told you last week that I was going to talk to Amanda, and then you go and fuck her at my brother's rehearsal dinner. Are you kidding?"

"That wasn't my plan. I went—"

"I don't give a shit if you planned it, it still happened. Then instead of owning up to it, you just show me her panties like some sort of trophy. What kind of fucking friend does that?"

"Okay, fine. I'll agree that maybe I didn't go about telling you the exact right way, but can I explain?"

Tired and with my head pounding, I conceded, taking a seat in his office chair. Conceding to hearing him out, though, didn't mean I was giving him a pass. He'd been a world-class dick when Amanda had left us both to tend to an emergency less than an hour before the ceremony. Once the door closed behind her, he cut his eyes at me and asked me, in an accusatory tone, what I planned to talk to her about.

After I told him that I was going to talk to her about us—her and I—he only nodded and paced back to the other side of the room to fill his empty glass with more scotch. Reed was not one to keep his mouth shut, and his lack of comment on the topic told me that something was off.

In a move that reminded me of something college-aged Reed

would have done, he lazily pulled Amanda's red panties out of his pocket and let them swing from his fingers.

"I didn't plan to have sex with her. I was going to the bathroom when I saw her," he started. "Turns out both of our dates were fucking each other. When we caught them, one thing turned into another, and it happened. But to be fair, you knew that I wanted to pursue her. This isn't news to you, and if it is, then it's because you haven't listened to a fucking thing I've said over the past year."

I took a deep breath and rolled my head along my shoulders, trying—and failing—to relieve some of the tension. I was frustrated because Reed was right.

For over a year, we had both—off and on—discussed Amanda. We were both open to the possibility of there being something more, but neither of us had acted on it for fear of a number of things.

Since that night two summers before, nothing had been the same. Not that it had all changed for the worse, but there was a connection the three of us had that wasn't there before. Personally, I hadn't gone into that night with any intention of sleeping with Amanda. One thing led to another, and she ended up pulling me up the stairs and into the bedroom she was staying in.

But I knew Reed couldn't say the same thing. Walking into that room and expecting it to be empty but then finding a dejected Reed waiting for Amanda at the end of her bed was shocking. And rather than have to decide who was going to get her attention, Amanda—with the help of some tequila—decided she wouldn't decide.

"What the fuck do you want me to say?" he asked.

"I don't know. This is all sorts of fucked," I responded, massaging my temples as I tried—and failed—to soothe my pounding head.

"You're telling me. Also, you had sex with her last night, so obviously my sleeping with her didn't fuck up your chances."

A knock on the door interrupted our arguing. "Yeah?" Reed called, still scowling at me.

A guy I recognized as one of his managers peeked his head in. "Yo, sorry to interrupt, but your interview is here."

"Thanks. I'll be up front in a minute. Get her something to drink while she waits," Reed instructed and the manager left with a salute in his boss's direction.

"I'm not sure now is the time to hash this out," Reed said after the door shut.

"Yeah, fine."

"Can we talk about it tonight? Are you working?"

"I may have to go in to do a few things."

He nodded, but I could tell he didn't want to drop the subject. After over a decade of friendship, it seemed like I knew Reed—and the rest of our group—better than I knew myself most of the time. He scrubbed a hand through his thick, dark hair and blew out a long breath but hesitated with his hand over the door handle.

Turning back, he opened his mouth to say something but stopped. He tried again, and when he still didn't speak, I jumped in.

"Just say it, dude."

He rolled his eyes. "I just think it's important for you to know that I'm not going to back down from this. I want her, and I've wanted her for a really long time."

I figured that much already, but to hear him say it out loud was nerve-racking—Reed always got the woman he wanted. Going up against him to try to win Amanda felt like a losing battle, but it would be worth it. She would be worth it because after being with her the night before, there was no way in hell I was going to just roll over.

I'd been hung up on her since freshman year, but until that July night, nothing had ever happened. Being with her felt more right than anything ever had, even if Reed was also there. And the second time solidified that our connection was deeper than friendship.

I just hoped that our friendship didn't completely fall apart in the process of figuring it all out.

"Yeah, me too."

# SIX

## Amanda

"HELLO?" I CALLED OUT AS I WALKED INTO MY PARENTS' HOUSE. The echo that reverberated back to me reminded me of my childhood. A shiver whipped through me.

"I'm here, as you requested," I tried again.

With no answer, I closed the door behind me and took a deep, calming breath.

My parents' house wasn't huge by my standards. I'd been to both Hazel's parents' ten-bedroom house and spent plenty of time in Reed's parents' two homes, which combined were likely over twenty-thousand square feet. I considered those homes huge. My parents' house was on the larger side, but the polished floor and lack of comfortable furniture or rugs meant it echoed like a house twice its size.

The click of my boots against the marble floor was uncomfortably loud as I made my way through the entry and peeked into the dining room on the right. The six-person table was set how it always was for family dinners with four place settings—one at the head of the table for my father, two closer to the door on the opposite side for Adam and me, as well as one for my mother.

Still finding no signs of life, I continued past the dining room and into the living room. Just as my mother liked it, not one item, pillow or decoration was out of place. The gray-and-white room was as immaculate as the day they delivered the furniture set. I remembered the day well because my mother scolded me for sitting on the couch with outside clothes.

She didn't think it was funny when the next day I proceeded to take off my clothes outside of the back door and walked into the house wearing only my strawberry-pink underwear and camisole. She was speechless at my near nakedness, so I told her that I thought outside clothes should stay outside. I was eight at the time, and it was the first time I clearly remember her calling me "uncontrollable and dramatic." Those were some of her favorites, although there were several she liked to use.

I made a sharp right and continued past the living room. Once I passed through the doorway to the kitchen, I finally heard hushed, whispered voices.

The clicking of my heels gave me away long before I entered the room, but even so, both of my parents, who were huddled by the sink on the opposite side of the open white space, immediately stopped talking once I stepped inside. They plastered fake smiles on their faces, and my mother navigated around the island toward me.

"Oh, you're here and only five minutes late!" she said, gripping my arms and kissing my cheek.

I decided to let the comment slide because, as was the case with every dinner, I knew there would be something more important to argue about later.

"Of course, I'm here. You invited me for dinner," I said as my dad took her place in front of me and kissed my other cheek.

"Well, the food is all ready, but I think your brother is still upstairs. Do you want to go grab him?" Mom hurried around the kitchen, grabbing the platters of food. Although the food was neatly arranged and placed in her white porcelain serving ware, I knew immediately that she hadn't cooked it. I couldn't remember the last time either of them cooked. The plates of food looked and smelled wonderful, but they were from a local place around the corner.

The smell was familiar because it was what my parents ordered at least twice a week for us or what they would pick up when we had guests. It could easily be made to look like one of them had slaved over a stove to prepare it.

Rather than walk all the way upstairs, I stood at the bottom and yelled my brother's name.

"Adam, dinner's ready!"

Mom scoffed as she placed one of the bowls on the table. "Well, I could have done that."

"Yes, well, then you should have."

Once I heard Adam's door close, I took my seat at the table across from my mother while my dad took his seat at the head of the table.

We sat in silence, awkwardly staring at each other as we waited for Adam to make his entrance. There wasn't any point in trying to start a conversation when I knew that they had little to no interest in my life or what was going on in it. I could have joined a convent or moved out of the country in the past few months, and they wouldn't have known until they invited me to a spontaneous family dinner.

Mom claimed the dinner invitation was because they missed me, but I knew better. Something was up, and the sooner my brother sat down, the quicker I would find out what it was.

"Let me go see—" I began.

"Oh, there he is," my mother cheerfully chimed, throwing her hands out wide. "Sit, sit."

Adam grunted in response and slid into the chair beside me. Not much had changed since I saw him the month before. His blond hair was still unkempt and sticking out in several directions, and he hadn't shaved in weeks. At least he smelled clean.

But at twenty-one, that was the bare minimum I would have hoped for. Being clean was required.

"Well, hello, James Dean," I quipped, watching him sink lower into his chair out of the corner of my eye.

"Lovely to see you, too, Heather." He reached for the green beans, but Mom batted his hand away.

"We should say grace first," she said, reaching for my father's hand, who took it with a smile.

Adam and I both scoffed at the same time and gave each other matching bewildered looks.

"Seriously?" he asked before I had the chance to.

"Yes, seriously. We should give thanks for this meal."

I was in the twilight zone. "Mom, when's the last time any of us stepped foot into a church?" I asked but reached for Adam's hand.

"I think if any one of us walked into a church, we'd be smote immediately," he said, and I suppressed a chuckle.

"Adam," my father said in his usual authoritative tone.

"Glenn," Adam said in the same voice, mocking my father.

"Amanda, why don't you say it?" Mom offered from across the table, and I couldn't bear to suppress my laugh that time. But she only smiled brightly, eagerly awaiting a prayer from her only daughter. They all bowed their heads, waiting for me to begin.

"Umm…" I stuttered, unable to think of anything that would even remotely sound like a prayer. Adam cleared his throat next to me and gave an expectant look, raising his eyebrows.

For several seconds, the room was silent as they all waited for me to begin thanking God and Jesus and whomever else for the food in front of us, but my brain didn't work that way anymore. I thought about thanking the restaurant where it came from, and then I contemplated pulling a full Aunt Bethany from *National Lampoon's Christmas Vacation* and singing the national anthem, but ultimately thought better of it.

So, instead, I dug deep into the recesses of my mind and remembered a prayer we said in Sunday School when I was no more than five years old. "God is great. God is good. Let us thank him for our food, amen."

Simple and to the point and it rhymed—I liked it.

They each raised their heads and looked at me like I had two heads, but she never specified how she wanted me to say the blessing, just that I should. At least I said it without too much of a fight.

Silence invaded the room once more. We each scooped food onto our plates and began eating without saying another word. It was when I was sipping my water, hoping it would suddenly turn into wine, that my father finally spoke up.

"Well, your mother and I have something we actually wanted to talk to you about."

"And there it is," Adam muttered around a forkful of chicken.

"What does that mean?" Mom sounded offended, and it was still too early in the dinner for arguing.

"Nothing, Mom. Just tell us," I chimed in before Adam could run off on the tangent he was so clearly begging to begin.

"We are moving to California!" she erupted excitedly.

The generous bite of chicken I'd stabbed with my fork hovered midair in front of my mouth. I couldn't say anything. I sat there silently, expecting something more than that or for them to elaborate.

"Congratulations?" The question in my voice wasn't intentional, but it was there, nonetheless.

"Aren't you excited or surprised?" my father asked.

Adam chuckled and set his fork on his plate. "Why would she be excited? *You two* are moving. We aren't going anywhere."

"You knew about this?" I asked Adam.

His only response was a shrug. I wasn't surprised the little shit hadn't informed me of the somewhat important development.

"Yes, you're right. But we thought you might be excited for us."

I gulped and looked at the liquor cabinet in the corner of the room that seemed to be calling my name. I wasn't an alcoholic, and I didn't depend on it in my everyday life. *But* during the odd family dinner, it made it all a little more manageable and kept me from getting the itch to stab a fork in my eye that seemed to creep up every time one of my parents spoke.

"That's great. When are you moving?" I asked.

"The movers will be here in three days."

My head whipped around to my father, who spoke like it was nothing of importance. He took another bite of food and smiled at me like it was any other normal day.

"Hold on. Like three days from now?" I asked, looking back and forth at both of them, hoping I was being punked.

"Yes, they'll be here on Wednesday and then this house will close on Friday," Mom said.

"When were you planning on telling me this? You've already sold this house."

Adam sat silently beside me, casually eating his green beans. His lack of snide comments made me even more concerned.

"Tonight."

"Adam, what are you going to do? Where are you going to live?"

My brother, who was ten years younger than me, was a few years out of high school and hadn't kept a steady job since he was sixteen. He wasn't interested in college—junior college or a university—and trade or technical school was also apparently out of the picture.

I'd tried to help him find a job several times, but they all turned out the same. I'd receive a call no more than a month later with another excuse on why it just wasn't "the right fit."

"Honestly, we thought he could stay with you for a while," Mom said.

"What?" I said flatly.

"At least until he can get on his feet. I'm sure you wouldn't mind putting up with your little brother for a few days."

"Did you know this was their plan?" I directed my question to Adam and held up my hand to my mother when she tried to interject on his behalf.

Adam sighed and finally put down his fork. "I planned to stay with a buddy, but when they mentioned the idea of me living with you, it sounded like a better option. It'll be temporary until I can figure something else out."

I laughed a dry, humorless laugh. "Mom, and no offense, bro," I said to Adam, who waved me off. "But it's going to take way more than a couple of days for Adam to find a job, save up enough money to afford a place on his own and then move into said place. It may be a month if we're lucky, but likely longer than that."

She shrugged like it wasn't any concern of hers. They were leaving, and as I watched them both stare at their plates, pushing food around but not eating, I realized that it was their plan all along. They planned to only tell me at the last possible minute so that I had no choice but to let Adam live with me because they both knew I wouldn't let my little brother be homeless.

Yes, he was a fucking pest and had no motivation, but he was my pest.

And I should have known something like that would happen sooner rather than later. Dad had retired a few months before, and Mom was getting anxious about traveling—or so she said. So, my surprise turned into contempt and anger. Their behavior was usual, and I should have suspected it, but I was angry at myself for not doing more to be proactive. I should have seen it coming.

No longer in the mood to act cordial or pleasant, I put my cloth napkin on the table and stood from the uncomfortable wooden chair. "Adam, start packing tonight. You can move in sometime before the movers get here. If you need help moving the bigger stuff, let me know, and I'll have one of the guys help you. We can talk about specifics after you move in."

Adam nodded, and I could see the sadness in his eyes. They

were darker blue like mine and swimming with emotion. He acted all tough and pretended that nothing affected him, but I knew better. It was all just that, an act, and I knew our parents up and leaving him hurt even if he didn't admit it.

"Where are you going?" Mom asked, like she was surprised I was leaving.

"Anywhere but here."

Dad sighed as I retrieved my purse from the side table, which was still decorated with Mom's ornate china. There hadn't ever been much "stuff" in the house, but they hadn't packed at all, likely waiting for the movers to do it all for them so they wouldn't have to lift a finger.

"Amanda, why must you always cause a scene? This is a good thing for your mother and me and that's what you should be focused on instead of storming out of here."

I didn't want to engage, but his dismissive tone grated on my last nerve. "I'm not storming, Dad. I am walking, striding, strolling—"

"Sauntering," Adam added with his head hung.

"Yes, good one. I'm sauntering out of here. Not storming."

Dad sighed again, and it sounded like my childhood. "Why must you always be so—"

"Oh, wait, wait," I stopped him with feigned excitement. "I know this one. 'Why must you always be so dramatic,'" I said, doing my best to drop my voice as low as my father's with the same disdain I felt drip from each of his words.

"Amanda," Mom started, but I held up a hand to stop her.

"Adam, I'll see you soon. Text me when you want to move in."

And then I walked, strode, strolled, and sauntered out of the house for possibly the last time and headed straight for the bar.

# SEVEN

## Reed

"*Expect the Unexpected.*" The weathered sign hung from its usual spot just above the entrance to Murphy's Law, rattling against the facade of the building each time a strong gust of wind whipped through. Even after renovations, Rhonda, the owner of the bar, left the sign hanging above the entrance like a warning to all who entered.

But other than the two signs, the place was almost unrecognizable. After Hazel was kidnapped by Luke's ex-wife, Valerie, and held hostage upstairs in the bar, and before Valerie was subsequently killed by Josh, Rhonda decided to expand her renovations to cover more than just the two bars themselves. She practically gutted the place but kept the same contemporary Irish pub style.

There was lots of green and gold, but with a more simplistic look to bring it into the twenty-first century.

It was our place in college and continued to be our place even after we all graduated. Me, Josh, Amanda, Luke, James, Devon, Blakely and at one time, Valerie could be found somewhere in the bar at least once each weekend. Although we had added

Hazel, our group had dwindled. Valerie was dead—good riddance—and Blakely had dropped off the face of the earth after she helped Valerie kidnap Hazel.

And as much as we all missed the familiarity of the old Murphy's, the changes were good. The fact that it looked completely different after so much bad had happened there was the fresh start that the place needed.

When I stepped inside the bar, I was greeted by warmth and immediately relaxed until I was accosted by the god-awful sounds of karaoke night.

The older man on the small stage was butchering "Don't Stop Believin'" as I made my way to the main bar in the center of the room. It was a huge, circular bar with more barstools than you could imagine and shelves and shelves of liquor in the center.

I shrugged out of my jacket and plopped my ass on one of the green stools, bracing my elbows on the dark wood bar top to wait for Josh.

Grady, one of our favorite bartenders, slid a beer in front of me, and I tried to summon a smile in return. He was in his midfifties and made his money in the oil business before he retired and started working as a bartender at Murphy's. After his wife died, he spent more time in Murphy's than anyone else. Rhonda finally told him, in her sweet, affable way, that he could either get the fuck up off the barstool and get behind the bar or find something better to do with his life than drinking it away.

So, he got behind the bar and has been serving us as well as providing unsolicited advice ever since.

I wondered what he would have to say about the predicament Josh and I currently found ourselves in. He'd probably tell us to get our heads out of our asses and that Amanda wouldn't want either of us so there's no point in arguing about it.

But I couldn't imagine anyone telling us anything that would persuade us not to go after her. I hadn't stopped thinking about Amanda since we'd been together at the rehearsal dinner, but it all started long, *long* before that.

We met in college, just as the rest of us had, but even then, I felt an instant connection to the bubbly, hilarious, yet slightly dramatic blonde that walked into my freshman biology class. She sat down next to me, frazzled that she was later than she wanted to be and immediately struck up a conversation about the proximity of parking lots and garages and the absurdity of the price of parking anywhere on campus.

Coincidentally, Josh, who was my freshman roommate, was also in that class. He was sitting next to me and was also listening to the cute blonde ramble on about the likelihood of ever making it to class on time since she had to "haul ass" from the other side of campus.

We were both immediately enamored, even as she prattled about bus and bike routes. And when the girl with her dark-rimmed glasses finally took a breath, we both promised that even if she was late, we'd always save her a seat.

I hadn't stopped wanting her since that day. She came into my life like a fucking tornado, and I've enjoyed every second of the chaos. It just so happened that my best friend also felt the same way, and we'd both finally decided to do something about it.

"Dude, do you see this shit?" Josh appeared behind me, pointing toward the opposite side of the bar. Lost in my own disordered thoughts, I hadn't paid attention to the rest of the bar since I walked in. One side of the place contained the stage, dance floor, and the circular bar where I was seated. While the other held a smaller bar with pool tables.

Josh was pointing near one of the pool tables, and it only took a second for me to understand.

Amanda was standing at one end of a table, the cue gripped tightly in one of her hands while the other one held the arm of the guy in front of her. He looked like a typical college frat boy, and based on the other guys surrounding him, he was there with all of his buddies. They were gathered on a few barstools at the high-top tables surrounding the pool tables and were snickering as Amanda spoke to the kid.

In a split second, his face dropped, and even from across the room, both Josh and I felt the mood shift. A quick look at my best friend was all I needed to confirm he shared my feelings. I was out of my seat at the same time Josh began charging for them. The little punk ripped the pool cue from Amanda's hand and tossed it to the side, then grabbed her upper arms. He looked like he was about to get in her face, but he didn't get further than that.

Amanda was yelling at him over the music booming through the place, struggling against his hold but mostly unfazed by his grip on her. We intervened only a moment later, but my blood boiled watching him touch her like that.

Josh stepped around Amanda's left and pried the prick's hand off of her as I stepped around her right side and shoved the guy's shoulder. With us between him and Amanda, the little douche stepped back but kept running his mouth.

"What the fuck is this? These your boyfriends or something, sweetheart," he slurred.

"Doesn't matter who we are, kid. We have a zero-tolerance policy for touching women like that or fighting in this place, so you and your friends gotta go," Josh said, waving his hand toward the front door. I didn't miss the way he seethed as he spoke or the anger that also rolled off of him.

"Are you kidding me right now? Chick hustled me! She said she'd never played before but didn't miss a fucking shot. Lost me fifty bucks," he cried, and I couldn't help but laugh. He didn't take that too kindly and tried to square up to me. But I was bigger and older and wiser, and I could see the doubt flash across his eyes.

"Sounds like you're just upset you lost, man. But either way, you gotta go. Now," I said, ready to be done with the bullshit and get back to the real reason I was there.

"Man, let's go." One of his buddies stepped up behind him

and ushered him out. He hurtled a few more slurred insults over his shoulder—mostly aimed at me and Josh—but we stayed between them and Amanda, just in case one of them tried something until they were out the front door.

As the door shut behind them, we both simultaneously turned to Amanda.

"Seriously, babe?" I asked as Josh scrubbed a hand through his hair.

"What? I just wanted a pick-me-up, and he was an easy target. I came in here prepared to play by myself, but then he started pestering me. I couldn't just let it go," she said. She reached behind her and grabbed her beer, which was surrounded by three other empty bottles that I assumed were also hers.

"How long have you been here? I've been upstairs for all of thirty minutes."

Amanda thought for a moment, then nodded. "Yeah, probably about that long."

"Why did you need a pick-me-up? What happened?" I asked.

She slumped onto the barstool behind her and took another long pull of her beer. I found myself drawn to the way her throat bobbed when she swallowed and how her lips formed around the rim of the bottle. I thought about the way her smooth skin felt under my lips, under my fingers and how her pouty, pink lips formed so perfectly to my own.

"My stupid fucking parents is what happened," she muttered and finished off her beer in one go. Josh and I glanced at each other—the last thing she likely needed was to be sitting alone in the bar after something happened with her family. She'd find a way to get herself into even more trouble.

"Let's go upstairs," Josh suggested and didn't leave time for Amanda to agree or disagree as he took her hand and led her toward the stairs at the back of the bar. She argued for a moment but conceded when she saw I was also following. Josh asked Grady to send three burgers with fries to his office upstairs as we passed, and I grabbed another beer for myself on our way up.

"Sit," Josh told Amanda once we entered the small space. His office was on the quaint side but was neatly organized. There weren't papers scattered everywhere as there were in my office, and it looked like he actually used his filing cabinet.

There was also a picture of him and Zach framed on his desk, which made me smile. That kid had turned out to be one hell of a spitfire.

With a huff, Amanda sat down on the older brown leather couch with her arms crossed in front of her. She was acting like she'd just been called into the principal's office or something. But the way her crossed arms pushed her tits up toward her chin, along with the practiced, contented look on her face, she looked nothing like a student.

Josh mimicked her and folded his arms over his chest as he leaned against his desk. With his ankles crossed and his serious expression, he looked like the damn principal. I rolled my eyes and plopped next to Amanda, throwing my arm on the couch behind her, which earned me a less-than-enthusiastic look from Josh.

"What happened?" Josh asked.

Amanda sighed and let her head fall back onto the couch cushion, her hair and the top of her head brushed against my arm and even that slight touch sent a jolt of excitement through me. I was dying to touch her with a need that was growing harder and harder to ignore.

"My parents are moving to California."

"Well, I guess that's good for them? But why are you—"

"They're moving in three days, and they just told me tonight."

I could tell by the look on Josh's face that neither of us understood why she was so upset until it clicked.

"Adam," I said. Her little punk of a brother had always been an issue. He was ten years younger than her, and a pain in the ass.

"Yes, Adam." She cut her eyes at me with an unamused look.

"How is Adam doing?" Josh asked, retrieving our food from one of the bartenders at the door.

Amanda eagerly accepted her food, toed off her boots and crossed her legs underneath her. Her attitude morphed right before our eyes. After the first bite of her burger, she said, "He's working on his audition for the *Breakfast Club* reboot."

"So, nothing's changed on that front," Josh mused.

"Where's he going to live? He doesn't have a job right now, right?"

Amanda shook her head and glanced back and forth between us before shoving several fries in her mouth. I waited for a moment for her to finish chewing and answer my questions, but she continued eating like she was hoping to avoid answering the questions at all.

When she reached for more fries, I blocked her tray with my hand.

"Withholding food from a starving woman is one surefire way to get your fingers chewed off," she quipped.

"Answer my questions, and I'll move my hand. No finger chewing needed."

She glared at me but sighed in defeat. "No, he does not have a job. But that's only item number two on the list of things to do after moving him into my apartment."

"You've got to be kidding me," Josh bristled.

"Babe, you can't let him do this again," I said.

Since I had known Amanda, her parents had always defaulted to her when they were tired of trying to handle Adam. They'd paid more attention to him than they had her, but that still didn't mean much. The guy couldn't keep a job, had no desire to go to school, or any ambition to do jack shit. But Amanda, being the big sister and person she was, would always be there for him.

When he dropped out of community college two weeks in, she helped him tell their parents. When he lost his job at James's office—the one Amanda pulled strings for him to get—she was up there pleading with Adam's manager to give him another shot.

It also bothered both me and Josh that Adam was so nonchalant about his treatment toward his sister—she had sacrificed a lot in the past twenty-one years to help him, and he acted like he gave zero fucks.

"What am I supposed to do? They are *leaving* in three days. I don't have a lot of time to figure something else out. He has no money, no job and no place to go. I can't just let him live on the fucking street, and that's where he'll end up if I don't intervene. Plus, my parents all but said, 'We figured you would take him.' What do you expect me to do?"

Her argument made sense, but that did little to change my mind when Adam was constantly involving her in his antics and stirring up trouble in her own life. Although I didn't have any siblings of my own—a fact that, at one point in my life, bothered me immensely—I understood her need to take care of her little brother. To keep him safe and guide him through the shit life could throw at a person, but after years and years of the same song and dance, it had come to the point where enough was enough. He was abusing his sister's kindness and generosity by constantly deferring to her.

"Does he have a friend he can stay with? Or don't you have an aunt that lives nearby?" Josh suggested.

"Gee, I wish I had thought of that," she said sarcastically. "I'd rather him live with me than one of his so-called friends. And my aunt is almost two hours away. Plus, she would be an even worse influence than his friends." She dropped her empty tray on the ground and let her head fall into her hands.

In her obviously stressed state, I couldn't help it anymore. I set my tray next to hers and ran my hand down her back. She shivered at the touch and peeked at me between her fingers but didn't comment on my attempt to comfort her. I let my fingers trace the length of her spine a few times before I squeezed at the base of her neck and shoulders, trying to relieve some of the tension. She ever so slightly leaned into my touch. The movement was barely a movement at all, as her shoulders tipped in my direction, but I felt like I wanted to celebrate all the same.

"So, he's moving in with you?" I said, and she nodded. "Do you need help moving him in? How much shit can one guy who lives with his parents actually have?"

She shrugged. "I'm not sure. I haven't seen his room in a few months at least, but yeah. If y'all could help, that would be really great. Otherwise, I'll ask James and Devon."

"No, we got it," Josh answered for the both of us.

"Okay, I'll text you both tomorrow morning and let you know the plan." She sighed, scrubbed her hands through her hair, and gave me a sad smile. Then she leaned forward, and before I could comprehend what she was doing, she kissed my cheek.

It wasn't totally out of the ordinary—she'd kissed my cheek before because Amanda was an affectionate person, even with her friends. But it was the first time she'd done it—or even voluntarily touched me—since we'd been together and since I had let myself actually feel whatever it was I was feeling for her. So the kiss made me eager for more.

Then she stood, as if I wasn't completely disarmed by one quick kiss, and did the same to Josh. She brushed her lips against his cheek, and I witnessed him have the exact same reaction I did. We were both well and truly fucked.

"I don't know what I'd do without you guys. I'm going to go get the guest room ready for Adam, so I'll talk to y'all tomorrow, okay?"

"We'll walk you out," I said as Josh also said, "We'll come with you."

Amanda looked at us like it was unnecessary, but I didn't

know if those guys were planning on coming back in or hanging in the parking lot until she left.

Downstairs, Amanda stepped into the bathroom, and Josh and I were left alone in the hallway to wait for her.

I leaned against the wall near the bathroom door and pushed my hands into my pockets so I wouldn't fidget. Josh leaned against the wall opposite me and worried his lower lip between his teeth, staring at the door intently.

"I think I have an idea," he said.

I immediately knew what he meant—an idea about our situation with Amanda—and I perked up, eager to come up with something. "Great, let's hear it."

"After we walk her out, we can talk about it. But at the same time, maybe it's better if we try to keep our hands to ourselves and back off a little while she's handling all of this Adam bullshit."

Sure, it made sense. She already had a lot going on, and the last thing we wanted to do was add more stress on top of it. "Her parents fucking suck. I wish I could say that I'm surprised, but I'm not."

He grunted in response and straightened as Amanda stepped out of the bathroom. Instead of continuing down the hallway, she stopped and looked between both of us like she knew we had been talking about her. Like our words were lingering in the air around us, hung up with the sound of someone butchering Shania Twain.

"You both look guilty. Why?" she asked.

"We do not look guilty," Josh said unconvincingly.

"You're just seeing things, babe," I said, tossing my arm casually over her shoulders.

"I know I'm not, but I don't have the energy to pry right now. You can tell me what the hell is going on another time. But until then, try to act like you aren't up to something," she said matter-of-factly, not leaving any room for argument.

Josh and I shared an impressed yet concerned look over her

head as we walked around a large group at the bar to the front door. Whether we were trying to spare her additional stress or not, she was too observant and was likely to figure it out sooner rather than later. She knew us too well, and to be honest, I don't think either of us would be capable of hiding much for long.

# EIGHT

## Amanda

"WHERE THE HELL ARE YOU GOING TO PUT ALL OF THIS SHIT?" REED asked on our tenth trip upstairs with more of Adam's stuff.

Reed and Josh had both volunteered to help move Adam's stuff into my apartment after witnessing and comforting me through my almost mental breakdown at Murphy's only the day before. And they were even generous enough to offer to go to my parents' house and load it all up in the U-Haul I'd rented.

I rented a midsize truck, figuring it may be too big for his belongings, but I didn't want to make more than one trip if it could be helped. So, when the guys pulled up to the closest door and into the parking spots I'd saved for them, I was surprised to see that the entire back of the truck was full. Like stacked-to-the-brim type of full. Like they had to brush off those Tetris skills to get everything to fit.

Although I'd told Adam he didn't need to bring all of his furniture, he'd done so anyway, claiming he had a sentimental attachment to it. Which meant we not only had to move Adam's stuff in but we had to move my stuff out. No one was very excited about doubling the workload, but luckily, Hazel and Luke had an entire house that needed furnishing and promised to return the furniture when I needed it back.

"I'll figure it out, just watch the corner on the wall," Adam said through gritted teeth as he and Reed tried to carry his huge, heavy dresser up the narrow staircase.

Reed, who was carrying most of the weight of the dresser at the bottom of the stairs, rolled his eyes and gave me a frustrated look over his shoulder. Adam was at the top of the stairs, slowly inching backward closer to the landing as Josh ran ahead to make space for the large piece of furniture.

I was carrying a box full of knickknacks and trying not to pee my pants from laughing too hard.

Reed and Adam had been at each other's throats all day. And I was surprised they hadn't broken out into a full-fledged fight, but the longer it took to move the damn dresser, the more likely a fight seemed.

"You've got to turn it a little more so I can step up," Reed said.

"Well, I'm pinned against the wall. I have nowhere else to go," Adam replied.

"Just lift it a little higher."

"You seriously think I can lift this shit above my head? Especially in this position?"

"I could do it."

"No, you couldn't."

"Are you fucking kidding me? Fine, I'm going to step back, then you need to lift it higher and turn more to your right."

Reed stepped back, Adam lifted the dresser slightly higher, and when he attempted to step onto the landing, the dresser again pinned Adam against the wall.

"Fuck!" Reed snapped. "You didn't lift it high enough. We have to get it over the stupid spindle thing here. Do it again."

And they did it again. Reed stepped back, and Adam lifted the dresser even higher and was nearly pinned against the wall.

"Okay, now, turn. Turn more. More!" Reed instructed as Adam heaved it onto the second—and last—set of stairs.

Unable to resist any longer, I hollered, "Pivot!" from the bottom of the stairs and behind Reed.

I heard Josh laughing from the floor above, but neither of the guys actually carrying the dresser thought I was funny.

Finally at the top, Reed dropped his side in front of Josh. "It's your fucking turn."

Josh rolled his eyes but picked up the dresser and shuffled it through the apartment door.

"Please be careful of the floors!" I warned.

I started to walk toward them but was abruptly stopped by Reed's hand on my shoulder. "Pivot? Really?"

I bit my lower lip to suppress my laugh. "It's from—"

He held up his hand while he took the bottom of his T-shirt in the other and wiped the sweat from his brow. As he lifted his shirt, I caught a glimpse of his perfectly toned abs and his tanned skin. His stomach was lightly dusted with dark hair that disappeared below his waistband in a neat line. I wanted to run my nails over each indentation of his abs, tracing the distinct muscles before doing the same thing with my tongue. I hoped he hadn't heard my sharp intake of breath at the sight of him.

"I know where it's from," Reed said as he lowered his shirt and cut off the good view. "But you had to make the joke while I was carrying a solid wood dresser all by myself?"

I scoffed. "First, look at you. That dresser should be nothing for you with the amount of time you spend in the gym, and second, Josh thought it was funny. Did your sense of humor get left in the moving truck or something?"

He chuckled and stepped toward me. Even with the small box still in my arms, he was close. His eyes darted from mine to my lips, lingering there long enough that I knew he was likely remembering what they felt like against his. I was thinking about it, too, as his tongue darted out and wet his lips.

He reached out, a mischievous smile playing on his lips, and pushed a piece of hair that had fallen loose from my ponytail behind my ear. "What do you mean, 'look at me'? I don't think I understand what you mean by that."

I rolled my eyes and hardened my expression. His featherlight touch was enough to undo me, but like hell was I going to let him know he had that kind of power over me. I wanted to retain at least a semblance of my dignity.

Like I was looking for something, I narrowed my eyes and peered around him and on the ground near us. "Hmm, yeah, looks like you forgot your rod and reel. You'll need them if you're going to go fishing for compliments."

He smiled but didn't respond, so I continued. "And probably some better bait because smiling and touching me won't do the trick."

"Is that so?" he said in a low voice, taking another step toward me. The fabric of his T-shirt brushed against the backs of my hands as I held on to the box for dear life, hoping that it would keep him at least a foot away.

"Yes, that's so." My voice was not nearly as confident as I hoped it would be, but I kept my chin high. With another step forward, I reflexively took one back and pressed my back against the concrete wall behind me. Sadly, the box did little to take up space between us, but I continued to grip it tightly, praying my expression didn't give me away.

Reed leaned in, planting one hand on the rough wall behind me next to my head while the other smoothed down the skin of my bare upper arm. The temperature was in the midfifties, but after hauling Adam's shit up and down the stairs for the better part of an hour, I quickly found I didn't need my jacket. I regretted the decision, though, because Reed's hand on my bare arm was enough to send goose bumps over all my exposed skin.

I hadn't pulled my eyes from his—although he continued to trace each feature of my face—and I recognized the moment he felt the goose bumps. His warm-brown eyes danced with humor and victory as his smile widened, showing off his perfectly straight white teeth.

He leaned in closer, placing his mouth so close to my ear I could feel the heat of his breath against my neck. "See, your mouth says one thing while your body tells a different story. I think with or without the rod and reel, my bait works just fine for you."

Then, as if he hadn't proven his point enough with my breath catching at each of his words, my heart pounding and the goose bumps, the asshole kissed my neck, darting his tongue out between his lips just enough that I felt its smoothness and was reminded of how it felt on other parts of my body.

When he lingered for more than a second, I stopped breathing altogether. My previously clear thoughts were muddled and confused by his intoxicating scent and proximity. And like nothing had happened at all, he grabbed the box from my hands and turned on his heels toward my apartment while I stood stunned, turned on, and mildly fuming in the middle of the hallway.

"Wait, where are you going?" I asked Adam for the fourth time, hoping it was the last time and I'd actually receive a clear answer.

He sighed. "Is this how it's going to be? You're going to turn into my mother since I'm living with you now? Do you want to track my location, maybe? Or," he said, sarcasm dripping from his every word. "That's probably not invasive enough, is it? Do you want to implant a dental tracker?"

I returned his eye roll with one of my own and blocked his exit. "Dude, I'm doing you a huge favor by letting you crash here rent-free while you look for a job. Not to mention it being so last minute, so cut me some fucking slack. I just want to know where you're going because I thought you might want to help us move my furniture to Hazel and Luke's house. You know, seeing as how the three of us helped you move your shit."

Thankfully, he stepped back, so I didn't have to crane my neck to maintain eye contact. I'm not sure why he received all of the height and size in the family, but I became increasingly frustrated when he used it against me.

He scrubbed a hand through his messy dirty-blond hair and shook his head. "I have an interview in less than an hour. That's where I'm going," he stated.

My eyebrows shot to my hairline as I glanced at his attire. He hadn't changed before trying to run out of the door with little more than a quick "bye!" in my direction. He was still wearing jeans that I would bet hadn't been washed in weeks, along with one of his gray high school hoodies.

"You're going to a job interview dressed like that?" No wonder he couldn't hold down a job if that's the way he was showing up for work.

"It's at an auto body shop, so what I'm wearing isn't necessarily important."

"An auto body shop? Which one, and how did you swing an interview there?"

He chuckled as Reed and Josh walked into the room. "You're doing a shit job convincing me that you're not going to turn into a mother."

I bit back my defensive response. Adam got the better end of that deal—my parents would have rather done anything than parent me. I was well and truly an unhappy accident, but Adam wasn't. They at least feigned interest in his life. He was lucky he didn't have to suffer monotonous, lonely days with strict rules set by inattentive parents. "Just," I began, backpedaling. "Are you sure you don't want to change?"

"Yes, I'm sure. Now can I go?"

I stepped to the side, and Adam immediately swung the door open, but before he left, he kissed my cheek and gave me a soft smile. My brother had some issues, but I knew he loved me.

Once he left, I turned back around to find Reed and Josh deep into what appeared to be a hushed yet heated discussion in my kitchen. They were huddled together by the fridge, each of them with a water bottle in their hand, speaking urgently.

Neither of them looked up when I approached, and I used their oblivious state to try to eavesdrop.

"... not the right time... maybe give it a week..." was all I heard when Josh glanced over his shoulder at me.

He cleared his throat and they both straightened, trying to appear casual and failing miserably.

"Secrets, secrets are no fun..." I sang, but both of the men ignored me, sipping their water.

"Are we going to head over to Hazel and Luke's to drop the stuff off?" Reed asked.

My eyes darted between the two of them, trying to piece together what they could have been talking about that they wouldn't share with me.

But I would be lying to myself if I said that after the wedding, everything felt the same. I'd done my best to not think about either of them in *that* way, but it was so damn hard. I had done well—or at least I thought I had—at appearing nonchalant about the whole thing and acting like I wasn't constantly thinking about getting them both back in my bed.

But the same couldn't be said for the two of them. I caught both of them acting cagey or giving me outwardly lingering looks. Which happened every once in a while since our one summer night together, but it was even worse and more obvious. Then the whole thing with Reed in the hallway was the icing on top.

We were all thinking about it, except I was the only one who was trying to act normal and play it off. Thankfully, each at least knew about the other, and I didn't have that hanging over my head on top of everything else.

"Sure," I said, deciding it wasn't the time to raise the question of what the hell was wrong with them.

We exited the apartment in silence. We entered the truck in silence. We drove the fifteen-minute drive to Hazel and Luke's house in near silence, save for the radio, which was turned so low that my normal breathing was louder.

And when we pulled into their driveway, we piled out of the truck like our asses were on fire.

Moving the furniture was also done mostly in silence, with only muttered phrases and quickly decided upon methods for moving the heavier pieces. When there were only a few more items left, I had had enough and found my way into the kitchen and the fridge, grabbing a beer and hopping onto the kitchen counter.

Hazel and Luke's home was cozy and welcoming. Hazel had decorated it well with warm colors and comfortable furniture, and all I wanted to do was curl up on the cream-colored couch and take a nap. I had promised her that while she and Luke were away on their two-week-long honeymoon road trip with their dog, Sadie, I would check in on the place. I knew it was likely that I'd be there more often since Adam was moving in. I would need somewhere else to go when he made me miserable.

I was in the middle of a daydream about napping on the large, comfy couch in the living room while idly sipping my beer when I heard hushed voices on the other side of the wall. To my left I could see over the half wall and into the living room and to my right was the entrance to the kitchen from the entryway. I peered over the wall, but they weren't in the living room, so I scooted to the right until I was close enough to almost clearly make out their voices.

"Where the hell is she?" one of them said.

"I don't know, but we're in agreement, right?"

I couldn't tell whose voice was whose when they were whispering, and I was already straining to hear them.

"Yes, for the millionth fucking time. We will wait a few weeks and then bring it up to her. But like I said, that means no kissing or touching or fucking until then."

I immediately perked up and was further intrigued and annoyed by the quiet conversation.

"I get that, but can you handle that?"

Someone scoffed and then said, "I can keep my fucking hands to myself. But I think the rule should only apply to initiating. If she kisses me, you've gotta be kidding if you think I'm not going to let it happen."

And with that lovely sentiment, I hopped off of the counter and turned the corner. "Who am I kissing?"

Never had I seen such genuine "deer in headlights" looks. Both men whipped their heads toward me, eyes wide with the realization that I was within hearing distance. For a long second, they both stared at me like they couldn't believe it.

"No one," Reed finally said, scrubbing a hand down his face while Josh shook his head.

"Yeah, that's not going to cut it for me. Obviously, you were talking about me, so you might as well fess up now."

Josh sighed as the two guys glanced at each other again, having a silent conversation with only the slight movement of their eyelids and minute changes in facial expressions. They were so close that they didn't even need words to communicate. They did it often, and part of me thought they didn't even notice it.

"This is a talk that we should probably have at your apartment," Reed offered, and I immediately shook my head.

"I'm not getting in the car with either of you until I know what the hell is going on and why you're talking about me in hushed voices. You've both been acting extra weird since…"

"Since you had sex with both of us within twenty-four hours," Reed muttered.

I narrowed my eyes at him but conceded. "Yes, since then. So, tell me, so I can also be in the loop."

With one final glance in each other's direction, they both nodded. "Let's sit," Josh said, leading the way into the living room.

Cautiously, I followed, and with each step closer to the couch, I began to dread the conversation to follow. Based on their attitudes and what they had said after our hookups, I could only imagine where their thoughts were. They had both been fairly vocal about wanting more than casual sex, but I had hoped their words were only said in the heat of an orgasm high. Or in an attempt to get in my pants.

The way they were eyeing me, though, as I sat on the far end of the sectional across from them, I knew it was only wishful thinking. I was immediately thankful for the glass coffee table between us. I needed space from them to think clearly.

"I guess…" Reed stuttered.

"We just…" Josh said with no confidence in his voice.

"I don't care who says what, someone just tell me what the hell is going on."

And without another second of hesitation, Reed blurted out, "We want more. With you, I mean."

"What?" I asked, gobsmacked by the sincerity in his voice and the seriousness I saw in both of their expressions.

"We want more than friendship. It's been something we've both been thinking about for a while now," Josh chimed in.

Before I could wrap my head around the words coming from their mouths, Reed continued, "We understand this puts you in a hard spot."

"A hard spot…" I muttered, lost in the maze in my own head.

"But we have a plan," Josh said.

"A plan…"

"And we think it'll work," Reed finished.

"A plan…" I said again.

They both watched me expectantly, but I couldn't tell what they wanted from me. I could barely make out the thoughts in my head, let alone say them out loud in full, coherent sentences. I felt scattered and ambushed.

My mind ran down the list—the very *long* list—of all the

reasons the entire situation was doomed and why I had to immediately undo all of the thinking they'd done. Because if they had
a plan, they'd actually thought about it.

But among the list of reasons why that couldn't happen, the
most glaringly important ones to me were the fact that more
than ten years of friendship was not something to just gawk at in
the face of a possible relationship with one of the men sitting in
front of me. And two, I didn't know if I saw a future like that
with either of them. Sure, the sexual chemistry was unbelievable,
but I had lived enough to know that a relationship would take
more than that to work. And finally, the idea of choosing
between the two.

"Okay, I can see the wheels turning, and before you think too
hard on it, I want you to hear our proposal," Reed said, the
nervousness I'd heard in his voice earlier long gone.

"Your proposal…"

"Are you just going to repeat everything we say?" Josh said.

I chuckled and shook my head, trying to clear the myriad of
thoughts. "I'm sorry, I'm just confused and surprised. And I'm
half expecting one of you to turn into a werewolf while the other
starts sparkling and has a sudden taste for my blood."

They both narrowed their eyes in confusion, but I waved
them off. "Just tell me what your proposal is, so I can turn it
down."

Josh scrubbed a hand over his mouth. "This will benefit you
more than you think. I would listen to what we have to say."

I blew out a breath and leaned back into the couch, crossing
my arms over my chest. "I'm listening. Please continue."

"Two separate dates with both of us," Reed said plainly. "We
were going to go with three, but four felt more reasonable. The
first one, we each plan a surprise date for you. We'll take you
somewhere, do something, pull out all of the stops—"

"Within reason," Josh added, glaring at Reed.

"We'll set a budget, but we'll each plan our own date. Then

the second date would be more relaxed—we'd make you dinner or order food and watch a movie. Something like that."

The bigger part of me told me to not even humor their ludicrous idea, but there was a small yet significant part that wanted to hear them out. I was morbidly curious. "So, I go on two dates with each of you. What happens after that?"

"Well, the idea would be that you would choose," Josh said.

And I laughed. Like seriously laughed because by the time I was done, my stomach was cramping and my cheeks hurt, and I could feel the tears pricking at the backs of my eyes. When I righted myself, tucking my legs underneath me and smoothing my hands over my legging-clad thighs, Reed and Josh were staring at me. They appeared only moderately annoyed at my outburst, but I couldn't care—I was the woman they wanted to date, so they'd have to learn to put up with me.

That realization hit me like a smack to the face or a bucket of cold water over my head.

"You want me to choose?"

"Yes," they both said simultaneously.

"You've both lost the plot. I'm not choosing, and who said I wanted to be with either of you? Huh?" Suddenly uncomfortable, I stood from the couch and paced in front of the fireplace. "Have you considered that? Maybe all I see is friendship between us. Did you think about that when you were scheming behind my back?"

"I would hardly call it scheming," Reed said, but I threw him a scathing look that quickly quieted him.

"Why did you have to do this? You both fucking ambushed me at the damn wedding and fucked it all up! Everything was fine before that—we all three pretended like that stupid night at the lake didn't happen, and it was fine. Why couldn't it have just been fine?"

"Because it wasn't fine, Amanda," Josh said, imploring me to hear him, and I stopped pacing. "We've both thought about that night every fucking day since, and nothing's changed. The feelings haven't gone away, so here we are. And you can say all you want that you don't feel some sort of way, but we know you're lying. Speaking for myself, I'm not willing to just let this go. And Reed has made the same statement, so this is the best we came up with—we both want a shot."

I shuddered a breath as I continued walking a hole in the hardwood floor in front of the fireplace. These men were going to be the death of me.

"I agree with everything Josh said. Speaking for myself—" Reed stood and stepped toward me, but I backpedaled quickly.

"Oh no, no, no," I said, darting around the couch, hoping to distance myself as much as I could. Space, I needed space to think clearly. All of their smells and hands and sounds made it hard to do anything besides focus on them. "Stay on that side of the couch. Do not come near me."

"Why?" Josh said, standing next to Reed near the coffee table, the two of them too damn attractive and mouthwatering for their own good.

"Because I need space to think."

"Why?" It was Reed that time.

"Because it's hard to fucking think straight when you're around."

"Who?" Josh asked.

"Both of you."

"But who?"

I groaned in irritation. "What are you two? Fucking owls? Or maybe it's Tweedledee and Tweedledum. Either way, just don't come near me."

"Because if we come near you, you can't think straight, right? We're distracting?" Josh said, taking a step around the coffee table.

I watched him pivot around the couch as my heart rate increased. The house was cool, yet my skin felt molten with each measured step he took. I had an exit to my back and to my right —into the entryway and into the kitchen—but I didn't move. I didn't move until Josh turned the last corner around the couch and was directly in front of me. Only then did I take a hesitant step back, directly into a hard chest. Looking over my shoulder, my eyes connected with Reed's as he looked down at me.

His stance was casual—hands tucked into the front pockets of his joggers and his shoulders were relaxed—however, the sharp line of his lips and the set of his jaw told me he wasn't going to let me escape.

As I turned back around, I wasn't surprised to find Josh had closed the short distance between us. I could feel the combined heat of them at my front and my back, a sensation I hadn't experienced in so long that I'd nearly forgotten how good it felt.

Then there was the mixture of their deep, masculine scents combined with the sweat from moving heavy shit all day that nearly drove me mad.

It was all I could do to suppress the quick breaths that wanted to escape through my lips, and as much as I wanted to pull myself from their orbit, there was an equal part of me that couldn't help but stay. Even with neither of them touching me, I was imprisoned by them—that's the pull they had, and it was the pull that scared me.

"We should—" I began, only to be interrupted by an odd sound to my left. There was a mechanical whir, then an odd mixing sound before I spotted the dog camera and a small, brown treat plopped out onto the wood floor.

"Umm…" Reed muttered behind me, but I braced myself for what I knew was about to happen.

"Hey, guys, if you're gonna fuck, could you maybe not do it where I can see you? I'm not much into voyeurism. Thanks!" Hazel's voice was clear as day over the small two-way speaker. I berated myself for forgetting the camera they set up to keep an eye on Sadie while they were out of the house.

"I think that's our cue to go," I mumbled to them and stepped around Josh to find the dog treat. I replaced it in the container at the top of the camera.

"A dog treat? You could have just called me or something," I said, knowing full well she could hear me.

"They were pawing all over you like dogs, so I figured it would distract them," she said and I couldn't help but laugh as I watched the two men mutter to each other and head to the front door.

# NINE

## Amanda

BEFORE WE EVEN GOT BACK INTO THE TRUCK, I ESTABLISHED A GAG order on all dating discussions until we got back to my apartment, which meant we mostly sat in silence because that was all the three of us could think about.

With the tension growing and my anxiety reaching a level I hadn't known in years, I considered what the conversation would be when we stepped through the door to my apartment. I couldn't imagine the two of them letting me off the hook, but I contemplated the possibility of locking myself in my bedroom for the foreseeable future and refusing to leave until they promised to drop it.

"Oh!" Josh said out of nowhere. "That was a *Twilight* reference you made earlier—the werewolf and the vampire."

I chuckled but nodded, glad he understood it thirty minutes after the fact.

"Wait, which one am I then? Because that chick ends up with the vampire, right?"

"I didn't mean to assign you one or the other. I said it because it's a love triangle situation."

Reed chuckled next to me, pulling the U-Haul back into the spot near the door to my building. "I'd be the vampire, then."

Josh scoffed, reaching behind me to push Reed's shoulder before he jumped out of the cab. "You wish."

"I'm just saying—" Reed began, but I held up my hand.

"Not until we get upstairs. Damn, guys."

They both trudged upstairs like teenagers being sent to their rooms, and the minute I closed the door behind me, they turned to me, leaning against the counter in the kitchen.

"You both seriously think this is going to turn out well?" I asked, taking up a spot on the other side of the kitchen island.

They nodded simultaneously, and I rolled my eyes at how in sync they were.

"There are so many issues with this whole idea," I said.

"Okay, name them," Reed instructed.

"You think you both can put aside your alphahole bullshit long enough to do this? Or to do this without ruining your friendship or our own? And I'm not saying I will, but what if I do pick one of you at the end? You can't tell me that isn't going to screw everything up, and I don't want to be put in that position."

"We've talked through all of this, Amanda," Josh said. "What's most important to us, in the end, is what you want. If you choose one of us, great, or if you don't, then fine. We've both come to terms with the fact that it may not be us, but we're tired of waiting around for an opportunity. We're making the opportunity for ourselves."

I huffed and scrubbed my hands through my hair, pulling the hair tie and letting it fall around my shoulders. It was a failed attempt at relieving some of the pressure growing in my head. It was on the tip of my tongue to repeat my earlier denial without any further argument, but I couldn't do it. They were so serious, watching me and trying to gauge my reaction or read my thoughts through the subtle changes in my facial expressions.

Their patience was admirable as we stood in silence. Neither of them showed any signs of agitation at my long pause. They weren't bouncing their legs or glancing at the clock. They didn't clear their throats or sneak looks at each other—they merely waited.

They waited, and I ran through every scenario. If I told them yes, it would mean our friendships would likely change forever. It could have caused animosity and grudges that may have never gone away, and there was also the terrifying possibility that I would get my heart broken. Or that I could even break one, or both, of their hearts.

I also knew the two men in front of me better than I may have ever known anyone. Through most of my adult life, they had both been there. And I had watched woman after woman, relationship after hookup after one-night stand, not change a damn thing. Neither of them was keen on commitment, which had never bothered me before. That was until I became the woman they were pursuing. Our night at the lake house and then the *nights* at the wedding were one thing.

And I didn't think highly enough of myself to believe I would be the woman to change that pattern for either of them.

But even with all of the reasons why I shouldn't do it, I found myself asking, "What are the rules?"

"At least two dates with each of us. We already know each other, it's just a matter of figuring out if there's more there," Reed said.

"Yes, but what else?"

"For the first date, let's say no more than two hundred fifty dollars," Josh proposed, and I immediately looked at Reed, knowing full well that his budget would have been at least double that amount if it were any other date. With a family that came from money, he had more disposable income and a small trust fund he'd had full access to after his twenty-fifth birthday.

As I suspected, Reed's eyes went wide for a moment, but he ultimately nodded in agreement.

"Second date, no more than a hundred," Reed said. Josh agreed that time.

"I want to pay for half."

"No."

"Absolutely not."

"Why not? It's the twenty-first century, and I can pay for half of it if I want to."

Josh grabbed a water bottle out of the fridge, handed one to Reed and then slid one across the island to me. "You're right," he said after finishing half of it in one gulp. "But this was our idea, so we should pay. Let us pay."

"Fine," I conceded, already preparing to argue about it during each date.

"Anything else?" Reed asked.

"We should probably discuss... umm... sex," Josh said.

I groaned and sank farther into the barstool, covering my face with my hands.

"What do you mean?" I heard Reed ask Josh, but I didn't engage in the conversation. Instead, I wanted to see where the two of them would take it.

"It should be allowed, you know, if it happens," Josh clarified, and I couldn't help the laugh that escaped between my fingers that were still covering my face. Both of them watched me, Reed crunching his empty water bottle between his hands while Josh fidgeted with the plastic cap between his fingers.

"I think that's a game-time decision. If it happens, it happens. If it doesn't, then it doesn't."

"Agreed. And is there anything specific you want to do or don't want to do? Do you have anything to add?" Reed asked.

"She hasn't even technically agreed," Josh pointed out.

"Just don't take me to a museum after hours and then to a Hollywood bowl where you give me a pair of diamond earrings you bought with your college money. I would also say you shouldn't let your best friend pose as our driver for the evening, but you don't have any other female best friends besides, I guess, Hazel, so that shouldn't be an issue."

"Yeah, but you'd look good wearing my future," Josh said with a smile which I easily returned. *Some Kind of Wonderful* was one of my favorite movies.

"So, that's a yes?" Reed asked.

"No."

I knew it wasn't the answer they were expecting, and they both looked at me like I'd kicked a puppy. It was almost enough to make me reconsider. Almost.

"You both have obviously come to terms with all of this, but I need a... a little more time to think about it."

"We understand," Reed said quietly.

"We'll wait. We've waited this long," Josh added.

They were both so dejected but attempted small smiles like they weren't upset about my initial denial. And it was on the tip of my tongue to change my mind until a fuming Adam busted through the door, letting it slam closed behind him.

"Hey, what the hell happened?" I called after him. He hesitated in the hallway that led back toward his bedroom and bathroom. He tugged off the black beanie and scrubbed a frustrated hand through his messy hair.

"I didn't get the job," he said through clenched teeth as he finally turned around.

"Well, that happens sometimes."

He scoffed and shook his head at me. "No, I was supposed to get the job. My buddy said I had the job and that the interview was just protocol. Turns out the job he told me about wasn't an option since I have no previous experience in a shop. They ended up offering me some shitty job cleaning up around the place for twelve an hour. I told them to shove it."

I groaned and felt my stomach flip. "But it was a job. It's more than you have now, and you could have had money coming in while you looked for something that was a better fit."

"I'm worth more than that, Amanda. I'm not going to sell

myself short. Are you telling me I should be working for twelve dollars an hour? I know I'm not fancy like you and have a college degree, but I deserve more than that."

"Adam, I didn't mean—"

"Look, I will find a job, okay? You can get off my back." His tone became more defensive, and I knew we were edging close to full-blown argument territory. I backed off, holding up my hands in surrender because I knew it had been a hard few days for him. His entire life had been uprooted.

Reed stepped around the island and slid onto the barstool to my right as Josh leaned against the counter on my other side, casually crossing his arms over his chest. Their eyes bounced from me to my brother, likely waiting for one of us to say something else, but I was done talking if it was going to cause Adam to blow up.

"You could come work for me." It was Josh that spoke up out of nowhere.

"What?" both Adam and I said in unison.

"Yeah, I mean, it would only be part time, but I need a barback to work Tuesday, Wednesday, and Saturday nights. I could pay you about twelve an hour plus tips. It would also give you the option to eventually become a bartender if you wanted to."

My mouth agape, I looked from Josh, who had his eyes trained on Adam, to my brother, who appeared to be contemplating the offer.

"You could also work for me," Reed spoke up from my other side. "I need a front desk guy to check people in and register new members. You'd also answer the phones, but it's not that bad of a job. You also get free access to the gym when you're off the clock. It'd be part time, too, just from eight in the morning until two p.m. on the weekdays. But I could do fifteen an hour."

My head swiveled back and forth between the two men, completely stunned by their sudden offers.

"You're both serious?" I asked, and they both nodded with straight faces. So, I turned back to Adam. "What do you think?"

"I guess that would work for now. I'm not promising that it'll be forever, though. Sorry, but I don't want to work in a gym or a bar for the rest of my life."

Josh laughed. "Wasn't my plan either, but hey, I run the place now, so it's not all bad. I'll text you and we can figure out a time to start training."

"That works for me." Adam looked at Reed.

"Same here. I need to look at the schedule."

Adam nodded and turned to leave but hesitated, glancing back over his shoulders. "Thanks, guys."

"Yeah, man."

"Of course."

Once I heard the click of the bathroom door and the water turn on in the shower, I looked back and forth at the guys. "Where the hell did that come from? You both have open positions?"

They shrugged, which wasn't enough of an answer for me. "No, seriously, don't do any favors for me or him. If you don't have an opening, then he will find something else. He's also not the easiest nor the best employee. And offering him jobs isn't going to further ingratiate yourselves with me—it's not going to sway me or make me say yes to your dates."

"My morning receptionist quit yesterday, so I do actually need someone."

"And my barback is being promoted to bartender, so I also need someone. And even if we are doing you a favor, it's not a big deal. That's what friends... are for." He stuttered over the word friends, and I watched a thoughtful expression pass over his features.

"Unfortunately, I have to go," he continued. "I have to get to the bar and meet with Rhonda. But"— he stepped forward and cautiously took one of my hands in his—"tell me you'll think about it. You don't understand how fucking eager I am to take you out on a date. And I promise it'll be worth saying yes."

"I told you I'd think about it," I said. "So, I'll think about it."

He nodded and kissed my cheek, lingering for longer than usual before turning toward the door.

"I've got to go," Reed agreed, also stopping in front of me. He brushed a hand down my arm, and I willed the blush I could feel creeping across my chest and up my neck to calm down. He opened his mouth, and based on the look on his face, I knew he was about to reiterate everything Josh had already made me promise.

"I promise," I began before he could say a word, "that I will think about it. I think I'm going to have a very hard time *not* thinking about it. But I will take everything both of you have said into consideration and give you an answer... soon. And I know whatever dates the two of you plan will be great, so you don't have to tell me again. And I know how so incredibly, insanely, utterly awesome you both are, so you don't have to reiterate that either. Now that we've covered all of that, you can both leave so I can think."

Reed chuckled, shook his head, and also kissed my forehead before the both of them left my apartment.

Think—that's all they wanted me to do. Easy enough. Just think...

# TEN

## Amanda

"FUCKING BEAUTIFUL," SOMEONE WHISPERED INTO MY EAR. HIS HOT breath tickled my skin while a set of hands groped and squeezed my breasts. Another hand tightened around my throat and then lips pressed against mine. His lips and then his tongue were urgent and confident against mine.

There were two of them—Josh and Reed—but I couldn't tell which hands or lips belonged to which man.

My eyes were firmly closed against the pleasure, and no matter how hard I tried, I couldn't open them.

Someone's finger began circling my clit in small movements, and I bucked and ground against it. And then there were two fingers inside of me. I gasped and clenched around them and once again tried to pry my eyes open.

There was nothing but darkness.

The fingers curled inside of me and pressed against the spot that made my entire body involuntarily shudder. Each movement was perfectly in sync, yet I knew each finger belonged to a different man. But it was like they were the same person—slowly and methodically

*moving as one person, drawing out my pleasure and coaxing me
unbearably close to what I knew would be an explosive release.*

*"Look at you. Falling apart around our fingers."*

*There was nothing else in the world but them—the three of us
together and moving as one. And I could feel my orgasm clawing and
begging. Was I begging? I was trying to beg, but nothing I said was
intelligible.*

*"Look at us."*

*"Open your eyes."*

*"Eyes on us."*

*And I tried again and again and again. But I couldn't open my
eyes. I could hear them, taste them, feel them, but I couldn't see them.
My body wouldn't let me see them—*

With a gasp, I jerked myself awake. My face pressed into the
pillow; I could feel the wet spot where the drool had collected.

Motherfucker.

It'd been two days, and all I'd done was think about Josh and
Reed's proposal. I'd barely slept, and when I did, I dreamed of
them. It was the most aggravating dream. It was one moment of
our summer night together on a constant loop, but I couldn't
open my eyes. And I'd wake up before we even got to the really
good part.

My brain was apparently anti-orgasm.

After a second sleepless night, I was irritated that I couldn't
shut my brain off. If I wasn't thinking about them, it was only
because I was trying to get Adam settled in, which didn't require
too much work when he was barely in the apartment to begin
with.

It was my final week off work for winter break, and I was
supposed to be relaxing. Yet my mind didn't get the memo. My
plan for the week had been to do absolutely nothing, which I
was still doing, but with nearly constant intrusive thoughts.

And, like my dream, the thoughts were on a constant loop—I
felt like I wasn't getting anywhere.

I would go over and over every reason why it was a bad idea. I'd remind myself that they were my best friends, that we had all the same mutual friends, and that it was bound to blow up in my face, just as every other relationship had before.

But then I'd remember that they were my best friends, and they knew me better than anyone really ever had and that had to count for something. And the sexual chemistry was off the charts. There weren't enough words in the English language to describe the electricity I felt in either of their company.

And then I'd loop back again—the bad and then the good, the bad and then the good.

I was mentally, physically, and emotionally exhausted.

I groaned, and like every millennial did first thing in the morning, I reached for my phone. It was a little past eight, and I had a few unread texts and spam emails.

But the first messages to catch my attention were in our "JAR" group text. We were unoriginal, so when naming the messages, we'd used the first initials of our first names: Josh, Amanda, and Reed.

There were two unread texts, one from each guy, but the last message before the new ones they'd only sent a half hour ago was from when we moved Adam in a couple days before. Reed was confirming that he'd returned the U-Haul, and after that, they'd both left me alone to think.

My head hurt from all the stupid thinking.

> Josh: These have been the longest two days of my entire life.

> Reed: We need a sign of life.

I was impressed they'd left me alone for almost forty-eight entire hours. I expected them to text me immediately the next day asking for an answer, but they were, again, being uncharacteristically patient.

So, I decided to let them flex that patience a little more and wait to respond until I'd had coffee and maybe a shower.

I pulled myself out of bed and made my way to the kitchen. There were no signs of life from Adam's room, and while my coffee brewed, I peeked through the partially opened door. His room was already in a state of chaos and disarray—boxes were still half-packed and any items that had been unpacked were thrown across the floor.

Each time he left the apartment or didn't come home, the sinking feeling in my gut grew. Since it was in the morning on a weekday, he was possibly at the gym with Reed and working his new front desk job. But since he'd moved in, I hadn't spent more than an hour with him.

I was in a state of constant worry when it came to him, and with him living under my roof, the feeling had tripled overnight. I just wanted him to succeed and do well. To figure out his life and ultimately be happy.

Feeling crushed by the weight of another sleepless night, I made an entire pot of coffee. I poured myself a generous cup, and my curiosity couldn't take it anymore. I texted Adam.

> Me: You at work?

The response came quicker than I expected.

> Adam: Ya

I was hoping for more than two letters, but at least he'd responded. Hopeful he was where he said he was, I found the "JAR" group text again and stared at the two same messages.

> Me: I'm alive. Although this could just be someone pretending to be me.

It was only seconds later that two new messages popped up.

> Reed: Only you would say something like that. If someone was pretending to be you, they wouldn't outright say that.

> Josh: You could prove it to us. Whose dick is bigger? That's only something Amanda would know. And yes, there is a right answer.

I shook my head and tried to suppress my smile.

> Me: That question requires verification on your part. Would you submit to a dick measuring contest? Unless you've already done that?

> Reed: I'm going to stop this conversation before it gets out of control.

> Reed: How are you?

I took inventory of how I was, but the answer was pretty simple.

> Me: Tired.

> Josh: Because you can't stop thinking about us? ; )

> Me: You wish.

> Reed: Yes, we do wish because that would mean we're one step closer to you giving in to our plan.

> Me: Mighty confident to assume that I'll eventually give in.

> Josh: We have every reason to be confident. You cannot resist us.

I scoffed and took another sip of my coffee. Their egos were overinflated, and the last thing I wanted to do was exacerbate the problem.

> Me: I did it for a year and a half. Wasn't too hard.

> Reed: That argument doesn't work. We have two very recent examples of when you couldn't resist either of us.

> Me: That was the exception not the rule.

> Josh: Should we come over and prove it to you?

I started typing a response at least five different times before I gave up and set my phone down. I'd been thinking for more than two days, yet I still didn't know what to do. I knew what I wanted to do, but what I *should* do was another issue.

I'd never had a hard time separating sex and feelings before or with anyone else. But with the two of them, they were completely intertwined. Although we were supposed to be a one-night stand, it was one night that had continued to follow me.

For nearly a year and a half, I'd tried so hard to forget. The effort I went through to erase it from my memory, or at least lock it away in an impenetrable box, was impressive. But it was useless. The more I tried to forget about it, the more I thought about it. And something told me there was a reason I couldn't let it go. Deciding between the two of them, or letting them both go, was something I knew I'd have to face if I wanted to explore anything with them. And it was something that didn't have to be decided in that moment while I stared into my quickly cooling coffee.

I picked up my phone.

Me: That's not necessary.

Reed: Worried you weren't going to respond.

Josh: Still thinkin' about us? ; )

Reed: Stop smiling at your phone like an idiot, Sunshine.

Me: Are y'all together?

Josh: We're mid-workout.

Reed: What are you thinking?

Reed doesn't have to include my name in the message to know he's asking me.

Me: That I should be institutionalized because I think I've gone crazy.

Reed: Are you saying...?

Josh: No. Fucking. Way.

I took a deep breath and tried to talk myself out of what I was about to do, but it was no use. All of the arguments I could muster were nothing compared to how much I wanted to try.

Reed: I'm not trying to rush you, but I'm trying to rush you. Josh is bouncing up and down like an idiot and I need you to make it stop.

Me: Plan the dates.

I held my breath and waited for their responses, but several seconds went by without any texts and I began to worry that maybe in the two seconds it took me to respond, they'd changed their minds. That would be just my luck.

Reed: That backfired. Now he's really jumping up and down. And whooping.

> Josh: THIS IS THE BEST DAY!!
>
> Reed: Thank you for giving me a chance. I already have the perfect date planned.
>
> Josh: So do I!
>
> Reed: You won't regret this.

Thank goodness no one was around to see the stupid smile on my face. I poured myself another cup of coffee and tried to soothe the gnawing worry in my gut with the steaming hot liquid.

> Me: I get total veto power and whatever I say goes. No matter what.
>
> Josh: Yes, ma'am.
>
> Reed: No problem.
>
> Me: Ok, then that's all I have to say.
>
> Reed: Our date is tonight. I'll pick you up at 7.
>
> Josh: WHOA. Wait a damn minute. You had to wait until I was in the bathroom to throw that out there. Why do you get the first date?
>
> Reed: Because I was the first to respond.

And then I watched for the next ten minutes while they bickered back and forth in the group chat about who should get the first date. One of my worries with dating both of them and them being such good friends was the alpha, jealous bullshit. But their bickering was all in good fun.

> Reed: One second, babe. We're going to handle this the way men should.
>
> Me: Duel to the death?

Josh: Pretty much.

Two minutes later.

Josh: He won. Stupid Rock, Paper, Scissors.

Reed: Tonight. I'll pick you up at 7.

# ELEVEN

## Amanda

GREEN OR BLACK? GREEN OR BLACK. I'D BEEN STANDING IN FRONT of the mirror, flipping back and forth between the two— throwing one off to put the other on, contemplating it for a few seconds to only do it all again. The green top was a little fancier and formfitting, but the black was my go-to on a first date. Because that's what it was, right?

I'd hung out with both of the guys numerous times, and I'd even slept with them both twice. Yet, we'd never been on a date. I wasn't necessarily traditional, but it was a little more backward even for me.

And I knew the night was going to go one of three ways. One, it would be an absolute nightmare, and we'd both know for sure that there would be nothing but friendship between the two of us. Two, it would be a decent-enough, good date but wouldn't lend itself to making any hard decisions, or three, it would be one of the best dates I've ever been on.

Of the three, I think the third option was the most terrifying and worrisome. The impact of a good date would be more widespread and the repercussions more severe. And make my life a whole hell of a lot more complicated.

So, I went with the black. Not for any good reason other than I was getting sweaty switching between the two tops over and over again. And sweaty before a date was not the look I was going for.

If it had been any other date with any other guy, I would have texted Hazel for advice on the fit. But I couldn't because that would elicit questions about the guy I was going out with and what we were doing and where we were going, and I only knew the answer to one of those questions and wasn't nearly ready to confess to my best friend that two of our other best friends shanghaied me into dating them.

She was also on her honeymoon, so there was no way I was bothering her. I'd lucked out that she hadn't mentioned catching me with Reed at the rehearsal dinner yet.

Then there was an ache in my chest. It was an ache that had been there for so many months that it was second nature now. Blakely was still MIA, and not knowing where my oldest friend was was painful.

Ever since she was caught up in Valerie's plan against Hazel and Luke, she'd been missing. She'd never made it to her parents' house in Arkansas and only called them every once in a while, never telling them exactly where she was.

She'd also left before she'd given a good explanation of her side of the story. It was something all of us wanted to hear. Blakely, as headstrong and stubborn as she was, wouldn't have thrown innocent Hazel under the bus to Luke's murderous and vindictive ex-wife for no reason. I refused to believe it.

But her absence didn't keep me from reaching out. Occassionally I would send her an email to which I'd undoubtedly never receive a response. And then, I'd text her and call her or send her a message on social media. All went unanswered, but I still tried. I didn't want to give up, but my messages had become fewer recently.

Hope was hard to come by, and as a group, we didn't really talk about Blakely anymore.

A light rap on the door drew me from my thoughts, and the ache in my chest was replaced by the nervous roll of my stomach. I glanced at myself one last time in the mirror and sighed— it was as good as it was going to get.

After a final shaky breath, I tried—and miserably failed—to also steady the shaking of my hands. As I approached the door, doing a substandard job of faking confidence, I chastised myself for my nerves. I knew Reed, and I knew even if we weren't romantically compatible, we would still have fun.

In one swift motion—like pulling off a Band-Aid—I swung the door open, and the chilly January air greeted me.

"Hi," I said quietly, the words catching in my throat. I started to step back and wave him inside but wasn't prepared for the sight of him. A black button-down shirt fitted around his chest and abs with the top button undone. And his jeans were nearly as dark as mine, as was his long black coat. My lips curled slightly when I noticed his dark-brown boots as his weight shifted. Texas boy through and through.

And gripped tightly in his hand was a bouquet of lilies.

He lingered in the doorway as his eyes raked over my body. From head to toe, his appreciative gaze sent a delicious shiver down my spine. It was like he was seeing me for the first time again.

In one second, we were staring at each other, and in the next, Reed mumbled something under his breath in Spanish and paced toward me like a man on a mission. He dropped the flowers on the table next to the door, and before I knew it, his hands were twisted in the hair at the base of my neck. The scent of his body wash, his cologne or whatever the hell it was, was heady and so potent I worried it would inhibit my cognitive abilities.

Our lips only an inch apart, he paused just long enough, I realized, for me to push him away or tell him no. But watching his intent, desire-filled eyes bounce back and forth between my eyes and my lips and the quickness of his shallow breaths against my skin, I knew I wouldn't say no.

And when he realized the same, his mouth covered mine in a totally different kiss than I was expecting. It was soft and purposeful. When his tongue pressed against my lips, I opened for him and the brush of his tongue against my own was thoughtful and languid.

I'd expected a heated, aggressive kiss filled with tension and the desperate clash of teeth. But for some reason, the delicate, meaningful kiss felt like so much more. Like with our lips pressed together, I could feel how much he wanted it. How much he wanted me.

It was too short. The second he pulled back, I missed the warmth of him, and it was altogether more terrifying than anything else I'd felt. It was too early to be feeling anything so intense—we hadn't even left my apartment.

"I couldn't wait until the end of the date to do that," Reed murmured against my mouth, still so close that his lips brushed against mine. "You're beautiful."

And with one final, gentle caress of his lips, he pulled back and retrieved the discarded flowers.

"Covered all your bases?" I laughed.

"Of course, who do you think I am?"

In the kitchen, I found a vase in the cabinet above the oven and filled it with water quickly.

"So, where are we going? What are we doing?"

Out of the corner of my eye, I caught the motion of Reed shaking his head. A nearly black piece of hair fell into his eyes with the motion as a playful smile tugged at his lips. Even the slightest movement of his mouth made my lips tingle with the memory of his stubble against my chin and his lips against my own. Trying to curb the tingling, I tugged my lower lip between my teeth, clamping down harder than usual, but it didn't stop the sensation.

Reed's smile widened, and I pulled my eyes from his mouth to his brown eyes, which mirrored the playfulness in his smile. Of course, he'd caught me staring at his mouth and knew the exact thoughts that were at the forefront of my mind.

I knew it was going to be a long night since the man knew my every thought with only a quick glance at my face.

"It's a surprise, but I promise you'll enjoy it," he said with enough confidence that I nearly believed him.

"Hmm, if you say so," I said with a shrug as I grabbed my purse and turned out the kitchen lights.

"Is this absolutely necessary?" I asked for the third time since we'd left my apartment only a few minutes earlier. Reed had come prepared with one of his ties and fastened it firmly around my eyes. Apparently our destination was so top secret that it required additional precautions.

"For the millionth time, yes, Amanda, it is necessary."

"But why?"

He huffed out a laugh, and I shivered when his warm fingers gripped my thigh. His thumb rubbed back and forth over the denim.

"Because you would know exactly where we were going if you were able to see."

"Ohhh," I said, like that was actually helpful in some way. "So, it's somewhere I've been before?"

Reed sighed and squeezed my thigh tighter, which I took as a sign that he likely wanted me to be quiet and stop trying to ruin the surprise. "You've been to a lot of places, Amanda. Not sure that little hint is helpful."

I shrugged and shimmied farther back into the seat, getting more comfortable for the indefinite amount of time we'd be in the car since he wouldn't give me that detail either. And to be honest, it seemed he had already put a lot of thought into the date, and I didn't want to be a spoilsport. I just wasn't a fan of surprises.

So, rather than continue the barrage of questions I had fired at him since he buckled his seat belt and fashioned the makeshift blindfold around my eyes, I settled in and let the seat warmer relax my nerves the best it could.

"What, you don't have any more questions?" Reed asked, and I could hear the smile in his voice. I imagined his perfectly straight white teeth glinting at me as he gave me a quick glance and a half smile. It's what I would have likely seen had I been able to see.

"I just figured I shouldn't try to ruin a surprise that you spent so much time preparing."

"Who said I spent a lot of time on this? This could have been totally last minute and we're just driving aimlessly."

I opened my mouth, prepared to deliver a snarky remark when Reed's phone began ringing through the Bluetooth in the car.

He declined the call because it suddenly stopped ringing only a second later.

"You looked like you were about to say something," he prompted.

"Yes, actually, I was going to say that I don't believe—"

Once again, the ringing rang through the car, and I jumped at least a few inches out of my seat. "Is it the same person?"

"Yeah, I can call her back later." A feeling I hadn't experienced in a while suddenly twisted its way through me, leaving in its wake an uneasiness.

"Her?" I asked cautiously, a verbal manifestation of the jealousy bubbling to the surface. A feeling I had no right to when I had staked no claim to the man behind the wheel with his hand steadfast on my thigh.

"Yes, her." Without any other explanation, the feeling wouldn't pass. I contemplated questions I could ask to pry the answer from him without sounding suspicious, but none came to mind.

It had been years since I'd been well and truly jealous. The last time I could remember was with my ex. Since him, my other relationships and hookups weren't important enough to get jealous over. And the feeling was foreign as I worried my lower lip between my teeth.

"What—" Reed began to say, only to be cut off by the incessant ringing for the third time.

"You should probably answer it. She must really want to talk," I said, cringing at the disdain that was clear in my voice.

"We're on a date, Amanda. I can't talk to my mom while I'm on a date."

I whipped my head toward him, like it was going to do much, and scoffed. "Reed, you cannot keep sending Mama G to voice mail. She's going to be furious!"

"I will text her when we get to the—when we get where we're going. She will understand when I explain."

Mama G was one of my favorite people in the entire world, without a doubt. She was a warm, gorgeous woman that had thawed—at least partially—Reed's stickler of a father.

They met in college, and according to them, it had been love at first sight. They were married only two months later—while still finishing their degrees—and had been together ever since. It was the perfect story of opposites attract. She was a lively, loving woman who cared unconditionally for the people around her. Her smile and vivacious personality lit up a room.

In the several years I'd been friends with Reed, I'd spent my fair share of time around Mama G and had grown to think of her as a somewhat surrogate mother. She was everything my own mother wasn't and then some.

But she was the exact foil to Reed's father, who was a harsh, quiet man except for around his wife. She worked as a successful architect while his father was an attorney and had opened offices throughout Texas. And although they didn't seem like the likeliest pair, they worked well together and *fit*. Instead of my own parents, Reed's parents were my blueprint.

He was a profound mix of them both; he'd become so diligent and goal-oriented that it was nearly a fault, yet he was so enthralled with life and the people in it that he was enigmatic and unencumbered.

"We're here."

I clapped my hands together and lifted my hands to the tie, ready to finally peel it away. But much to my dismay, Reed's hand caught one of my wrists. "Not until we get inside."

I huffed and was prepared to argue until I heard Reed's door close and then silence. "Reed?" I said quietly.

More silence was my only answer, so I said again, "Reed?"

And nothing. Not a single peep and my anxiety that I'd been left in an unknown place for an unknown amount of time ratcheted up a notch or five. Just as my breathing quickened, the passenger door to my right swung open, letting in the chilly air as a hand encircled my upper arm. I jumped at the sudden touch and pulled away.

"It's just me, babe. No need to freak out."

"If I'm going to be blindfolded, can you at least tell me what you're doing before you do it?"

In a move I wasn't expecting, Reed's thumb found my lower lip and pulled it free from between my teeth. The next thing I felt was his lips, firm against my own.

"You know I wouldn't do anything to hurt you, right? You'll always be safe with me," he said, still hovering his lips over my own. He lifted me onto the concrete, and the car door closed behind me and echoed through what I believed was a parking garage. It was an interesting development but didn't lend itself to learning our location.

Reed's large palm enveloped my own as we began walking. "Okay, so you're going to step down right about now," Reed instructed, and I did as he said but lost my balance all the same.

He chuckled and helped right me before we continued. The

short heels of my boots clicked against the concrete and was the only sound around us as I concentrated on not falling.

"Now there's another curb, so just step up right now," he instructed again, and with little grace, I stumbled again but was caught in Reed's strong arms.

"And that's about enough of that. Hang on, babe," he said, which was my only warning before I felt the world fall away. Reed gripped me at the bend in my legs with one arm as the other held me at my upper back. I wasn't prepared to be carried and let out a pathetic, unsuspecting squeak as I landed in his arms.

"I've got you," he said, as though it was usual to carry a perfectly capable woman.

"If you just take the blindfold off, then I could walk on my own."

"Yes, I know."

I sighed but found my arguments dying on my tongue as I slid my hands over his chest and wrapped them around his neck. I felt weightless in his arms and settled closer to his chest as we came to a stop. He leaned in one direction and then righted himself quickly.

"Just don't drop me," I said.

"Wasn't planning on it."

There was a ding, which meant we were in an elevator, and Reed stepped forward before turning us around and leaning to press another button. Or so I assumed.

"And don't run me into anything either."

"I hadn't planned on doing that either."

I took a deep breath as I heard the doors shut and the elevator moved upward.

"And if you could not—" But once again, my words were suddenly cut off by the feeling of his lips on mine. And in less than a second, I couldn't even remember what my last request was as he kissed me breathless.

I returned the urgency of the kiss, pulling myself even closer to him and tangling my fingers at the short hair at his neck. A breathless moan slipped from between my lips as the elevator doors dinged open.

Without breaking our kiss, Reed stepped forward and didn't move again until I heard the doors whir shut behind us.

"I've realized," he began in a husky, low voice, "that's the best way to keep you quiet. I have to give your mouth something else to do. Something else to focus on."

Maybe if he hadn't just had his tongue in my mouth and delivered a kiss that left me feeling weak and light-headed, then I may have taken offense to his comment, but I was feeling all of those things, so I let it slide.

I did, however, think of about ten ways to make his comment even dirtier and was contemplating which one fit the situation best when he set me down and removed the tie from my face.

Thankfully, the lights were low in the room, and it only took a few seconds to adjust. And when I did, my breath caught in my throat. I didn't know what to look at first, so I found myself whipping my head from one side to the other and then up toward the tall ceilings.

To the right was the gift shop filled with items and knick-knacks I'd perused a million times and to my left was the ticket area where I'd stood several times and waited an ungodly amount of time for new exhibits when I was a kid and buying tickets online wasn't an option.

In the black rafters, several feet above us, were sculptures of animals, planets, and dinosaurs, dangling from the ceiling from clear wire, giving the illusion that they were floating in midair. The large entrance hall was cast in dim, warm light, and I peered at everything a second and third time before I whirled around to the man standing behind me.

With his hands tucked effortlessly in his pockets and a sly grin on his lips, he seemed proud of himself.

"We're at the Museum of Natural Science."

He chuckled and smoothed a hand over his mouth and jaw to subdue his smile. "Yes, we are."

"But… but it's late. They're closed."

"Yes, they are."

I looked around again and made sure my eyes weren't deceiving me. But everything was just the same as I had seen it only a few seconds before. There were signs in the middle of the hall displaying the various new exhibits and the tables at the far end where the small café was were covered in overturned chairs.

"How are we here?" I said loud enough that my voice echoed in the otherwise silent space.

"I called in a favor," he said with a shrug like it wasn't a big deal.

"What the hell did you do that meant the return favor got us into the museum after hours?"

"Does it really matter? We're here, and we have the whole place to ourselves until midnight." He waved one hand out like he was showing me how much of the place we had.

For likely only the second time in my life, I was nearly beyond words. It had to have been closer to eight, which meant we had four hours to explore. Hopefully that would be enough time.

"Oh, Mr. Gregory, I'm glad to see you've made it. Good evening, Ms. Allan." A man in a black suit and a white shirt sauntered our way from near the ticket area. He held out his hand, which Reed quickly shook with an affable smile. The man offered his hand to me, and with a slight reluctance, I took his hand, still stunned that I was standing in the middle of one of my favorite places on earth after hours.

"Well, as we discussed, the place is yours until midnight. I just ask that you don't touch any of the exhibits and leave the place just as you found it. Oh, and as a treat, there are two bottles of champagne at the table nearest the entrance of the first exhibit. But otherwise, I hope you both have a great time."

"Thank you, Mr. Charles," Reed said. And with a smile and wave, he disappeared back the way he came.

"Start talking," I said as Reed grabbed my hand and led me to the little table with the champagne.

As he popped the bottle and filled the two glasses, he began to explain. "Charles is the manager, or equivalent, here, and I train both him and his boss. When I mentioned that I may want to bring you here and explained that this was the most important date of my life, he said he would make an exception. We have free rein of the place."

Reed handed me my glass of bubbles and tapped his own glass against it before taking a small sip. All the while, my mouth was agape.

"Let me get this straight: you help the guy lose a couple of pounds or help him lift weights a few times a week, and in return, we get the museum?" I let the full amount of my uncertainty fill my words.

"Well, that's not necessarily how it happened, and I do more than just help people lose a couple pounds. But yes, more or less, and for the sake of argument, that's what happened."

"I just... this is amazing, Reed. Truly, this is one of the coolest things someone has ever done for me. I'm honestly shocked." With my hands nearly shaking, I took a sip of the champagne, hoping that the bubbles and alcohol would calm me. But I was swept up in the awe I felt for the man in his perfectly tailored suit standing in front of me. My heart constricted and felt like it was beating overtime as he stepped up and brushed my hair from my face.

"There's nothing I wouldn't do for you, Amanda. And this is just the start."

And if it weren't for Reed's eager expression as he gripped my hand, grabbed the bottle of champagne, and urged me forward into the first exhibit, I was sure I would have stayed rooted to the spot in the large room.

# TWELVE

Reed

THE EXCITEMENT IN AMANDA'S VOICE AS SHE PRATTLED OFF FACTS about the body and the joy that lit up her face meant I was suppressing my desire to sprint in the opposite direction. And I'd taken to staring at the dark, carpeted floor, following her by only watching her little black boots and listening to her voice.

"Okay, so this is cool because—" she began but didn't finish, and I chanced a look up toward her face, hoping I didn't catch a pair of beady eyes from one of the cadavers or whatever the hell they were called.

But it wasn't beady eyes I found, just Amanda's skeptical stare, her eyebrows raised and her arms crossed over her chest.

"What?" I asked, feigning confusion.

"Why are you staring at the ground?"

I huffed and did my best to look only at her, which was never that hard since the woman always pulled my attention to her without even trying. "I feel like they're all looking at me," I muttered, feeling a little childish but unsettled nonetheless.

She laughed and relaxed as she closed the distance between

us, pressing her small palms against my cheeks. "Reed, are you scared of the plastinates?"

"The *what*? Have you named them?"

Her laugh tinkled through the air once again as she threw her head back. It was the most beautiful sound in the world and did wonders at easing my nerves.

"No, they preserved the bodies using plastination. The water and fat in the bodies are replaced by plastics, which means they don't decay or smell, but they look the same."

An involuntary shiver ran through me, slipping down my spine and making me shudder at the thought of bodies being preserved at all.

"I'm really not trying to kill the mood, but it just kind of freaks me out—all of their eyes watching us. But I love that you love this stuff, so please continue. I'll be fine. I'm just going to stare at the ground and your ass."

I dipped my head again, but little fingers gripped my wrist and tugged me around a few glass cases that were likely filled with plastinates and through the exit door. Which elicited a deep sigh of relief once it closed behind us with a satisfying click.

"Let's go see the dinosaurs instead," Amanda said with the same enthusiasm she conjured when talking about the types of muscles in the human body.

"*Yes!*" I said, matching her excitement, and we took the staircase back down to the first floor and onto the last exhibit before my penultimate surprise.

She'd spent the entire time naming random facts about anything we saw that she found even remotely interesting. We spent the most time in the Ramses the Great exhibit discussing the lifestyle and culture of the ancient Egyptians. Only an insane person wouldn't be enthralled with the priceless artifacts and the descriptions of their use.

"I love dinosaurs," Amanda murmured quietly to herself the moment we entered the vast room. The lights were dim, with only the uplights on the numerous exhibits and features illuminating the key attractions.

"I think you've said that every time we've walked into a different exhibit," I said as I pressed a kiss to the side of her head, lingering just long enough to smell her clean hair and warm perfume.

She laughed and gazed intently at the massive T.rex in front of us—the primary display and the first thing you see when you walk into the room.

"I'm like a kid in a candy store in this place," she sighed before continuing farther into the exhibit, pausing to read the plaque with the T.rex information.

"Actually, you're like a science teacher in a science museum."

She rolled her eyes and chuckled. "Touché."

For a few minutes, we wandered around the exhibit, stopping to read the plaques to which Amanda would add random information or pose questions that I wouldn't even dream of knowing the answer to. And as excited as I was at being there, and as interesting as each display was, it was Amanda I couldn't tear my attention from.

Her blonde hair was warm in the faint light and there was something about the way her heels clicked against the tiled floor that was very satisfying. Or maybe it was because her ass looked even more fantastic in the heels. She was stunning, no doubt, and I appreciated every second she let me be close to her, but my favorite part was watching her reaction.

There was a thoughtfulness in her expression when she read about a fossil or an artifact and as she processed the information —her eyes darted back and forth between the object and the plaque, piecing it all together as her brow furrowed slightly.

Then when she saw something she was even more excited to see, the excitement overtook her entire face. Her mouth spread wide in a grin and her eyes were alight with glee and intrigue. She'd bounce on her toes as she explained why she was enthusiastic and tried to dumb down the more intensive topics to my level.

The museum was cool, and I'd tried to pay attention, but she was my favorite part.

"Umm, Reed, what's that?"

I'd been so focused on watching Amanda that I hadn't realized my next surprise was directly in front of us. I stepped around the corner and eyed the table in the center of the room. Just as I'd requested, it was covered in a white tablecloth and there were a few candles in the center along with two cloches covering—hopefully—the dinner I'd specifically instructed should be underneath.

"What kind of date would this be if I didn't feed you?" I asked, brushing her hair off her shoulder so I could place my hand on the back of her neck. The skin-to-skin contact made her shiver subtly, and I pushed my fingers lightly into her hair to see if I could elicit another reaction.

"It would have been an awful date, so I'm glad you remembered."

Taking her hand, I led her to the table, and like the gentleman I was, I pulled out her chair. The entire time she watched me with eyebrows raised and an unbelieving smile playing on her lips. And before I sat down, I lifted the cloche dramatically with a flick of my wrist and waved to the warm meal on the plate.

Her mouth dropped open in surprise and her eyes darted between me and the plate a few times before she threw her head back and laughed. The sound was even better than usual as it echoed in the large space and bounced back to me for a second time.

"Burger Joint? Really?" she asked, covering her mouth with her hand in an attempt to stifle her laughter.

"Yes, of course. It's your favorite."

"And you even remembered the bacon," she said after lifting the top bun to inspect the toppings.

I scoffed. "Yeah, I absolutely did because that really would have ruined the date."

Without further delay, Amanda took a huge bite of her burger and moaned just as loud as I'd ever heard her moan. The sound barreled straight through me like I'd made it happen myself, and my dick didn't seem to care that it was from a burger and not anything we had done. Subtly, I readjusted in my seat, unable to keep myself from watching her eyes shutter closed as she chewed the moan-inducing bite.

"Do you remember the first time we went to this place?" She asked between bites.

Of course I remembered it—I remembered every second I'd spent with Amanda because all of them were memorable.

I finished chewing a handful of curly fries and nodded. "Yes, I do."

"Really?" she asked. Her tone was doubtful, and she cocked her head to the side like she was challenging me to prove how much I remembered it.

With a smug grin on my face, I refilled her champagne glass with the new chilled bottle on the table. That's where most of my two-hundred-and-fifty-dollar budget had gone; to champagne and burgers, a classic combination.

"It was our sophomore year of college, and it was the first time you'd used your fake ID at Murphy's. *And* it was the first time you'd done shots, so it also turned out to be the night you got so drunk that you persuaded the band to let you on stage to sing Britney Spears," I began, swelling with pride when Amanda's doubt morphed into shock. "The seven of us stood at the very front and cheered you on while everyone else in the bar booed you to high heaven. God, and you were wearing this skintight black dress with red heels and Blakely gave you so much shit about being overdressed, but all I could think about all night was that you looked fucking fantastic. My little twenty-year-old brain couldn't stand that you looked that good. And after you'd had enough and we sobered you up as much as we could, we went to Burger Joint to hopefully soak up the rest of the alcohol. That was when they were open at all hours of the night. Everyone else went home, but me, you, and Josh sat at a booth in the far back corner. I think we annoyed the shit out of almost everyone there since we couldn't stop laughing."

"You—you remember every single detail of that entire night?" She cautiously took another bite of her burger.

"Yes, I remember all of it."

"I can't believe you remember that whole night. I mean, you were drinking, too. That has to mess with your memory at least a little bit."

I shrugged. "I remember nearly everything, babe."

"What do you mean, everything?"

"I remember the important things."

"So, you're telling me that the first time we went to Burger Joint was important?"

"Every moment I've spent with you is important, so I remember almost all of it. I would say I remember everything, but you're right—alcohol really changes memories. Time does that too, sadly."

She pushed a few pieces of her curled hair behind her ear as her jaw dropped. She shifted in her seat, sitting up taller, her back pin straight. "That's impossible."

With my burger gone, I leaned back in my chair, propping my foot on my opposite knee, with my container of fries in my hand. "Do you want me to prove it to you? I can tell you exactly what you said when you sat down in our freshman biology class. Or what you were wearing on your first day of teaching, because I'm not sure I've ever seen you that excited. I could also probably tell you about every fight you had with your parents in the past several years because you've almost always confided in me about them. So, what do you want to start with?"

Mouth still agape, Amanda cleared her throat and tried to straighten in her chair even more. "I don't need you to prove it to me. I already know you wouldn't say that unless it was the truth. But I'm just surprised that you would remember all of that. That I'm that imp—"

"Important, yes," I said, finishing her sentence for her as the word caught in her throat.

Several seconds passed and we just silently stared at each other across the table. No matter the pressure I felt in that moment, I didn't look away from her eyes, which were bluer than a summer sky, for fear that it would all come crashing down around us. That she wouldn't believe what I was saying. But she did, and I watched as the confusion morphed into understanding. Slowly she realized that the dates weren't just some harebrained idea to continue getting in her pants or to keep me and Josh occupied. I saw when she recognized that we were serious, that I was serious. And I felt a little triumphant that I'd made the point I'd set out to at the onset of our date.

She was the first to break eye contact. She cleared her throat and fidgeted with the cloth napkin in her lap for something to do. "Did you know that I actually spent most of the rest of the night throwing up the burger and fries we ate? Blakely sat with me on the bathroom floor of our en suite the entire time, dabbing at my head with a wet washcloth." Her tone was grim and sorrowful as she remembered a fond memory of a friend none of us had seen in several months. I opened my mouth to ask if she'd heard from Blakely or been able to contact her like she'd at one point been so diligently trying to do when Amanda plastered an attempt at a smile on her face and looked up at me. "It's a wonder I can still eat them. Although I don't remember much from that night after the two of you left me with her. I guess I was still drunker than I thought."

I noted her effort to steer the topic away from our lost friend and decided a date was not the place to broach such heavy topics.

"Broccoli cheddar soup," I offered instead.

Her brows furrowed in the cutest confused look, so I continued, "When I was a kid, I got this horrendous stomach bug—I was out of commission for a week, at least. I'll spare you the gory details, but it was rough. My parents tried everything in the book to get me feeling better, but nothing was working. I couldn't keep a lot down, but my dad actually made broccoli cheddar soup. Apparently his mom always made it for him when he was sick and it helped, so he thought he'd do the same for me. And thankfully, you've met and know my dad, so you know how out of character that is for him."

She nodded, both in understanding that simple acts of care were few and far between for my father and in understanding that she likely knew where this was going.

"And since it was so out of character, I was going to try it no matter what. Even though I knew the second I smelled it, it wasn't going to stay down for long. And sure enough, halfway through the bowl, everything I had managed to choke down came right back up. I haven't been able to even smell broccoli cheddar soup since, and it's been like twenty years."

"I love broccoli cheddar soup," she said while laughing. My anecdote had done the trick and moved the conversation back to less serious topics and replaced the forced smile on her lips with a genuine one.

"Yes, well, most people do. But it's a no-go for me."

"I couldn't imagine having that reaction to a burger and fries. That would be tragic."

"I wholeheartedly agree."

"I'm surprised you even ate one, honestly. Even if it is a special occasion," she teased, knowing that I tried to keep my diet as clean as possible since it was my job to lead others in a healthy, achievable lifestyle.

"Like you said, it's a special occasion. And I'm not a crazy health nut. I enjoy a burger and fries just like anyone else. It's all about balance."

"Sure." She shrugged. "I'm still surprised."

"Speaking of surprises..." I said, cringing at the ungraceful transition. But we were only an hour and a half from midnight, and similar to Cinderella, we had to be out of there by then. Otherwise, there'd be pumpkins or something. "I have one more for tonight."

She gave me a quizzical look but took my hand when I offered it, lacing her small fingers between my own. "Do we just leave this here? Or…"

"Yes, I paid one of the maintenance guys a hundred bucks to put everything back the way we found it. But bring your champagne," I said, grabbing my empty glass and the nearly full bottle before leading her back out into the main entryway.

"I understand we have to be out of here by midnight, but why are we running?" she asked breathlessly next to me. I hadn't even realized that I'd been walking nearly twice my normal speed, eating up the distance between one exhibit and the other at a pace Amanda couldn't keep up with without almost jogging.

"Sorry, I'm just excited," I said truthfully and slowed my pace. But along with excitement, there was a nervousness buzzing through my veins, just below my skin, that wasn't there before. I knew at any second Amanda would recognize what our final exhibit was—it was her favorite part of the museum and I'd made sure we would have access to it.

I thought about asking her to close her eyes or fishing the tie I'd used as a blindfold out of my pocket, but it was too late.

"No way," she muttered quietly. I chanced a look back at her and was proud of the genuine excitement on her face.

"Yes way," I said as I pushed the doors open to the planetarium.

Once inside the room, it appeared that the screen went on infinitely. Displayed on the screen was what appeared to be a video of the night sky as seen through the strongest of telescopes. It was filled with hundreds of individual stars, some organized in detailed constellations. Between the stars were colorful galaxies of blues, pinks and yellow, each of a different shape and size.

But my focus was pulled from the massive screen around us to the woman who was craning her neck to take in each minute detail. Amanda was glowing in the dim light, the colors of the stars bathing her in a rainbow and reflecting off her hair.

It was a sight I knew I'd remember forever, but the image in my head would never live up to the real-life thing. And neither would a photo, but it was the best I could manage since it was impossible to bottle a point in time to replay it over and over again.

I held my phone in front of me and focused it on Amanda, who was peering up and to her left. I snapped a few photos, then once I'd felt confident I'd captured the moment to the best of my ability, I switched to video and recorded her quiet dance. As she spun in place to analyze each astronomical object with a look of pure enchantment and wonder, I committed the moment to memory and film.

The last two seconds of the video were of when she turned back to me, a wide grin spreading across her face and when she'd caught me videoing her.

"Are you recording me?" she asked, confused but with the smile still in place.

"Yes, I am. I'm not even going to try to hide it," I said as I came up with a ruthless yet brilliant idea. Clicking on my text messages, I pulled up the chain with Josh and sent him one of the photos I'd just taken of a starstruck Amanda. It was sure to make him jealous and irritate the ever-loving shit out of him. Just the way I liked it.

"Okay, now what the hell are you doing?"

"What do you mean?" I asked, still peering down at my phone, waiting for the dots to appear and let me know he was typing.

"You have a maniacal look on your face."

Instantly I pocketed my phone and scrubbed a hand over my mouth to wipe the smile from my face. "I sent one of the photos I just took to Josh."

She raised her eyebrows at me, and without a word, I knew what she was thinking. That I was being overly competitive and that it would cause an issue.

"A little bit of competitiveness never hurt anyone. And it's all in good fun."

"Yeah, until I pick one of you over the other," she muttered, which stopped me midstep. I felt my face drop before I could control my expression. Of course, Amanda saw the hurt, and although I quickly corrected it and closed the space between us, she had an apology poised on her tongue.

Instead, I took her hand and led her to two random seats in the middle of the sea of hundreds.

"It's the truth," I said when she attempted to apologize again. "Anyway, isn't this amazing?" I asked, hoping to move the conversation back to the extravagant date I'd planned and not the reality-TV-show-type scenario we found ourselves in.

Amanda contemplated for a moment, deciding whether or not to accept the subject change. "So, we're seeing one of the shows?" she finally asked, and I breathed a sigh of relief.

When around Amanda, it was easy to forget that this could very well be temporary. She could suddenly decide after her date with Josh, or hell, even before the date, that I wasn't the one. That our connection was one-sided or only relied on sexual chemistry and wouldn't be anything more. And whether I liked to admit it or not, I was a guy who was used to getting what he wanted, especially with women. I could count on one hand the number of times I'd pursued a woman and been rejected.

Each of them seemed meaningless, though, with the possibility of losing Amanda looming over me. The possibility of losing her before I ever really knew what it was like to have her seemed even more terrifying.

"Yes, we're going to watch something called *Unseen Universe*. It sounded the most interesting," I said in my best attempt to feign casualness while my insides twisted with every possible outcome.

She plopped down next to me and gasped, lightly smacking me on the arm in excitement. I couldn't help but smile. "That's the one I've been wanting to see! It's new and they talk about..." She stopped abruptly, waved her hand, and turned to face the front without finishing her sentence.

"Wait, why'd you stop? What's this one about?" I asked, urging her to continue.

"I feel like I've been talking about nerdy science stuff this entire time, and I'm sure you're sick of hearing me go on and on. And we'll see in a few minutes, anyway, right? No need for me to spoil it before it begins."

Immediately, I replayed the entire night and tried to think of a moment when I said or did something to make her feel that way.

"What makes you think that?"

"Makes me think what? That you're tired of hearing me drone on and on about science shit?"

I nodded.

"Well, because it's not like you're interested in all of this like I am, and I know that if you're not interested in it, then it can get boring or annoying when I talk about it." She shrugged like it was just a fact of life that someone would find what she's passionate about annoying.

"I can tell you're speaking from experience, and it's fucking infuriating that someone, anyone, would ever tell you that you're annoying or boring. So, just so we're clear, I'm not sick of hearing you talk about something you love. It's the exact opposite, actually. So go ahead and tell me about the show," I said, motioning to the screen. "I promise I want to hear about it."

I settled back into the cushy black seat and reclined slightly, prepared to hear about the show. But what I wasn't prepared for was one of Amanda's hands cupping the left side of my face and urging me to look back in her direction. Her smooth fingers were a harsh contradiction against my rough stubble, but it felt so fucking good to have her touch me.

Her eyes roamed my face, raking over my forehead and my cheeks, pausing on my eyes and thoughtfully considering my mouth. I couldn't remember the last time I blushed, but my cheeks warmed under her scrutiny. She licked her lips, her bottom one pulled between her teeth as her focus bounced between my eyes and mouth. Her thumb brushed my lower lip as her gaze settled there, and I watched as she made her decision.

The next thing I knew, her lips had replaced the feeling of her eyes on my mouth. At first, they were soft, barely a whisper against my own, and I let her take the lead, although every part of me was itching to take over. To push my tongue against hers and pull her onto my lap, so she could grind against me and take her pleasure. I wanted to claim every inch of her and in every way that counted.

And the opportunity presented itself when she reached her other hand around my head and weaved her fingers through my hair, pressing her tongue against my lips, eagerly requesting entrance. I parted my lips and without a moment's hesitation, she brushed her tongue against mine. The sweetness of the champagne tasted so much better on her tongue.

Her moan was immediate, and I swallowed it down as the little self-control I had snapped. In one swift movement, I pushed up the armrest between us and gripped her hips, guiding her to straddle my lap. And without any prompting, she settled directly on top of me. Even between the denim of her jeans and my own, I could feel the warmth radiating from between her legs as she pressed herself against my rapidly hardening erection.

She ground herself against me and pulled away slightly to gasp at the pressure. I took the opportunity to bite her bottom lip, sucking it into my mouth and hoping it might mark her. That she could wear and feel the evidence of me long after I took her home.

My name fell from her pretty little lips with a pleading sigh.

In response, I used my grip on her hips to push her harder against me as I pressed up, guiding her hips back and forth.

"We can't do this, Reed," Amanda murmured against my mouth. Her words said one thing, but her actions said another. Her hips didn't stop as she shamelessly ground herself against my very obvious bulge and her hands clung to my neck and shoulders as her mouth moved eagerly with my own.

I wasn't strong enough to tell her to stop. There was an aching want deep inside of myself that craved her pleasure and her release as much as I wanted my own.

"We really shouldn't," she sighed as my lips found their way over her jaw and down the smooth planes of her neck. I paused to suck lightly on the spot behind her ear that I knew made her crazy, and her nails dug into my scalp as she tugged at my hair.

"Reed," she said again, that time with a sternness she hadn't mustered before. And with the change in her tone, I reluctantly pulled away from her neck, letting my head fall against the leather headrest behind me.

Her hands didn't move from my hair, and I suddenly worried they would. That she would move, and I wanted her in my lap even if nothing escalated past making out. So, with my left hand, I held the spot where her hip met her thigh, and with my right, I ran my fingers up her arm and covered her hand with my own, making sure she didn't let her hand leave my hair.

"Why can't we do this?" I asked and wasn't surprised by the lust dripping from my voice.

"I told myself when I agreed to y'all's crazy plan that I wouldn't let anything distract me from it. This isn't something I'm taking lightly, and after tonight, I'm concerned that sex is going to complicate all of it even more than I thought. We know that the physical part isn't an issue, but it's the rest of it that we have to make sure works. And I know myself well enough to know that my vagina overrules my head more often than not. So in order to be able to make an intelligent and level-headed decision, she's gotta stay out of it," Amanda nodded in finality after motioning to between her legs where she was still pressed against me.

She was right—I knew everything she said was correct, yet that didn't keep me from groaning when she plopped back into her seat.

She let out a little laugh but curled into my side as the screen changed around us.

"Did you know that it was this place that made me want to become a science teacher?" she whispered as more prominent and vivid galaxies morphed around us.

"I actually didn't know that," I remarked, studying the complexity of the images.

"Yeah, it was one of the few places my parents would allow Adam and me to go in the summer. Most of the time, we were stuck inside because..." She trailed off. Her expression was distracted and reminiscent, but it quickly vanished. "Well, just because, but I convinced them to let the two of us come here. For a while, one of our neighbors would drive us, but once I turned sixteen and got my license and a car, I'd bring us both all of the time. We'd spend hours here."

The show had actually begun by the time she finished, which meant having a conversation over the loud narrator and sound-track was nearly impossible. In response, I kissed the top of her head and pulled her closer to me. She nestled in and fit perfectly into my side like that's where she was meant to be. And to me, it was. She was supposed to be not only in my arms but in every part of my life.

"Thanks for bringing me back here," she turned her head and whispered into my ear before placing a chaste kiss on my jaw.

# THIRTEEN

## Amanda

LIVING WITH A MAN-CHILD MEANT BEING WOKEN UP BY SLAMMING doors. The morning following my date with Reed, I'd woken to Adam slamming the bathroom door. He then returned to his room and slammed that door.

Luckily, I'd fallen back to sleep for another hour before my phone insistently buzzing on my bedside table pulled me into the world once again.

There were several missed texts: one from Justin, who I hadn't actually thought about since I watched him walk out of that room with Reed's date, then another from Reed, one from Josh, and several from Hazel.

Hazel calling me was the reason for the incessant buzzing. Before answering, I chanced a look at the clock on the opposite side of the room and groaned when I saw it wasn't even eight.

"Hello?" I said in a voice still drenched in sleep.

"Oh, shit, I'm so sorry, I didn't want to wake you up. I keep forgetting that y'all are an hour behind us, and—"

"I told you she wasn't going to be awake!" I heard Luke

shout from somewhere in the background, and I couldn't help but laugh.

"No one asked for your input, husband dearest," Hazel yelled back before clearing her throat. "Anyway, I'm sorry, but since you are awake, I need a favor."

I grunted in response as I tried to scrub the sleep from my eyes. Hazel took my grunt as confirmation to continue. "One of my cousins sent a late wedding gift. I'm not sure what the hell it is, but he just told me that someone has to be there to sign for it. Luckily, I would just need someone there between noon and two this afternoon, and I was wondering if you could go to our house and wait for it."

"Yeah, I guess I can do that. But what the hell did your cousin buy you that requires a signature? Is it alcohol?" I asked, pulling myself from my comfortable bed only because my bladder was screaming for relief.

"I'm not even sure, but he's one of the cousins that…" Hazel kept talking, but I groaned when I opened my bathroom door, excited to relieve the pressure in my bladder, only to remember that my toilet was broken. It had taken three days for the mainte- nance guy, CJ, to find the part needed, and after only a few days of sharing a bathroom with my brother, I was already more than over it.

Begrudgingly, I opened my bedroom door and crossed the hall. Without muting the phone or asking Hazel to hold on, I peed as she moved on to topics about their road trip and where they were headed next. The several missed texts from her that morning were apparently photos from their time in the Rocky Mountains.

"But we'll be back by the end of next week," she said as I stepped out of the bathroom. I was already thinking about crawling back into bed when Adam intercepted me in the hallway.

"Hey, sis. I'm heading to the gym for my first day, but how

was your date last night? I gotta tell you the fact that you're dating both Reed and Josh is fuckin' crazy if you ask me."

I whipped my head in Adam's direction and proceeded to give him my most withering, scathing "big sister" look I could muster through my shock. His comment was like a bucket of ice water over my tired mind and body.

"*How...?*" I began to ask but stopped when I realized it had to have been Josh since he was at the bar last night with him.

In my head, I began plotting how I would get back at Josh for letting it slip about our situation, or whatever you wanted to call it. I was lost in my thoughts for a moment until I jumped when Hazel spoke up again on the other end of the phone that was still cradled to my ear.

"Did he just say you're dating Reed and Josh?" she asked in a surprised whisper.

"I... uh... we—" I stuttered for a second, trying to come up with the best, simplest explanation, but nothing was coming. Instead, I insisted that I would call her back over her hurried arguments and pleas to not hang up the damn phone.

I tossed my phone on my bed as it began vibrating with what I assumed was another call from Hazel.

"How the fuck did you hear about that?" I asked, turning to Adam, who had the decency to at least appear a little apologetic.

"Okay, to be clear, I didn't notice you were on the phone and had I known, I wouldn't have just blurted that out. But I caught Josh staring at a picture of you last night and then saw that it was Reed who had sent it to him. At that point, he was caught, so it was either fess up to your little contest or me assume they were stalking you."

I scoffed, crossing my arms in front of me. "Stalking me, really?"

He laughed and brushed past me, heading past the living room and into the kitchen. "I didn't think they were stalking you, but I knew Josh wouldn't hide the truth when I was accusing him of that. So, tell me, how'd the date go?"

"It was fine," I lied. The date was great, magical, actually, and had kept me up most of the night because it had been nearly perfect.

"Eesh, that bad, huh? So, it's probably gonna be Josh?"

I rolled my eyes and pulled a coffee mug from the cabinet as I turned on the coffee maker.

"That's not what I meant. What I meant by 'fine' is that it's none of your business."

Adam chuckled as he filled up a reusable water bottle and tugged on his beanie. "Like hell is it none of my business. I need to know if you're going to have those two in and out of your bedroom. At least give me a warning so I can wear my headphones to sleep or find another place to crash for the night. I'm not sure listening to my sister—"

"Adam, holy shit, enough! That's not going to happen."

He made another unimpressed noise. "So, it's not good, then. Or..." He sucked in a breath. "You're not saying you're a virgin, right? Is that why it's not going to happen, because you haven't—ouch! Shit, Amanda. That hurt," Adam griped when the apple I threw landed square in the center of his back. "You should really—"

"Uh-uh. Say something else about my sex life, and I'm throwing the fucking pineapple next," I threatened, and Adam held up his hands in surrender.

"Okay, okay," he muttered as he grabbed his keys and water bottle. "All I'm saying is that you're aware this isn't going to end well, right? Whether you pick one of them or neither of them. So, you should be careful—look out for number one."

He wrapped up his unsolicited advice with a kiss on the top of my head. I stood, still fuming, as the front door slammed shut behind him.

Frustrated, I sipped my coffee while still stewing in my anger. Being ambushed by my little brother about my sex and dating life was never something I wanted to experience, let alone before eight in the morning when I was off of work.

Hoping I could smooth things over with Hazel, I retrieved my phone from my bed to find seven missed calls and five new text messages from Hazel.

The woman was relentless, and as I contemplated what exactly I could tell her (because ignoring her wasn't an option), another text came through with several exclamation points and expletives.

Most of her texts were asking various versions of the same question, *What the fuck is going on?*

And oh, how I wanted to give her an answer to that simple yet insanely complex question.

When the guys proposed the idea, I knew they were serious. I'd had a fleeting thought that maybe they were just joking, but it was just that, fleeting. And I'd considered several possibilities and outcomes, which included both the good and the bad: hearts could be broken, friendships could end, lives would likely be altered, and World War III could begin. And I understood that the dates would lend themselves to my ultimate decision but that our friendships would also prove to be the basis for any relationship that may begin.

And what I'd failed to consider in my moments of deliberation before the fact was that everything would change immediately. In my mind, I would have four dates and through those four dates, things may or may not progress and then we'd go from there. But I had four dates to get through before anything significant would happen.

My date with Reed had proven that my thinking was more wrong than I could ever imagine.

Everything was already different.

My phone vibrated in my hand once again, and I sighed before answering it.

"Hi," I said quietly.

"Don't 'hi' me!" Hazel bellowed over the line. "Are you dating both Josh and Reed?"

I sighed and prayed that I could get out of the conversation with as little explanation as possible.

"Technically, I guess I am."

"Technically?" she questioned.

"Well, I've only had a date with Reed so far, and—"

"What?!" she screeched, and I pulled the phone from my ear, cringing in pain. "I thought y'all just slept together at the rehearsal dinner—that it was a one-off. That's what I told Luke, too. You're welcome for that, by the way. But start from the beginning and tell me everything."

The excitement in her voice was genuine, and I started from the beginning—at their rehearsal dinner.

Hazel held all of her questions and thoughts until the end, thankfully, which made it somewhat easier to recount all of the details. And I had to admit that it was nice to confide in someone who knew the three of us fairly well.

"So, yeah. Tonight is my date with Josh, and it's becoming very real, you know, the situation that we're in."

She was quiet for a long moment, so long that I peered at the phone to make sure she was still there.

"Hello?" I asked, and she cleared her throat.

"I'm here. I'm just… processing."

My heart constricted, and nervous energy pumped through my veins. I knew it was likely that she would tell me that I was crazy, and she had every right to. But I didn't need to hear what I already knew.

"Well, can you process faster because you're freaking me out?"

"I mean, to be completely honest, I'm not totally surprised. I picked up on something going on between the three of you the first time I met y'all and before you told me about the night at the lake. It was only a matter of time before it all came to a head," she said and then chuckled at her obvious innuendo.

I groaned and swept my hair into a bun at the top of my head. "What the hell am I going to do, Hazel? This is just all sorts of screwed up, and now it's going to be my fault when everything goes wrong."

"Okay, I understand your concern, but look at it this way: you have some sort of feelings for both of them, right? You care about them?"

I nodded and then realized she couldn't see me, so, in a quiet voice, I mumbled, "Yes."

"Now, what would have been worse, taking them up on their somewhat strange offer and seeing where things go, or not doing it and possibly regretting it? Even if it doesn't go great, at least you tried. Otherwise, you may have regretted never pursuing the option."

Although I was nowhere near convinced that I hadn't made a crucial error, she was kind of right. But would I eventually regret trying if it turned out as horribly as it could?

"But—" I began, preparing to announce my possible alternative regret when the doorbell interrupted me. "Shit, I think that's the maintenance guy. I'll call you back later."

"Okay, let me know when the gift is delivered to the house, *and* be prepared to tell me all about your date tonight." She laughed.

"Wait," I said before she had a chance to hang up. "Don't tell Luke about this just yet, okay? I need to figure everything out first before we tell everyone else what's going on."

"Fine, fine. I will keep secrets from my husband, but only for you."

"Thank you so much. Enjoy your honeymoon!"

I hung up the phone as I peered through the peephole. I composed myself and refrained from doing a happy dance when I opened the door for the maintenance guy. His usually shaggy blond hair was covered with a beanie, and he was wearing a bulky blue jacket over his usual worn black T-shirt.

"My favorite tenant." CJ gave me a flirty wink and sauntered past me. "Got the part that we need, so it should only take a few minutes to fix."

"Great. That sounds amazing," I said, my voice higher pitched than usual from my excitement. No more sharing a bathroom, thank goodness. "Do you want something to drink?" I asked from the kitchen as the banging of tools began from down the hall.

"Nah, I'm good. Thanks," he hollered from the bathroom as I continued picking up the living room and kitchen, trying to stay out of his way. I wasn't the best at keeping my apartment tidy and with Adam around, it was even worse than usual. It was always clean—the dishes went in the sink, at least, and there wasn't anything dirty lying around—but there were often clothes piled on the couch and my bed after I'd washed them and sometimes folded them. And I wasn't the best at straightening the pillows on the couch.

I was picking up a throw blanket from the floor while simultaneously contemplating the last time I'd cleaned the blinds when I heard the thump of CJ's work boots on the wood floor. He appeared from around the corner, and I smiled hopefully.

"Done?" I asked, and he nodded with his attention still on something down the hallway.

"Umm, yeah," he said, distracted. "You get a roommate?"

"Yeah, my brother moved in with me for a little while."

"So not a boyfriend. Good, I would've been heartbroken." He smiled.

I quickly changed the subject. CJ was always a flirt, but it was harmless. "Yeah, so I'm glad you were able to fix the toilet. I was tired of sharing a bathroom with him." I chuckled, and he glanced at the console table underneath the TV—which housed most of my extensive DVD collection—his eyes landing on a photo of Adam and me from a few Christmases before.

He picked it up and tapped the glass with a large finger. "This him? Looks just like you."

"Yeah, that's Adam," I said with a half smile. A look passed over his face, one that I couldn't easily identify and didn't have the chance to, as it was replaced by a soft smile.

"Well, you're good to go," he said, replacing the photo on the console table and slinging his tool bag over his shoulder. He gave me a quick wave before he slipped through the door.

Immediately, I straightened the photo and smiled. Adam was sixteen, which made me twenty-six. At that age, he still seemed so young and innocent, but it was around that time that it all went south. Each decision he made was worse than the one before.

Staring at that photograph would have upset me at one time but seeing how far Adam had come, I had the opposite reaction. I wanted to believe he was close to a breakthrough.

My phone buzzing in the pocket of my oversized sweatpants jolted me from my memories, and my smile widened when I saw the text message.

> Josh: I know you're going to ask, so here are your answers.
>
> 1. Dress comfortable and warm
>
> 2. Be ready by 5:30 and I'll pick you up
>
> 3. No, I'm not going to tell you where we're going. But I promise you'll love it

My heart thumped wildly in my chest, and I breathed out a steadying breath.

Whether I liked it or not, I had made my decision to go along with their dates. And I wasn't going to back out. Yet.

# FOURTEEN

Josh

"Didn't she say that she didn't want us to take her to a museum after hours? That was seriously her one request, man." I scoffed, trying to gather my belongings and get out of our apartment on time.

Reed had finished giving me the rundown of their date, which was as over the top as I assumed it would be. He was over the top in most aspects of his life, and dates or pursuing women were no different. He was all about grand gestures.

Before I'd learned what he had planned and pulled off, I was wholly confident in my plan. But afterward, I had to admit that I was a little rattled. The only thing that was keeping me from completely freaking out was the fact that I knew Amanda didn't care as much about being wooed. She'd care more about the thoughtfulness of the date rather than the spectacle of it.

"She didn't seem to mind," he said with a sly smile and a wink. I rolled my eyes at his ever-present cocky attitude and tugged on my beanie. I'd found my thick jacket at the back of my closet and dug it out for the night as well. Thankfully, even after being tucked away for most of last year, it still smelled like fresh, clean laundry when I threw it on over my long-sleeve T-shirt.

I slipped into the kitchen and fished the small cooler out of the pantry as Reed closed the refrigerator door with a fresh beer in his hand. He was in the middle of proclaiming that my date would never top his when I righted myself and set the cooler on the counter. Reed's words cut off midsentence as he glanced over at me. I watched as his brow furrowed momentarily, only to straighten out as he shook his head and twisted the cap off of his drink.

"Either way," he continued. "You've got some catching up to do." His words didn't hold the same sharp challenge they had only moments earlier, but I still gave him my middle finger in response.

"I'm confident that Amanda is going to love my date, asshole. And hey, aren't those my sweatpants?"

Reed shrugged and turned on his heels, striding into the living room. "Probably," he muttered around the opening of the beer pressed to his mouth. "Found them in the laundry room with your clean clothes, so…"

It's not like I cared—we shared clothes occasionally, which was a perk of being nearly the same size. But those were my favorite gray sweatpants.

"You have so many of your own expensive clothes. Why are you wearing a pair of my old sweatpants?" I filled the cooler with a few beers and ciders I remembered Amanda wanted to try as well as some wine and a couple bottles of water. I was going to cover all of my bases.

"Laundry day," Reed hollered from the opposite side of the island, where he was reclined back on the couch, his feet propped on our wooden coffee table. I took a second to peer around the apartment and sighed. The apartment itself was damn nice—upgraded everything, exposed brick on the outer wall, and stained concrete floors in all the main spaces—but we had furnished it with only the bare necessities. We had a coffee table, a couch and a chair in the living room, along with a TV stand that easily fit our eighty-inch TV.

Besides that, there weren't any decorations or knickknacks. When we were moving Adam into Amanda's apartment, I'd notice that it was full of knickknacks and photographs and a few plants. It made it feel homey, unlike our place.

"We should put up some pictures or something," I commented once the cooler was full of ice.

"Why?"

"So this place feels homier, I don't fucking know. Wouldn't that be nice?"

"And you think pictures are going to do that?" Reed fired back.

"It would help, yeah."

He chuckled and finally settled on something to watch after clicking through options for the past several minutes. "When I buy a house, then I'll make it homey."

Reed had been saying he wanted to buy a house for years but still hadn't. He claimed it was that he wanted to get the gym up and running first before he took on another project. But I wasn't positive that was entirely it.

He'd lived in that apartment for several years—I couldn't even remember when he'd actually moved in, that's how long it'd been. And I'd been living there for a while without adding anything of my own to the place. Something about that didn't sit right with me, like I'd just placed myself into Reed's premade living space.

"Okay, well, I'm heading out. I'll see you tonight, maybe," I shot him a suggestive smile and by his middle-finger response, he knew what I was talking about.

"Not very likely, man. She said she had to keep a clear mind, which means no sex and no orgasms." He raised his eyebrows like he was waiting for me to react, but I had sort of expected that from Amanda.

"Honestly, that may make things worse for you then," I

chided, grabbing the cooler and my keys. "That's the only thing you had going for you, honestly. And now that she's taken that away…" I didn't finish the thought and took pride in the irate expression Reed's face morphed into.

"Yeah, we'll fucking see about that, Sunshine," he muttered, and I shook my head at the old nickname. You have shaggy blond hair in high school and play football, so that means the only viable nickname is Sunshine.

Pulling into Amanda's apartment complex, the last thing I expected to see was her ass in the air as she dug around in the back seat of her little white sedan. I parked in a spot a few over from her car and got a front-row view of her jumping up and down with something gripped tightly in her hands in front of her.

I hopped out of the truck as she slipped a gray beanie over her mess of blonde hair. I couldn't wipe the smile from my face and wasn't surprised that Amanda seemed embarrassed when she turned to find me standing by the passenger door of my truck.

"You're early," she whined, straightening the beanie and stuffing her hands into the pockets of her black jacket. She looked cozy, and it was seriously fucking cute.

"I'm only five minutes early," I corrected her.

"Well, five minutes was enough time for me to run down here, find my beanie, and run back upstairs before you got here. But now you're early."

"I apologize. Next time I will be perfectly on time or how about this: I'll be two minutes late. Better?"

"Yes, that would be great, actually."

"Fine, I will implement that on our next date," I said with a wink, and she smiled. "So, you need to run back upstairs?"

"Yes, I'll just be a minute or two. I need to grab my phone and my purse." She began climbing the concrete stairs but stopped on the second step. "Is what I'm wearing okay? The outfit guidance you gave me wasn't very specific."

She held her arms out at her sides like she was presenting her outfit to me. Besides the gray beanie and black fleece jacket, she was wearing dark jeans and white sneakers.

I smiled. "You're perfect."

She bit her lower lip just the way I wanted to and nodded before running the remainder of the way up the stairs.

While she was gone, I turned the truck back on and made sure her seat warmer was on. All of the supplies we needed for our date were shoved onto the back seat floorboard, and I hoped she wouldn't turn around to see them. They would most likely give up our destination rather quickly.

I slipped out of the truck as Amanda hurried back down the stairs and met her at the passenger door.

She murmured a small "thanks" as I opened the door and made my way back to the driver's side.

It wasn't even a full second after I shut the door that she asked, "So, where are we going?"

I chuckled and rolled my lips to suppress my grin. Out of the corner of my eye, I caught her mischievous smile as she straightened her seat belt over her chest.

I pulled onto the street. "It's a surprise, baby girl. I thought we talked about that."

She sighed and let her head fall back onto the seat in defeat. "Yeah, I know, but I thought I'd try. You do both realize that a good date doesn't require a surprise, right?"

"Yes, but you have the best reactions to surprises," I clarified and reached over to grip her neck, urging her to look at me.

"What is that supposed to mean?" she said in a bored tone. However, I could see the excitement in her eyes, dancing along the surface of the blue.

"It's your excitement and joy—it's contagious."

She pursed her lips and tried to hide her smile but failed miserably. My fingers twitched against her hair, and I palmed her cheek as she leaned into my touch. I attempted to split my attention between the road and the woman who was openly accepting my affection. It sent warmth through me that she wanted me to touch her.

"Can you at least tell me how long it'll take us to get there?"

"Nope."

She groaned and playfully pushed my hand away from her face. I caught it, though, gripping her small hand in my own before she could pull away.

"About fifteen minutes," I said, dropping a kiss to her knuckles and settling our intertwined hands on her lap.

We sat in companionable silence for several minutes, and as we drove farther out of town and away from the city, the more relaxed we both became. The weight of our lives washed away as the miles passed.

"How's Adam doing so far?" she asked as we neared our destination.

I shrugged and stopped at a four-way stop in the middle of nowhere. "Fine. He's been mostly helping Grady behind the bar."

Amanda raised her eyebrows at me in surprise. "So, you're telling me Grady didn't go all... *Grady* on him?"

I chuckled, knowing exactly what she meant. Grady, in his wise old age—his words, not mine—enjoyed spreading the knowledge he'd obtained in his nearly seventy years on earth. Especially to young barbacks and bar patrons that unsuspectingly found themselves in his path. He was the king of unsolicited advice, which usually turned out to be useful even if it didn't seem that way at the moment.

"I'm sure he probably did, but your brother didn't say much about it. It was also only his first day, so there are plenty of other opportunities for Grady to *Grady* him."

Amanda's laughter tinkled through the cab of the truck, settling in my chest. "We've now turned his name into a verb? I'm not sure Grady would appreciate that."

"No, I think he would love it. Means that his influence has exceeded the confines of the English language."

"Well, when you put it like that... I want my name to be a verb, too. What do you think it would be?" For a moment, I contemplated what kind of verb Amanda would convey. Sifting through all of the emotions she made me feel and the things we did together, nothing seemed to fit. Everything was too mundane.

"Josh?" she asked, squeezing my hand. "What do you think?"

"Sorry, I was thinking. Um..."

"Did it hurt?" she said, straight-faced, and for a second, I didn't catch her joke.

"Ha ha." I feigned a dry laugh. "Now I'm not going to tell you."

"No." She laughed, tugging on my arm. "I'm kidding. Please tell me?"

If we hadn't been pulling into the driveway of our date location, I would have probably conceded.

"We're here," I said, excited that she was too busy begging me to realize where we were, and I was rewarded with watching the surprise cross her face.

"Where is—" Her words cut off as the two large screens came into view behind the low-lying trees. Slowly, her head turned in my direction as her eyes grew wide and a smile split her face. "No fucking way."

"Yes way, babe," I said with an equally wide smile.

I paid for the movie tickets as Amanda sat in excited shock.

"Wait," she said, suddenly gripping my forearm. I drove toward the back screen and parked as close to the center as I could a few rows back. We were several feet from the cars on either side of us, meaning we'd have a decent amount of privacy and no one would have to walk too close. "What's playing?"

I waited until I put the truck in park to tell her because I wanted to watch her face as I did.

Her hands were clasped against her chest, and her eyebrows were raised in excitement. The heat permeating the cab of the truck had warmed her enough to give her a light blush on each of her cheeks. That was good, too, because we were about to be sitting outside in the cold for hours.

"The first movie is *Ghost* and then *Pretty Woman*," I said with a smile.

Her mouth dropped open, and her eyes danced with pure excitement. "Patrick Swayze *and* Julia Roberts?!"

Her attention moved from me to the screen behind us and then back to me like she couldn't believe I'd found a drive-in with two of her favorite movies of all time. She made a surprised noise and threw her hands up in the air. I had surprised the woman who always had something to say beyond words. The smug smile I knew I was wearing said it all—I was genuinely impressed with myself.

"Josh, this is umm… perfect," Amanda said with a suddenly serious tone, scooting closer to the center console. Instinctually, I leaned in as well, my elbow propped on the leather between us as her eyes darted back and forth between my lips and my eyes.

The woman was always overwhelming and dominated my attention in every situation, no matter how many people were around, but in the smaller front seat of my truck, she was all-consuming. Her warm, clean smell wrapped around me as I watched her contemplate kissing me. We both knew what it felt like to press our lips together. Each time hers were plump yet yielding against my own, and just thinking about the brush of her tongue against mine and the electricity that would follow was enough to propel me forward.

My palm landed against her cheek at the same moment her small fingers curled around my open jacket. The second we touched, all hesitation was gone, and utter relief washed over me at having her mouth against mine once again. She must have also experienced it because I heard and felt her sigh against my lips. I took the opportunity to guide my tongue between her lips and deepen our connection.

My fingers twisted in the hair at the base of her neck as she pulled me closer by my jacket. What I wouldn't have given to lift her from her side of the car and settle her on top of me in the driver's seat. The position would give me free rein to touch her and cherish her.

And when my thoughts continued to wander further from the drive-in and to the way one of her pebbled pink nipples would feel and taste on my tongue, which was ravaging her mouth, I reluctantly pulled back.

When I pried my eyes open, utterly amazed at my self-control, it almost all went out the door. Amanda's lips were parted and wet with the evidence of our kiss. Against my lips, I could feel her quick breaths, which did nothing to help my cause.

"So," I began in a thick voice. "I did good?"

Her smile began in her eyes. "With the kiss or the date?"

"Is there a different answer for both? Is one good and one just okay? Don't break my heart before the movie even starts, babe."

She threw her head back and laughed toward the ceiling before she straightened and tugged me closer for a quick peck.

"*So* good. It's so good, I almost peed my pants!"

"Umm… what are you—what?" I stuttered, completely thrown by her admission. For a second, as her grin widened, I contemplated showing her where the bathroom was located or calling it a win because she at least said it was good.

The look on my face must have been priceless because her smile turned into another laugh. "It's a line from *Pretty Woman*, Josh. When they go to the opera? Don't look so terrified."

I couldn't admit to her that although it was one of her favorites, I had actually only seen the movie once or maybe twice. Both times were with girlfriends of mine in high school and then in college. And there wasn't a whole lot of *watching the movie* going on.

With Amanda, though, I knew we would definitely be *watching* the movie. There wasn't a chance she would let me go far during two of her favorites. If Amanda was serious about anything, it was enjoying a movie.

"On that note," I said. "I figured I'd leave it up to you what we do. We can either watch the movies from inside the truck and in the warmth, or we can sit in the bed of the truck. I brought blankets and pillows and a bunch of other shit from the apartment if that's what you want to do. It's just going to be cold."

With a quick glance out the back of the truck and toward the blank white screen, Amanda seemed to ponder the decision only for a moment before she said, "Bed of the truck."

With a nod, I hopped from the truck and instructed that she could stay in the warmth while I set everything up. The first show started just after sunset, which was less than thirty minutes away. I opened the back door and fished out the thick blankets and all of the pillows I could find in our place.

Reed was going to be furious when he went to bed tonight, only to realize he didn't have a single fancy pillow left.

The timing couldn't have been more perfect. The moment I fished the cooler out of the back seat along with the insulated bag of food, the lights around the screen dimmed, signaling the movie was about to begin.

I jogged around to the passenger side of the truck and retrieved Amanda who was nearly bouncing in her seat.

With her hand tucked protectively in mine, I led her around the truck and waved a hand at the bed, which I'd expertly lined with an array of cozy and colorful pillows and blankets.

I gave her a moment to take it all in and hopefully appreciate the work I'd put into the spread, but I couldn't give her too long because the movie was beginning behind us. In one swift motion, I gripped her under the arms and hoisted her onto the truck.

She let out a surprised gasp but quickly righted herself and toed off her shoes, leaving her in fuzzy blue socks.

"This is absolutely amazing. I'm honestly in shock," she said as she scooted back into the pillows, her eyes darting back and forth around us, taking it all in.

"Why is it shocking? Didn't think I could pull this off?"

She rolled her eyes and grabbed a thick blanket that she tucked under her chin. The content smile on her face was one I always wanted to see there.

"No, that's not what I meant. I just didn't realize that..." She trailed off, staring at the screen but not paying attention to the trailer of a new action movie. Behind the screen, the sun was nearly below the horizon and painted the sky in muted pink and red hues that bathed everything in a warm glow. It was like one last work of art before the night rolled in.

"What didn't you realize?" I asked as I grabbed the cooler and bag of food.

She sighed, and it sounded sad, but when I looked up at her, positioning the things in front of us, she was smiling softly. "I didn't realize that it was going to be like this—that you both cared enough to plan these perfect dates."

My excitement waned as I caught on to her meaning. "I can promise you that this"—I waved my hands around, motioning to everything that went into getting us there—"will be the norm when we're together. Weekly, biweekly, whatever you want, I will make it happen because you're important and so is your happiness. And as much as *I* want you, and as much as I want you to pick me at the end of this, I know the same goes for Reed. He cares just as much as I do. We're fucking crazy for you."

She sucked in a shaky breath. I held her stare and let the gravity and seriousness of my words wash over her. Much to my surprise, she didn't look away from me either, like she was silently communicating with me that she understood.

As much as I needed her to choose me, and as fucking devastated as I knew I would be if she didn't, I also had to admit that both of us would treat her right. No matter who she chose, whether we would treat her right didn't need to be part of the decision because it was an even tie.

The moment the subtle orchestral music erupted from the truck speakers and from the cars surrounding us, Amanda pulled her eyes from mine and glanced at the cooler and bag in front of me.

"What's in there?" she asked, the soft smile returning to her lips.

I positioned the bag in front of her as I took up a seat beside her and peeled it open first. The mouthwatering aroma of Italian food wafted toward us both.

"Oh my gosh," she gasped. "You're not playing fair."

I laughed and pulled out to-go containers of every type of pasta we would ever want. "How does the saying go? 'All is fair in love and war,' I think I heard that somewhere."

"Hmm…" she mused, popping a breadstick in her mouth, "not sure I've heard that one before."

Fishing out the largest container of fettuccine alfredo I'd ever seen, I handed it to her. I couldn't get the fork to her quick enough. Had I delayed a second more, she would have likely used her hands to scoop the noodles from the container.

With a mouthful of food, she mumbled, "This is *so* good."

And my heart expanded several sizes. Amanda's emotions were big. She lived hard, and there had always been something about her that made life better. But not just better—she made life *more*. And it was that characteristic or personality trait, or whatever the hell you wanted to call it, that consistently drew me to her.

You want to hold on to the people who make your life *more*.

"I'm glad you like it," I said around my own bite of rigatoni.

We ate our weight in pasta as the movie played, slowly finding ourselves gravitating closer to each other. And with the empty containers collected in the bags and ciders for each of us, I pulled Amanda into my chest. I was propped against the pillows at the back of the bed, and Amanda curled herself around me. One of her legs tossed over mine and her cold hands pressed into the fabric of my T-shirt on my stomach. I couldn't remember a time when I'd felt more content, and the only thing that would have made it better was having my son on my other side. Two of the people I cared about the most so close.

Amanda peered up at me from where she was lying on my chest to say, "You know, you kind of have Patrick Swayze eyes."

"Is that a good thing?" I questioned, hoping it was a strange compliment. But I shouldn't have been surprised since the strangest things sometimes came out of Amanda's mouth.

"I think so. I love Patrick Swayze."

"Hmm… well, that's good at least."

She popped up a little farther, propping herself on her hand. "You really don't see it?"

I shook my head. Amanda turned back to the screen and, with a serious expression, watched the movie intently until there was a scene where you could easily see the guy's entire face for a few seconds.

"See," she said, pointing at the screen and glancing back at me over her shoulder to make sure I was watching. "You both have this insane blue-green eye color. And his are a little more deep-set, but yours are too kind of. And you just both have this… soulful, serious look sometimes. They're similar enough to make a comparison."

I studied his face again while Amanda tucked herself back into my side, pulling the blankets taut. The air was cool around us, but the body heat and pounds of blankets helped insulate our warmth. There was also no way I wouldn't be happy with Amanda pressed up against me and using me to keep warm.

"I guess I can see it," I muttered and pulled her beanie back to press a kiss to the top of her head. My lips hovered over soft hair, and *fuck*, she smelled so good that I couldn't pull away. I felt like a sociopath or a drug addict taking hits of the fresh, clean smell of her hair, but I couldn't be helped. Thankfully,

Amanda didn't notice but eventually grabbed her beanie from where it was fisted in my hand and tugged it back over her head.

For the rest of the movie, we watched intently and without exchanging a word, except every few minutes when Amanda would nudge my chest or point at the screen, telling me it was her favorite part or favorite line. Her excitement was palpable and contagious, and all I wanted to do was experience it with her.

At the end of the movie, Amanda had been silent for several minutes until I heard her sniffle quietly against my chest.

"*It's amazing, Molly,*" Patrick Swayze (Sam) said on-screen as he faded into the light. "*The love inside, you take it with you.*"

Another sniffle and Amanda resituated herself, pulling the blankets slightly higher.

I knew full well that it was just the movie making her cry, that it was a movie she'd seen a thousand and one times, yet still cried every time. She'd told me as much before the movie started, but even so, her wet tears against my shirt and her muffled sniffles drove an overwhelming need to comfort her through me.

Like Amanda crying sad tears was the worst thing in the world. Especially since she never cried.

My hand was already tracing down her back every so often, but as the tears continued, I pressed her closer to me and kissed her beanie while I continued rubbing soothing patterns on her back.

We stayed like that until she briefly sighed and chuckled softly when the movie came to a close. The sound of her small laughter was like a balloon of relief expanding in my chest. When she peered up at me through damp lashes, her eyes still rimmed with nearly shed tears, there was at least a small smile on her face.

"I've seen this movie a million times, but I still cry. That part gets me every time."

"It's a great movie," I remarked. "And I forgot how freaking amazing Whoopi Goldberg is in this."

"She's the best. This is probably one of my favorite movies she's done, and she won so many awards for it."

Amanda grabbed two more ciders from the cooler, handed one to me, and then carefully rearranged the pillows on her side of the truck as she rattled off facts about the movie and the awards it won.

"So, pretty much everyone else, including the critics, also agree that Whoopi was the best part of that movie," she finished, pulling the blanket back up around her lap and settling into the fluffed pillows. She cracked open the new cider, but before it could reach her lips, her eyebrows darted up in suspicion. "Why are you looking at me like that?"

"I really fucking like you." Did I think before I spoke the words out loud? No, but there wasn't a chance I was going to keep my feelings to myself. Playing hard to get or like I didn't give a shit weren't options when a future with her wasn't guaranteed. Especially when I also knew that Reed was good at laying it on thick.

Something even as simple as listening to her talk about movies gave me a giddy, heartsick feeling. It made me feel like a teenager, but I was old enough to at least be able to identify the feeling. And it wasn't something I could ignore. I wanted to continue reminding Amanda that I was serious about her, and the best way I could think to do that was by telling her every chance I got.

"I like you, too," she whispered.

"I just wanted to make sure you knew that." I shrugged as she took a long sip of her cider.

"I've actually wanted to ask you about something. Being in your office the other day had me thinking about it and then you offering Adam the job."

"Sure. Ask me anything."

She hesitated for a moment. "Is it hard to work at Murphy's? It's just that your office is right down the hall from…"

From the room where I killed Valerie. Where I saved my brother and Hazel and accidentally shot Valerie in the head during our struggle for the gun.

A familiar chill ran through me as my thoughts drifted to that night.

I swallowed thickly and shook my head, trying to dislodge the memories. "Most of the time, no. I have my good days and bad days. But as of the past few months, there are more good than bad."

Most of the time, I was fine, but then there were times it was like a tidal wave, and I was back there: trying to keep my breathing quiet so Valerie wouldn't hear me; the weight of the Taser in my hands, the sound of the electricity buzzing through her body as I tried to keep her subdued; the deafening bang as the gun went off, followed by the mind-numbing silence; and the color of the blood draining from her bullet wound and pooling around our feet.

The same thing happened when my parents died. One minute I was fine, and the next, I was overcome by images of my dad shooting my mom, my mom fighting my dad, and sending two shots through his chest before they both died.

Even though I wasn't there, the knowledge that it happened was enough. That and watching my mother be tortured daily by his incessant abuse.

"Have you ever thought about leaving? Finding a job elsewhere to get away from it? Start over?"

I sighed and thought for several long seconds before responding. "I've thought about it, but I won't."

"Why?" Her question was automatic and a good one. It didn't make sense to most people why I would stick around after so much bad had occurred.

"Because," I said simply. "I don't give up that easily."

She nodded thoughtfully and we eased into a loaded silence, like each of us wanted to say more but didn't know how.

Wanting to move on from the topic, I said, "I need to Face-Time Zach. He's in Michigan with Sam and her boyfriend. Do you mind?"

Amanda immediately whipped her head in my direction and smiled. Watching the corners of her mouth tick up, I knew we were in the clear. There was hope yet, and relief washed over me.

"Yes, I'd love to see that kid."

I held out my arm, inviting her back to her earlier spot tucked into my side as she scooted closer. She didn't hesitate in pressing her body against me.

# FIFTEEN

### Amanda

WHY DID HE HAVE TO SMELL SO GOOD?

We'd been sitting outside for nearly two hours and yet he still smelled like he'd just hopped out of the shower.

And *God*, why did he have to be so honest? So heartbreakingly honest that it actually made my heart hurt.

"Auntie Manda!" Zach's little voice squealed over the phone.

"Hi, Z-man. How's it goin'?" I laughed as he completely ignored his father and squealed my name over and over again.

"Pretty good. It snows a lot here, and I played in the snow almost all day! It was really super fun until I got so cold that my fingers hurt. But then we went inside and Travis made a fire and that helped my fingers *and* my toes. It gets so much colder here than it does at home, but I don't think I like it very much. You have to wear too many clothes, and it takes too long." He spoke on one breath and took a huge gulp of air when he'd finally finished his long thought.

The kid was cute and had so much energy he was hard to keep up with. He also spoke a mile a minute and only correctly pronounced approximately half the words he used. Along with his slight Southern accent, you had to pay close attention to catch every word.

"Bud, I'm here, too," Josh stated, waving his hand in front of the phone and tilting the camera to show more of his partially hidden face.

"I saw you, Dad. Hi," Zach said with a halfhearted wave. "So, Auntie Manda, what are you doing? Why are you with my dad?"

"We're actually at the drive-in. Remember when we went last summer? We sat in the truck and watched the movies?" Josh offered, hoping to insert himself back into the conversation between me and his son.

"Ooo!" Zach cried. "Yes, that was so much fun! Are you having fun, Auntie Manda?"

I chanced a look over at Josh, who I caught peering at me as well, probably anxiously awaiting my answer.

Everything was changing so quickly. But change was the point, wasn't it? Both of the guys hoped something would change and had created a plan to make it happen. Change was the name of the game.

"Yes, I'm having lots of fun," I confirmed, and for my honesty, I was awarded a lopsided smile by Josh. His arm tightened around me and his palm flattened against my waist.

"So, you're still having fun, bud? As long as you don't get too cold."

Zach bobbed his head unenthusiastically. "Yeah, it's okay. But I miss you, Daddy. Mama said we're coming home soon and I get to see you right when we get there, right?"

Even in the small box at the corner of the phone screen where we were displayed, I could see the emotion wash over Josh's face at hearing his son confess that he missed him. And then, out of the corner of my eye, I watched Josh's throat bob before he cleared his throat.

Why was it that watching him be a dad—and be a good one, at that—such a turn-on?

"Yeah, I'll see you as soon as you get back on Sunday. Do you want me to bring pizza?"

Zach was in the middle of shrieking about the kind of toppings he wanted on his pizza, jostling the phone every which way when it was steadied and pulled from his hands.

As evidenced by our faces, neither Josh nor I were prepared for Sam's face to replace Zach's on the screen.

"Sorry, he's gotta go to bed. He's absolutely exhausted from playing in the snow all day," Sam spoke as she walked around the house they were staying in. We could still hear Zach in the background, whining that he hadn't finished telling his dad about the pizza he wanted.

"Okay, can I at least tell him goodbye?"

She huffed out a breath. "Yes, Josh, of course I will let you say good night."

"You did just snatch the phone out of his hands," Josh mumbled low enough that Sam couldn't hear him.

"I will give him the phone back. But can you just listen to me for a second? I have some news I want to share." And then she thrust her hand in front of the camera, flashing the shiny new engagement ring wrapped around her finger. "Travis proposed this afternoon, and I said yes!" By the high-pitched tone of her voice, I could tell exactly where Zach inherited his intense squeal.

Josh stiffened slightly, but his expression was unwavering. "Congratulations, Sam. I'm very happy for you," he said, even his tone was unflappable against the news. But I hadn't expected much different—Josh hadn't harbored feelings for Sam in several years, so her engagement wouldn't have affected him all that much. Except for the fact that Travis would now be his son's stepfather.

"Yes, congratulations!" I said with a little faux enthusiasm for her benefit. "That's really exciting, Sam."

"Thank you, Amanda," she said quickly, turning her attention back to Josh next to me. "Anyway, I just wanted you to hear it from me first."

Josh shot me a look that said he wasn't convinced of her unselfish intentions, but his words belied something different. "I appreciate that, Sam, and I'm genuinely happy for you. I'll say good night to Zach and let y'all go."

Sam gave the phone back to her son, who accepted it with a huge smile.

"Daddy, I gotta go to sleep, but you'll see me soon, right?"

The shift in Josh's mood was noticeable. "I'm going to see you so soon, bud. And I'm bringing pepperoni and pineapple pizza."

"Yes! Because that's my favorite!" Another squeal and as my eardrums burst so did my heart.

"Yes, that's exactly why." Josh laughed at Zach's excitement.

"Mama told me I have to go to bed now. She's giving me that crazy-eye look. Good night, Daddy, I love you."

Scratch my earlier heart-bursting comment. Hearing Zach telling Josh he loved him, that actually did it.

"Good night, bud. I love you more."

"Not possible!" Zach hollered and then hung up the phone.

The timing couldn't have been more perfect. The moment Zach's face disappeared, the large screen in front of us came to life.

Josh promptly locked his phone, tossed it down next to him, and used both of his arms to press me into his chest. I let him tuck me closer and reveled in the warmth of his body as the temperature of the night around us dropped.

And although I didn't think Josh so much cared about Sam's news, I could still feel the tension in him, which prompted me to ask, "You okay?"

"I'm great. Why?"

"Sam's engaged."

He made a less than enthused sound in the back of his throat. So, I tried another tactic. "Zach's going to have a stepfather."

*Bingo.*

His arm tensed around me, and I looked up just in time to watch his jaw tense and his eyes narrow into slits. The look was fleeting, but it was there, nonetheless. Betraying his thoughts about what would likely be a profound change in his own life, too.

"Yes, he is." His voice was matter of fact, and his eyes didn't look away from the screen that was rolling through movie trailers. Using my hand on his chest as leverage, I sat up. At eye level, it was easier to identify his unease.

"It's okay to be worried, Josh."

"I'm not worried. What Sam does with her life is her own business. I haven't cared about her in *that* way in years."

I shifted again, finally pulling his attention from the screen. "You know that's not what I meant."

He sighed, pushed his beanie off of his head, and subsequently pushed a frustrated hand through his blond hair. After he'd tugged the hat back on, his hand found my hip once again and tugged me closer until my knees were pressed against the outside of his thigh.

"I know what you meant, but I don't want to talk about it right now. It's not really first-date worthy. You know? I just want to enjoy this time with you. We'll only ever get one first date, and I don't want to spend it talking about my ex." A ghost of a smile tugged at the corners of his lips and with it, the weight of the heavier topic disseminated.

"I mean, I didn't lie to Zach. I am having fun."

That granted me a wider, Josh-like smile. As the first notes of "Oh, Pretty Woman" filtered from the speakers of the truck and the cars surrounding us, Josh hauled me closer to him. With little convincing, he had me straddling his lap and his hands were roaming over my back. One hand slipped beneath my jacket and my shirt, pressing against my warm skin with his cold fingers. I tried to retreat from his icy hand but ended up pushing my chest directly into his face.

"Josh, your fucking hands are freezing cold. *Shit.*" Pressing against his shoulders in an attempt to flee was futile.

He chuckled and weaved his other hand beneath my jacket, too, removing all the warmth from my skin. The cold of his fingers chilled me to the bone.

A shiver buckled down my spine as his hands slowly, and I mean *slowly,* began to warm.

"You're such an asshole," I pleaded.

"Can you blame me? Your skin is so soft," he muttered, less than an inch away from my mouth. His hot breath ghosted over my slightly parted lips.

"We're missing the movie," I whispered back. My eyes fluttered shut the moment his lips connected with the corner of my mouth. His hands on my bare back were finally warm and an exquisite sensation on my skin.

"How many times have you seen it?"

"More than you can count, but that's not the point."

"Then what's the point?" he asked, ready to negotiate and prove his point. But more than his words, it was his hands gently caressing tiny patterns on my back that were doing most of the convincing. And the effort to not press myself against his lap and feel him hard underneath me was overwhelming. Especially when I already knew how good it felt. How good it felt to have every part of him against every part of me.

The longer my thoughts lingered on it, the quicker the pulsing between my legs grew.

How did I constantly find myself in that position?

"I made myself a promise that I can't go back on. I told myself that there wouldn't be any sex involved. The physical stuff isn't concerning; I already know I'm incredibly attracted to you," I explained. And even though I was telling him he wouldn't get further than first base (or was it second base? I could never remember), the confession that I was attracted to him earned me a small smile.

"But we can't let sex get in the way," I continued, letting my fingers drift through the stubble along his jaw. "Of making clear-headed decisions." And then, like my words meant nothing, I made the fatal error of allowing my body to fall directly onto him. No longer hovering over his erection threatening to tent his jeans, it was pressed against me right where my body craved it the most.

"You do realize that orgasms don't have to come from sex, right? It would be fairly easy to slip my fingers inside of you and let you ride them just like you would my cock." His words were whispered directly into my mouth, and I gasped at the pleasure I knew would come from his dirty ideas.

But I needed to be stronger than what my pussy wanted. But *God* did he ever make it fucking difficult.

"You have no idea how good that sounds," I whispered over his lips and kissed him softly. "But it can't happen."

Thankfully, Josh didn't resist too much when I slipped off his lap and fell beside him again. Our legs were still touching and his arm was pressed against mine, but he still felt too far away.

We were at least fifteen minutes into the movie—Edward had already picked up Vivian on Hollywood Boulevard, and they were entering the swanky hotel.

"*Well, color me happy, there's a sofa in here for two,*" I murmured along with Vivian as she entered the hotel elevator.

"*I bet you can see all the way to the ocean from here,*" I repeated.

"*Well, now that you have me here, what are you going to do with me?*"

"You know every word to this movie, don't you?" Josh quipped. I chanced a look in his direction, only to find him watching me out of the corner of his eye with an amused grin tugging at the corners of his lips.

Lips I craved to taste again. The memory of them against my own was almost too much—I bit my lower lip, trying to suppress the thoughts, but the pain did little to ease the craving.

Doing what I could to steer away from the thought of Josh's gorgeous mouth and all of the things I wanted him to do with it,

I crawled to the end of the truck and grabbed two more drinks from the cooler. Not that the alcohol would help, but it was something else to do and focus on.

"Of course I do. Are you surprised?" I said, finally answering his question.

"Not one bit actually. It's amazing you can fit anything else in your brain with all of the movie quotes you store up there." He took the cider from me, our fingers only brushing the slightest bit, yet there was still a jolt of energy up my arm.

"It's not just movie quotes. Honestly, there're quite a few song lyrics *and* TV show quotes, too."

For several minutes we watched the movie, and I quoted nearly every other line.

Although I knew Josh would only be amused by my skillful recollection of the movie, I still murmured quietly to myself to not disturb him.

There was something about Vivian's spirit that called to my own. She was unflinchingly honest and authentically herself. Characteristics I hoped to find in myself even from a young age. Had my parents been around more often or paid more attention, maybe I wouldn't have been watching the movie with my two-year-old brother, but that's the way it was. It came with the territory of consistently leaving your child in front of a TV with zero adult supervision.

But it wasn't until I was nearly twelve that I fully grasped that she was a prostitute and Edward was paying her for her "company." Even then, that didn't dissuade me from seeing parts of myself in her. This was especially true when my mother began calling me wild, uncontrollable, and dramatic. Or telling me that I was too loud or too much.

Vivian was loud, but Edward didn't think that she was too much. He actually reveled in the fact that she was different. So, the whole prostitution part never mattered much to me.

"*It was so good, I almost peed my pants!*" Vivian erupted from the screen. I was so lost in my own thoughts that I'd missed one of my favorite lines and one that I had quoted to Josh earlier.

I laughed and turned to look behind me, where Josh was still quietly leaning against the back of the truck.

"See! I didn't make it up," I said, pointing to the screen.

But Josh wasn't watching the movie. His eyes were locked on his phone screen, which he held in front of him.

"You're not even watching," I said with a roll of my eyes.

"Sorry, I was busy watching something even more interesting."

"What on earth could be on your phone that is more intriguing than watching *Pretty Woman*? This is a classic and should be treated as such."

Rather than tell me, he scrubbed a hand over his jaw, seeming to contemplate his next move and then offered me his phone. I was inclined not to take it and just turn back to the movie, but my curiosity got the best of me. As it always did.

Queued up on the screen was a video that he'd taken of me. And I only hesitated a second before I pressed play.

The movie was playing in the background, slightly blurry since that's not what Josh was focused on. It was taken only a few seconds before, and to anyone who watched me, it would appear that I was absorbed in the movie. Although my thoughts were—in that moment—stuck on memories from years before.

And then Vivian delivered my favorite "I almost peed my pants" line, and I threw my head back laughing. In another second, I turned to Josh to make sure he'd heard it as well. My face was cast in odd shadows from the bright screen behind me and the subtle car lights all around us. You couldn't completely discern all of my features, but I was definitely smiling.

"What's so interesting about a video of me? Besides the fact that both you and Reed have some weird thing with videoing me when I'm not looking."

I reached forward to hand him back his phone, but Josh gripped my wrist and tugged me from my spot a few feet away.

His arm wrapped around my waist was the only thing that kept me from narrowly missing his family jewels with my knee.

Josh seated me between his legs, my back pressed against his chest and facing the screen.

"You could have just asked me to come sit by you," I grumbled.

With one arm wrapped around my waist, he repositioned the blankets to cover us both.

Once the blankets were arranged to his satisfaction, he reached for his phone once again and held it in front of us. He pressed play, and I did what I could to hide the tiny gasp that escaped my throat when he leaned forward and I felt his hot breath on my neck.

"You are more interesting to me, Amanda," he said and then ghosted his lips over my exposed skin. A shiver worked its way through me. I could feel the smile pull at his lips as they continued to dance over my skin. He trailed an intentional path up to my ear and back down my neck.

"That moment was so perfect that I needed to save it. And when you were on your date last night, Reed sent me a photo and then a video of you. You were smiling, and you had this amazing look of... wonder on your face. It was beautiful. Actually, it was breathtaking, and *fuck*, it made me so jealous. I saved it and replayed the video over and over again. I wanted to be there, too. I wanted to see that look on your face and help make you smile. And that asshole knew exactly what he was doing. So, I decided to give him a taste of his own medicine."

My breath hitched in my throat. As his words surrounded us, his mouth continued sucking and kissing my neck. Each time the video would stop, he would press play again, and I'd watch myself laugh and swing my head around to look at him.

I did look happy. I was *so* happy.

And the fact that he noticed it and had the idea to video it so he could relive it over and over again was almost too much.

Not a single coherent thought was possible for several long

seconds. His words and hands pressed eagerly against my stomach, along with his lips and tongue lavishing my neck, were all too much.

With one deep, painful breath, I was able to open my mouth and pull myself from his orbit just enough to make one simple statement.

"A little competition is fine, but if it escalates..."

"Baby girl, it's all in good fun. Just a little friendly competition between friends. And you can't blame us either when you're the only thing either of us has ever wanted."

At the same time, he nipped at my ear and then soothed it with his skillful tongue, my heart leaping into my throat, the emotion bombarding me.

In two dates, they'd both shown me the best they could that what he said was true. It was all too good. They'd been the best dates of my life. Which is why my stomach sank. The emotion in my throat morphed into something different. It was simultaneously hopeful and daunting.

Nothing would ever be the same again.

# SIXTEEN

Reed

No matter how high the volume, I couldn't get the music in my headphones loud enough.

Usually a hard workout, with cardio and weight training and loud-ass music, did the trick to clear my head. But it wasn't fucking working.

My muscles were aching—the kind of ache I lived for—and my lungs were on fire. Each breath was more difficult than the one before as I pushed myself harder on the treadmill. My labored breaths, the hum of the machine, and my pounding footfalls were all drowned out by the music blasting in my ears.

I'd long since lost my shirt. The sweat quickly drenched the thin material during our third set with the battle ropes.

I glanced over to the treadmill next to me and found Josh also had his treadmill nearly as high as my own. His headphones were also in, and like I'd found myself only a few seconds earlier, he was staring off into the distance, not looking at anything in particular but lost deep in his own thoughts.

When he'd walked into the gym late that morning for our workout, we hadn't discussed the workout nor had a conversation about what we wanted to do. With only the looks on both of our faces, we'd agreed to the workout we needed—something that would push our bodies to the brink and hopefully keep our minds occupied for an hour or two.

Although I suspected that neither of us was feeling much better, we were at least thoroughly exhausted and had expended the energy we were wasting on worrying about our predicament.

My palm slammed down onto the stop button, probably too hard, but the belt immediately stopped.

Without the movement, and my legs pumping underneath me, I felt the nearly two-hour-long workout and six miles on the treadmill throughout my body.

As I tried not to double over to catch my breath, instead clasping them on top of my head, I caught sight of Josh out of the corner of my eye, also slamming the stop button on his machine. He'd run nearly as far as I had—just shy of six miles—and mimicked my posture, folding his hands and placing them on top of his unruly blond hair. It was plastered to his forehead as the sweat dripped down his face and chest.

The effects of his more regimented workout schedule were evident. When I'd opened the gym, Josh made it a point to work out with me at least four or five days a week, and the lean muscle mass and sculpted shape of his body was a product of his consistency.

He'd told me to shove it, though, when I'd explained that laying off the beer during the week and extra fries would show even more pronounced results. Then he'd lifted his shirt and flexed his abs to prove that he was doing just fine.

Josh had stepped off his treadmill and his lips were moving, but with the rock music still blaring in my ears, I hadn't caught a word he said.

"What?" I asked, pulling my headphones out and trying to get used to the much quieter atmosphere of the gym.

"I said, 'do you like what you see?' because you're fucking staring." He laughed, still trying to breathe normally, but I didn't return his chuckle.

I hadn't even realized that I was openly staring at my best friend and his abs that I'd help carve. It wasn't my fault they were damn good abs.

"I was just thinking that I'm a damn good trainer. And as your trainer, I'm impressed with your results. That's all," I said, maybe too harshly.

"Damn, dude. I was just giving you shit." He headed past me to grab his water bottle where we'd dropped them, and I made it a point to look anywhere besides at him. That's when I saw one of my managers, Collin, jogging toward me with an intense set to his face.

"Hey, boss. I think you need to have a little chat with New Guy up front," he said in a hushed whisper. Although everyone in the place knew Adam's name and how he got the gig, they still referred to him as "New Guy." It was some kind of hazing shit that I didn't have time to worry about.

I outwardly groaned and closed my eyes. We'd made it nearly a week without issue, and although that was far longer than I thought he would last, I still wasn't looking forward to what I knew would happen.

"What happened? Why do I need to talk to him?"

I held my breath as my manager cringed, obviously not keen on having to tell me. "Well, you see… he was actually… okay, let me start over. I was going to—"

"Oh, for the love of God, spit it out, Collin. I don't have all day."

He took a deep breath. "Sorry… umm… he set his bag down on the counter, and it fell over, and well… several smaller bags fell out of it."

My mind went a million different directions as I waved my

hands, prompting him to continue and silently asking him to hurry the fuck up.

"Weed. Quite a bit of it."

I should have been more surprised. Actually, I wished I had been surprised, but it was classic Adam behavior: someone gives him an opportunity and he does some stupid shit like bring drugs to work.

"Where is he?"

Collin's eyes went wide as an incredulous look passed over his face. He was likely concerned by my lack of reaction.

"Umm… in your office," he stuttered.

"What's happening in your office?" Josh asked, stepping up to my right and using his shirt to wipe off the sweat still lingering on his face.

"Adam brought weed to work."

"Classic," Josh said with a casual shake of his head.

Collin's confused expression deepened, and he too shook his head at us.

"Let's go have a chat with Mr. New Guy," I said, jerking my head toward my office in the back. Like I knew he would, Josh followed me, mumbling "fucking kid" under his breath a time or two before we made it to my door.

Before opening it, I said a silent prayer that Adam was fucking sweating. That he was terrified I was going to rip him a new one when I walked through that door. That he feared me like the Grim Reaper coming for his soul.

Whether I would rip him a new one was something I hadn't yet decided. It all depended on his reaction.

I glanced quickly at Josh, who just raised his eyebrows in return and gave me a friendly pat on the back. A silent sign that he was on my side.

I pulled my shirt back on over my head—the fabric awkwardly sticking to my slightly damp skin. In the next second, I opened the door to find Adam reclined in my desk chair, spinning and staring up at the ceiling like I'd kept him waiting.

Yeah, I was going to tear him apart.

"So sorry we kept you waiting," I murmured, stepping into the room and leaning against my desk next to him.

Josh shut the door behind us and stopped right in front of Adam, kicking his foot out to stop the chair from spinning.

"*Fuck*," he groaned. "Both of you, really?"

I taunted him with an amused smile and crossed my arms over my chest. "What, New Guy, so you can do stupid shit until it's time to answer for it?"

"Okay, wait, can you let me explain before you start jumping to conclusions?"

Josh scoffed and glanced up at me. "Do you have an explanation that isn't absolute bullshit?"

Adam nodded convincingly.

"Go for it then."

"You know that I smoke recreationally every now and again, and since it's not legal yet in this fuckin' state, I've gotta get it somewhere. So my guy just got back from Colorado and told me I could pick it up tonight but changed the plan on me last minute. So, he had to drop it off to me. I was going to leave it in my car, but I haven't had a chance to go out there yet. I was going to go on my break—which is in fifteen minutes. I'm not—"

"Wait a second," I stopped him, moving the chair so he was facing me. "You bought weed in my gym? You didn't just bring it here, but you bought it on the premises?"

Adam shrugged, which pissed me off even more, and then tried to excuse his behavior by saying, "Well, actually, I paid for it ahead of time. Sent the guy the money, so technically, he just dropped it off."

With that absurd excuse, I had to take a deep breath and try to tamp down the frustrated anger I could feel prickling at my skin.

"You know, Adam," I began and watched as Josh rolled his lips to suppress a knowing smile. "Amanda told Josh and me a lot about your life growing up. We've been friends for so long I almost consider you like a little brother. You're sure as fuck as annoying as one most of the fucking time. But you know what Amanda didn't mention about your childhood in *all* the years we've known her?"

I eyed him and raised my eyebrows until he huffed out an exasperated, "What?"

"She didn't mention the several hundred fucking times you must have been dropped on your head to make you so insanely stupid."

At the same time, Adam sighed, and Josh laughed and nodded in agreement. "Okay, that's not fair—" Adam began, but I cut him off with a wave of my hand.

Worried that my anger and frustration would get the better of me, I took to pacing on the other side of the room near the door.

"Look, both Josh and I gave you a job, not only as a favor to your sister but to you as well. And at some point, you've got to get your shit together. I thought you were heading in the right direction because you've done well all fucking week, but then this shit happens. If you were anyone else, I would fire your ass immediately. There would be no argument about it because if someone figures out that I knew you had that shit here, I'd also have to answer for it."

"I get it, and I'm sorry for not thinking about that. But it's just a little weed. I didn't think you'd have such an issue with it since I know both of you have smoked before," Adam tried—and failed—once again to argue.

At a loss for words, I glanced over at Josh, who seemed just as surprised by Adam's shitty attempt at arguing. His messy blond hair was sticking up in every direction as he continued to run his hands through it in frustration.

"Fucking hell, Adam," I groaned. "I don't give a fuck that you smoke weed, but it's not legal in Texas. And whether you or I agree with that doesn't matter. But I care that you bought an illegal substance at the business I own and still fucking have it here on top of that. It's not about what you do in your free time, but what you've done while you're here. So, I need to know that this is the last time we'll be having this conversation, otherwise, you can get the fuck out now."

Adam looked between Josh and me, probably considering if he could make another half-assed argument, but thankfully, he thought better of it when he saw the stone-cold expressions on both of our faces.

The worst part was that I'd seen Adam grow up. All of us had watched him go from a hyper kid with an overactive imagination who always wanted to be around when his sister was home from college to a classic teenager that questioned authority at every turn. But Amanda believed he would eventually grow out of it and find his way. Sadly, at twenty-one, he was still nowhere near capable of doing anything on his own.

"It won't happen again."

I breathed a tiny sigh of relief and let myself believe he was telling the truth for a few seconds.

"Okay, good. Now, just take your break early and get that shit out of here."

Adam stood, and I stepped to the side so he could open the door.

"Could we agree not to tell my sister about this? She'd go ballistic."

The last thing either of us wanted to do was lie to Amanda, but the fact that she wasn't talking to either of us made it easier. And telling her was just going to cause more issues and that's the last thing she needed.

I looked at Josh for confirmation, and he nodded, crossing his arms in front of him.

"Fine, but if it happens again, all bets are off."

Adam agreed and was prepared to make a speedy exit when Josh added, "I guess it goes without saying that the same goes for the bar."

"Yup, goes without saying," Adam mumbled back before he all but ran out of the office.

I sagged back against the door and tried to take a deep, calming breath. There wasn't a chance I was going to calm down, though. My two-hour-long workout to calm my anxiety and nerves had been completely undone in a matter of minutes by Adam Allan.

"When's the kid going to fucking learn?" Josh asked.

"Maybe never. Not sure what the fuck he's going to do, though, if he can't even do this simple-ass job correctly."

Josh plopped himself in my desk chair and spun a time or two before leveling me with a look. "Not sure it's our problem, man."

"Well, if it's Amanda's problem, then I think it's our problem, too."

I didn't think it was possible, but I sagged farther against the door.

It had been nearly four days. Four miserable and uneventful days without hearing from Amanda. Neither of us had received a single text or phone call or email or fucking carrier pigeon from her in the days following our dates.

Actually, that was a lie. She'd texted us both to say she was busy preparing for classes starting back up for the spring semester and would have to take a rain check on the other two dates we'd had planned.

Both Josh and I had been understanding, but I don't think either of us realized that preparing for the new semester meant she wouldn't respond to us *at all*.

"Maybe we can give her a heads-up if she ever talks to us again," Josh grunted, saying out loud the words we'd both been thinking for the past several days. We'd tiptoed around the topic, not wanting to confirm what we thought could be happening— that she was ghosting us both.

"She'll talk to us again. She's just busy," I said unconvincingly, looking away from the dejection forming in Josh's eyes.

"You don't sound so sure," he murmured.

"Does that surprise you? It's usually me who's the pessimistic, realistic person between the two of us. Where's all your usual optimistic sunshine bullshit?"

Josh's response was a sigh that was laced with frustration and confusion that I'd also felt bone deep.

"Don't feel like being optimistic about the fact that she won't speak to either one of us. She hasn't made her decision already, right? It would be one thing if she had already decided that it was you or whatever, but she hasn't, right?"

The hurt in his voice reminded me of how much it meant to each of us that we were the one left standing. That if she picked one of us over the other—or neither of us—we would be irrevocably changed. And I registered the fact that if she picked me, it meant she wouldn't pick Josh. And my heart broke for my best friend.

"No, she hasn't said anything to me. We're in the same boat. I don't know where her head's at either."

"What are we going to do, then? I can't just sit around and wait for her to decide to talk to us. If she doesn't know yet, then fine, but I need to know." The volume of his voice slowly climbed. His frustration with our situation—with his situation— mounted with each word.

"It's Amanda," I said by way of explanation, like it all made sense because she was who she was.

"Yeah, but Reed, we've only ever known her as a friend. She's our dependable, funny, fucking beautiful *friend*, Amanda. And now, we've changed everything."

"You're right," I muttered, caught off guard by the glaringly obvious truth.

I took up pacing the length of my small office, chastising myself for the piles of papers and old equipment lining the walls. At least it was fairly organized chaos, but it made pacing difficult, having to step around them and be careful not to knock them over.

"I know I'm right." I glared at him and caught sight of his abs flexing as he chuckled softly. Guy still hadn't put on a shirt.

"Thanks for that, Sunshine," I said, fishing a new RG Fitness shirt from a pile in the corner and tossing it in his direction.

"God, you really want me to cover up, don't you, babe?" I gritted my teeth, trying to contain my annoyance and ignore his provocation.

"No, you're just sweating all over my chair." Josh winked in response and all it did was further irritate me.

As he pulled the shirt over his head, further messing up his already disheveled hair, I felt myself relax slightly.

"So, what are we going to do?" he asked.

I scoffed and took up the chair he'd vacated, easing myself back until it was as far as it could go. I'd sprung for the ergonomic chair, which my dad had told me was an extra expense I shouldn't have incurred. Little did he know I spent more time in that chair than I did in my own bed sometimes.

"We?"

He crossed his arms over his broad chest, looking down at me over his nose. "Yes, we, fucker. We," he said, motioning between the two of us. "Decided and agreed on this plan to begin with. We're in this together and need to figure out a way to fix this shit. I'm not okay with Amanda not talking to me. Are you?"

"Seriously? How can you even ask me that? Of course I'm not okay with this, but I'm not going to force her to talk to me."

Josh waved me off. "Maybe I just want this more than you do then. I'm not going to force her to talk to me, but I'm also not going to just roll over. There's a difference between showing her how much she's missing and forcing her to respond."

"You're fucking delusional," I said, barely restrained anger dripping from each word.

"If that's true, then prove it. Help me figure this out instead of sitting on your ass." With that comment, he'd pushed me too far. I pushed from my chair, slamming it into the desk behind me as I shot to my feet and got into Josh's face. My palms met resistance against his chest, but he staggered slightly, stepping back closer to the door. Only inches apart, the only thing I could see was the smug grin pulling at his lips.

The grin told me all I needed to know: he didn't believe any of the bullshit he was spewing. He was merely saying it to coax a reaction from me. And of course it worked—unsurprisingly, my best friend knew me better than nearly anyone.

"You annoy the shit out of me."

The grin he was trying to suppress turned into a full-on, Josh-like smile. "No, actually, I don't think I do."

# SEVENTEEN

Josh

REED DIDN'T TAKE A STEP BACK AND CONTINUED TO WATCH MY mouth long after I'd spoken. Uncomfortable under his scrutiny, I wetted my lips. An odd look passed over his face—one I couldn't exactly pinpoint—twisting his eyebrows and setting his mouth in a deathly straight line. The only word I could think of that might accurately describe it was surprise, but that didn't even make sense.

What the hell did he have to be surprised about? The fact that I knew challenging him would make it impossible for him to say no to me? That shouldn't have been a surprise since it was my usual MO when he was being more difficult than usual.

I cleared my throat and stepped forward. Thankfully, he took a half step back and lifted his eyes to mine. We were still close enough that there was no missing the dark-whiskey color of his eyes. The same whiskey he often ordered at Murphy's.

I opened my mouth to speak but felt the need to clear my throat again. I did it again—a little louder—and finally found my voice. "Tomorrow's her first day back at school, and I have something planned for tomorrow morning. I'll let you know how it goes."

Done with the conversation and having said all I needed to say, I headed for the door.

"Wait," Reed spoke up from behind me. His hand wrapped around my upper arm, keeping me from moving any farther to the exit. When I looked back, waiting for him to start talking, he wasn't looking at my face but at his hand and where he was touching me.

There was a wrinkle between his brows again like there was a minute before. His hand felt heavier against my skin the longer he left it there.

He cleared his throat and pulled his eyes from where he touched me. "Why do you get to see her first? Who decided that?"

I tried not to smile at his usual competitive nature and the need to make all equal.

The entire time we'd known each other, it always had to be fair. If we were both interested in the same girl, we'd play Rock, Paper, Scissors to figure out who would approach her. If we wanted to watch different movies, we'd flip a coin. When we'd go out, we'd have to find someone to pick a number between one and twenty. Whoever's number they were closer to was where we'd go.

"Because you got the first date, and actually, I decided," I said as I crossed the space to the door. His hands slipped from my arm as I stepped around the box of shirts he'd pulled mine from and another box of fancy water bottles.

"See you at home," I called before the door clicked shut behind me.


Six in the morning was exceptionally early when I usually finally fell into bed at around two or three a.m.

But I couldn't let my exhaustion affect my plan, so I carefully grabbed the cup of hot coffee—a large, caramel latte with cinnamon—and the salad I knew she enjoyed from a local grocery store from the passenger seat.

I'd arrived early enough that I knew she'd still be at her apartment, likely frantic to gather her things in enough time to still get her coffee and be at school earlier than necessary.

I hurried up the stairs and paused for a moment at her front door, saying a silent prayer that she wouldn't be pissed off that I'd shown up unannounced before knocking.

Depending on what she was doing, I thought I might have to knock a few times, but it was only a matter of seconds before the door swung open.

Amanda was already dressed in colorful pants and a sweater, with her school lanyard around her neck. But my favorite part was her black-rimmed glasses that framed her wide blue eyes that were looking at me like I'd turned purple and grown five heads.

"Good morning," I said as I squeezed past her, not waiting for an invitation to enter.

Quickly her shocked expression turned into one of frustration. One I knew very well.

"What the hell are you doing here? I have to leave in like ten minutes." She pushed the door closed and threw her hands in the air as it slammed a little too hard for six in the morning.

"Is Adam here?" I asked, preparing for a very pissed-off twenty-one-year-old to come storming out of his room any minute.

"No, he's… out." Her hesitant explanation made me pause for a moment, but I continued.

"Well, I brought you coffee and lunch, which means you don't actually have to leave for closer to thirty minutes." Treating it as a peace offering, I held the still very warm coffee cup out to her.

Not dropping her death glare, she took it with both hands and smelled it before taking a sip. When her expression eased slightly—the tension between her eyebrows settling—I knew I'd won a few brownie points having nailed her order.

She took a long sip, and I left the salad next to her purse on the island.

"What are you doing here, Josh?"

For a second, I contemplated my response, but I sidestepped the sarcastic response I had on my tongue and decided to tell her the truth.

"I'm here to talk."

The truth earned me an eye roll, and she immediately turned and headed back to her bedroom. I followed, of course, and ended up leaning against her bathroom counter as she applied the finishing touches to her makeup.

"Thank you for the coffee, but I really am trying to get ready for work."

She swiped her glasses off her face and made a cute "oh" face when she applied more mascara.

"I understand, but I'm not planning on making you late. I even brought you coffee and lunch to make sure you weren't late."

"So you could talk to me?" There was a slight waver in her voice and when she replaced her mascara tube in the drawer next to her sink, there was a small tremble in her hand.

*Fuck.* The last thing I wanted to do was upset her.

"I just miss my best friend. We don't have to talk about anything in particular, but I do want to talk to you."

Her head was tilted down, mindlessly moving things back and forth in her small makeup drawer, and her only response to my confession was a glance up in my direction. She peered up at me through her now darker lashes and behind the lenses of her glasses.

"You really want to do this right now, Josh?" she said quietly.

"Not necessarily, but in the ten years we've known each other, I can't remember the last time we went this long without at least texting and saying 'hi.'"

She closed the drawer and paced into her closet, returning with a pair of tan boots. As she slipped them on, she said, "The last time was during our fight junior year about that stupid girl who thought I was into you."

I chuckled at the memory and at how upset Amanda was that the girl would even think she'd do something like that. Interesting how things turned out.

"And look at us now," I said, and immediately regretted it when I saw her face.

"What does that mean?"

"I'm just saying that we've slept together twice now and been out on a date. We obviously have feelings for each other, so maybe that chick wasn't all wrong."

Her scoff echoed in the bathroom. Once she'd finished zipping her boots and taken one final look in the mirror, she flicked off the light and left me standing in the dark bathroom.

So... she was mad, and it was not going well.

"Amanda, wait," I pleaded, following her quickly retreating steps into the living room and back into the kitchen. "This is not how I planned on this going at all."

I approached her from behind, and she whirled on me, crossing her arms and staring up into my face. "Is that so? Then how did you imagine it going when you showed up at my apartment unannounced when we hadn't spoken in several days? Because this is about what I would expect. Actually, I'm surprised I haven't kicked you out yet."

"I was running out of options. What the hell else was I supposed to do when you wouldn't answer the fucking phone?"

"I don't know, take the hint, maybe? I don't have anything to talk about right now. I need to get through these first few days of school and then..." She chewed her bottom lip, debating her words and looking everywhere except at me. "And then, if you want to talk, then we can. Just give me a little more time. Today's Wednesday, we can discuss it this weekend if I'm feeling up for it."

That statement simultaneously felt like both progress and several steps back. I wasn't sure what had changed after our date, but something had.

"Another three days feels like forever. Why do I feel like you're just going to turn around and tell me that this isn't happening?"

She darted around the kitchen, grabbing a water bottle and throwing the bag I brought the salad in into a lunch box container. But she didn't say anything. And her silence seemed so much louder than anything else she could have or would have said.

By the way she hurried around her apartment, I knew she was worried about getting to school on time and was also probably keen to get away from me as quickly as she could. So, I didn't say anything else.

I hung back close to the door as she proceeded to gather her things. When she turned the kitchen light off, grabbed her keys off the table in the small entryway, and lifted her purse over her shoulder, I opened the door.

I offered to carry something, but she waved me off.

She didn't spare a glance at me as she hurried out and waited for me to exit before she locked it behind us. I trailed a few steps behind her as we headed toward the stairs and watched a shiver run through her. It was chilly, and I felt pulled to wrap an arm around her and tuck her into my side, hiding her from the wind.

But I refrained from touching her no matter how badly my hands itched to do so.

I did, however, rush ahead of her to open the back door of her car, so she could slide her arms full of belongings onto the seat.

And when she pivoted to the driver's side door, I reached my hand out to the handle. I was a second faster, which meant her cold, soft hand landed on mine. Finally, she looked up at me, and there was so much doubt in her deep-blue eyes.

"I thought our date went well. What happened?"

"It did go well," she said, and then she muttered to herself. "That's part of the problem."

I searched for something to say. Anything that would mean I wasn't going to lose her before I'd even really gotten her.

"Look, I just need time and space to think."

"Amanda, I just—" I stuttered, struggling for the right words. "*Fuck*, I can't, actually, I won't lose our friendship. That's the most important thing to me. So, even if nothing else happens, we will still be friends."

She sighed deeply and rolled her neck, releasing some built-up tension. "Can you really promise that, though? Can you stand here and tell me that our friendship hasn't already changed?"

"Yes," I lied. And I could tell that she knew I didn't believe it. "Please, just don't shut me out. I want to talk to you, even if we don't talk about us."

"Good," she said, prying her fingers from beneath my own and gripping the door handle. "Because, Josh, there is no *us*."

And then she left.

I watched her car pull out of the parking lot and then disappear down the street. I stared in that direction for a while, and only when the sun finally peaked over the horizon did I begin walking to my truck.

# EIGHTEEN

Reed

The sun had set nearly an hour before and the cold air chilled me to the bone.

But even as my teeth chattered, I stood steadfast. I'd waited in my car for nearly half an hour, and once I'd realized Amanda wasn't going to be leaving school at a decent time, I felt bad about the gas I'd wasted. So I'd taken to leaning against her car door, praying she'd appear from the glass doors sooner rather than later.

Instead of staring at the door and awkwardly making eye contact with each person that left the school, I busied myself with my phone. I'd scrolled through all of my social media apps and responded to a few work emails before I texted Luke for an update on their honeymoon and Josh letting him know that I was going to wait as long as necessary.

Luke responded only a few minutes later with an eggplant and a heart-eyes emoji. I decided to leave that one alone.

Josh, however, had read my message and ignored it.

I was already heading to work by the time he left earlier that morning to intercept Amanda before she left her apartment, and by the time I returned, he'd left for Murphy's. He'd also made it a point to read, yet ignore, all of my texts asking how it went.

With his silence, I assumed it didn't go according to plan. We were both competitive, and between the two of us, I was far more vocal about it. But, if he'd gotten the result he was hoping for, he would've texted or called to gloat.

Which meant Amanda would either tell me to fuck off or maybe she'd already made her decision. And although I fucking prayed that she'd choose me, my stomach plummeted when I thought about what it would mean for Josh.

If she said yes to me, that would mean he'd get a no, and it was hard to be happy about my own success when I knew my best friend would be devastated. The possibility of his being heartbroken nearly overshadowed my hope that Amanda would light up when she saw me.

My phone vibrated in my hand, the screen having gone black while I contemplated Josh's broken heart. Eagerly, I unlocked it, but instead of seeing the response from Josh I was hoping for, it was a text from my mom.

Her first text was simply my full name, and then another came through a second later.

> Mama: Reed Alejandro Gregory.

> Mama: Come visit your Mama.

I texted her back and promised to visit that week, to which she responded that she'd believe it when I walked through the front door.

What I wouldn't do to visit her more. My mom was my best friend and biggest supporter but going to their house across the city meant I'd also have to see my father. And it took all of my energy to field his questions and concerns for even an hour. His constant confusion over my life choices and annoyance that I hadn't chosen his preferred path for me was more than I could usually handle during a casual family dinner.

I shrugged my shoulders and rolled my head from side to side, attempting to relieve the tension that had been building there for the nearly hour and a half I'd been waiting for Amanda.

The moment I pocketed my phone and looked toward the front door of the school for what seemed like the millionth time, I finally saw what I'd been waiting for.

Amanda stepped out of the glass doors with her phone in her hand, smiling down at whatever she saw on the screen. She had her purse slung over one shoulder while carrying a large tote on the other. And it wasn't until she'd stepped off the curb and was several feet into the parking lot that she looked up and stopped.

I made a mental note to talk to her about her lack of awareness later, but in that moment, I pushed the thought out of my head and smiled.

Even with her glasses on, I could see her squint in my direction and look around like she was waiting for Ashton Kutcher to jump out from behind a bush and tell her she was being punked. I watched as her smile faded and she glanced back to the school doors she'd just exited, appearing to contemplate heading back inside instead of approaching me.

That hurt, and it would have hurt more had I not had to quickly compose myself when her steps quickened in my direction.

"You and your friend have some really shit timing," she mumbled, grabbing the door handle of her little car and chunking her bags in the back seat. They landed with a thud, and she slammed the door with enough force that it rocked the car. "Go ahead," she prompted. "Say whatever you came here to say and make it quick. I want to go home."

God, she was angry. Her arms were crossed over her chest, and she squared her shoulders like she was ready for a showdown.

"If you want to go home, I can meet you there. My intention wasn't to—"

"Wasn't to what, Reed? Force me into a decision I'm clearly not ready or willing to make? Because that's kind of what Josh said this morning, too, yet that's what you're both doing. You show up here and try to bamboozle me into talking."

"This is not a bamboozlement," I stuttered out.

"First of all, no way in hell is that a word, and second of all, you didn't answer my question. What is this, then?"

"I *miss* you," I said, letting all of the pent-up emotion and hurt and concern flood out in those three little words.

Amanda heard it all, too—what those three words said and didn't say—because her face fell and her shoulders dropped.

"I haven't gone anywhere, Reed. There's no reason to miss me."

"Are you sure? Because it feels like you're somewhere else completely."

"How can you say that when I'm standing right here?"

It took all of my strength not to roll my eyes at the way she twisted my words.

"Why can't y'all just give me a little time? Why is that so hard?"

"Because it feels like we've been waiting for this opportunity for forever," I pleaded, chancing a step closer to her. She didn't step back—which I took as a win—but she continued to watch me warily.

"Look, I'll tell you what I told Josh this morning: I just need some time, okay? Let me at least get through this week, and then maybe this weekend, I'll be in a better headspace to talk."

"You mean to tell us that you're not interested? That you're not feeling it?" I clarified, and she didn't hold back her eye roll.

"No, Reed, that's not what I'm saying. *God*, you are both so infuriating. I just have a lot going on right now with school starting back up and Adam moving in. Not to mention I have a new fucking wrinkle every time I look in the damn mirror and am now contemplating Botox."

"Well, you show your emotions all over your face, so I'm not surprised about the wrinkles."

She scowled in response, and I motioned to her expression. "Yes, exactly like that."

If looks could throw daggers, I would have been dead. But she withheld the verbal lashing I knew she wanted to give me and instead settled for a deep breath. Her eyes closed, and I chastised myself that my eyes went directly to her chest as it rose and fell with her breath.

"This conversation isn't going anywhere, so I think we're done. If it makes you feel better, and you can mention this to Josh as well, I haven't made my decision yet, and I don't know what the fuck I'm going to do. But that's all I have to say. So, just give me the rest of the week," she pleaded, and when I opened my mouth to respond, she whispered, "*Please.*"

There was this invisible pull to wrap her in my arms and tell her that it would be okay. That no matter what happened, I would make sure we were all okay. I wanted to run my hands over her back and soothe away the concern and frustration that was twisting her soft, beautiful features.

I felt horrible that I'd been the one to make her feel that way. So, I only nodded and backed away from her car, giving her ample room to open the door and slip inside without another word or glance in my direction.

# NINETEEN

### Amanda

"WE REALLY DON'T HAVE TO GO HERE, YOU KNOW? THERE'RE A million other bars in this city," I explained as Hazel pulled into the parking lot of Murphy's Law.

It was packed as it usually was on a Friday night, and even more cars pulled in behind us.

"Yes, I know. But the renovations have helped." She put the car in park and glanced over her shoulder at the front door. "And I'm not going to let a place have that kind of power over me anymore."

Only a little over a year later, Hazel was, in her words, "done being scared and trapped by her past." She hadn't died, although that had been Valerie's intent when she kidnapped her. And Murphy's, being the place where it all came to a head, was an overwhelming reminder of how close we'd all come to losing her.

"If you're sure," I said, watching her watch the door.

Her eyes flashed to mine, and thankfully, there wasn't an ounce of hesitation. And the smile she gave me was genuine.

"I'm sure," she said and promptly hopped out of the car. "It's also a bonus if one of your guys is here," she added with a wink.

I groaned and contemplated throwing a fit until she agreed to go somewhere else. I'd missed her something fierce while she and Luke had been on their honeymoon, and the last thing I wanted was for our girls' night to be commandeered by my boy drama. But she didn't give me a chance as she opened the passenger door and all but pulled me from her car.

I wobbled on my heels for a moment and threw a glare in her direction. Her response was a long eye roll. "Leave the glares for the guys. Let's go!"

By the time I turned around to grab my purse and close the car door, Hazel was already halfway to the front door, her little black boots clicking on the newly paved parking lot. I knew it was under Josh's direction that Rhonda had finally decided to pave the lot after decades of the same gravel. And my feet and balance thanked him at that moment because heels and gravel were a really shitty combination.

Hazel stopped next to the door before turning her attention back to me.

"You look a little like a baby giraffe," she commented as she swung the door open.

"These are new heels, so I feel like a baby giraffe."

Loud pop music greeted us as we stepped inside. The room with the pool tables to our left was packed, and the back bar was crowded with several people waiting for drinks.

"I didn't think they did karaoke on Friday nights," Hazel whisper-yelled into my ear.

The stage in the corner of the place was set up with the karaoke equipment and the large screen that projected the lyrics. Across the top of the screen was a banner that read "Happy Birthday, Grady!" and it all made perfect sense.

"Looks like it's special for Grady's birthday."

"Is he seriously still working on his birthday?" Hazel pointed to the older man who was in his usual place behind the bar. Only he had a huge grin on his face watching and listening to the woman on stage butcher a Taylor Swift song.

I grabbed Hazel's hand and pulled her along as I beelined for two seats that had opened at the bar. We made it to the empty barstools a split second before two other guys who'd also seen the opening. Hazel threw them an apologetic smile, but I was more worried about saying hi to my favorite bartender.

"That is not who I think it is sitting at my damn bar," Grady said brightly and loudly over the music and butchered lyrics.

"Hi, Grady," I said with a smile, only the second genuine one I'd felt in a while. The first one was when I'd reunited with Hazel and the second one was when I saw the pure joy on Grady's face. The wrinkles around his eyes and mouth evidence of a well-lived, happy life.

"It's been too long. And you brought my other favorite girl." He smiled at Hazel, who returned it with ease. She had that deliriously happy, newlywed glow about her. And I was over the moon excited for her, yet the nagging jealousy I'd felt at the rehearsal dinner hadn't gone away. I was throwing myself a pity party because of my own disastrous love life.

I was truly happy to see my best friend happy. But I was envious of her easygoing smile.

"I was in here two weeks ago, Grady. It hasn't been that long."

"Two weeks is way too damn long. Hazel, how were the wedding and honeymoon? Josh showed me some pictures, and they looked beautiful."

Hazel was radiant. "It was perfect. The wedding and the honeymoon."

"I'm glad to hear it. So, what are y'all drinking tonight?"

"Margaritas," Hazel proclaimed, and I nodded in agreement. Our classic girls' night go-to.

"Coming right up." Grady tapped his knuckles on the dark wood bar top and pulled two glasses and a shaker.

"So, you're working on your birthday?" Hazel asked as Grady found the tequila and the Cointreau.

"Well, technically, my birthday isn't until tomorrow. I'm heading to my daughter's up in Colorado to celebrate tomorrow morning. Get to see my grandson for the first time in a while, but I persuaded Josh to set up karaoke for tonight. Give me something to laugh at while I'm back here."

Hazel opened her mouth to respond, but we all cringed as the woman on stage screeched out the final note of the song, and the music thankfully cut out.

"Wow, thank you so much for that," the guy running the karaoke cut in. "On that note, I think it's time for a break."

And without delay, a steady rock beat filtered through the speakers and reenergized the bar patrons.

"Well, happy early birthday and safe travels," Hazel said, raising her margarita in a toast. I tapped my glass against hers and then Grady added in his water glass.

I took a long gulp and savored the burn of the tequila. Like he knew I needed it, Grady made them extra strong. Hazel spluttered next to me, squinting her eyes at her glass in surprise.

"Damn, Grady. I was hoping to have more than one drink tonight, but I may be flat on my ass after just this one."

Grady cut his eyes at her as he wiped down the bar and grabbed a few beers for a group of guys next to us.

"Looked like Amanda needed something a little stronger. I can rein it back next time—"

"Nope," I chimed in before he could finish. "This is perfect and exactly what I needed."

"Good bartender always knows without anyone ever having to say a word." Grady winked and flashed me an understanding smile before he made his way to the other side of the bar.

"Okay, take another sip, and then I need you to fill me in on everything that's gone down in the past week."

"Do we have to?" I groaned, still taking the sip as she instructed.

"Yes, we absolutely have to. I told you all about our honey-moon and even gave you a rundown of Rebecca's birth. So, it's your turn."

"We're trading information now? Is this what our friendship has come to?" I commented and then caught Grady's eye across the bar and pointed at my nearly empty glass.

"Yes, now spill."

Earlier in the day, Hazel had not only given me a play-by-play of their honeymoon, including all of the destinations they'd visited, but she'd also included pictures that correlated to each stop and story. And she'd spent extra time on Delilah's labor with Hazel's new niece, Rebecca. She and Luke had been only a few hours away in Memphis when Delilah went into labor and made it to the hospital in time to see little baby Becca born.

Those photos I hadn't been as keen on seeing.

"There's nothing new to tell," I said with a grateful smile to Grady, who dutifully refilled my glass. "I haven't spoken to either of them. They haven't even texted me. I told you that they both came to see me. I told them I needed space, and they gave it to me."

"So, at this point, you've cut off all contact?"

I shrugged by way of an answer, but Hazel cut her eyes at me from behind her straight brown hair.

"Until I can figure out what the fuck I'm doing, yes. Talking to them just complicates everything."

"How does it complicate it?"

Whether it was the alcohol or I'd finally hit my breaking point, I wasn't sure. But I was tired of bottling in the emotions that had been driving me mad for weeks.

I pivoted in my chair and looked Hazel directly in the eyes. "Because when I'm around them, I feel shit I didn't even know was possible. And that is absolutely terrifying. I am terrified."

Hazel's eyes widened with my honesty, but other than that, she didn't react to my confession. In all of our conversations, it was the most candid I'd been about my feelings. And it was the first time I'd said out loud what I'd been warring with inside.

"Say something, please," I pleaded, slowly becoming more and more concerned by her silence.

"Why is that so bad, babe?"

My deep breath did little to settle my intense nerves, but I'd already opened the can of worms. There was little I could do to take it all back, and I knew Hazel wouldn't have it.

"Because it's both of them, Hazel. I feel the same way about both of them. My feelings are just as intense when I'm around Reed as they are when I'm around Josh. Choosing between the two would be nearly impossible."

"For now," she added.

"I'm not so sure my feelings are going to change that much, especially on their short time line."

She placed a soothing hand on my exposed thigh and squeezed. The comforting gesture kept me from bouncing it in nervousness, something I hadn't even noticed I was doing.

"I know this is cliché advice, but I really do believe it will all work out the way it's supposed to. And I know for a fact that both of those boys are fucking crazy for you. I would just talk to them and tell them that you need to extend the time line a little. Maybe change the rules of your agreement and add a few more dates. Or hell," she said, throwing her hands out, "do away with the agreement altogether and just be casual. Don't put a time line or a date limit on it."

My chuckle was rueful. "You really think they'd go for that?"

She nodded emphatically and swigged her drink. "Because you know what they care about more than anything? More than time lines and rules and competition?"

It didn't take me any time to figure out where she was going, but I still asked, with a lilt of a question in my voice, "Me?"

"Yes, you dumbass. They care about *you*. Not only as their future partner but as their friend and as a person. So, just talk to them, okay? I promise it won't be as miserable as you've cata-strophized."

"So, you're telling me that I won't have to fake my own death or make my apartment a fortress they can't penetrate?"

She gave me a quizzical look and then sighed. "That's another obscure movie reference I'm not going to get, isn't it?"

"*Heathers* and *Fear*."

"Okay, I probably could have gotten the *Heathers* one if I wasn't on my second margarita. And on that note, I really like this song."

Hazel downed the rest of her nearly full margarita, and I did the same as quickly as I could before she tugged me off the barstool.

"No more boy talk!" she shouted and wrapped her arms around my shoulders.

I threw my head back and laughed at her proclamation. It had been amazing to watch the timid, terrified woman I'd met over a year ago, and who Luke rescued from her own hell, turn into a confident, badass chick and my best friend.

And I decided to push it all away. For one night, I wouldn't worry about my missing friend, parenting my twenty-one-year-old brother, the start of the school year, or my love triangle.

I grinned at my bestie, who wore the purest smile as she flung her hair back and forth before screaming the lyrics in my face. I did it right back, and we both dissolved into hysterical laughter.

A girls' night could cure all.

# TWENTY

Amanda

"How many margaritas are too many margaritas?"

"The limit does not exist!" I chanted back as Hazel and I picked up our third margarita from the bar top. After over an hour of dancing and drinking, I was at that perfect level of tipsy. Where everything was funny and I felt like there was nothing I couldn't do.

"No, I definitely think there's a limit and you two are close to finding it," a voice interrupted from behind us, and on instinct, I swiveled to give the jackass a piece of my mind. But I stopped short when I was met with the smiling face of my brother.

"And that's exactly why I brought fries for both of you and water." He placed two servings of fries on the bar in front of us, as well as two full glasses of water. I stuck my nose up at the water, but the fries I immediately dug into.

"I didn't know you were here tonight," I admitted, with fries stuffed into my mouth.

"Josh asked me to help out since it's Grady's birthday. Guy pulls a pretty big crowd," Adam clarified.

"It hasn't been too bad," Grady countered. Refilling the water Hazel had already sucked down.

"It's the busiest I've seen it since I've been here."

Grady chuckled and nudged the water I hadn't touched closer to me, silently urging me to drink. "Just wait until St. Paddy's day. It's always chaos, which means all hands on deck."

"Oh, yes!" I exclaimed at the memories. "St. Patrick's Day here is the best! One time in college, Blakely and I—actually, maybe Devon, too—but we all drank *so* much green beer that our puke was green that night. We thought it was fucking hilarious until we passed out on the bathroom floor." I chuckled around a mouthful of fries at the stupid college memory. "There was green glitter all over my bathroom floor for weeks."

Not that I could say much, though, because I was pretty positive that the glitter was my bright idea.

Unsurprisingly, it was usually me, Josh and Reed that came up with the crazy shit and usually took it too far. There was a multitude of dumb ideas and half-assed plans that wound up with someone injured, but all of us laughing our asses off.

"You were the life of the party, weren't you, sis?" Adam joked, shouldering me with a disbelieving look.

"Actually, she was." Josh smiled as he saddled up next to Grady and leaned his forearms onto the bar in front of me.

The goose bumps on my arms were proof that my body's reaction to these men was insane. It was nonsensical that my body would have that type of reaction just to Josh's proximity.

Although I would have been lying if I hadn't admitted that the short-sleeved black *Murphy's* shirt perfectly hugged his toned biceps. And it wasn't fair that his dirty-blond hair was messy in all the right ways, pushed back from his tanned face and showing off his blue-green eyes.

And for some reason, I found myself mesmerized by his mouth. His lips were plump, and his teeth were straight but not perfectly straight, and that fact made him even more personable and charming.

When my eyes flitted back to his to once again gawk at the ocean-like color, it was Josh's wink that made me suddenly realize I'd been staring and appraising him for far too fucking long.

It was the fucking alcohol, so I broke eye contact and chugged my water like I'd been stranded in the Sahara for weeks and weeks. I nearly choked, that's how fast I gulped it down. And with raised brows, Grady refilled it without any *verbal* questions.

"You should have her tell you about the time—"

"Oh, no!" I interrupted Josh midsentence. "We are not going to tell my little brother about my college shenanigans. I refuse to be that much of a shitty influence."

Josh chuckled and shook his head. "No offense, but I really think that ship has sailed. He's already got enough of his own bad ideas. Hearing about the bullshit we got up to isn't going to change him. Right, Adam?"

Adam shrugged and tossed a white dishrag over his shoulder. "Yeah, I can agree with that. So, tell me. I was too young to really have paid much attention when you were in college. Did you get arrested?"

"Twice," Josh answered, and I swore in that moment I could have killed him. Or, at the very least, pinched him.

"Twice?! Why the fuck did you get arrested? I was mostly fucking around, but now I need to know."

I rolled my eyes and groaned. "We really don't need to make any trips down memory—"

"The first time was when she broke into a professor's office because—*Fuck!* That hurt!" I actually pinched Josh that time instead of just thinking about it.

"No one wants to hear about that. It was like ten years ago." I threw my hands out in exasperation.

"Actually, I kind of do," Grady added.

"Same here," Hazel quipped.

The betrayal I felt at Hazel's agreement I let show all over my face and in my bewildered expression. She shrugged and ate another fry.

"You talk a lot about the crazy shit Josh and Reed did but not so much about your part in it all."

The fact that all it took was Hazel wanting to know more about me to get me to cave, I, again, blamed on the alcohol.

"Fine," I conceded. "One of my professors took my backpack with all of my shit because she thought I was cheating and when she refused to give it back, I went and got it. Only to be caught by campus security."

"Wait a second. You have to tell the whole story."

I glared at Josh.

"That's most of the story—those are the most important details. And besides, you can't really call it getting arrested. Technically, I was only detained by campus security for two hours."

"Pretty sure it was closer to four, and why don't you tell the class why you were detained for so long, babe?" Josh's knowing look and crooked grin were evidence enough that if I didn't cop to it, he would spill it all for me. Probably in greater detail, too.

With a sigh, I said, "Because they caught me using her favorite bright-ass red lipstick to write on her wall, 'Free the orgasm.'"

There was a look of pure, unadulterated horror on Grady's face while both Hazel and Adam were doubled over in laughter. Josh's knowing look hadn't faltered, and all I wanted to do was wipe it from his face. The little shit stirrer he was.

Hazel nearly fell off of her barstool, cradling her stomach. I held on to her arm as she righted herself and wiped at the tears running down her face.

"Why that? Why'd you write that?" she croaked out.

"She heard me say something to a girl in my class about how she needed to buy a vibrator and then basically called me a whore. It happened right before she took my bag. She deserved it."

Hazel erupted into a whole new laughing fit, and Josh's crooked smile slowly inched across his face. His dimples were prominent because of the shadows that were cast across his face in the dim bar light.

I found myself returning his smile, and even biting my lower lip couldn't keep it from spreading across my face. It was the same look he always gave me when I did something that maybe wasn't as thoroughly thought through as it should have been but was warranted nonetheless.

It was a smile that said he saw me and my intentions and liked both.

With his forearms still braced on the bar, Josh leaned forward even farther, the smile never slipping from his face. One of his hands slid into mine that rested on the bar, fidgeting with the napkin under my water as he moved closer. For a second, I thought he was going to kiss me, and by the look that flashed across his eyes, I knew he was contemplating it.

My chest heaved with anticipation, and the thought that he was going to throw everything out the window about keeping us quiet and simply kiss me right in the middle of the bar was maddening. But at the same time, I didn't move. His approach was slow and measured and gave me plenty of time to jerk away if I wanted to.

But I was sucked into his orbit and wanted to know where this would end up.

When he casually ran his tongue over his bottom lip, I knew I was right. I could feel the memory of his lips on mine. Plump and perfect and urgent for more every time. And then his soft tongue would brush against mine, stoking our twin flames of desire to an astronomically high level.

But that was not at all what happened. At the last second, and as I sucked in a deep breath to ready myself for the kiss, he turned his head to the side and kissed my cheek.

His hot breath covered my ear and fresh goose bumps pebbled my skin.

"That's my girl," he whispered as he squeezed my hand.

Abruptly, he pulled back, and the sounds of the bar and the chaos around us were apparent once again.

I knew I had to look as ridiculous as I felt. My breathing was labored, and there was an obvious flush to my skin. I could have blamed the latter on the alcohol, thankfully, and with a shaky hand, I pressed my water glass to my lips.

He didn't even kiss me, yet I looked and felt like I'd been properly fucked by him whispering in my ear.

I glanced at Hazel next to me, who was nearly recovered from her laughing fit and watched her eyes eagerly search the crowd for her husband. He was easy to find, though. Luke was so large that people usually got out of his way before they could even be in his way.

"There's my beautiful wife," he boomed and threw his arms wide. Hazel didn't hesitate to leap into them, and like the lovesick newlyweds they were, Luke spun her around in a bear hug. And when he gingerly set her back on the ground, he planted a long, lingering kiss on her mouth.

"I thought you were supposed to stop that shit after you two got hitched. Doesn't marriage change everything?" Devon remarked, striding in behind James.

Devon circled around to my right and kissed my temple before waving to Grady for a beer.

"How's it goin'?"

"It was going great until we took a trip down memory fucking lane," I mumbled, contemplating switching back and ordering my seventh margarita.

"Let me guess: the professor and the lipstick?"

"Oh, that's the best one." James laughed, sidling up on my left and next to the barstool Hazel vacated.

"No, I think the one when she—"

Tired of hearing about my past transgressions, I slapped my hand over James's mouth and glowered up at him. His blond hair was perfectly styled as usual and he was still wearing the suit he'd worn to work. He'd probably only just left the office and met the boys at the bar.

"We're done reliving my past. Can we all agree, please?"

James rolled his eyes but nodded, so I slowly removed my hand. I jerked my glare to Josh, who nodded and then to Devon, who innocently sipped his beer.

"Thank you all. Anyway, Grady, I think I need another margarita after dealing with these guys."

"You know you love us, Manda," James quipped.

He perched his head on top of mine and smoothed his hand down my opposite arm.

"You trying to steal my girl, Larson?"

James turned and a smile broke across his face. "Oh yeah, Gregory? You callin' dibs?"

"You know it," Reed said and slapped our friend on the back.

In another second, his golden-brown eyes were on me, and I suddenly forgot how to breathe. The scruff along his jawline was longer than usual, and for some reason, the first thing to cross my mind was the memory of how that scruff felt against my inner thighs.

A delicious shiver coursed through my body as I remembered the roughness.

And like he knew what I was thinking, Reed flashed me a wicked grin.

"You having fun, baby girl?" His voice was low, and I nodded as James and Devon went to find an open pool table. Reed took up the barstool to my left, and his thigh brushed mine.

I turned farther to the front and took my water between my palms.

"Hey, Sunshine. I think I need a shot of whiskey and a beer." It was Reed's go-to order no matter where we went because you'd have to be the worst bartender in the world to fuck it up.

Josh's eyes bounced between me and Reed, his hesitance

obvious, but he ultimately turned to pull the whiskey from the glass shelf behind the bar.

"Girls' night was good?" Reed asked when Josh turned away.

"It was until all of this testosterone showed up."

He tilted his head back and laughed, showing off his perfect Adam's apple and toned neck. There was a vein running from below his ear and disappearing under the collar of his shirt, and my tongue tingled with the reminder of his reaction when I'd run my tongue over the line of it. He'd lost his mind with desire and tossed me to the bed when I'd bit into his chest muscle.

Unfortunately, I knew I'd never forget that damn night. It was going to haunt me for eternity.

Josh slid the drinks across the bar and replaced my water. "Looking a little thirsty there, babe. Figured you could use another."

My face flamed. Of course Josh had seen me watching Reed. Those men watched and dissected my every move and word like it was going to tell them some essential information about me. Or about what was going on in my head, which I knew was what they both wanted.

The frustrated set to Josh's eyes was made even worse by the jealousy burning within them. He hadn't missed my gawking, but hadn't he also noticed earlier that I was doing the same thing to him?

I was caught between two insanely attractive men who seemed to sincerely want me. And not just want in my pants as I'd once thought—they wanted me in every way they could.

I'd asked for space the first few days of classes, and they'd listened to me. There was something about their listening that felt important. And while the distance was good and exactly what I'd asked for, they still hadn't been far from my mind. All week I'd been dreading the conversation I knew they'd make me have. I knew we'd get to Friday—or maybe they'd give me until Saturday—and they'd be ready to talk.

And the fact that they were both in front of me and available was enough. I was ready to get it over with and get it all out in the open, like Hazel had suggested.

Reed tipped back his shot and, like the seasoned drinker he was, didn't make any sort of face as the liquor went down. His fingers twitched around the shot glass as he set it back on the bar top. With the tap of the glass against the bar, I turned to Josh.

"Are you busy right now, or do you think you could stand a few minutes away?" A nervous energy ran through me, and my foot bounced on the barstool, trying to release it before the conversation ahead.

"Sure, I can ask Grady to hold down the fort for a little while."

I nodded. "Can we talk?"

Josh's eyebrows lifted, and his eyes darted to Reed. "All of us," I clarified, looping Reed into the conversation.

"Your office?" Reed asked. I couldn't watch Josh's response because Reed was too busy taking my hand in his and pulling me from the barstool.

Reed's hand was firm against mine as we headed to the dark hallway at the back of the place. And then I felt Josh's presence behind me as we ascended the stairs to the second floor.

There were still so many people crowding the bar that I didn't think anyone noticed our hasty exit. At least I hoped no one saw it.

None of us said anything even after the door to Josh's office was closed. The silence was thick and loaded with tension. And it was a stark contrast to the music and energy downstairs that could still be heard through the thin walls. Then, suddenly my mouth was dry, and the room was so small around us.

The alcohol in my system was all but gone and with it went my courage.

Reed leaned against the wall near a filing cabinet to the left while Josh leaned against the front of his desk. I decided to hover near the door not only for a quick exit but also because I'd lost the ability to walk under the weight of their stares.

They both watched me expectantly, and I fidgeted with the strap of my purse still slung across my body.

The words I'd planned on saying were stuck in my throat. No, actually, that wasn't true because that would have meant I remembered them. But looking between the two men in front of me, not a single coherent thought crossed my mind.

"We've missed you this week." I didn't catch which one of them said it because my eyes were downcast, staring at a deep knot in the wood floor.

I swallowed around the emotion, disbelief, and uncertainty lodged in my throat and murmured back, "I missed you, too. Both of you."

# TWENTY-ONE

Josh

I'D NEVER SEEN AMANDA SO NERVOUS. HER HANDS WERE TREMBLING against the strap of her bag, and she was standing on unsteady legs.

I loved to watch her legs tremble but for wholly different reasons.

My statement—that we missed her—was the total truth and was meant to relieve some of the tension in the air. It hadn't worked, though, because she'd gone back to staring at the floor and shuffling her weight from foot to foot in her heels.

Even filled with nerves and seemingly unsure of herself, she looked like a goddamn goddess. Her blonde hair was curled and falling around her shoulders. And the tight black dress was meant to show off every one of her curves. The fabric wrapped around her arms, down to her wrists as the bottom of the dress hovered a few inches above her knees. It did a fantastic job of showing exactly what I'd been missing for the past week.

Nothing was like having Amanda in my arms. Being able to touch her and follow the contours of her body, memorizing each with as much precision as I could. Feeling her shake with need beneath my palms was a sensation I craved to feel again.

She continued to fiddle with her purse strap, and I could hear her quick, labored breaths even from across the room. Reed and I looked at each other quickly, and I saw in his eyes the same concern I was feeling. I inclined my head to her, and he nodded his response, pushing off the wall.

While he closed the distance between them, I kept my position leaning against the desk.

Reed stood in front of her and dipped his head to whisper into her ear. His voice was low enough that I couldn't hear what he said, but it did make her look up from the ground.

"Take a deep breath," Reed instructed, removing her purse from her shoulder and hanging it on an empty hook near the door. "Why don't we just sit, and you can—"

"I don't think I can sit. Just—I'm fine."

She rolled her shoulders and pushed her hair behind her.

"Okay." Reed took a step back and tucked his hands into his pockets as Amanda eyed us both warily.

"Okay, first, I wanted to say thank you both for giving me space this week. I really appreciate it, and you don't know how much it means to me that you listened when I said I needed space. That couldn't have been easy, so thanks."

I caught Reed's glance in my direction and knew he was also freaking out about where this was going. We were both terrified she was going to say we were done—like a breakup without ever having been together.

"And this week has really given me time to figure out what's going on in my head. Since all this started, I've been really confused and frustrated at myself for being confused. We're all such good friends, and the last thing I want to do is fuck up our friendship or our entire group dynamic. Friends like y'all are hard to come by, and that's why—"

"Are you saying you're done? That it's neither of us, and we should stop?" Reed interrupted her, saying out loud my exact thoughts. Each time she said *"friends,"* my chest tightened, and I felt like we were inching closer and closer to her final confession that that's all she'd ever want to be.

Amanda whipped her head in Reed's direction and glared at him through lowered lids.

That's my girl.

"If you would let me finish, I promise it will all be crystal clear."

Reed huffed and shifted his weight on his feet but didn't say anything more.

"Like I was saying, you both are my best friends, which makes all of this incredibly difficult." She took a deep breath, closed her eyes and grounded herself. My anxiety shot to new heights before she continued, "But I can't pretend that I don't have feelings for you both."

The smallest sliver of hope wiggled between the fear and anxiety in my chest. But I didn't let it blossom into more, and I wouldn't until I heard all she had to say, especially since her eyes had once again cast down to the floor.

"And that's fucking insane."

"Is it, though?" I asked.

She sighed and threw her arms out to her sides. "It is. I know you've both come to terms with all of this, but I've spent the last year and a half trying to ignore and forget what happened. But it's not fucking working, especially with the two of you being so insistent. So, here I am."

There was a tense silence between the three of us.

"Here you are?" Reed questioned.

"Yes. What I'm trying to say is that the way things are going isn't working for me. All of the rules and time limits and other shit just don't work."

"Okay then, what do you want?" I asked. At the same time, Reed said, "Tell us what you want."

"I want to be done with the time limits. I'm in no position to make a decision and even thinking about doing that makes me sick to my stomach," she said emphatically. She'd begun pacing the length of the room, her heels clicking against the wood. When she reached one end, she would turn slowly and head back in the other direction, talking to her hands.

I wished she would look at us.

"So, I don't want that hanging over our heads. And I know that's a lot to ask, and I promise I won't keep you both in this in-between period for too long. But the idea of trying to sort out my feelings while also having this decision hanging over my head is impossible."

Finally, she looked up, her deep-blue eyes brimming with hope. But there was still fear lingering there. And seeing it and hearing her be so open and honest after closing off from us completely broke what little self-control I had left.

In a few strides, I ate up the space between us and gripped her face in my hands. At first, she was startled by my quick approach but easily melted into my touch in the next second. My thumbs rubbed against the smooth skin of her cheeks, and I watched the tension release from her features.

It felt right to touch her again.

"We'll give you anything you want." My voice was steady, although I was waiting for her to pull away any second. Her words were one thing, and it was great to hear that she wanted more. But it was another to see it firsthand. To talk and touch and feel without the pressure of her holding back her feelings. Reed and I had both felt it—it was hard to miss her uncertainty and the way she questioned every interaction.

"You want to date us both without the rules and pressure?" Reed added, approaching Amanda from behind and pressing himself against her. She shuddered as he ran his hands down her sides and gripped her hips.

"Yes," she breathed out and relaxed further into both of us.

I caught Reed's eyes over Amanda's head and the devious smile tugging at his lips was enough of an agreement.

Amanda's eyes never strayed from my face, and when I

looked back down at her, she'd pulled her bottom lip between her teeth. Using my thumb, I pulled it free and covered her mouth with my own.

A startled moan escaped her, and I quickly deepened the kiss, sliding my tongue into her open mouth. She conceded and tilted her head to the side. She tasted like tequila and fucking happiness.

Behind her, Reed pressed in closer, which in turn pressed her harder against me. A groan I couldn't contain vibrated through me at the first press of her body against mine.

Her tongue and lips were fervent and confident against my own, but her hands felt hesitant when they clutched the fabric of my shirt at my chest. Then her nails trailed up my neck and dug into my hair, tugging me closer. The heat of her body was like a drug, and the way she slowly gained confidence in her mouth and hands was hypnotic.

My cock was fucking steel, pressing against the zipper of my jeans.

"I think we need to relieve some of this pressure, don't you think, Josh?" Reed's voice was dripping with the same desire I felt coursing through me.

On a gasp, Amanda pulled away, and her eyes fluttered close as Reed's lips trailed a line up her neck. Her own lips were wet and swollen from our kiss, and I took the lower one between my teeth, carefully nipping until she gasped again.

"Yes, we should relieve the pressure. What do you think, babe? Do you want us to—?"

"*Yes*," Amanda pleaded against my lips, simultaneously pushing against me and grinding back on Reed.

Another look above Amanda's head, and we were on the same wavelength, making the woman between us feel incredible.

Reed continued peppering kisses up and down the side of her neck as his hands splayed out on her ribs, teasing the underside of her breasts with his thumbs. My eyes trailed down her body, enjoying the euphoric look on her face and the way her chest heaved with each breath. A light sheen of sweat was already covering her chest, so I leaned down and licked the curve of her breast. Flattening my tongue against her soft skin, she still tasted sweet, but there was a slight tang of saltiness.

I drew back and continued my perusal of her body. Reed cupped one of her breasts in his hand while the other gripped her hip, guiding her back toward him as she searched for some friction and a release of the growing tension I knew was between her gorgeous legs.

"Are you going to let Josh finger you while I play with these perfect tits?" Reed whispered into her ear.

And *God*, the sounds that broke free of her lips were like the most melodic music I'd ever heard.

"I think that was a yes," Reed said with a smile before he claimed her lips.

Lost in my own desire, I took a moment to run my hands up the outside of her thighs, pushing her dress up higher and higher. Trying to commit to memory everything about the scene in front of me—the way her kiss with Reed grew more frantic the closer my hands got to the apex of her thighs, and the way his hands tugged down the front of her dress, revealing a lacy black bra.

I pushed her dress up until it collected around her hips, exposing a matching black thong. And because teasing her was my favorite pastime, I ran my hand up one of her inner thighs and then did the same to the other.

I smiled at the goose bumps pebbling her pale skin.

"Josh, *please*," Amanda broke away from Reed and pleaded with both her words and eyes.

"Tell him what you want," Reed instructed, playing with a peaked nipple through the lace of her bra.

"Fuck me with your fingers." Her voice was strong, and I tried to suppress my smile.

"Say please." Reed tweaked her nipple harder, and she pushed her chest into his hand.

"*Please* fuck me with your fingers, Josh."

Well, fuck, who was I to say no to the woman? And hearing my name roll off her lips was like the sweetest prayer.

I pushed her panties to the side, and she leveled me with a confident, challenging stare through heavy-lidded eyes.

Never one to back down from a challenge, I stepped closer to her and ran my middle finger down her center. She eagerly spread her legs wider, her breath catching as I gathered her wetness and pressed against her swollen clit.

Starting with slow circles, I played her up higher, watching as her legs nearly gave out beneath her and Reed banded an arm around her stomach. He held her up as I continued to torture her with the lightest touch.

"What is he doing, baby? Playing with your clit and teasing you? Is he getting you ready to fuck his fingers?" Reed bit her earlobe, and she went even more limp in his arms.

"Yes," was all she could manage between struggling breaths. I was struggling to breathe, too. Watching her give herself over to us for the first time in what felt like forever was nearly enough to undo me.

"Are you ready for his fingers?"

She nodded eagerly, and although I wanted to extend our time together as much as I could, I also needed to feel her around my fingers just as much as she needed them inside of her.

Abandoning her clit, I lifted my middle finger to her mouth, pressing it against her already parted lips. "Suck," I instructed.

Her eyes flared, and she obediently opened wider and stuck out her tongue. When her lips closed around my finger, I thought my legs would give out too. She hollowed her cheeks and twirled her tongue around it, tasting herself and giving us a show.

"Can you taste yourself on his finger?"

She nodded, and I removed my finger, ready to come in my pants if she didn't stop.

Not that my finger needed to be more wet, she was already dripping by the time I pushed my finger inside of her.

She buckled when I crooked my finger and pressed the heel of my hand against her clit.

"Did he hit the perfect spot?" Reed asked against her lips.

She nodded and began grinding against my hand. I added another finger, and she gasped as her inner walls clamped down harder. Just like I knew she wanted, I massaged against her G-spot with my fingertips, picking up speed as her breaths came quicker. The sounds of her arousal mixed with her moans filled the small space around us.

"Are you already going to come for us? Are you going to make sure everyone downstairs knows who made you come?"

Each time Reed spoke, she clenched down harder. "She likes it when you talk dirty. Her needy, little cunt squeezes my fingers nice and hard."

As I spoke, she bore down on me, one of her hands finding the back of my neck while the other grasped for Reed's behind her.

She hung on to us as her pleasure neared its peak. With my hand that wasn't occupied, I grabbed her hip and kept her in place as I fucked my fingers into her.

Reed kept one arm around her stomach, essentially the only thing keeping her standing, but he snaked the other up the center of her body. He teased one exposed nipple and then the other. He twirled his fingers around the dusky-pink peak and then pinched it roughly.

She seemed to glow as the pain morphed into pleasure. Reed's hand continued upward and settled loosely around her neck. As my fingers found the perfect rhythm, enjoying the heat surrounding them, Amanda grasped my arm, a silent plea to keep going, to not stop.

Then her eyes opened and found Reed's. I watched her nod

to him, another silent request to keep going. His hand tightened around her throat and she let her head fall back to his shoulder.

He licked the shell of her ear as I squeezed her hip harder.

"You're so beautiful when you come undone for us. When you let yourself go and give yourself over. There's no reason to be scared, baby. We've got you; we'll always have you. Now, I need you to come on Josh's fingers and show us how badly you need us. How good does it feel to be between us? Do you know how crazy you make us? We're both so hard right now watching you fall apart."

Then he began muttering in Spanish as I continued to call her our dirty girl and tell her that she felt so good around my fingers.

The sexual tension between the three of us was like a piece of thread, or a string, ready to snap at any moment. Unable to stretch anymore against the unfathomable intensity. But it was Amanda's orgasm that finally snapped it.

Her pussy clenched and gripped my fingers so perfectly. Pulling me deeper as her hips bucked, grinding her clit against my palm.

Reed continued to hold her up with a hand around her midsection and the other wrapped around her throat. Her cries were strangled by the pressure against her throat, but I could still make out both of our names and the word "yes" over and over again, chanting like she was thanking a higher power.

And watching her come apart, her release generously coating my fingers and my hand as her face contorted in blissful ecstasy was the most perfect sight.

It was several seconds before she blinked her eyes open and I removed my fingers. Reed released his hand from her throat and tentatively let her hold her own weight. She wobbled slightly, but we stood firm around her until she found her balance.

"Fuck," she whispered, hands against my chest. "That was…"

"Amazing," Reed said.

"Incredible," I added.

"Crazy."

"Perfect."

"Unbelievable."

"Intense."

"The best ever."

Amanda erupted in a fit of laughter, and the sound was tied for first place in the best sounds I'd ever heard.

"Yes, all of the above," she agreed. But there was still a slight hesitancy in her eyes as she looked between us. "You're both really okay with this? Me not choosing and dating you both... for now?"

Reed and I nodded simultaneously, and she relaxed.

"God, what the fuck have we gotten ourselves into?" she asked.

I leaned in to kiss her, but a knock at the door interrupted us. Instead of kissing the beautiful woman, I groaned and glanced around to make sure all was right in my office. Reed opened the door.

On the other side was Adam, holding a box of straws and napkins.

"Umm... Grady's looking for you, boss," he said and then peered behind me. "Also, you may wanna spray some Febreeze or something. Definitely smells like sex in there. Good on you, sis. See you downstairs."

And then he was gone. I closed the door and turned back around to find a red-faced Amanda hiding behind her hands.

Reed and I both laughed and lowered her hands. "It's just Adam. He's not going to say anything for fear of our wrath. He's also going to see us around more often, so not sure how long we were going to be hiding it anyway," Reed reasoned.

"Okay, fine. But let's try to be careful around everyone else until we figure this all out. We don't need to complicate things prematurely."

We both agreed, and Amanda headed downstairs. Reed and I

followed like we were the cats that got the canary. The grins on our faces easily betrayed what had happened.

Once downstairs, Reed stopped off in the bathroom, so I took our unusual moment alone to turn to Amanda.

"Hey, I'm actually taking Zach to the aquarium tomorrow. Do you want to come with us?"

She wrung her hands in front of her and nervously tucked a few stray pieces of hair behind her ear. "Are you sure? I don't want to impose on your time together."

I smoothed my hands down her arms, and she dropped them to her sides. "I'm positive. Ever since we FaceTimed him at the drive-in, he's been asking about you. I think this week he's asked me how you were and where you were at least four separate times."

Every time my son brought her up, my heart further constricted in my chest, knowing he liked her nearly as much as I did.

"Seriously?" she questioned, eyebrows shooting to her hairline.

"Seriously."

"Well, if he wants me to come, then I'm in no position to tell him no."

And then she smiled and I couldn't help but kiss her. It was the thought of the three of us spending time together as well as the knowledge she wanted to go, that really made it impossible to resist the temptation of her mouth.

"That's the exact opposite of keeping this quiet," Reed said over the sound of a new karaoke song.

"She's hard to resist. I know you know that." Throwing an arm around Amanda's shoulders, I led us back to the front of the house, but I didn't miss the ticcing in Reed's jaw and the flare of jealousy in his eyes.

Too fucking bad.

# TWENTY-TWO

## Reed

Josh was pissed, but what else was new? He'd been all flared nostrils, scowling glances, and grunted responses since the moment Zach proclaimed that I should also go with them to the aquarium.

Josh's initial response was to tell Zach that I had things to do that day. Which, to his credit, I did, but all of them could be rescheduled or wait until later.

Zach had been so insistent that Josh could do nothing but concede after nearly twenty minutes of begging and negotiating. I wasn't much help either. The thought of seeing more of Amanda meant I sided with Zach and agreed that I should go with them.

"I'm not going to forget this," Josh muttered low enough that Zach, who was skipping in front of us toward Amanda's apartment, couldn't hear the annoyance in his voice.

"It's not like I could've told him no. Did you see the faces he was making? And you can't deny his thinking was hard to argue with."

Josh made an unamused sound in the back of his throat and scrubbed a hand through his unruly dirty-blond hair.

"If you can't hold your ground with a six-year-old, we have bigger problems," he whispered.

"He's not a normal six-year-old. He's *your* six-year-old, Sunshine." I flashed a smile at him, trying to dismantle his frustration piece by piece.

"What is that supposed to mean?"

"It means that he knows exactly how to get under my skin in the same way you do."

Josh stopped suddenly as we made it to the top of the stairs, Amanda's apartment a few doors down to our right. I looked back at him and he was looking at me through narrowed eyes. Under his intense stare, I didn't know what to do, so I shoved my hands into the front pockets of my jeans and straightened my posture.

"I get under your skin?" he asked in a voice so quiet I could barely hear him.

My throat felt tight, and my skin prickled with awareness. Josh studied me with an intensity in his eyes I hadn't witnessed before, darting his attention from my feet, up my legs and over my midsection before landing again on my face.

His jaw, covered in scruff from the past few days, clenched several times, and his Adam's apple bobbed as he swallowed.

I was paying so much attention to him watching me that I'd forgotten he'd asked a question and was waiting for my answer.

"Yeah," I croaked out and cleared my throat of whatever was blocking it. "Yeah, you do."

He nodded and acted like he was going to say something else but was distracted by Zach pounding on Amanda's door.

It was going to be a long day.


"Auntie Manda, what does an octopus eat? Do they eat fish?"

It was Zach's millionth question of the day for Amanda—

when he'd remembered she taught science, he began posing all of his questions to her. And as I knew she would, she took them in stride, answering what she could and covertly googling the rest.

"They eat crabs, snails, fish, and even other octopuses."

"Octopuses? Is that right?"

"Yes," she said, but it still sounded wrong to me.

"Octopi sounds more correct."

"Both work. Now, shush. Zach is learning." She held her finger to her lips and shushed me as Zach asked ten follow-up questions.

In two hours, we'd made it most of the way through the exhibits. Zach had found his "Nemo" fish and also discovered what an eel was. The eel had prompted several questions—more than I'd ever thought to ask about an eel. But to watch his face light up every time he saw a new animal was priceless and worth the hours of questions.

We turned another corner and were met with tiny shrieks and echoing laughter. Zach's jaw dropped and Amanda and I suppressed a chuckle at his stunned silence.

He excitedly tugged Amanda's hand, which he hadn't let go of for most of the day and turned back to us. "We... we get to feed the stingrays?" he stuttered.

"Yes, you want to?"

"That's a dumb question, Auntie Manda," he quipped and took off for the small stingray enclosure. It was a low glass pool that was completely open at the top and surrounded by children and their parents.

Amanda was being tugged to the enclosure but took a moment to look back. "Where's Josh?"

We both quickly looked around, but there wasn't any sign of him.

"I'll go look, you deal with the hellion."

She didn't have time to respond as Zach lurched forward and yanked her in the opposite direction.

I turned around and scanned the large room, expecting to see him hovering near one of the several eye-catching exhibits, but he was nowhere to be found. Navigating around people and exhibits, I retraced our steps, searching for his face in every blond-haired guy over six feet tall.

It wasn't until I stepped into the room we'd wandered around before that I saw him tucked into a corner. Between an oversized tank filled with a variety of fish and a cutout of a shark, Josh pressed his phone to his ear. A scowl contorted his features, and in the few seconds I watched him, he rolled his eyes, shook his head a few times, and ran a frustrated hand through his hair.

For a moment, I contemplated approaching him.

His frustration had waned throughout the day. By the time we'd made it to the aquarium, bought our tickets and began exploring, his frustration with my attendance was nearly nonexistent. We even shared a few laughs at Amanda's expense, as usual.

But Josh had been on edge since Amanda refused to speak to us the week prior, and I was concerned that one misstep on my part would put him right back into that mindset. Because although Amanda ignoring us wasn't completely my fault, he'd acted like it was. Just as she was ignoring us, he ignored me.

Not to mention, Josh, who was normally carefree and wore a smile ninety-nine percent of the time, hadn't been the same since Hazel and Luke's wedding. We were all eager to have him back to normal. Me most of all.

So, when he turned deeper into the corner and gripped the back of his neck with his hand, I headed to him. Politely smiling at a couple and their little girl that sprinted around my legs, I approached Josh just in time to hear as he laughed humorlessly and quickly ended the call.

"Let me guess," I said by way of greeting, "Sam?"

Josh whirled, startled, but quickly righted himself when he

realized it was just me. He shook his head as he pocketed his phone and leaned against the wall behind him.

"How'd you know?"

"When y'all argue, you always have the same look on your face. Kind of like you're constipated and seriously hungover all at the same time. But not a regular hangover, I'm talking a whole night of drinking nothing but Jäger. That kind of hungover."

He cringed and then let out another sad chuckle. "That's kind of how it feels too," he said with a sigh I felt in my bones.

I'd been there through all of it. When he started dating Sam, when he found out she was pregnant, when Zach was born, when they tried to make it work, and when it all went to hell. To say that we were all surprised they'd ended up where they were would be an understatement. It wasn't until almost two years before that they'd finally figured out co-parenting enough that they could stand the odd conversation about their child's well-being or manage a change in their schedules.

"What'd she have to say?" I leaned against the wall next to him, crossing my arms over my chest and preparing to wait until he was ready to spill.

With another sigh, his head fell back to the wall and he groaned. "She called me last week sometime and asked if I wouldn't mind picking Zach up on Saturday morning instead of Friday after school as I usually would. Apparently they had this engagement party thing with their friends and wanted him there. I told her yes, and when I picked him up this morning, she said she wanted him back early tomorrow for something else they were going to do with her family. She wants me to drop him off tomorrow morning instead of at six. But I can't do that. That means I'm missing so much time with him after he's been gone an entire week. We ended up compromising that I would drop him off at her parents' house at two instead of dropping him off at their house at eleven tomorrow morning. But I just don't understand why everything has to be so hard. I get why she wants him there, but I don't want to give up my time."

Never having been in the situation he was in, I knew my words wouldn't do much to console him. I didn't have any life-altering advice, and I was fresh out of words of wisdom.

So, I settled on, "That's really rough, dude," which felt ridiculous and wholly unhelpful the second it left my mouth.

But Josh did laugh, and it was a genuine one that I hadn't heard in a while. He even smiled wide enough for the lines that usually gathered around his eyes to appear.

I eyed him suspiciously but laughed along with him.

"It really is. And honestly, I got lucky with Zach. I didn't think in a million years I'd have a kid half as freaking awesome as him. But at the same time, I wish the circumstances were different. I'm worried Sam and I are going to fuck him up with our bullshit."

Before he even finished talking, I was shaking my head. "No, that kid is just as lucky to have you, too. And I know Sam isn't always the best co-parent or whatever, but she is a good mom. And you're a great dad, so you shouldn't be concerned. He's happy, and from the little I know about parenting, I do know that's like the golden rule."

His smile faltered slightly, but he nodded. He began to speak, but shrieking children running by us and heading directly for the octopuses, octopi, whatever, interrupted him. We both cringed at the sound as they faded into the distance. The sound of screaming was replaced by high-pitched voices, excitedly talking about the colors and sizes of the animals.

"I appreciate that. Being a parent is fucking terrifying. Every second I'm with him, and even when I'm not, I'm terrified I'm going to screw him up."

"Nah, there's no way you will."

"You seem pretty sure of that."

"I am," I said, looking him in the eye, so I knew he saw how sure I was.

A brief look of recognition, and maybe belief in my words, washed over his expression. We weren't more than a foot apart, if that, and I could clearly see that his eyes were greener in the dim lights than they usually were.

And this foreign feeling weaved its way through me, tightening my chest and circling my stomach, when our stare finally broke, only for his eyes to settle on my mouth. My lip twitched under the weight of his attention, and I ran my tongue along it to eliminate the sensation.

Abruptly, he looked past me like I'd slapped him or like someone had called his name.

"Well, at least that's something you have over me."

"What do you mean?"

"I mean that I'm not sure Amanda is ready to be anything more than 'Auntie Manda' to Zach. Being with me means I'm a package deal. She could very likely see it as more than she can handle. I've… had to prepare that that might be the case."

Dumbfounded, I gawked at him, too caught off guard to think of a response. How could he even think that? Amanda already loved Zach more than nearly anyone, which was the first step in being a stepparent for him. Just thinking that term, though, "stepparent" or "stepmother," felt serious in a way I hadn't yet contemplated.

But if anyone would make a good stepmom for Zach, it would be Amanda.

Was I standing in the way of that?

"Where are they anyway?" he asked after clearing his throat, and I started at his voice.

Even as he asked the question and stared at the exhibit where he'd likely left us to talk to Sam, I surveyed his face. The tension in his jaw and shoulders was back. But it was the quick rise and fall of his chest that made me weary.

"They're umm… feeding the stingrays. Or at least that's where I left them."

Josh nodded, tucked his hands in his pockets, and headed in that direction.

Not one to be left behind, I followed, shoving my own hands in my pockets.

But before we could make it to the final corner, we heard Amanda's voice yell, "Zachary Gregory, are you serious?!"

In a split second, we were both racing for the corner, dodging people left and right, and skidding to a stop in front of them.

Standing before us was a disheveled Amanda, frantically pulling a soaking-wet Zach away from the exhibit.

"What the hell happened?" Josh asked, squatting down in front of his son.

"Excuse me, we'll get you a towel, but you can't attempt to swim in the exhibit," a worker wearing a bright-blue polo and pristine white sneakers commented as she approached the three of them huddled together.

Amanda whipped her gaze to the worker with a look that I knew all too well. "Yes, trust me. He's very well aware that you aren't supposed to swim with the stingrays. He's six, not two. You said you were getting a towel?"

The unprepared woman stuttered and looked around at the other bystanders. Thankfully, a younger guy, also wearing the same blue polo and white shoes, trotted up with two towels.

"Hey, buddy," he said, crouching down to Zach's level. "You doin' okay?"

"Yeah, I'm okay," Zach said with a shiver.

"Here." The young guy wrapped the towel around his shoulders, and Amanda gave him a grateful smile. "I think you scared your mom and dad."

"Oh, that's his dad," Amanda corrected, pointing at Josh, "but I'm just the aunt."

"Oh." The guy's voice was filled with hope that was coupled with a huge smile.

Before I knew what I was doing, I stepped up beside the kid shamelessly flirting with our girl and placed my hand on his shoulder.

He quickly looked up at me.

"Good try, bud, but there's no way it's going to happen. So, thanks for the towels, but bye."

He stood and lifted his hands in surrender as he made his way back to his place on the other side of the stingray pool.

By the time I finished eyeing him down, I caught the end of the question Josh had asked Zach, *Why?*

"Well, I accidentally dropped all of the food they gave us into the pool, and I was worried that they were going to get sick. Because that's what Mommy tells me: she said that if I eat too fast or eat all my food at once, then my tummy will get sick. So, I tried to grab it before they got it, but it was too far down. Auntie Manda had to pull me back up."

He tilted his little head back to peer up at Amanda. "Thanks for saving me," he said with a distinct quiver in his lip.

"Anytime, buddy. You just scared the crap out of me." She smoothed down his damp hair and pushed it out of his face.

"Are we done with the aquarium for today?" I asked Zach. I think we were all ready to be out of there.

"Yeah, can we go to your house, Daddy?" Josh promptly scooped Zach up and asked the worker if we could take the towels.

She nodded and waved, probably eager to get us out of the place and off of her plate.

"You okay?" I asked Amanda as we dropped behind Josh and Zach.

She sucked in a deep breath. "Yes. After I knew he was okay, all I could see were what the headlines might have looked like: *'Woman lets young boy swim in stingray tank.'*" Her voice goes deep, like she's mocking a news anchor.

"*'Schoolteacher urges child to explore more hands-on learning with deadly animal,'*" I added.

She groaned. "Me being a teacher makes it so much worse. And a science teacher at that! *'Science teacher fired after incident at the aquarium.'*"

"But then there'd be ones like *'Teacher throws student into stingray tank.'*"

She acted surprised at the turn, and she slapped me in the stomach with the back of her hand. I took the opportunity to take her hand in mine.

A contented smile crossed her lips as she glanced down at our intertwined hands. There was an innocence and comfortability in our touching.

"Hey," she said. "Is he okay?"

She pointed to Josh, and the best I could do was shrug. "I think he will be. Just normal drama with Sam, but… I think it might be good if you talk to him."

"About Sam?" she questioned quietly since we were still only a few feet behind Josh. Although he was preoccupied with Zach's continuous questions about what would have happened had he fallen all the way in the stingray enclosure.

"Yes, but also about Zach. Just, I think it would be good for both of you."

"Okay?" There was still a question in her voice, and the closer we got to the car, the more certain I had to be that she was going to heed my advice.

"You promise you'll talk to him?"

She eyed me curiously but nodded. "I promise."

# TWENTY-THREE

Amanda

"Hey, I have an idea," Reed said as we all piled out of the truck. Reed squatted down next to Zach and tightened his jacket around him. Zach's clothes were mostly dry, and thankfully, his jacket hadn't made it into the water since I was holding it nearly all day. "Why don't you and I go to the park around the corner while your dad and Auntie Manda go check on something in her apartment?"

Shocked by his offer, I remembered his comment at the aquarium and my promise to discuss Zach and Sam with Josh. He meant immediately, though? I couldn't think of a reason that the conversation would be urgent enough to warrant it happening that instant, but just in case, I wasn't going to argue.

"Check on something? What are you—" But Josh stopped arguing when Reed widened his eyes in a look that quickly conveyed that his idea was for Josh's benefit.

"Can I?" Zach turned, seeking Josh's permission. All it took was a nod from him before Zach gripped Reed's hand and tugged him along.

Reed gave me a look similar to the one he'd given Josh, and I nodded my understanding.

Once the pair was out of sight, Josh turned to me, confusion knitting his brows together. "What was that all about?"

I was hesitant to throw Reed under the bus, but he hadn't said not to tell Josh that he thought the talk was necessary.

"Reed may have mentioned that we should talk. I think he's worried about you."

Josh closed the back door of his truck and crossed his arms over his chest. The rapid change in his demeanor and his sudden guarded body language clearly communicated that he wasn't keen on the topic.

"Why don't we go upstairs and talk? This doesn't feel like a parking lot type of conversation."

I turned to the building without waiting to see if he followed. Climbing the stairs to the second floor, I wasn't exactly paying close enough attention to where I was going and ended up running smack into a hard chest.

"Oh, shit. I'm so sorry!" I threw my hands out to steady myself against the railing and apologized immediately, preparing to come face-to-face with a disgruntled resident.

"No worries, Mandy." And I looked up to find CJ smiling down at me, helping steady me with his large hands on my shoulders.

"Hey, man." CJ peered behind me. "I'm CJ, maintenance guy."

"Josh. Nice to meet you." They shook hands in the way men do—puffing out their chests and standing a little taller. I refrained from rolling my eyes and went to continue up the stairs.

We slipped past each other, Josh following close behind me, but before I got to the top, a thought stopped me in my tracks.

"Hey," I said to CJ. "Did you ever watch *Twister*?"

His lack of immediate response told me he hadn't watched it.

"We're going on a month now, CJ. Watch it or give me my

DVD back!" I shouted over my shoulder while climbing the stairs and heading to my apartment door.

"I'll watch it tonight, Mandy!" he yelled back.

I swung the door open to my apartment and tossed my keys and bag down on the catchall table in the small entry.

"Best friends with your maintenance guy, huh?" Josh questioned.

Warily, I eyed him, noting a hint of jealousy in his tone.

"I wouldn't say 'best friends.' He just saw my DVD collection and took an interest in my taste in movies."

Kicking off my boots, I beelined for the fridge and pulled out two of my favorite ciders. Josh eagerly took the one I offered him and used our proximity as an excuse to tug me closer. I stumbled closer to him, our chests nearly touching, and he smoothed a free hand down one of my arms.

The light touch of his fingertips, even over the fabric of my sweater, along with the heat of his body so temptingly close, was enough to send a shiver through me.

All day it had been lingering looks and stolen touches as we wandered through the aquarium.

I'd even turned around a few times to find not one but both of their phones trained on me. Their attention excited me but was also a tease—and hopefully, a promise of what was to come. And after a day full of it, I was feeling the effects. I was needy and even the slightest touch from Josh was more than I could bear.

"You won't even let me borrow a DVD," Josh muttered, his eyes dropping to my mouth, which curved around the cider bottle.

I threw my head back and laughed. He couldn't have forgotten the one and only reason why he didn't get access to my collection.

"There's no way you forgot one of the biggest fights we got into in college; it was the whole reason I don't let you borrow DVDs or literally anything anymore."

Without an ounce of recognition on his face, I continued, "I let you borrow three DVDs, and after nearly four months, I had to convince Reed to let me into your dorm when you weren't there. Then I went through all of your shit to finally find the damn DVDs. I vowed to never let you borrow one again."

He frowned down at me. "That's not the way I remember it."

"Of course it's not, but that's what happened."

"Can I see the collection?" Josh asked, knowing full well it was mostly stored in the three drawers of the living room entertainment center.

I waved my hand in front of me, inviting him to see for himself.

Methodically, he opened one drawer after the other, scanning the titles that were packed side by side for optimal browsing and storage.

"Still impressive." He smiled up at me from where he was crouched on the floor, leaning over the last and bottom drawer, which held the action and horror movies.

Unlike most people who witnessed or heard about the insanity of my collection, Josh didn't say a word about the irrelevance of DVDs. He didn't mention that DVDs were defunct and mostly useless with the number of streaming services available. And he didn't comment on the absurd amount of space they took up.

If he did think any of those things, he kept them to himself and his facial expression neutral because he knew what they meant to me. He knew, along with the rest of my friends and Adam, that inside those drawers and within the worn, loved plastic cases was the entirety of my childhood.

They were gifts from my parents for every occasion—birthdays, holidays, celebrations—because they were the most likely to be used.

"You know what I find funny?"

I raised my eyebrows as he closed the drawer and stood.

"This collection is perfectly organized—not one DVD out of place. But your apartment is another story."

My jaw dropped, and I scoffed at his brazenness. Whether it was the truth or not, he didn't have to say it out loud.

"That's not true. It looks so nice in here." I waved my hand around to the somewhat tidy room.

"Sure, the living room and your classroom are always neat, but what about your bedroom?"

My hand that I was waving around, showing him proof that he was wrong, limply fell to my side.

*Touché, asshole.*

And before I had time to react, Josh moved around me and headed straight down the hallway toward my bedroom. As I took off after him, mumbling obscenities, I did a mental tally of the state of my room. Then my pace picked up, but I was far too late.

Damn it, little legs.

Out of breath from the short sprint down the hallway, I contemplated my life choices—literally all of them—as I braced myself against the doorframe and Josh examined the chaos.

The cream carpet was covered in clothes—clean clothes—that I'd thrown from the closet while trying to get dressed to go to the bar with Hazel and then again that morning for the aquarium. The chair in the corner had also fallen victim to a pile of clean clothes. And the white sheets were a tangled mess at the bottom of the bed, along with the yellow blanket I'd used for years. Two of my pillows were at the top near the headboard, and the other two were nowhere to be seen.

There was jewelry scattered over the weathered wood dresser on the opposite side of the room along with a few odd and end things I hadn't found an actual place for yet.

But besides the clutter, it smelled good. The sweet rose water scent from the plug-in in one corner was fresh yet subtle.

"Looks about right." Josh smirked, standing amid the mess.

"Thought you knew I wasn't perfect, babe. Sorry to disappoint."

I proceeded to kick the clothes across the floor and closer to the closet door, which I refused to open lest I wanted more comments about my inability to keep my shit organized.

"Your imperfections make you all the more perfect to me," Josh murmured into my ear, his hot breath brushing over my neck. His hands snaked around my waist the moment his lips found the tender spot beneath my ear.

A shaky moan escaped my lips, and Josh's hold tightened. Nearly lost to his touch, it was the press of his hard length against my lower back that made me jerk out of his hold.

"We," I said, taking a deep breath and stepping back to add more space between us, "are supposed to be talking."

Josh rolled his eyes and took a step forward, which I mirrored with a step back.

"I think we could just tell Reed that we talked and then use this time to do *other* things."

The dark glint in his eye was too much for me to handle while trying to keep my composure and remember my promise, so I averted my eyes. Looking anywhere but at him, I continued.

"I promised Reed."

With a heavy sigh that told me he understood, Josh took a seat at the edge of my bed. He propped his elbows on his knees and then looked up at me expectantly, big blue-green eyes taunting me.

"What did the man say we should talk about?"

"Zach... and Sam."

As soon as I said his ex-girlfriend's name, the tension in the room grew thick, and I had an eerie suspicion that in focusing on Zach that day, I'd missed something with Josh.

"I think we should just tell Reed to mind his own damn business. That sounds like a better idea to me."

"He's just worried, Josh. Does he have a reason to be worried?"

With his elbows still propped on his knees, he pushed his hands through his hair and gripped the back of his neck. Taking a few more steps back, I closed the door with a soft click before crossing back to him.

His brow furrowed when he peered up at me, letting his hands fall back to his lap.

"Adam could come home at any time, and I don't want to be interrupted. Or if Reed decides to bring Zach up here, it's just a precaution. Now, spill. Tell me what's going on."

A small piece of his dirty-blond hair had fallen forward in his frustration, and my hand itched to push it back into place. And rather than resist like I had for so long, I gave in to the urge and swept my fingers through his soft hair, putting the piece back where it belonged.

But my hand lingered, brushing down the side of his face and resting on his cheek, enjoying the stubble along his defined jawline.

When God made that man, She did a damn good job.

"Amanda, we don't have—"

But I stopped his argument by leaning down and teasing my lips against his. It was just a taste, a promise even. And yes, I was going to use whatever methods necessary to get the truth and figure out a way to make it better. Even if those methods were sometimes frowned upon.

The touch of our lips was fleeting, and Josh groaned when I stood back up.

"You're playing dirty," he remarked, eyes finally fluttering back open.

"Tell me what's going on, why Reed thinks it's absolutely necessary we talk now, and I will gladly show you just how dirty I can play."

His chuckle was my sign that I was getting somewhere, as was the way he wrapped a palm around my thigh and scooted me closer. Positioning me between his open legs.

There was a contemplative look on his face as his left hand

came up to wrap around my other thigh, and his thumbs massaged into my skin.

"Sam's giving me a hard time. It's nothing new—the usual wanting me to drop him off or pick him up at odd times that we never agreed upon. And then wanting me to cut my time short for something she has planned. We've figured out all of the financial stuff involved in co-parenting, and we communicate fairly well on a regular basis, but there are still some issues we've run into, especially lately."

He gulped and shook his head, that same damn piece of hair falling forward, so I again pushed it back into place and cupped his cheek. I used the pressure of my hand to force his gaze back to me.

Maybe I was going crazy, but I thought I saw a sheen of unshed tears in his eyes.

"All of that, along with everything happening between us, has got me thinking about... the future. And before you freak out, I'm not talking this year or even next. I'm just saying *sometime* in the future because when you have a kid, you have to think long term even if you don't know exactly what tomorrow is going to hold."

I nodded, but only to urge him to continue, not because I actually understood where he was going with his future talk.

"Since he was born, I've had to contemplate every relationship more than I ever would have before because now he's the most important thing. If I ever get serious with someone, it comes with a lot of thinking about how that person would fit into our lives. *Both* of our lives."

A sense of clarity washed over me that I was thankful for. It was a heads-up to what was coming next.

"I'm worried that there's a possibility you won't choose me. And not just because you care more for Reed or because we don't have something because, at this point, both of those things would be bullshit. I'm scared you won't choose me because choosing me also means choosing Zach. It means you would be a stepmom and love my son like I do. At least, that's what I would want out of this. And I get that's a lot to take in, but like I said, these are the decisions I have to make. Things I have to think about."

I swallowed around a knot in my throat and croaked out, "You're scared?"

His nod was slow and genuine. "Because Reed doesn't have that. He would be the easy choice, honestly. You'd easily fit into his life without having to worry about Sam or learning how to be a stepmom to a six-year-old. Reed's one person, albeit he's a lot to deal with," he said with a weak chuckle. "But he's one person. I come with a whole fucking football team worth of shit."

# TWENTY-FOUR

Amanda

I OPENED MY MOUTH TO SAY SOMETHING BUT IMMEDIATELY SNAPPED it back shut. Because who the fuck was I kidding? I didn't know what to say.

I was embarrassed to say that I hadn't even contemplated what I would be walking into with Josh. He was right—if I wanted to pursue something with him, I'd better be damn sure it was the real deal. He had Zach to worry about and even Sam to an extent.

I could feel the flush creeping up my cheeks, embarrassment at my lack of forethought rolling through me.

But although I was annoyed at myself and would later chastise myself relentlessly for not thinking about the one person Josh always put first, the anxiety and fear I thought I'd feel didn't come.

Was I ready to be a mom? Absolutely fucking not. I'd just gotten a new IUD, which meant there were no babies happening in at least the next three years. But being a stepmom, being *Zach's* stepmom, was something different. Especially if it meant doing it with Josh.

And that's the thought that stopped me. The anxiety I was waiting for nuzzled its way into my stomach, but it was mild. It wasn't Zach or Sam or anyone else that was the cause. It was the idea that making the decision—picking Josh—would mean I'd have to think years into the future. Because I wouldn't put either of them through having me in their lives unless I was certain it would be for a long time. At least.

It went beyond what felt good in the moment, but I felt confident that it was a decision I could make when the time came. And being in Zach's life as a stepmom, or having to co-parent with Sam, wasn't going to dissuade me from choosing Josh if that's what I decided.

"Zach would only be a bonus," I said, my voice surprisingly steady. And the look on Josh's face was priceless. It was apparent in the way his jaw went slack and his eyes suddenly widened that he wasn't expecting that out of me.

"Really?" His question was a whisper, and I smiled.

"Yes, really. I can't promise that I'd be good at it, but if the time comes when I'm Zach's stepmom, I *can* promise that I'll give it my best. I already love him so much. He's just like you, which makes him one of my favorite people ever."

In the next breath, Josh's mouth was on mine, and the whole world ceased spinning. All I could think about was how his tongue pushed through my lips and how easy it was to give myself over to him. His hands were everywhere—in my hair, running down my back and then cupping my ass. He urged me closer to him, and I willingly fell.

My hands found the hair at the base of his head, and I pressed myself against him, feeling the hard planes of his muscles against me.

That kiss confirmed that I was lost to him.

Reluctantly we both pulled away. I could feel the quick beat of his heart against my chest. It mimicked the intense pace mine relentlessly carried.

"You're fucking everything." And I felt his words like I'd felt his hands.

Although I was resigned to the fact that I was in way deeper than I knew, there was a part of me that still wanted to protect my heart.

"Are you a little less stressed now? A little less worried?" He laughed and playfully nipped at my lower lip before kissing my nose.

"A little, yes."

With a mischievous smile and adding a playful lilt to my voice, I asked, "Can I show you the other way I enjoy relieving your stress?"

I dropped to my knees in front of him and peered up at him. The surprised yet excited look on his face made my stomach twist in anticipation.

It'd felt like a lifetime since I'd been in that position, but being the source of his pleasure, watching Josh come apart at the seams from my mouth and my hands alone was the stuff of my fantasies.

As I tugged at his belt, unfastening it and slipping the worn, brown leather free, his hands were already tangled through my hair.

My eyes didn't leave his when I slowly unbuttoned his jeans and eased down his zipper. His jaw was slack, and I wanted to draw it out as long as I could. I wanted to tease the shit out of him until he was begging me for my mouth around his cock, but I knew our time was limited. So I quickly pulled down his jeans just enough until I could see his impressive length straining against the fabric of his dark-gray boxer briefs. I placed a hungry open-mouth kiss against him, and the moment my mouth pressed against the fabric, his head tipped to the ceiling.

"*Fuck*," he whispered.

A smile pulled at the corner of my lips, and I slipped my fingers under the waistband of his briefs. His cock sprang free as

I pushed his briefs down. His hand, still tangled in my hair, tightened.

I broke our eye contact long enough to appreciate the length and thickness of him in front of me. The veins running up and down his shaft were too tempting not to lick. And when I did just that, flattening my tongue against the underside of him and licking him down and up, he sucked in a harsh breath.

"I never thought I'd see this again: you on your knees in front of me." His words were dripping in desire, and I could hear that he was on the brink of losing control. "But I dreamed about it all the time, and I'm telling you, the dream has nothing on the actual thing."

My lazy licking and perusal complete, I licked the palm of my hand and gripped him in my fist.

I glanced back up at him, and the way he watched my hand twist up and down around his cock, the smooth skin of him slipping against my palm, was like a drug. One that made me feel ten feet tall, which was a horrible combination of my already confident disposition.

"You have such a pretty cock," I murmured, wrapping my lips around the head and sucking only hard enough to give him a taste of what was to come.

He mumbled a few things I couldn't make out, and I pushed him deeper. Sliding him against my tongue until he reached the back of my mouth, I felt my gag reflex strain.

Then I pulled back, fluttering my tongue around the head of him, only to do it all over again. Licking and sucking him as my hand followed the movement of my mouth.

"This is going to be embarrassingly quick," he huffed out between groans.

The fingers he'd tangled in my hair were merciless against my scalp, pulling at the root and sending a delicious bite of pain through me. Everything about him was turning me on, and when his other hand traced the outline of my mouth stretched around his cock, I couldn't take it anymore.

The seam of my jeans wasn't doing me any good in relieving the pressure growing between my legs, so I made a split-second decision to unbutton my own jeans and slip my hand inside.

In my position, it was a tight fit between the unforgiving denim and my body, but the second my fingers touched my clit —the same fingers that were wrapped around Josh's dick only a moment before—I moaned low and deep.

"Fuck, baby. Are you—you're touching yourself."

Another moan was my only response, my eyes shut against the intense pleasure growing inside of me as I urgently twirled my fingers over my clit.

Josh adjusted in front of me, popping free of my mouth, but when my eyes opened, he quickly righted himself.

"Use this," he instructed. In his left hand, only inches from my face, was my neon-pink vibrator, affectionately known as Patrick. Patrick Swayze.

I glanced up at him, preparing for the punch line, but his expression was deadly serious.

"Use this to get yourself off while you suck my cock," he panted, and I wasn't in the position to deny either of us what we wanted.

Quicker than I ever had before, I undressed from the waist down and then chucked off my sweater for good measure. Then, in only my black lace bra, I reached for the toy. Josh willingly handed it over and replaced his hands in my hair. He held my head back from his proudly standing cock so he could look down his body to where I teased my entrance with the vibrating toy.

I clicked the button three times before I found the exact vibration pattern I wanted. It was a medium-high, consistent vibration, which I teased around my dripping pussy before latching back on to Josh's cock and pressing it to my clit.

My moan was a vibration around his shaft, and he bucked back into my throat. Swallowing around him, I realized he wasn't the only one that was going to be done in only a matter of seconds.

Multitasking was already a challenge but trying to focus on sucking Josh at the perfect rhythm while also grinding against the toy was nearly impossible. Thankfully, Josh was so consumed with pleasure that he took over, fucking my mouth and using my hair to guide me up and down his length.

My lips burned as they stretched around him, and my hand that was gripped around him fell to his balls. I squeezed them, massaging them with enough pressure that he lurched forward.

"Fuck, yes. That's it. Are you going to come with your mouth wrapped around me?"

*God, yes.* The dirtier the talk, the better, in my book. And his tempting, taunting words only heightened my arousal to a level I hadn't achieved in what felt like ages.

My answering moan was loud, even if it was slightly muffled by his cock, and I pressed the toy harder against my sensitive clit. I ceased moving my hips, feeling the release barreling toward me at an unbelievable speed. My whole body was tense and primed, but I wanted to get Josh closer. I wanted him to fumble over the cliff as close to me as he could.

So, I tightened my hold on his balls and hollowed my cheeks around him. His reaction was instant.

His hands yanked at my hair, shooting sparks of pain that flamed into pleasure down my spine and straight for my cunt.

I gasped as my orgasm finally won, and I shook with the effort to keep my mouth around him. I nearly shrieked, the pulsing between my legs overpowering every other sense.

"I'm coming. *Fuck.*" I vaguely heard Josh only a second before I tasted his release on my tongue. Just as I had, Josh shook and vibrated with each pulse of his orgasm as I drank him down.

My eyes had closed against the power of our combined pleasure, but when I opened them, it was Josh's face I saw first. He was kneeling down in front of me and then he was kissing me.

His tongue dove into my mouth without concern as he

pressed me closer to him, one hand on my lower back and the other at the base of my neck. The kiss, unlike so many of the others we'd shared, was gentle. His lips carefully stroked my own, teasing a whimper from me. The kiss seemed to say so much more in the few seconds we'd been connected than so much else had.

Sitting back on his heels but keeping me in his arms, Josh sighed contentedly.

"I—" he began but was immediately cut off by the sound of the front door slamming.

"Sister, you here?" Adam sang from the front of the apartment.

Josh and I jerked our gazes to the door and then back to one another.

"Now aren't you glad that I closed the damn door?" I chided, but we were both up and moving. In the mess that was my bedroom floor, I lost the jeans I had been wearing when I tossed them behind me in the heat of the moment. So, I grabbed the closest thing, which was a pair of leggings and yanked them on before pulling my discarded sweater over my head.

"Amanda, what the fuck? I gotta talk to you!" Adam yelled.

"Little brothers are the worst," I mumbled angrily. Stopping by the mirror, I cringed at my reflection. There was mascara gathering under my eyes, and my hair was sticking up in a million different directions. Quickly, I swiped under my eyes, removing what little mascara I could, and brushed down my flyaways.

"Hey, I take offense to that—I'm a little brother."

"My point exactly."

Adam's pounding footfalls were hurrying down the hallway, and the last thing I wanted was for him to find us in my room together, looking the way we did and it reeking of sex—again. There was something so wrong about being caught with my... *friend* in such a compromising position. Like we were teenagers being busted by our parents while trying to act like absolutely nothing had happened.

I contemplated asking Josh to hide in my bathroom or closet, but those two spaces were as messy as my room. So, I sucked it up and rushed out of the room.

"Yep," I said, trying to appear casual as I leaned against the doorframe. "I'm here. What do you need to talk about?"

"I knew you were here. I need to talk to you… oh… hey, Josh. What's up, man?" Adam said skeptically as he looked up and over my shoulder at Josh, who I assumed had finally righted himself enough to also come out of the room.

"Adam. Nice to see you." Josh's front was so close to my back that I could feel the heat of him through my clothes. And given both of our disheveled appearances after coming out of *my* room, there was little left to interpret.

"Great to see you, too, Josh. Is Reed about to pile out of there, too? Probably need to get you a bigger bed, sis, if you're going—"

"Adam, seriously?" I said, cutting him off as he smirked down at me. But the moment he looked behind me again, his face suddenly dropped.

I glanced over my shoulder to see Josh's hand drop from his mouth and direct a murderous stare at my brother.

From the small part of the movement I caught, it appeared that Josh was miming smoking weed to my brother, but I wasn't in the mood to investigate further. The important part was it got Adam to cool it on the threesome jokes.

"What did you need to talk to me about?" I asked Adam, giving Josh a pointed look.

"Umm… I'm going to visit Mom and Dad next weekend. She called and wants me to see their new place. I figured I could do some recon for both of us."

It didn't matter if I had given up on our parents caring about me as much as they did Adam a long time ago. Which still wasn't much. The pain in my chest was still very much real at hearing his words.

I hadn't spoken to my parents since they'd left. The little I knew about their move and new life in California was what I'd heard from Adam. Part of it was my fault, I guess. I also hadn't reached out, but I was so angry. The type of anger that had accumulated over years and years of being treated as a second-rate person and a nuisance.

So, I wasn't surprised that they'd invited Adam but left me out of the little family reunion.

"How are you affording a plane ticket?"

Adam scrubbed a hand over his jaw and immediately shifted his feet, obviously uncomfortable with my question.

"Mom sent you money," I said flatly, and the pressure of Josh's palm appeared against my lower back.

The small touch did wonders for my nerves as he stood steady behind me. My stomach still plummeted, but I didn't feel like I was going to fall with it.

"Please don't be upset. If you don't want me to go, then I won't."

I did my best to muster a smile, but I knew it fell short.

"No, I want you to go. It'll be good to see them and where they live now. I know you've also always wanted to go to California."

His smile looked almost as sad as mine felt as he said, "Yeah, okay." He brushed past us both and disappeared into his bedroom, the door clicking shut behind him.

"You okay?" Josh wasted no time spinning me around the moment Adam was gone.

"Yeah," I said, offering a soft smile and laying my hands flat on his hard chest muscles. "It's nothing new."

"Doesn't mean it doesn't hurt all the same." He pushed all of my hair behind my shoulders and wrapped his hands around the sides of my neck.

Frustratingly enough, I knew he was right. Even after years

of the same shit, I knew what to expect—or what not to—from my parents. I figured at some point I would become numb to their lack of emotion or interest in my life, but the opposite was true. It always stung and hurt just the same.

"You're right, but at least it's not a surprise anymore."

He used his thumbs to push beneath my chin, my face lifting up toward him. Josh's eyes raked over my features for a moment, likely looking for a sign that I wasn't okay before he kissed me.

It was intentional and methodical, like he was trying to undo all of the hurt my parents had caused with a simple brush of his lips against mine.

"I think you're the one that deserves some stress relief now," he mumbled against my mouth, and that time, my smile was honest.

"For some reason," I said, hearing pounding footfalls from tiny feet against the concrete in the hallway, "I don't think we're going to have enough time for that."

"Auntie Manda!" Zach shouted, bursting through the door. He looked left and, after not finding me in the kitchen or living room, whipped to the right, where he spotted both me and his dad in the hallway.

"Auntie Manda, I have to go potty!" He raced to me with his hands in front of him.

Sensing the emergency, I quickly ushered him through my room and into my bathroom.

Back out in the hall, I rejoined Josh just as Reed also came through the door.

"Dude," he panted, with his hands perched on his hips. "I work out all the fucking time. Hell, I own my own goddamn gym, for Christ's sake, but when that kid took off saying he had to pee, there was no way I was keeping up."

Josh and I both laughed as Reed rolled his eyes, nostrils flaring.

"You're both assholes."

I could see the torment on Reed's face—he saw my smile and wanted to return it. And a second later, he lost his inner battle, one corner of his mouth tugging upward.

Then his eyes dropped lower, perusing my body until he stopped at my legs. A different expression passed over his face, and I frowned. Looking down, I realized he'd noticed my change of attire.

A blush crept over my cheeks, and I could feel it down my neck and chest. I didn't know why I was suddenly embarrassed when I'd made my intentions completely clear only the day before.

"You guys get the chance to talk?" he said, and I couldn't decipher his tone. Was his tone weird, or was I reading into a change that wasn't actually there?

"Yes, and thanks for that, by the way," Josh responded with sarcasm dripping from every word. "Didn't think I was telling you so you could run and tell everyone else."

Reed chuckled and glanced between us. "I know you're being sarcastic, but you're welcome. Looks like it all turned out for the best, since our girl is wearing different pants."

He gestured to my legs and my blush from before was magnified.

*Our girl.* Oddly enough, I didn't mind the sound of that at all.

"Auntie Manda," Zach's voice startled me as he exited my bathroom.

"Yes, bud?" I asked in a weary voice.

"Your bedroom and bathroom and everything is really messy."

My jaw dropped. Like father, like son, apparently.

"Trust me, bud. Daddy already told Auntie Manda that she should clean her room."

"Okay, good. Daddy, can we go get something to eat? I'm hungry."

"Yes, we can." Josh turned to me. "Want to come with?"

There was something about the idea that he included me—

that Josh wanted me around him and his son—that made my breath catch. And as much as I wanted to say yes, I had to decline.

"I have papers to grade, and I promised Hazel I would help organize all of my shit we just threw into her guest room. Rain check?"

"It's an open invitation—whenever you want to spend time with us, we'd be happy to have you."

How I didn't end up in a puddle on the floor, I would never know.

"Thanks," I breathed out, hoping to stay steady on my feet.

"Bye, Auntie Manda!"

"Bye, Zach. I had so much fun today, and I'll see you soon, okay?" I stooped down to his level, and he threw his arms around my neck without hesitation.

The kid had hugged me a million times prior—I'd seen him and been there through every stage of life. But that hug felt different and more loaded with the possibility of the future after our conversation.

Would Zach want me as a stepmom? He loved me as "Auntie Manda"—he'd declared it loudly and often. But dating and eventually... *marrying* his dad was something else altogether.

"Love you," he crooned into my hair next to my ear.

"Love you, too."

When he let go, I stood and looked at Josh. His smile was broad, and the emotion swimming in his eyes was enough to tell me his thoughts mirrored my own.

"Okay, Daddy, let's go. Uncle Reed, are you coming? I want a hamburger!"

There was a conflict in his expression as Josh's eyes bounced from me to the two standing at the end of the hall. I knew he was worried about Zach seeing too much, so I made the decision for him.

Pushing to my tiptoes, I wrapped my arms over his shoulders and pulled him into a hug that could have been considered a friendly goodbye. He chuckled softly into my hair as his arms banded around my lower back.

"Thanks, babe."

"Anytime, Sunshine," I said, using Reed's favorite nickname for him.

And with a kiss on my cheek, he let me go. There was a hint of reluctance in both of us, but Josh walked down the hallway. Zach took his outstretched hand and waved to me as I slowly walked to them as well.

"Bye, Auntie Manda."

"Are you coming?" Josh asked Reed, who'd barely taken his eyes off of me since he'd walked in.

"Yeah, I'll be right there. Give me a minute."

Zach huffed and then proclaimed, "Okay, you have one minute, but that's all. You come downstairs in one minute, or we're going to leave without you."

Reed promised he'd be down there in a minute, and with one last glance at me, Josh led Zach out the door.

"Did you know that there are sixty seconds in a minute, Daddy? I knew that because…" The door closed behind them, and Reed's whiskey eyes turned back to me.

There wasn't a word between us as he took two quick steps, gripped my upper thighs and hauled me up into his arms.

He sealed his lips to mine, finally releasing the pent-up desire we'd collected throughout the day. My fingers tangled in his hair, which was slightly longer than Josh's yet just as soft, and I huffed out a breath when my back collided with the living room wall. Pinned between the wall of a man and the actual wall was mind bending.

I tilted my head slightly, deepening our kiss and trying—but failing—to suppress the moan inching up my throat.

Only minutes before, I had come undone thanks to Josh and my trusty toy, Patrick, but subject to Reed's hands and mouth and intoxicating smell, I still ground against him. My body urged me to find another release.

The fireworks I'd experienced with Josh did a little to release our growing tension, however, it was separate from my connection with Reed. We had our own desire and tension building between us that had to be released by him alone.

"Is this how you wanted to use your minute?" I panted against his mouth, his teeth nipping at my bottom lip.

"Yes, but it won't be enough. It won't be enough until I'm buried inside you again. And even then, I can't say I'll ever be fully satisfied."

My entire body was a live wire under his touch, and my core clenched. I wished he was inside of me at that moment, so I could clench around him.

His lips, hot and urgent against my skin, migrated across my jaw and down my neck as his hands released my hips, propping me on the wall. His palms slid up my sides and found purchase against my ribs under my shirt.

I pressed my chest out and bowed my back off the wall. The touch of his fingers on the underside of my bra was a delicious tease.

"So, you talked?" he asked without stopping.

"Yes."

"About Sam and Zach?"

I nodded because one word was difficult when he was doing that thing with his tongue against my neck.

"And then what?"

My body suddenly tensed under his speculation, and I found myself again questioning if he was upset. But he continued to lick and suck at my neck, taking my earlobe between his teeth and biting.

I gasped, and he chuckled.

"Tell me."

Since he was asking, I threw caution to the wind—if he did get angry, then maybe that would dissuade him from asking in the future.

"I got myself off with my vibrator while I sucked his cock."

Reed reared back, and I immediately missed the pressure of his lips against my neck. I waited to see any sign of resentment in his eyes. But they were too busy carefully eyeing the quick rise and fall of my chest, displaying nothing but a needy intensity. Then they ran the length of my neck.

"He needed you to get off, too?" he guessed, and I nodded. "Always so giving, our Sunshine."

And I shook at the revere in his voice. Like he was more than okay, more like he was happy Josh also thought of me in the moment.

He shifted our position, wrapping an arm around my lower back, supporting most of my weight with it, to wrap his right hand loosely around my throat.

My eyes fluttered closed, and I was so close to asking him to stay and begging him to put me out of my misery.

"Where did he come?"

Another question I wasn't expecting, but it seemed to be a part of his game. His dark, twisted, and dangerous game that I enjoyed participating in. Especially when I didn't answer right away, and his grip tightened around my throat. With a smile that made his eyes flare, I reveled in the way his fingers dug into my skin and restricted my airway.

"Answer me. Tell me where he came."

"In my mouth."

My answer was slightly muffled, but with it, his hand disappeared from around my neck to tug at my bottom lip. He dipped his thumb inside my mouth and pressed it against my tongue, pushing it deeper and running the pad of it back and forth. Like he didn't believe me completely.

"Did you swallow?" His voice was a low, barely restrained whisper.

I nodded, and his finger triggered my gag reflex. As I swallowed, he removed it and rested his hand around my neck once again.

"Does that bother you?" I asked for some unknown reason.

Mostly because each of his reactions surprised me more than the last. I wasn't used to a man expressing desire or need when hearing about the woman he wants being touched by—or touching—another man. Even if that man was his best friend.

"Quite the opposite actually," was all he said before his lips covered mine and his tongue was immediately urging them apart. Like nothing I'd ever experienced before, he explored my mouth, tasting me and likely some of Josh.

And then his phone vibrated from his jeans pocket and our minute was up.

# TWENTY-FIVE

Amanda

It was the Spice Girls blaring in the background that made it impossible to hear the knocking on my apartment door.

And it was also possible that my aggressive singing to "Spice Up Your Life" had something to do with my inability to hear, or focus on, anything besides the lyrics and rapid beat.

After spending the afternoon the day before organizing Hazel's guest bedroom, which was packed to the brim with my stuff, I was motivated to tame the chaos of my own place. And organizing or cleaning of any kind meant the volume of the music was supposed to be at an uncomfortable decibel to anyone inside the apartment and only slightly annoying to any of my neighbors.

The kitchen was only partially done, and I'd taken a lengthy break to refill my margarita and scroll through the music app on my phone, picking out the perfect songs that fit my mood. It wasn't until "Buttons" by The Pussycat Dolls filled the space that I'd finally gone back to sorting the Tupperware cabinet—pairing lids to their respective containers.

The song was nearly half over when I heard a sound behind

me and assumed it was my tall tower of Tupperware containers precariously stacked on the island about to go cascading to the floor.

Much to my surprise, it wasn't the containers, and instead, I turned around to find someone standing on the opposite side of the island.

My scream reverberated off the walls, and my hands flew in front of me, catching the edge of the island to keep myself from slipping on a lid on the floor. The force of it caused the tower of Tupperware to go crashing to the floor.

But it was the least of my worries as my eyes flew back to the intruder, who ended up not being an intruder at all. At least not exactly.

"CJ, you scared the shit out of me!" I yelled, reaching for my phone and turning the volume down several notches.

That's what I got for trying to organize—random people walking into my apartment and a near-death experience from the heart attack I almost suffered.

"I was knocking for nearly five minutes, but you also put 'enter at any time' on the service request," he said calmly with an amused smirk.

I clutched my chest and attempted to settle my racing heart. My breaths were coming in short gasps, and it took several seconds for my fight-or-flight response to dissipate.

"I didn't submit a service request," I said flatly.

From his back pocket, CJ pulled out a sheet of paper, reviewed it, and then pushed it to me over the island. "See, it says here there's an issue with a bedroom window and to enter at any time."

I scanned the printed version of the service request and shrugged. "It must have been Adam who requested it, which means it's probably his bedroom window."

Clarity washed over his face. "Shit, I'm sorry. I forgot you have a roommate now. After years of you livin' alone, it must have slipped my mind."

I waved him off, my heart rate finally back to normal, and took a long sip of my margarita. "Not a problem. It's still kind of weird for me, too."

With a polite nod, CJ hiked his thumb over his shoulder and headed down the hallway and into Adam's room. I didn't realize my baby brother knew how to submit a service request, let alone knew our apartment complex had a website at all.

In the few weeks we'd lived together, we'd done fairly well. Our schedules meant that we didn't see each other but for an hour or two in the evening before he had to leave for his shift at Murphy's. And like the twenty-one-year-old he was, he was rarely in the apartment any other time.

Like me, though, he was a little messy, which wouldn't have been an issue until you put the two of us together. Two messy people doubled the disaster.

I'd mentioned that he needed to pick up his half of the mess before he left for California the next weekend. He'd agreed, but there was a twinge of sadness in my chest at the topic—that my parents couldn't bother to invite me.

The day before, when I was discussing the entire situation with Hazel, the sadness became so much more than a twinge that I broke down and texted my mom.

It had been eighteen hours and thirty-two minutes, and she hadn't responded. But I wasn't counting.

"Okay, all fixed," CJ announced. "It was jammed a little bit, so it wasn't opening all the way. Easy fix."

In the midst of my thanking him, the front door swung open.

"Whoa," Adam said and pulled up short, nearly running into CJ. His eyes darted back and forth between me and the big guy. "What the hell are you—who is this?"

I balked at his rudeness and stuttered a response.

"Adam, seriously? This is CJ," I said as I motioned to him. "He's the maintenance guy *and* the guy who's saved my ass on more than one occasion."

The glare CJ threw at Adam was completely called for, and if

CJ had something to say about Adam's attitude, I wasn't going to get in the middle of it. Adam likely deserved it for more than one reason.

Adam returned CJ's glare, his jaw ticcing as CJ crossed his arms over his chest. The tension in the air was palpable and quickly rose to a level I was scared would erupt until someone else pushed open the door behind Adam.

"Babe, you really shouldn't—" Josh's booming voice called out the moment he burst through the door, but his statement died on his tongue when he noticed CJ and Adam. "Leave your door unlocked," he quietly finished.

And, like usual, Reed was right behind him.

They both immediately noticed the agitation in the air and found me across the kitchen. Their eyes were filled with questions I didn't have answers to, so I pursed my lips and shrugged.

"What's going on, guys? Everything good here?" Reed stepped forward, and Josh flanked him.

It was CJ that looked away first, although it appeared to be a struggle for him. "Yeah, we're good. Right?" He held out his large palm to Adam, who glanced at it like he'd never witnessed the gesture before, but he didn't hesitate too long before taking it and pumping once. That was all CJ was getting, though, because Adam turned down the hallway.

"Well, I'm glad to see everyone's done swinging their dicks around—someone was bound to lose an eye," I quipped.

"Sorry, Mandy. Won't happen again," CJ muttered apologetically and peered down at his watch. "I've got a few more stops to make before I'm done for the evening, so I'll see you later."

I gave him a polite wave, and as the door closed behind him, I crossed the room to lock it.

"I'm so tired of people walking into my apartment without announcing themselves," I mumbled.

"What the hell did we just walk into?" Josh asked, plopping onto the couch and kicking his feet up on the coffee table I'd already cleaned.

I went back into the kitchen and surveyed the destruction of my Tupperware tower. "I'm not sure. Adam just walked in with guns blazin', asking who the hell CJ was. Then they had a stare down that I thought would end in fists flying if y'all hadn't walked in."

"CJ would've laid Adam out." Reed chuckled, taking a seat at one of the barstools and eyeing the chaos on the other side of the island.

"Yeah, I've got twenty on the big guy," Josh murmured from the living room.

"I don't disagree, but it was just weird. Adam's a fuckhead on the best days, but he's not usually downright rude to people he meets. I'll... ask him about it later."

The idea of asking him about it wasn't at the top of my list. We hadn't argued since he'd moved in, but the conversation I had in mind was bound to stir things up. His favorite comeback anytime I brought something up—no matter what it was—was to remind me that I was not his mother.

"Does CJ know Adam is your brother? Not your boyfriend that just moved in?" Josh asked, and my eyes went wide.

"Yes, of course. Why?"

"Seems like he was sizing up the competition, is all."

"I agree. I still think he's into you, Amanda. But does Adam know CJ then? Things were a little tense for two guys who have no history," Reed asked, and my eyes met his when he stooped to assist me with the mess.

"Another question we'll have to ask Tyler Durden in there."

I heard Josh's laugh before I saw him round the corner of the island. "Okay, I got that one." And I could tell by his tone and cocky grin that he was proud of himself.

"Isn't that the guy from *Fight Club*?" Reed asked innocently.

Josh and I both locked our glares on him as I reached out to smack his arm. "What is the first rule of Fight Club, Reed?"

His unamused stare bounced back and forth from me to Josh before he sighed and scooped up the remaining Tupperware in his arms. With no care, Reed unceremoniously dumped the several containers into my thankfully clean sink and turned back to me.

"Anyway, did you forget why we're here?" he asked, and I stilled.

I opened and closed my mouth several times, like a fish out of water, and racked my brain for any idea before I resigned myself to the fact that I'd forgotten. I'd been so focused on cleaning and properly organizing that everything else had slipped my mind. Grading the previous weeks' assignments was the only thing I remembered that had to be done before Monday. There was a stack of them a mile high, and I'd been up late finishing the final assignment.

The fancy private school I worked for didn't care that it was the first week of spring semester and expected us to implement as rigorous a schedule as we always would.

"Sunday dinner," Josh said, coming to my rescue, unlike Reed, who would have waited forever if it helped him make his point—I was forgetful sometimes.

"Oh shit," I muttered, quickly throwing myself into action and hurrying toward my bedroom to get ready. Glancing at the clock over the stove, I saw we had roughly thirty minutes until we had to be at Hazel and Luke's house.

Sunday night family dinner was a tradition we'd started in college. Every Sunday, we prioritized dinner with our group as a way to start the week on a high note surrounded by our friends. In college, it was usually pizza or tacos because we were all students and were often only scraping by.

Once we graduated, we'd mostly traded in the cheap, greasy food for potluck meals. But the idea was the same—spend time with each other, catch up on our busy lives, and start the week off right.

Sadly, in recent years, the tradition had fallen off. More often, one or more of us were busy with unshakable commitments, which meant our weekly tradition turned into a monthly one. And then monthly turned into every couple of months.

It had been nearly a year and a half—maybe longer—since our last formal Sunday night dinner. And if it wasn't for Hazel, we may not have revived the tradition. When she caught wind of the previous gathering, she proceeded to scold us all for letting it die off and then led the charge in renewing it.

And I was the dumbass that forgot.

Scrambling to get dressed, I contemplated skipping a shower since I'd taken one the night before but realized I smelled like bleach and a variety of other cleaning supplies. I groaned, turned on the water, and proceeded to take the quickest shower of my life.

After throwing on some mascara and tossing my hair into a bun on top of my head, I stared at my newly clean closet for a few minutes before I settled on black jeans, black boots, and a maroon top that cinched in at the waist.

It was an outfit I'd worn several times, but without the time to put together something new, it was the best we were all going to get.

No more than twenty minutes later, I was striding back into the kitchen to find Reed and Josh stacking the Tupperware containers neatly in the cabinet.

"You didn't have to do that. I would've figured it out when I got back."

Reed scoffed, and Josh suppressed a chuckle. "No, you would've left them in the sink for days, and when you finally got tired of looking at them, *then* you would've thrown them back into the cabinet."

I pretended to act offended, but he was right.

Ignoring him, I turned to the fridge and pulled out the dessert I'd prepared for the dinner. Although it'd slipped my mind that day, I had the forethought the day before to make the dessert.

Even the Amanda from the day before knew I was likely to forget.

"Are we ready?" I asked, turning back to the men and taking them in.

Reed leaned against the kitchen island, a navy-blue pullover straining across his muscular chest and down his arms. His jeans were a light denim, and his ankles were casually crossed, showing off a small amount of his dark-brown boots.

Josh stood in the middle of the kitchen with his hands pushed in the pockets of his dark jeans. His blue-and-green flannel shirt was tight in all the right places and matched his eyes so well.

There was something about the flannel, though, that made me do a double take.

"Like what you see, babe?" Josh joked with a playful wink.

"Is that the shirt I bought for Reed last Christmas?"

Josh looked down at the shirt and shrugged. "Maybe."

"Do you share clothes a lot?" I asked as Reed pushed Josh's shoulder, forcing Josh to turn and face him.

"Dude, that is definitely my shirt. What have I told you about wearing my damn clothes?"

"Not sure why it's such a big deal. You wear mine, too."

We all made our way to the door, and I hollered to my brother that we were leaving without a response. Reed grabbed the dessert out of my hands, still scowling at his friend, while Josh handed me my purse and opened the door for us.

"Kinda think it looks good on him, Reed. Maybe you should let him borrow it more often," I chided, knowing I was just adding fuel to the fire, but I couldn't resist.

"Borrowing it would require asking first. He straight up stole it."

"But I have every intention of giving it back, so I agree that I borrowed it."

The guys bickered back and forth about the fundamental

differences between stealing and borrowing as we headed to Josh's white truck.

"You can have shotgun," I told Reed as I hurried ahead and slipped into the back seat of the truck so there wasn't any further argument.

They were both still arguing when they approached the car, and I rolled my eyes. They were the best at getting on each other's nerves, but it felt like more than annoyance—it bordered on actual anger and frustration, which was unusual.

Josh shook his head and pulled open the driver's side door at the same time Reed rounded the truck. But he completely bypassed the front seat and yanked open the door to the back.

"Mind if I join you?" He smirked, and I scooted over as he climbed in.

"Seriously?" Josh scoffed. "What the fuck am I? Your chauffeur?"

Reed set the dessert on the floor between his feet and reached across the seat to wrap his arms around my waist. With a swift tug, he moved me to the middle seat and smiled when I put on my seat belt.

The warm weight of his hand found my thigh, and I tried not to audibly sigh.

"No, if you were our chauffeur, and I was paying you to drive us, I'd also include in your instructions to keep your thoughts to yourself."

I smacked Reed in the stomach and gave him a look that said he was taking it too far. The smile he threw my way was far too cocky, and I knew he wasn't planning on heeding my silent warning.

"Anything to flaunt your money, right? Especially to us little people."

The sun was near the horizon, so it wasn't easy to see from the back seat, but I still watched the hurt flash across Josh's eyes in the rearview mirror.

"What is that supposed to mean?"

"You know exactly what it means. You've done the same shit the entire time I've known you."

"And what might that *shit* be, Josh? If you're going to accuse me of something, you better have some evidence to back it up."

Their voices were growing louder and the tension in the truck was nearing an unbearable level. Josh pressed harder on the gas as Reed's hand tightened around my thigh.

They both began speaking at the same time, each of them on the brink of saying things they couldn't take back, so I took that as my cue to step in.

"Okay! That's enough."

Thankfully, they both shut up.

"Thank you," I sighed. "I don't know what the hell has gotten into the two of you, but I'm not going to listen to this bickering anymore. If you don't have anything nice to say, don't say a damn word."

I had a flashback to saying the same thing to the twelve-year-olds I taught, but never did I think I'd be having the same conversation with two grown men twenty years their senior.

They were both silent, and I took it as a win.

"You used your teacher voice," Reed said and was smart enough to look a little scared.

"I don't want to use it again, so don't make me."

"I kind of liked it," Josh said from the front seat, peering at me with a mischievous glint in his eyes through the rearview mirror.

"Me too," Reed agreed. And we were back to normal—mostly. Hopefully.

# TWENTY-SIX

Josh

SHE WAS ACROSS THE ROOM, SITTING WITH HAZEL AND JAMES, laughing so hard there were tears spilling from her eyes.

We'd been at Hazel and Luke's house for nearly two hours. The food was gone and the drinks were flowing, but I couldn't keep my eyes off her. And I wasn't the only one.

Quite a few times throughout the night, I'd caught Reed also watching her. We ate around Hazel and Luke's long oak table and both found ourselves opposite her. It was amazing that no one noticed that neither of us could keep our eyes off of her. Without interrupting or drawing attention, we watched her interact with our friends. Her laugh was contagious, she was engaged in every conversation, and she gave us all the same amount of attention and enthusiasm.

James announced he received another promotion at work— the workaholic asshole—and Amanda cheered like she was the one that got the raise along with it.

And when Devon mentioned his sister had been accepted into the college of her dreams, she'd wrapped him in a hug. One we all knew he needed—mixed with his excitement was also plenty of doubt and nerves.

With his mom still fighting the cancer ravaging her body, Devon felt like it was his job to put his sister through school and make sure she didn't miss out on anything. The guy had more on his plate than any of us really knew, even being his best friends.

"Josh, have you heard a word I said?"

Shaking off my Amanda-filled thoughts, I turned back to my brother.

"No, sorry. What'd you say?"

He laughed and gave me an incredulous look. "That has to be the tenth time you've done that tonight. So, what the hell is going on? Where's your head?"

I glanced between him and Devon. They were both looking at me expectantly, and I knew there was no getting out of it. And I had to admit that the idea of talking to someone about the situation was tempting.

Amanda—and, as a result, Reed—hadn't been far from my thoughts. It was simultaneously a nightmare and a blessing. At one moment, I was thinking about her on her knees, her blue eyes staring up at me as she sucked me like she was made to do it. And then the next, I was trying to calculate the probability that, against all odds, she'd pick me in the end.

It was fucking exhausting.

"There's this woman," I started and watched the smiles grow across both of their faces.

"Go on," Luke urged.

"She's literally perfect and everything I could fucking want, but… there's another guy."

Devon groaned. "Please, for the love of God, tell me she isn't married. Or engaged. Or in a relationship at all."

Ardently, I shook my head. "No, it's not like that."

"Okay, then…" Devon questioned.

I glanced around to see if anyone else was within hearing

distance. Amanda, Hazel and James were still talking in the living room, and Reed had stepped outside a few minutes before to talk to his mom.

It was just me, Luke and Devon alone in the kitchen, hovering around the island. "She has feelings for me and this other guy."

"That fucking sucks," Devon said, taking a long pull of his beer.

"You're telling me. She said that there was no way she could choose. Or at least she can't right now or anytime soon."

"So, what are you going to do? If that's the truth, then it seems like you're stuck," my brother asked.

Out of all the questions I had, what I would do wasn't one of them. There wasn't a doubt in my mind that I was on the correct path. "I'm going to keep fighting for her. Until she makes a decision, I'm not bowing out."

Devon and Luke shared a look that I knew meant they thought I was crazy. Hell, *I* thought I was crazy.

"Seems to me like she's just stringing you both along. Does she have any intentions of choosing one of you?" Devon grabbed the three of us another round of beers from the fridge.

"What are we talking about?" James asked from behind me and made me jump about ten feet in the air.

"Josh's caught in a love triangle and is in denial about it," Luke spoke up, and I swore I couldn't have scowled harder if I tried. Leave it to my older brother to announce my business to anyone.

James cringed and grabbed his own beer from the fridge.

"I just wouldn't take her word for it, man, or get your hopes up that she's going to choose you. That's not to say you wouldn't be a hell of a choice, but…" Devon trailed off and shrugged.

The more they talked, the more I changed my mind—I actually didn't want to talk about it at all.

"Yeah, love triangles never turn out the way you want them to," James added.

Luke eyed me curiously, then asked, "Do you know the other guy? What's his deal?"

That question, I thought, was the one I dreaded the most. God's honest truth wasn't going to happen when the implications of our situation could have been tragic for our group.

So, I decided to go with as much of the truth as I could without pointing large, red arrows toward Amanda and Reed.

"He's a good guy, which makes it even worse. But she's worth the fight."

At that, they were all silent, which said something. I couldn't remember the last time I confided in my friends about a woman like that—it was possible that I never had. Because I'd never felt that way about any other woman.

Their silence was louder than if they'd said anything at all, and the weight of their stares was heavy.

Devon and James only appeared concerned for me, but it was Luke's stare that felt like he saw through all of the lies. Like he knew there was so much more to the story than what I'd said.

"Either way, don't pass that information around," I requested, spinning the beer bottle on the counter. "Not everyone needs to know everything about my life."

Without missing a beat, Luke asked, "Reed know?"

What a loaded fucking question. And he knew it, too. I usually appreciated having such a close relationship with my brother—we read each other better than anyone could and anticipated what the other was thinking—but it made lying to him difficult.

I didn't want to lie to him, but it was in everyone's best interest that we all lied.

"Yeah, guess so. He doesn't know all of it, but we live together, so it's kind of hard to keep secrets." My vague reply wasn't going to slide with him, and I watched his eyes narrow as he contemplated pushing me.

But Hazel came to my rescue, yelling from the other room, "Babe?"

"Yes, Angel," Luke immediately responded, and James made a sound and motion mimicking a whip. We all laughed as Luke shoved him on his way out, and I was relieved the conversation was over.

"Their house is so nice," Amanda said again from the back seat where she was cuddled up with Reed. "It makes my little apartment look like a fucking hostel."

She and Reed were both tipsy, and I would have been too, if I wasn't the DD for the night. Every second I was growing more frustrated that I'd lost that stupid coin toss to Reed before we left our apartment to pick up Amanda.

They were cuddled up in the back seat and wouldn't stop fucking touching each other while I was driving them around.

After the conversation with the guys and their lack of support, combined with the sounds coming from the back seat, I was at my limit. The renewed hope I'd felt the day before from my conversation with Amanda was completely nonexistent.

The more I watched the two of them interact, the more uneasy I became. They had an unquestionable chemistry that I tried not to compare to me and Amanda. But I was failing miserably.

I was doing my best not to glance in the rearview mirror, but apparently, I liked to torture myself.

Approaching a red light, I slowed down and glanced in the mirror.

The light the controls and streetlights provided were muted. But I caught Reed's hand running up and down the length of Amanda's inner thigh. Her legs were slightly spread, inviting him to tease her, but each time he approached the seam of her jeans, the perfect place that was hidden behind the fabric, he changed directions.

Her breathing was quick and shallow, and the way she bit her lip, I knew she was holding back a moan and all of the other lovely sounds that escaped her lips when she was in the throes of pleasure.

Even held down by the seat belt strapped across her lap, Amanda tried to push herself up into his hand, urging him closer to where she wanted him most. But he didn't cave.

Instead, Reed kissed and licked at her neck. The same skin I'd also felt beneath my lips. I knew it was soft and slightly sweet. I knew that you could feel her pulse if you pressed your lips against the spot just beneath her jaw.

And he was pulling from her the same reactions she gave me. She was eager and willing and pining for more. It wasn't by my hand, but her reactions were still just as captivating.

I couldn't bring myself to stop them.

Somehow I managed to notice when the light turned green and centered myself enough to slowly ease the car forward.

The distance between red lights seemed infinite. Quick glances in the mirror did nothing for my morbid curiosity. And when we finally approached another light, I prayed it would turn red.

Apparently, God answered prayers when you were eager to watch your two best friends get it on in the back seat of your truck.

I tilted the mirror down and found Amanda's eyes reflected back to me. Turning slightly in my seat, I saw it was Reed this time, with his head thrown back, lost in her touch. She was running her palm over the bulge in his jeans. Just as Amanda had, Reed was attempting to press up into her hand but was restricted by the seat belt.

My eyes locked on the sight. Her hand was urgently rubbing him, giving him some sort of friction as he eagerly chased a release. But from experience, I knew it wouldn't feel like enough. It was the perfect tease because the woman was a wonder with her hands, mouth, and cunt. And he'd be thinking about how good it would be when she wrapped her hand around his bare shaft or when he pushed into her.

My own erection was throbbing against the seam of my jeans, wanting to be back there, too. And it wasn't lost on me that my dick was growing harder the longer I watched the woman I wanted pleasuring another man. But I was past caring.

"Light's green, Sunshine," Amanda purred, and I regretfully straightened in my seat.

We were less than ten minutes from her apartment, but that felt like another eternity.

Idling at a blinking yellow light for a left turn, I peeked into the mirror once more. I immediately caught Amanda's eyes, and when she had my attention, she quickly flicked her gaze from me to Reed.

I understood her question and didn't hesitate before nodding my head once. The sexy smile that slid across her face was enough of a reward.

Sadly, it was my turn to go, and my attention was back on the road. But I heard the unmistakable sound of Reed's belt, followed by the zipper lowering.

"What—" Reed questioned, but the argument—if that's what it was—was short-lived. The next thing I heard was a gasp, a mumbled "*fuck*," and a deep groan.

It was eerily similar to my reaction when Amanda's mouth, wet and eager, wrapped around my cock. Drowning under the pressure of my own need, I pressed the palm of my hand to my erection. But it didn't help as the definitive sounds of sucking and licking filtered to the front.

One last light. I could see Amanda's apartment just past it, but I couldn't wait to park the fucking truck there.

When I turned around again, Amanda was bent over Reed's lap, her blonde head bobbing up and down. Her hand gripped the base of him, twisting her wrist as she followed the path and speed her mouth set.

"Your mouth is perfect," Reed muttered in a low voice that felt like it vibrated through the truck and continued through me.

Amanda hummed around his cock, taking him deep and to the back of her throat. I agreed—her mouth was perfect.

As she gagged on his dick, the light turned green, and I fucking gunned it.

Reed continued to mutter curse words under his breath and complimented her technique as I swerved into the parking lot. His breathing was loud, and I barely registered Amanda asking him, "Are you going to come in my mouth just like Josh did yesterday?"

"Fuck yes," Reed answered through gritted teeth the moment I put the truck in park.

Every part of me wanted to jump in the back seat with them. I wanted to join in the fucking party, but Amanda popped off Reed only long enough to give me a small shake of her head. I didn't know what she was playing at, but I wanted in on whatever she had in mind.

Restraining myself was nearly impossible, and I knew if I turned around completely, I wouldn't be able to resist. So, I positioned the rearview mirror where I could see them both and white-knuckled the wheel.

My head hit the seat behind me at the view. Reed had pulled Amanda's hair away from her face, holding it together at the back of her head, which meant I got to see everything.

His thick, tanned cock was dripping with her spit and fully disappeared into Amanda's mouth again and again and again. She was relentless. Her cheeks hollowed, and she worked him harder. And the moment her hand slipped into his jeans, Reed hissed.

I would've bet the bar that she'd cupped his balls, squeezing and tugging with the perfect amount of pressure.

"Just like that." The words were mumbled as he struggled for his next breath, and I found myself struggling right there with him. "Cielo. Mi Cielo," he chanted.

I didn't know a lot of Spanish, but it was hard to not pick up on some of it being around Reed so often. And what he'd muttered to Amanda, cupping her head reverently, I understood.

"*Heaven. My heaven.*"

There was a mix of emotions in my chest—jealousy, arousal, happiness, and concern all made an appearance. But I refused to look away.

And the emotions only became more confusing when Reed's hooded eyes found mine through the mirror. Like finding me watching was a shock to his body, his mouth parted, and he jolted.

His nearly golden eyes were barely visible in the muted light of the parking lot, but they were steadfast on my own. And as much as I wanted to glance back down and watch Amanda, I was held hostage by him. Like I couldn't tear my gaze away even if I wanted to. And I was as much a part of what they were doing as the two of them.

There was a deep furrow in his brow and a light sweat collected along his forehead, just below his messy brown hair. The same sweat glistened above his full top lip. My fingers twitched on the wheel, for some reason wanting to reach out and brush his hair back and wipe away the sweat.

The feeling startled me almost enough to make me look away. Never had I wanted to touch him like that.

But I didn't, and he groaned low and deep in the back of his throat.

"*Yes*, fuck!" he cried, pumping into Amanda's mouth harder and shooting into the back of her throat.

And the entire time, his eyes stayed on mine. He fought against the overwhelming pleasure I knew he was feeling to hold my stare. From experience, I knew it would have been easier for him to close his eyes.

Several seconds passed, and Reed's breathing slowly returned to normal. I figured he'd look away, and I prayed he'd be the first to do so. Then I'd feel like I'd had the upper hand somehow if he was the one to break this insane connection. But the last thing I expected was the slight upturn of his lips, followed by a playful wink.

I didn't have time to react, though, as Amanda's head came into view. She was wearing the same mischievous grin Reed was as she wiped at the corners of her mouth.

"That was fun. Good night, boys," Amanda said in a singsong voice.

Finally, I turned around at the same time Reed tucked himself back into his pants.

"Just gonna suck and run then, baby girl?" Reed asked.

"I have an early morning. But I'm sure I'll see you both soon since I haven't been able to get rid of you yet."

I opened my mouth to respond, but it died on my tongue. What was I going to do, beg her to follow her up?

Could have been worse. But I knew me and my hand were going to have a late-night rendezvous.

"We'll see you very soon," Reed promised and pulled her in for a kiss.

Amanda hopped out of the back seat and turned to my window, where she motioned for me to roll it down.

I did as she asked. "You know, we'd be more than happy to walk you upstairs. We are gentlemen, or at least I am," I said, unable to resist throwing a jab at the guy still in my back seat.

"You can see my apartment from here. And I know you'll sit here and watch until I make it inside anyway."

"Okay, but—"

Her finger covered my mouth and cut off my argument. She shook her head slowly twice as a warning she wasn't hearing anything more of what I had to say.

"Just kiss me, Josh."

And who was I to deny her? She stood on her toes and reached into the truck, gripping the back of my neck to pull me closer to her mouth. My hand found her cheek, and the moment our lips touched, she was already opening for me.

I pushed my tongue inside her mouth, and the taste of Reed immediately hit my tongue. It was different than I expected.

I was kissing Amanda after she'd had Reed's dick and cum in her mouth. And my reaction wasn't one that I was prepared for. I didn't stop.

Instead, I let my tongue push deeper, sweeping along hers and drawing out the most delicious moan. It was Amanda that pulled back first.

"*Damn*," she said, settling back onto her feet, a glazed look of desire spreading across her features. "Good night, boys."

With a last wave, she hurried up the steps, unlocked her apartment door, and slipped inside.

I didn't move until Reed opened the back door and slid into the front seat.

Usually on a drive like that one, we would turn on some music, maybe sit in companionable silence, or discuss whatever came to mind. But that drive, although silent, was still different from any time before.

We weren't going to talk about what just happened. Or at least I wasn't, since I wasn't positive what it was. And based on Reed's behavior, I couldn't imagine he knew either.

I found myself laser-focused on the road ahead of me, yet unable to stop thinking about the guy to my right. Reed's knee bounced, and he fidgeted with his seat belt a few times before he thankfully pulled out his phone. His fidgeting only elevated my own anxiety that I was doing a shit job of managing.

Sadly, the music was only a low hum in the background, and I couldn't force my attention from the road to turn it louder. The button being only a few inches from my hand didn't matter when I was already straining to keep my eyes forward.

The tires spinning against the street sounded louder against the quiet. A quiet that was loaded with something.

# TWENTY-SEVEN

Reed

"We should've probably called or texted her first. She's going to be pissed that we just showed up."

I lumbered up the stairs carrying my duffel bag along with a bagful of food while Josh followed behind me carrying his own bag and another full of other supplies. Against the wind, we climbed to the second floor and toward Amanda's apartment.

The winter storm was still hours out, yet the temperature had dropped nearly twenty degrees throughout the day. The possibility of snow and ice had shut down most of the state, including schools and most businesses.

"Finding new ways to annoy her has always been our job."

Amanda told us she was prepared for the incoming storm, but her texts were vague and unconvincing. We had to see it for ourselves. Actually, I was going to see it for myself, and Josh was separately going to see it for himself. We ran into each other in the kitchen, both preparing to go to her apartment.

With a bag slung over each of our shoulders, it was clear that was both of our intentions. And the argument that ensued was pointless. One of us didn't deserve her more. We couldn't know who she'd want to see more.

And our usual methods of breaking a tie or making a decision—Rock, Paper, Scissors or flipping a coin—didn't seem sufficient. So rather than spend our time arguing in circles, we reluctantly decided to go together.

Our drive was silent—neither of us knew what to say, although it felt like there was so much we needed to talk about.

We hadn't said a damn word to each other all week. When we'd happened to be in the apartment at the same time, we'd barely managed to grunt a hello or look at each other.

I think we'd all lost our minds in Josh's truck. But I couldn't think straight when Amanda's lips were wrapped around my cock. When she pressed her palm against my growing erection, I was surprised. But when she quickly undid my belt, unzipped my jeans, and slipped my dick out, I was lost to everything else around us.

And it wasn't like we hadn't been in a similar situation before. All things considered, Amanda giving me a blow job in the back of Josh's truck *while* he was driving was relatively tame compared to our threesome at the lake.

But I wasn't expecting to re-create any of the things we did that night at the lake. Ever.

That night and the three of us together were supposed to stay firmly planted in the past. Forgotten.

And then Josh looked at me.

I was so close to coming down Amanda's throat that I'd looked up to see where we were. We'd stopped, but I hadn't paid attention the entire ride. I was thoroughly overwhelmed by each sensation and the waves of unending pleasure. So, when I glanced up and saw we were parked in front of Amanda's apartment, the lights scattered throughout the parking lot doing little to illuminate the cabin, I expected Josh to do anything besides stay in the front seat and watch. His hands mercilessly gripped the wheel, and his jaw ticced with dwindling restraint.

One second, his eyes, which were reflected in the rearview mirror and shrouded in near darkness, were trained on Amanda's head in my lap. But in the next, they were on me.

Again he undid all my expectations because what I saw in his eyes wasn't jealousy. It was the same desire he'd likely seen in mine.

His look was ultimately my undoing. I'd come down Amanda's skilled throat while staring in my best friend's eyes. In that moment, there wasn't anything that could have torn my gaze away from him.

And I'd thought about it every second of every day since then.

*Fuck me.*

"What are you waiting for?" I asked Josh, realizing we were both standing outside of Amanda's apartment staring at the door.

He took a deep breath and glanced at me over his shoulder. The blue of his jacket deepened the blue in his eyes.

I swear I was going crazy.

"What the hell crawled up your ass and died? She's going to be even more pissed if you act like that, so figure your shit out."

"I don't know what you're talking about," I said, shifting uncomfortably and putting a few extra inches between us. It was the longest he'd looked at me in several days.

"I see. Okay, good to know." He turned back to the door like the conversation was over, but I wasn't done.

"What the fuck does that mean?"

He scrubbed a hand through his hair and gripped the back of his neck like I was causing him stress. Didn't he know what he was doing to me?

"You're going the denial route. That's good to know."

"Just shut up and knock on the damn door."

He knocked hard twice, and we waited in complete silence, trying not to shiver against the harsh cold.

Before she even opened the door, Amanda's irritated voice filtered through the wood.

"You've got to be fucking"—she swung the door open and stared us down—"kidding me."

"Nice to see you, too, babe," Josh said and stepped inside after kissing the top of Amanda's head. She stood, mouth agape and eyes wide, as Josh slipped past her. Before I also stepped inside, I gave her a moment to process.

She noticed the duffel bag slung over my shoulder and the other sack I grasped in my opposite hand. Her eyes narrowed in suspicion, but she stepped aside to let me enter when a strong gust of wind pushed down the exposed hallway.

When I walked past her, I also pressed a kiss to the top of her head in nearly the same spot as Josh.

Josh was already unloading groceries when I joined him in the kitchen. Setting my bag down next to his, we methodically worked to unload everything into the pantry and the fridge.

Amanda slid into a barstool across the island and eyed us both curiously like she couldn't totally believe we were actually there. Or was at least uncertain what our intentions were.

She propped her elbows on the granite countertop and rested her chin on her intertwined hands. Only the tips of her fingers were exposed under the sleeves of her oversized gray sweatshirt, and she looked relaxed with her hair precariously sitting on top of her head and her black-framed glasses balanced on her nose.

"Did you say you were coming over?" she finally asked.

"No," Josh and I said in unison.

"So, this is a surprise visit?"

"Yup," Josh answered for the both of us. "Great surprise, right, babe?" The wink he threw her barely melted the tough, icy exterior she'd developed. But I could see a hint of a smile tugging at the corner of her lips.

"It's definitely a surprise. But, great? I'm not so sure about that. Did you both just come over to restock my fridge and my pantry? Not sure if you can tell now with all of *your* food shoved in there, but I *did* go grocery shopping yesterday. I'm not completely unprepared for this winter apocalypse."

"We needed to see for ourselves," I said, tossing one of the empty bags at the bottom of the pantry.

"What kind of men would we be," Josh added, "if we didn't ensure our girl was taken care of during a time like this?"

He'd said it so easily and casually, *"our girl,"* yet the possessiveness was evident in the two little words. But not possession for himself, he'd declared that she was *ours*. Together. The both of us.

My stomach clenched at the thought, and rather than look at Josh, Amanda's eyes found mine across the kitchen. There was a silent question there, and I assumed she was waiting for my reaction.

But I didn't know how to react. There were a myriad of emotions and thoughts and concerns spinning so fast in my head that I couldn't figure out which made the most sense or felt the most right. None of my thoughts had been clear since Josh and I had both decided to pursue Amanda. And every day, they seemed to grow more and more uncertain.

Amanda was waiting for a reaction, and so was I—one that would help me understand exactly how I was feeling and what I wanted to do. Because I couldn't decipher it any more than they could.

So, I decided not to react at all.

"It's supposed to be pretty bad. Possible power outages throughout the city and state. You've got to remember Texas isn't built for this weather. You only had enough water for maybe a day or two."

Josh chuckled to himself and shook his head. I didn't want to know what he was thinking.

"Well, I wasn't preparing to be an extra in *The Day After Tomorrow 2*."

"Isn't that the one with Jake Gyllenhaal?" Josh asked, tossing the flashlights, tea lights and other candles on the counter.

"Yes, such a good movie," Amanda commented.

"We should watch that one tonight, and then maybe that other apocalypse movie with Dwayne Johnson?"

"Umm…" Amanda hesitated, looking between Josh and me and then eyeing our bags with suspicion. "I don't remember inviting the two of you to stay."

"Well, good thing we don't always wait for an invitation."

"Right, because you wouldn't have gotten one," she muttered. "You're both staying here?"

"Yes," we both said simultaneously.

"Together?"

We nodded.

"And that's going to be okay?"

"Why wouldn't it be okay?" I asked, and Amanda raised her eyebrows. She darted her attention to Josh, who was conveniently reorganizing the food in the pantry and had stopped participating in our conversation.

"Who's going to take the couch?" Amanda added, and I tried to suppress my chuckle. Always stirring the pot.

"We'll flip a coin for it," Josh finally added as he closed the pantry door.

With a groan, Amanda tried to slip past me, but I was quicker. I darted my hands out and caught her by the waist, pulling her back into me. My lips easily found the sweet spot beneath her ear, and I pressed a lingering kiss there. The shudder that worked its way through her was enough proof that she wasn't upset at our intrusion.

"We're just worried about you," I whispered into her ear, slipping my fingers an inch or two under her sweatshirt and smiling when I felt the goose bumps on her soft skin. "But if you want us to leave, tell us now, and we'll go. Just say the word."

She hummed, and the sound was likely meant to sound like she was thinking, but it was oddly reminiscent of a suppressed moan.

"I guess you can both stay," she relented as Josh took a seat directly in front of us on the arm of the couch. Amanda reached out her hand in offering, and he quickly took it, lacing their fingers together. "But I get to pick the movies. All of them. Without complaints from either of you."

Josh's smile was immediate, and it was bizarre how watching his face light up made me smile.

He'd always had a contagious smile. I thought it was the dimples.

"Deal," he said. And Amanda leaned her head back to look at me.

"Deal," I repeated with a smile before I closed the short distance between us and pressed my lips to hers. They were soft and yielding, but I didn't push to deepen it, no matter how difficult it was.

We both pulled back with matching smiles, and I squeezed her once before I let her go. The instant my hands released her, she stepped between Josh's legs and kissed him. It was similar to the one we'd just shared—soft and genuine.

And my heart somersaulted in my chest because they looked good together. And I didn't mind it. I wanted to be right there with them.

# TWENTY-EIGHT

Amanda

As the final credits rolled on our first movie, I began scrolling through options for the next movie and asked, "How's Zach holding up?"

"He's doing well. I called him right before we left the apartment. He's excited about the possibility of snow again and gave me a rundown of all the activities he plans to do if there is snow. Sam is freaking out, though. I offered to go over to their house and help them prepare, but apparently, Travis had it covered. I don't think Sam wanted to be stuck with me for possibly days."

He popped another piece of popcorn into his mouth, but I didn't miss the slight shake of his head. He didn't believe Travis had anything covered, and it was probably eating away at him that he wasn't there to take care of his son.

"I'm sure they'll take care of him."

Josh nodded in agreement, very little of the tension dissipating. "I'll call again in the morning, and Sam promised me she would call me if they needed me."

"That's good. I'm sure she will," I said and settled deeper into our mat on the floor.

We'd taken all the blankets I could find in the apartment, excluding those in Adam's room because like hell was I going in there, and had thrown them on the living room floor in front of the couch. Under my specific direction, both of the guys had stacked the pillows and positioned the blankets for the optimal movie-watching experience.

It was what I'd planned to do before they randomly showed up, but it had been more fun with them. And so much more entertaining.

"And the gym is good to go?" I turned to Reed, who was seated on my right. He had his own bowl of popcorn because the boys couldn't share. I was eating out of both of them as my heart desired.

"Yeah, we've wrapped all the pipes and followed every other precaution. One of my managers, Collin, lives in the apartments right around the corner, so if anything, he'll be right there."

"And your parents?"

He laughed and sipped his beer. "They aren't even in the country. Mom said they were somewhere in South America. I think she said Chile until next week. Then I've been told I'm required to be at their house next weekend for dinner."

"I love Mama G." That woman was a saint.

"She loves you, too. Trust me. She actually wanted me to, and I quote, 'bring my date from the other night' with me."

I was confused for a second, then remembered when she called before we made it to the museum. I guess he'd let her know what he was up to and why he declined her calls.

"Oh, so you mean me?"

"Yeah, baby girl, I mean you," he said, throwing an arm over my shoulder and pulling me into him. He placed a kiss on my temple and the smile that slipped across my face was completely out of my control.

"What do you think?" he added with another kiss. "Want to meet the parents?"

I tossed my head back and laughed. "Reed, I've met your

parents hundreds of times. It would hardly be like taking any other girl home to meet your parents."

"You're right, because you're nothing like any other girl."

Josh snorted on my other side, and I glanced over at him. My heart clenched when it dawned on me that Josh's parents were dead. There wasn't anyone in his life—besides his brother—that he'd "introduce" me to, whether it was a pointless introduction or not.

"Is something funny, Sunshine?" Reed quipped, and I groaned internally. With all the fucking fighting, I swore I was going to lose it on them.

Before a full-on argument broke out, I cut in. "It was kind of cheesy, Reed. But either way, I'll be there."

He smiled and kissed me, lingering just long enough to make me want more.

"Speaking of parents," Josh began, slipping his hand under the blanket and finding my upper thigh. "Adam made it to California before all of this shit started blowing through?"

For a second, I lost the ability to speak. Reed's hand ran idle circles along my shoulder, which was now exposed since I traded my sweatshirt for a tank top, and Josh's hand was squeezing my thigh. His thumb dragged back and forth against the soft fabric.

"Yes, he texted me a few hours ago that he touched down and he'd gotten a ride to their house. He's already in love with it, so I'm sure he'll come back here making plans to move there."

"Would that be the worst thing? Get him away from all the shit he can't seem to sort out?" Reed asked.

Although that seemed like the best idea for my sanity, it was the exact opposite. With Adam in the same city, I had—or at least pretended I did—some sort of control or say. It was easier to stage interventions when his idiocy reached new heights or he needed me to bail him out.

It would have been infinitely more difficult to get him out of trouble if he was thousands of miles away.

"I don't know if I could handle that."

"Maybe," Josh added, giving my thigh another reassuring squeeze, "a little independence would do him some good?"

It was a question, but also not one at the same time. They were both fairly outspoken on my relationship with my brother —I was too overprotective of a kid that didn't give a fuck. I knew they only had my best interest in mind, but that didn't change mine.

Being his big sister meant I was there. No matter what.

"Anyway," I said, immediately changing the subject. "What do we want to watch next? I'm thinking a romantic comedy."

They both stifled their sighs, and I smiled for real.

"Can I?" Josh asked, holding out his hand for the remote.

Hesitantly, I placed it in his hand and waved for him to continue scrolling. "I get full veto power, though," I confirmed, and he nodded.

"He's going to pick something fucking sappy," Reed murmured next to me, and Josh's hand, still on my thigh and dangerously close to a place I was eager for him to be, tensed.

*Fuck.*

"If I do, it'll be because it's a good movie. *And* Amanda has to agree, remember?"

"Okay, how about this? You pick one, I'll pick one and then Amanda can choose."

Josh scoffed and continued scrolling. "She already agreed to let me pick, so why don't you just sit over there and eat your damn popcorn quietly? What was it you said to me the other night? That you'd pay me to keep my thoughts to myself. Well, I've got a twenty with your name on it in my wallet if you do just that."

"Okay, well, I think a romantic comedy sounds great, and we're going to pick..." I yanked the remote out of Josh's hand and scrolled quickly through the section. "This one. Oh, perfect, I love Sandra Bullock."

Neither of them commented on my choice, and I tried my

best to relax back into my comfy cocoon, even with the tension hanging around us.

After witnessing them argue for days, I'd finally come up with a plan to ease the tension. Or at least I hoped it would because if it didn't ease the tension, it was bound to make it a million times worse—there was no in-between.

I'd dissected and scrutinized each argument since they began a few weeks before. It wasn't a coincidence that they hadn't been able to see eye to eye on virtually anything after they agreed to the stupid dates. The last thing they agreed on was pursuing me. And since then, tensions have been flaring.

The friends that never fought were constantly bickering, and at first, I thought it was because of me. But I was beginning to believe that it had more to do with them.

My plan was to shatter all their walls. The start of which had been my unexpected blow job in the back of Josh's truck.

You know, sometimes the best things in life are unexpected— orgasms being some of the best.

And whether phase one of my plan had been a success, I still wasn't sure. But that night, with the wind howling and the storm threatening to push Texas into a deeper winter than we'd ever experienced, seemed like the best night to initiate phase two.

# TWENTY-NINE

Amanda

"I THINK OUR NEXT MOVIE NEEDS TO BE SOMETHING FAST-PACED. Something with action and drama," Reed said, trying to feign that he wasn't interested in the romance that was nearly over. But I'd caught him once or twice trying to slyly wipe at his eyes or shake the emotions off.

"You can say that you like the movie, Reed. It won't hurt your fragile masculinity to *like* the movie."

He pinched my side and gave me an unamused look. "I *do* like the movie, babe. But I also like action. Sue me."

I shrugged and glanced at Josh, who was grinning at us both. "I guess I'll allow it."

As the final credits began to roll, Reed pulled out his phone and sighed. I leaned over his shoulder and watched Collin's name scroll across the screen.

"Sorry, I have to take this."

I nodded and tried not to look too excited that the perfect opportunity had finally presented itself.

"Go ahead. Josh and I are going to grab more blankets. I think there's some in my closet." Quickly, I leaped from the floor and reached for Josh's hand. The two of them shared a confused look as Reed answered the phone, brushing it off to tend to whatever Collin needed.

"I thought we already grabbed everything you had," Josh argued as I tugged him down the hallway.

Standing in the middle of my room, which had stayed rather clean, much to my surprise, I could still hear the low murmur of Reed's voice. When I turned back to Josh, his wide blue-green eyes were cautious and slowly appraising my disheveled state.

"Okay, what the hell is going on?"

"We're not getting pillows or blankets."

He rolled his eyes and shook his head. "Yeah, I got that much, but it doesn't answer my question."

I took a step closer to him, closing the short distance between us with two sure strides. With my front pressed up against the hard planes of his chest and stomach, a warmth settled in my lower stomach. As my hands found purchase on his shoulders, he reflexively gripped my waist, steadying me on my toes.

Pressed up onto my toes, there were still a few inches of height difference, but I'd managed to close the gap enough that I could ghost my lips over his. Teasing the possibility of a kiss by letting my breath linger over his parted lips for a short moment.

I pulled back just enough to look him in the eyes. "Do you trust me?"

His nod was instant, and his answer of "Yes" was rough.

"I think," I began, tightening my grip on his shoulders, "we need to do something to relieve the tension between the three of us."

Watching for any change in his expression, and not finding one, I continued, "And I think that we"—I motioned between us —"can do just that."

There was a slight furrow in his brow as he pondered my proposal carefully. It wasn't the entirety of my plan, but it was the first step I needed him to get on board with.

When he didn't try to interrupt me or tell me to fuck off, I took that as silent agreement.

"You remember the other night in the truck?" At that, he tensed under my hands, but I pushed on, hoping the other details would relieve some of his hesitance. "I want to do that again, but with you. I want Reed to walk in here and see me with you. Or at least, that's how I want it to start. I think it will push him to open up. I think it'll be good for all of us."

He was still visibly tense, and I tried to appear calm and patient as he thought. But internally, I was hoping he'd hurry because any moment Reed could walk into the room and it wouldn't work. I prayed Collin was a talker.

Ever so slowly, Josh nodded, and I sighed in relief. "Okay, but I need to ask. Is this—" He cleared his throat, and anxiety replaced the arousal in my stomach. "Are you using me to get Reed? To make him jealous? Is it him? Because if it is, I just need to know. I'm not strong enough to tell you no, but I need to know going into it if—"

"No, Josh," I cut him off, rushing out the words. My heart broke at the concern marring his features. Concern that I'd put there, diminishing the light and hope in his eyes. "I want you, too. And this isn't me choosing at all. This is me... this is me trying to break down the walls that we're all so eager to build."

His torment waned slightly, and so I said the only thing I knew with my entire body and heart. Something I'd only recently given myself permission to contemplate. "I need you, Josh. I *need*... both of you."

Out of everything I was feeling, of that, I was certain—that I needed them both. I wanted them both again.

Finally, a smile graced his full lips, and I couldn't stand not to kiss him. An unfamiliar optimism coursed through me. But as quickly as our kiss began, Josh pulled back and pushed a few stray strands of hair that had fallen from my bun back away from my face.

"Do you want to make a bet about how long it takes for him to break?"

"Ten minutes."

"Five," he countered and instead of shaking on our bet, we sealed it with a kiss. A kiss that led us to my nearly empty bed. We collapsed onto it, all tongues and lips and teeth. He smelled like the beach after it rained. And I wanted to drag it out and feel all the ways Josh could touch me and wind me up. He was so good with his hands and long, skilled fingers, but we were on a time limit.

And I had a feeling we'd have plenty of opportunities in the future to take it slow.

I didn't let him settle between my legs like he wanted to. Instead, I slipped under his arm and pushed his shoulder. He landed on his back with a curious smile and I planted myself between his thighs. He propped himself up with a decorative pillow we'd left behind earlier.

Until I began fumbling with his belt, I didn't realize my hands were shaking slightly.

I'd been so confident in my speech to Josh because I knew if he sensed any amount of hesitation, he would've told me we could find another way. Which might have been possible, but the plan I'd concocted felt like the quickest way.

I knew both of these men better than anyone, and my gut told me to do it. My gut told me to suck Josh's cock and put on a hell of a show for Reed.

My fingers pulled the button of his jeans free, but his hands stopped me.

"Take your shirt off," he said, our eyes meeting. "And then your sweats. It'll be a much better picture when he walks in here, your ass up in the air while my cock is in your mouth."

I liked his thinking and quickly shed my loose tank top, thankful I'd put on one of my more attractive sports bras when I changed. It was a black front-zip bra that pushed my boobs up higher than normal.

I tossed my shirt to the side of the bed and ungracefully yanked my sweats off next.

"God, you're fucking beautiful," Josh murmured as I worked his zipper down and slid his jeans off his legs.

I smiled under his praise and pressed my palm against his large erection. He was already straining against his black boxer briefs, and he hissed at the pressure, pushing up into my hand.

As his body eagerly searched for more, I heard Reed's conversation a little louder at the front of the apartment. I knew he was nearing the end of the call, so I pulled the boxer briefs off at the same time Josh tugged his shirt over his head.

I licked my lips at the sight of him—the head dripping with precum and the veins running along his shaft, thick and pulsing.

My fingers wrapped around the base of his strong, proud cock, and I let my tongue sweep up his slit, licking the bead of precum and relishing the salty taste. And as much as I wanted to tease him, I wanted him in my mouth.

I sucked the thick tip, swirling my tongue around it before pushing him deeper. I found my pace easily, letting my hand move up and down in tandem with my mouth. He was soft yet heavy against my tongue, and his fingers appeared against my cheek, tracing the outline of my lips stretched around him.

His touch was reverent, and I was lost to the motion and feeling until footsteps sounded behind me.

Josh stiffened underneath me, but I didn't stop. I ran my free hand along his thigh, hoping my touch was soothing as I lifted my eyes to watch his face. He was in a stare down with Reed, and I tried not to smile around his dick.

"Well, this doesn't look like grabbing more blankets and pillows," Reed said. I assumed he'd stopped in the doorway based on how far away his voice still sounded.

With a louder-than-necessary pop, I popped off of Josh and threw him a wink before looking over my shoulder at Reed.

My breath caught at the sight behind me. He was cloaked in darkness, leaning casually against the doorframe with his arms crossed over his chest. There was a playful smirk tugging at his lips, and his eyes were hooded.

"There's a chair in the corner: a front-row seat."

"Is that so?" he asked, raising one dark eyebrow in question.

"It is," I said, turning back to Josh, who watched me slip my tongue over his head and lick up his shaft from balls to tip in one long swipe. "It's going to be great. You won't want to miss it."

I heard Reed shift behind me, and I sent up a silent prayer that he'd play along. The man loved a challenge, so when I peeked to my left and saw him relaxed back into the chair, I wasn't surprised.

The man dwarfed my little pale-gray chair. But he made do by bracing his arms on the short armrests and reclining back slightly.

When I was sure he was settled and willing to play along, I got back to work.

Turning all of my attention back to Josh, I took him to the back of my mouth in one movement. He hit the back of my throat, triggering my gag reflex, but I quickly swallowed around it. Pressing my tongue against the underside of his cock, I shifted my hand to his balls.

One squeeze and his labored breathing and quiet words that I could barely make out over the rain splattering against the windows exploded into a loud groan. It reverberated through the quiet space, and I heard Reed rustle behind me.

"*Fuck*," Josh pleaded as his fingers found their way through my hair. He tugged out the scrunchie holding it all back, and it fell in waves around my face. Quickly, he gathered it and fisted the strands all in one hand.

"She has the best mouth," Reed said in a voice riddled with restraint. I imagined he was having the hardest time keeping his hands to himself—probably fisting them against his thighs to keep from joining in.

"Yes," Josh hissed in response. "So warm and eager, and *God*, her fucking tongue." Just for that, I ran my tongue around his head, then up and down his shaft. His deep groan was my reward, and I returned it with a moan of my own around his cock.

There was a slight bite of pain at my scalp, where Josh tugged at my hair, guiding me up and down his length. The pain was minor and quickly twisted and morphed into a pleasure that only added to my growing arousal.

Having both of these men at my mercy and so entranced by what I was doing lit my entire body on fire.

"My favorite is when she pushes me all the way to the back of her throat and gags around my cock." Reed's confession wasn't news to me, it was the trump card I knew I could play anytime to get him there quickly. "What do you think, Josh?"

The added question made Josh tense once again. The hand in my hair fisted tighter and pulled harder, burning my scalp and eliciting an unexpected moan from my throat.

"Mmm," was Josh's only response as he teetered on the edge of bliss.

"There you go, force her deeper," Reed instructed, and without hesitation, Josh complied. I opened my eyes to find him watching me with heavy-lidded eyes as he pushed me farther down his cock.

"Don't stop until she starts gagging."

He'd reached that point where he was deep enough my gag reflex was triggered. He pulled my head up only half an inch, just to push up again and again, hitting the tip of his cock against the back of my throat.

Tears streamed down my face and spit ran down my chin and gathered around the base of him where I still held him loosely in my hand.

Josh mumbled incoherent words and groans, and with each thrust, I could feel him barreling toward a release I wasn't yet ready to let him have.

"You're doing so good, Amanda. He can't even form words anymore." There were a few seconds where all you could hear was the wet sounds of my gagging combined with Josh's heavy sighs and groans. And then Reed added, "I think he's going to come. Do you want him to come yet?"

Immediately I pushed up against Josh's hold on my head and replaced my mouth with my hand, stroking him slowly. He groaned in frustration, but I smiled.

"No," I said breathlessly. "Not yet."

Before I had a chance to think through my next move, the desire clouding Josh's eyes shifted. It wasn't completely replaced but was overshadowed by a mischievous glint. In one swift motion, he reached forward, gripped my hips, and tugged me closer.

"I'm going to win this bet," he whispered into my ear before running the tip of his tongue down my neck and nipping at my collarbone. "Turn around." There wasn't room for argument in his voice, and he said it loud enough that Reed could also hear the command.

There was a flutter of nerves in my stomach, but they disappeared as quickly as they emerged. Eagerly, I pressed a kiss to Josh's lips and turned.

Knowing Reed was seated in the corner watching us was one thing, but it was another to see him. In the shadowed corner, he was comfortably reclined like a king presiding over his people. His face was mostly hidden, as was most of his upper half, but his legs were spread in front of him.

And when I noticed his belt open and his jeans unzipped, my breath caught. One of his hands gripped the armrest with immense force while the other had disappeared into his jeans.

Behind me, Josh scooted closer to the headboard and pulled me back into him, positioning me between his legs and in the perfect position for Reed to see everything.

"Look at what you've done to him," Josh whispered into my ear. Every tiny hair over my body stood at attention as his warm breath washed over me.

"What *we've* done to him," I corrected, and he chuckled.

"Did sucking my cock make you wet? Did Reed *watching* you suck my cock make you wet?" Josh said before nipping at my ear. His hands were firm against my hips, and I squirmed against him, wanting him to touch me anywhere and everywhere.

"Yes," I breathed, and I heard a shuffle in front of me. My eyes had fallen closed, and I didn't have the strength to open them again.

"Let's show him how wet you are." Josh's thumbs hooked under the lace fabric of my thong, and I helped him remove it. Like we'd done with the rest of our clothes, he tossed them on the floor beside the bed and forced my legs apart.

Each of his hands squeezed my inner thighs and pushed them open, baring and presenting me to the other man only a few feet away. Reed sucked in a breath and mumbled a curse the moment my legs parted. His hand on the armrest twitched, and the smile that tugged at my lips probably looked maniacal.

Josh ran tender hands along the sensitive skin of my inner thighs. He massaged the skin at my knees, only to gingerly dance his hands lower and closer to my pussy, throbbing and needy. But he continued the torture, getting to the apex of my thighs, only to turn and move upward once again.

A depraved moan ripped from my throat and both men chuckled darkly.

"Is someone needy?" Josh asked in a hushed voice directly into my ear.

A nod was all I could muster as my head fell back on his shoulder and I looked up at him. He brushed the hair from my face and traced the outline of my features—outlining my eyebrows, running his finger down the bridge of my nose and pausing for a few seconds to admire my lips. His eyes watched his fingers, but when they finally returned to mine, there was a depth to them I hadn't seen. The look they bore nearly stole my breath.

When we finally disconnected, I found it hard to breathe, but

Josh immediately pushed his hands lower, sweeping over my collarbones and over the tops of my breasts.

*Please take it off,* I thought as he paused at the zipper.

Before he did, though, he glanced up at Reed and my eyes followed. He was in the exact same position he was in before— slowly losing the modicum of control he still retained.

"Show me," Reed requested, and like before, Josh answered by slowly lowering the zipper and letting it fall open.

"*Fuck*," came from the corner, and I took a second to lean forward and tug the bra free. A woman could get used to that kind of response.

My body was alive under their attention and praise. Nothing had ever come near feeling the way it did when it was the three of us.

I sucked in a sharp breath when Josh's hands cupped my breasts, pushing them together and massaging them somewhat roughly. My head fell back once again, landing on his firm chest and in the perfect spot for me to press an open-mouthed kiss to his neck. His pulse was quick under my lips.

Shifting slightly, I attempted to litter more kisses along his neck but sucked in a sharp breath, instead turning my attention forward. He'd pinched each of my nipples between his fingers, and it was like a straight line to my clit, which was already pulsing uncontrollably.

"*Josh*," I pleaded, pushing up into his hands as he stroked. There must have been something in my voice, or he'd finally had enough teasing because it was less than a second before his fingers were at my pussy. A finger—one long, skillful finger— ran down the center of me.

God, I was so wet and ready for whatever he wanted to throw at me. Never had I felt the need to come so badly from one minor touch.

I'd gone into the entire situation prepared to be in charge. I was prepared to coax both of the men to the three of us being together once again. But under Reed's intense stare and Josh's touch, it didn't seem necessary anymore.

"How wet is she?" Reed asked, and my eyes fluttered open at the new edge to his voice.

My heart stuttered when I saw the sight before me. Reed's full attention was on where Josh's fingers teased my clit in small, languid circles, and I'd missed him freeing his cock from his pants. It was hard and thick in his big hand, and he stroked himself at the same pace Josh moved his fingers over me. The circles he played against my clit were purposeful and slow, as were each of Reed's strokes.

It was the tease, the warning before the explosion.

"She's so fucking wet and ready. Aren't you, babe?"

I think I nodded in response, but I was too far gone to really know.

I do, however, remember Josh's fingers stopping for long enough that an irritated groan slipped free of my lips. But I wasn't without him for long.

His left arm banded over my chest and grasped my opposite shoulder, effectively holding me against him and keeping me in place. Then he whispered into my ear, "Hook your legs over mine. Show Reed how wet and needy our girl is."

There was no hesitation in my movements. I placed my feet on either side of his legs that were spread around me and opened myself up for Reed's scrutiny. The position left nothing to the imagination, and I enjoyed the hard press of Josh's hard cock in my back. It was proof that he was enjoying it as much as me and Reed, which did more than I could comprehend to further heighten my arousal.

Because if the three of us were going to be together, we all had to enjoy it equally.

"Open," Josh ordered, pressing two fingers to my lips. Greedily, I sucked them into my mouth and treated them as I would have his cock—weaving my tongue between them and lavishing them with attention.

A deep chuckle escaped Josh's lips the moment he pulled his fingers free. He took no time returning between my legs, resuming the tight circles over my clit.

I bucked up into his hand. It felt so good, but I wanted more. I wanted all of it.

With a final pinch to my clit, he ran his drenched fingers over my opening and plunged the two I'd just had in my mouth inside of me. I cried out at the intrusion and was overcome by sensations.

His fingers pressed into me again and again, hooking up and grazing the spot that made my eyes nearly cross while he sucked and nipped at my neck. Knowing exactly what I needed, he kept his thumb poised on my clit, applying a delicious pressure as he rubbed.

The sounds of my arousal and moans filtered through the air, and I suddenly had the urge to look at Reed. My eyes had fallen closed the moment Josh's fingers entered me. But I forced them open to see the dark figure in the corner.

His hand on his cock had stilled, and his breathing appeared labored. The knowledge that it was his eyes on me while Josh skillfully and forcefully coaxed my orgasm closer was nearly too much to bear. His eyes on me—his careful, unwavering scrutiny —felt as physical as Josh's touch.

I could feel his eyes everywhere, and in their wake, they left an acute and intoxicating desire. A desire that Josh stoked higher and higher with his hands and fingers and mouth.

"*Fuck*, Josh, that feels so good. Don't—don't stop," I stuttered the words, but even my own voice sounded so foreign and distant.

The chair hit the wall—that's the first thing I heard—when Reed's razor-thin restraint finally snapped.

"Fuck it. I need to taste you." He approached me like a predator would its prey. Dropping down onto the bed between my spread legs, he gripped under my hips and tugged me lower.

There was a needful glimmer in his amber eyes that made me shiver.

Josh's arm stayed around my chest, and he whispered where only I could hear, "Look what you did. He looks starved."

I shuddered a breath because he was right. Reed peered down at my pussy like he'd never seen anything more mouth-watering.

"Spread her open for me." Reed's eyes shifted to Josh behind me. Josh hesitated, and although it wasn't more than a second before he complied, I noted it.

Josh's legs pushed farther out, taking mine with them and spreading me farther. But the man took it to another level, using his fingers to spread my lower lips, opening my pussy and presenting me to Reed.

So slowly I thought I would combust, Reed's eyes slid from my pussy to my face, then behind me to Josh, whose breath against my ear was hot and quick. Like he was barely holding on to the control Reed just disregarded.

Reed held Josh's eyes for a second, then, with a smile, slid his attention back to my face. When his tongue finally appeared from between his perfect full lips, I was frozen and not nearly ready enough. He licked me from bottom to top, savoring the first taste with an appreciative groan.

My jaw fell slack while every muscle in my body tightened. Swirling his tongue around my pulsing clit, he flattened it against me and went for it.

His hands were unforgiving against the tender skin of my inner thighs as he pressed them wider yet. And his tongue and lips and teeth lapped and sucked at every part of me. All while his best friend held me open and made sure my pussy was easily accessible.

It was utterly erotic.

With each plunge of his tongue inside of me, I felt myself coming apart. His tongue was eager as he penetrated me as far as he could. Then he licked upward where he'd press against my clit and suck it into his mouth.

And then Josh began to murmur into my ear. He kept me flush against his chest, his forearm pressing into my neck and inhibiting my airway enough that the pain elicited a new type of pleasure. One that was depraved and sought the danger.

Josh's words fell over me and spurred me onward, infinitely closer to the release I could feel spreading through me.

"So fucking beautiful spread open for us."

"Open your eyes. Watch him eat your pussy."

"You're doing such a good job. Such a dirty girl. Yes, moan and tell him how much you're enjoying it."

"Are you going to come on Reed's tongue?"

They were trying to kill me. Reed's fingers teased my opening as his tongue continued to assault my clit. And when he finally pushed two inside, I immediately clamped down around them. My impending orgasm was no longer on the horizon, it was tight in my stomach and controlling my entire body.

Reed growled against me, and Josh held me tighter to him, his erection still incredibly hard in my back. He was whispering something to me again, but I couldn't hear his exact words.

As Reed's fingers curved inside of me, his teeth grazed my clit, and I was gone. One of my hands found Josh's thigh on my right side, and I used it to keep me on the bed while the other gripped Reed's hair. I held him to me, writhing and shaking as I rode his face.

All the while, the man between my legs didn't let up. He sucked and licked, keeping a steady rhythm with his fingers as the world exploded around me. The orgasm overwhelmed my entire body, consuming me in unabashed pleasure.

Sounds I'd never heard myself make escaped me.

And each wave was euphoric.

I might have blacked out because I didn't remember Reed removing his fingers and climbing up toward my face. But when

I opened my eyes, there he was in front of me, smiling crookedly but with a heat in his eyes I wanted to fall into.

"So fucking sweet. Watching you come is my new favorite thing." Then he kissed me, brushing his tongue into my mouth, and a desire stirred within me again.

The answer was yes, they were trying to kill me.

"You going to take us both?" Josh asked while Reed's tongue was still in my mouth.

I pulled away and turned my head, my nod of agreement immediate. I'd prepared for that moment. And the thrill of being between the two of them sent a shiver down my spine. I tilted my head farther back, and Josh quickly captured my lips. His hand drifted up my chest and throat before cupping my cheek and deepening the kiss. A moan I had no control of slipped into his mouth and someone growled.

Realizing it was Reed, I smiled against Josh's lips.

"I need to be inside of you," Josh said, barely breaking our kiss.

"Yes, please."

He gripped my hips and flipped me around like I was weightless. My knees planted on either side of his legs, we were chest to chest, and I could see the effect of it all on him. His pupils were dilated, and there was an overwhelming hunger in his eyes. Like he was a prisoner to it.

Then he touched me like he was touching me for the first time again. He cupped my cheek and pressed his lips to mine as he slid his cock back and forth through my wetness, pausing over my clit.

"*Please*," I pleaded. I needed him—them—inside of me like I hadn't needed anything before.

"You sound so pretty when you beg," Reed commented from behind me.

And I nearly combusted when Josh lined himself up with my opening. His fingers teased a trail down my jaw, my neck and over my chest before coming to rest beneath my breast as the other hand gripped his cock and he positioned himself beneath me. My hips shifted, and I began to lower myself onto him until Reed's hands gripped my hips and guided me the rest of the way down onto Josh's waiting cock.

He filled me completely, and although they'd prepared me with their fingers and an orgasm, that was nothing compared to feeling his thick length. It was the best kind of stretch.

With him buried deep inside of me, I stilled and gave my body a moment to get used to his size. Reed's hands tensed on my hips, and I could feel the heat of him at my back. They both gave me a second, then his hands flexed, urging me to move over his friend.

I braced myself against Josh, my hands gripping his shoulders as I leaned forward and lifted my hips. I slid up his cock until only the tip was inside of me, and his resounding moan was exactly what I'd hoped for. When I let my hips fall once again, plunging him into me, we both groaned in unison as he grazed my cervix.

"Fuck, yes. Ride him," Reed instructed, guiding me up and down his friend's cock.

Josh's hands were higher, braced around my rib cage as I bounced up and down. Every so often, I'd change it up, grinding down harder onto him and relishing the pressure against my clit. And each time he grazed that place deep inside of me, a bolt of pleasure careened through me.

Josh's jaw was slack, but the hunger in his eyes hadn't diminished. It grew the longer I rode him.

"Are you going to let me in here?" Reed asked as his fingers spread me apart and brushed between my cheeks. When he paused against the place I'd only ever allowed the two of them, I pushed back into his touch. My walls clenched around Josh at the thought of taking them both together again.

"*Oh fuck.*" Josh sucked in a breath beneath me. "Yes, she is," he clarified, feeling my reaction to even the mention of the possibility of having both of them at once.

Reed held his thumb in front of my mouth and pressed it against my lower lip, forcing me to open. "Suck," he instructed. And I did, giving him the same attention I had to Josh earlier.

He didn't let me go too far, though, before he pulled it from my mouth and pressed it against my ass. Once, twice, he circled the entrance and ran his other hand adoringly up my back as he slowly pushed inside. To give him better access, I leaned forward over Josh, who took the opportunity to suck one of my nipples into his mouth. He continued his deep, long strokes up into me and easily distracted me from the uncomfortable feeling I knew would come.

But I let myself relax into it, knowing that neither of the men inside of me wanted to do anything besides make me feel good. And the uncomfortable sensation would eventually give way to insurmountable pleasure.

"There you go, let me in," Reed murmured, pushing past the second ring of muscles. Stilling, he let me adjust to the feeling before he pulled out and pushed back again. And quickly, the odd feeling morphed. I continued moving up and down on Josh as Reed moved with me.

"More," I pleaded, and both men chuckled.

"Lube?" Reed asked, and I pointed to the bedside table. He leaned over, pulled the top drawer open, and paused behind me.

Instead of coming back with the lube, he had Patrick, my vibrator, in his hand. He eyed me but put it back before he retrieved the small bottle of lube I was so glad I'd kept there.

"That," he said, referring to Patrick, "will be used later."

I nearly made a smart-ass comment, but it died on my tongue when I heard the snap of the lid to the bottle and two fingers prodding my entrance. Not giving me as much time as before, he pressed inside of me.

As he pushed deeper, touching a place he hadn't yet reached, all thoughts evaporated from my mind. His fingers scissoring inside of me, stretching and preparing me. But I was done waiting.

"I'm ready. I'm there. Just please get inside of me." I wasn't above begging when it came to pleasure. I knew what I wanted and was more than prepared to ask for it.

"Yes, ma'am," Reed quipped and withdrew his fingers. Immediately I missed his warmth but was greeted by the sound of the lube bottle again. Behind me, Reed prepared himself while I focused on Josh underneath me.

I slanted my mouth over his, and we melted into one another. He pulled me down onto his chest and tangled a hand into my hair. We both fought for control, our tongues dueling and teeth scraping, but I willingly gave it over when Reed's cocked nudged me.

His hand resumed his adoring touch down my back, leaving a warm trail in its wake as he pressed forward. Josh continued his assault on my mouth, sucking on my bottom lip and biting. All the while, his hand, with its skillful fingers, slipped between our bodies and found my clit.

He strummed it and slowed his strokes until he was buried deep inside of me, only pulsing up into me.

The moment Reed's cock breached the tight outer muscles, I couldn't help but tense. His dick was so much bigger than the two fingers he'd used to prepare me, even with my previous preparation, but I wanted to feel them both inside of me. So, I focused on Josh's fingers on my clit and tugging at my hair. And his tongue licking at mine.

"You're doing so good, beautiful. Taking us both at once," Reed said. His voice sounded as adoring as his touch felt against my back. With each thrust, he paused, giving my body enough time to relax and welcome him before he pushed in farther.

There was a heat blazing through me with every inch. But with the pressure and tightness that came, I forced myself to relax. I wanted it. I wanted them both at the same time, and a little pressure wasn't going to stop me.

"*Holy fuck,*" Josh cried, breaking our kiss. "I can feel you."

"Yes," Reed responded in a tight voice. "*God,* you're so tight."

And then he pushed the rest of the way in. Josh stilled underneath me except for the pressure he kept against my clit, and Reed froze behind me.

There was pain mixed with the pleasure, and it magnified everything. With both of them inside of me, I wasn't sure where one or the other began or ended. And I couldn't care. I breathed deeply and welcomed any and every feeling they'd give me.

"How do you feel?" Josh asked, cupping my cheek.

A smile danced across my lips, and I stared into his ocean eyes.

"Full. Now, fuck me."

# THIRTY

Josh

With both of us buried inside of Amanda, I could feel Reed's cock between the thin wall separating Amanda's cunt and her ass.

Above me, Amanda's face contorted momentarily in an expression that bordered actual pain, but quickly it morphed. The deep lines between her eyebrows smoothed and her jaw went slack.

And then she demanded that we fuck her.

My eyes met Reed's from over her shoulder and the uninhibited desire I felt in my blood I saw reflected back to me in his eyes.

Simultaneously we both pulled out and slammed back into her. She cried out a string of unintelligible expletives followed by a low moan. And then we did it again, slowly picking up speed.

She was tight and warm, and each time I grazed her G-spot as Reed plunged into her from behind, she grew more wet and urgent. Her nails dug into the skin on my chest, and I welcomed the bite of pain.

Our hands were all over her, not leaving a piece of skin

untouched. And the moment I suctioned my lips around one of her dusky-pink nipples, she tossed her head back, thrusting her chest into my mouth. I licked around the perimeter of it, enjoying the sweetness of her skin before I bit down on the rigid peak.

"*Yes*," she cried. Her nails sure to leave behind marks when we were through, but I'd wear them proudly. "More. *More*."

"Come for us." Reed's voice was deep and strained. And the command made her pussy flutter around me. "You love having both of our cocks buried inside of you. Don't you, dirty girl?"

She speared herself with my cock and pushed back into Reed, chasing an imminent orgasm I could feel in the way her walls strangled my cock. The sounds of our fucking, skin slapping, and heavy breathing filled the room and drowned out the cadence of the storm outside.

Reed tightened his bruising grip on her hips as I massaged her breasts, switching my mouth to the other nipple. And together, we sent her over the edge. Coming apart around us both, her back arched, and she stilled with both of us buried deep inside of her.

She cried out, nearly screaming. But I continued to pulse up into her as Reed did the same.

Her release coated my cock and made slipping into her that much easier. We fucked her through each wave of pleasure, and I was barely holding it together. The best thing I'd ever seen was her face when she came. The best thing I'd ever heard were her moans and the sound of her screaming our names—both of them —as she came apart.

She rocked with pleasure for several seconds, and I did my best to hold off my own release.

"Don't come," Reed demanded. Startled, I glanced at him over Amanda's shoulder, and sure enough, he was staring down at me. "She gets one more."

Not used to taking commands in the bedroom, I hesitated. But something in me wanted to agree.

The taut muscles in his chest rippled with both the force of fucking Amanda but also the restraint of holding himself together. And the sweat that collected on the surface of his tanned skin glistened in the little slivers of light coming from between the blinds. His face was contorted in pleasure, similar to Amanda's, but his black hair tumbled forward against his forehead and skimmed his eyebrows.

He looked good fucking our girl.

I swallowed thickly and shuddered when Amanda's pussy fluttered around me again, but then I nodded.

"You gonna give us one more, babe? I know you can." I barely recognized my own rough voice.

"I don't know if I can," she argued breathlessly and attempted to fall onto my chest. But Reed caught her around the waist before she could. With one toned arm around her middle, he tugged her up and pressed her back to his chest, cutting off my view of most of his body but replacing it with Amanda. Her tits bounced as we both fucked her mercilessly.

Looking down at me through hooded eyes, she licked her swollen lips.

She was a fucking siren pinned between us, and she was loving every second of it.

Reed's hands palmed her breasts as he licked up her neck, and my own squeezed her thighs. She enjoyed the pain, that much was clear in the way her eyelids fluttered closed when I gripped her legs with bruising force.

But they immediately widened when Reed's hand continued up between her breasts and closed around her throat. The moment he squeezed, Amanda responded with a throaty, strangled moan.

"You're going to come again. You're going to cream all over Josh's cock and then you're going to lick him clean." I picked up the pace of my strokes at the image—her on her knees for me once again, with Reed watching nearby.

She nodded, and he rewarded her with another squeeze. Her

responsiveness was addictive. Each touch or word out of one of our mouths was like an electric shock to her body.

"Such a dirty girl for us," I said, testing my theory and proving myself right when she whimpered and clawed down my stomach. Something we had in common was the pain—how it heightened every other pleasurable sensation.

Reed grinned behind Amanda, and my attention was torn between the two. They were both breathing hard and lost in the depths of pleasure, but they also looked so good together, each other's foils in so many ways. Reed's dark hair, muscled physique and tanned skin were the perfect contradiction to Amanda's blonde locks, curvy yet small frame and creamy white skin.

They were quite the pair. And watching them enjoy each other, and me, twisted my stomach. There was a connection between the three of us that we'd tempted the first time around. We'd only gotten a taste and now that we'd gone back for seconds, I didn't know if I could return to the way things were before.

As I watched them, Reed leaned to Amanda's ear, not pausing his deep, methodical strokes for a moment, as he whispered to her. Between my own labored breathing and the sleet pounding the window, I couldn't hear what he said, but I witnessed the small smile pull at Amanda's lips.

Feeling slightly left out and unable to control myself, I licked my thumb and pressed it to her clit. She jolted as I circled the pulsing spot and her hand struck forward, closing around my throat. Shocked by the move, my thumb stopped and my thrusts stuttered.

They both wore twin conspiratorial smiles. Reed had told her to choke me.

There was still a hint of a smile on Amanda's lips until Reed slammed into her harder, keeping her upright and pressed against him. My eyes shifted to him.

His eyes held mine and then narrowed on Amanda's small

hand around my neck. It wasn't doing much—her hand was too tiny to fit even halfway around my neck—but the intention was still enough. Amanda was dominant in the bedroom but enjoyed being made submissive. She liked being used but was vocal about her pleasure.

And in that moment, it was like she was the conduit—like Reed's hand was actually around my throat.

As Reed's hungry eyes swapped between staring at Amanda's hand and my eyes, my own attention ping-ponged between the two of them as our thrusts became chaotic.

Amanda's hand tightened around my throat, slightly restricting my airway, and I increased the pressure against her clit, feeling my own release barreling down my spine and pulling at my balls. She cried out and a second later, she tensed between us once again and was overwhelmed by an earth-shattering orgasm. Between us, she writhed on our cocks, searching for more friction as her beautiful face contorted.

Her second orgasm was somehow stronger than the first and she strangled my cock. The tightening of her pussy made it exponentially easier to feel Reed's substantial length rubbing inside of her. The thought that only a small wall separated us made my balls draw up tight.

His cock was so close to mine and the idea was maddening.

Amanda panted with the aftershocks of her release and then I felt the change.

With her third release, our girl was sated. And so we both began the chase for our own. Our thrusts, although still in sync, were harder and faster.

Amanda collapsed onto my chest, and she buried her head into the crook of my neck, where she licked and sucked at my skin. Her tits pressed against me nearly had me flying over the edge, but it was even better when Reed also lowered himself over us. The added pressure pushed her harder against me.

His hand planted next to my head and my eyes caught on the veins pulsing under the skin of his forearms. My attention followed the shape of his defined arms, over his chest, and up his neck until I found his eyes.

There wasn't a second's hesitation before his mouth was on mine.

My brain short-circuited for a second, and I couldn't tell if I was again fantasizing about kissing Reed or if it was actually happening. But his tongue, strong and sure pressing against my closed lips, told me it was real.

I could have guessed that Reed would be a dominant kisser, that his tongue wouldn't willfully yield to my own. I could only imagine that his breath would be hot and sweet against my skin, like flames licking over me. And I'd contemplated that he'd like to nip at my lip with his teeth and then soothe it with that skillful tongue.

I'd only ever imagined it. But the real thing didn't compare— it was so much better.

His tongue slid against mine, and my hand weaved into his dark locks.

My balls drew up, and when I felt his large, calloused palm smooth over my thigh and grip my hip, I let go. Thrusting up into Amanda's tight heat, I pumped my release deep into her. Pleasure zapped through every inch of me, alighting every nerve in my body. It was harder than I'd ever come in my entire life, and my orgasm seemed to provoke Reed's, too.

His lips hovering over mine, we both groaned and cursed. I could feel his cock twitch inside Amanda's ass at the same time mine did. Like I could feel his orgasm in my own cock.

Seconds passed and we were all a tangled mess. Reed was still poised over us both, our eyes locked through a stunned silence. I don't know if either of us completely realized what had happened until it was all over. Part of me was immediately worried, but the other hoped the shift in his eyes was one that led to more of what had just happened.

For once, I could barely read the man. His dark brows and

the lips that were only seconds earlier eagerly tasting mine were both set in firm, straight lines.

Between us, it was Amanda that broke the tension. "That was fucking amazing," she muttered in her satisfied, orgasm-drunk state.

I couldn't help my smile as I turned to her and kissed her nose. A blush crept up her skin and warmed her cheeks. She returned my smile, but when her eyes shifted to Reed, his smile was tight.

Tenderly, he removed himself from her but kissed the back of her head before heading in the direction of the bathroom.

"Clean him up," he added over his shoulder. The click of the bathroom door was followed by the light underneath it.

Amanda gingerly pulled herself off of me and poised between my legs. My dick was coated in a mixture of our releases and before I could tell her she didn't have to listen to Reed, she took all of me into her mouth.

I gasped and then groaned. I was overly sensitive, but she licked me clean as Reed had instructed. While she was still running her tongue up and down my shaft, Reed stepped back into the room. He froze at the sight before him, a muscle in his jaw flexing.

For a moment he watched Amanda eagerly licking my cock, which was rapidly hardening again between her lips. But he quickly snapped out of his trance and stalked to the end of the bed. One hand poised on Amanda's ass, I noticed the washcloth in the other. Gently, he wiped between her legs, and she gasped, letting go of my dick.

"We don't deserve you," Reed said, finishing cleaning her and rubbing her ass that was still up in the air.

"Feeling's mutual," she said with conviction.

She pressed one final kiss to my shaft, winked at me and turned to Reed. On wobbly legs, she stood from the bed right in front of Reed, who kept her from falling. Folding my arms behind my head, I watched our little seductress push up on her toes and slant her mouth over Reed's.

There was a moment where he hesitated, probably tasting a combination of both me and Amanda on her tongue, but that moment didn't last long. He pulled her into his arms and deepened the kiss, diving his tongue into her mouth and groaning.

Between them, his cock hardened and pressed against her stomach.

But as soon as it began, Amanda stepped away. "I'll be right back," she said, slipping into the bathroom and leaving Reed and me alone.

The tension from before was back in full force, thickening the air around us with every possible unknown. And although there were so many questions floating around in my head, I knew it wasn't the right time to voice them. Hell, there may have never been a right time, but I knew it especially wasn't then.

For all I knew, it was the heat of the moment, the impending orgasm, that had driven Reed to kiss me. No matter the fierceness and confidence I felt in his lips, I knew at the height of pleasure, it was easy to do things you'd regret afterward.

I wasn't one of those people, but Reed could have been.

Hoping to dissipate some of the tension, I pointed to the washcloth hanging limply in his hand.

"Can I borrow that?"

He glanced down, looking at it like he'd forgotten it was there. For a second, I thought he was going to tell me to fuck off based on the look on his face, but eventually, he refolded the small blue towel and stepped around the bed to my right.

Poised and as still as a statue, he held the washcloth in his hand as his attention turned from my eyes to my cock. It lay against my stomach just below my belly button, and it jumped under Reed's gaze.

His hands flexed around the damp material in his hand, and I had half a mind to ask him if he wanted to do it for me or if he saw something that he liked. But the door to the bathroom opened, and I felt the material hit my stomach.

Moment lost.

Cringing against the cold, I used the washcloth to wipe myself down a little more and then tossed it into the laundry basket in the corner.

Then it hit me. "We didn't use condoms." At the bottom of the bed, Reed's eyes widened as he tugged on his boxer briefs. He looked from me to Amanda and then back again.

Never had I forgotten a condom before.

"The beauty of an IUD. And since we're all clean, there's not much of a point, right?"

I nodded and so did Reed. Neither of us was going to argue with fucking our girl raw.

"And I didn't want anything between us anyway," she added and eagerly climbed back into bed. I scooted over to give her some room, and her naked body curled around me. I welcomed the feel of her curves and smooth skin against me.

"I want you both in bed with me tonight," she murmured into my neck. Every muscle in my body tensed, but Amanda ran her nails gently down the center of my chest and stomach. Her touch eased every worry.

"There's nothing on the bed besides a few pillows," Reed said and tossed my own boxer briefs at me. I caught them midair and didn't argue when I slipped them on.

"Will you grab the comforter and a few pillows from the living room, please?"

Like me, Reed was far from immune to Amanda. What our girl wanted, our girl got. So, with a little huff, he went back out into the living room, returning a few seconds later with blankets and pillows.

We arranged everything to Amanda's specifications, giving her her favorite pillow and laying another blanket down underneath the comforter.

When everything was the way she wanted it, she patted the

spot on her other side and motioned for Reed to join us. He hesitated, looking between the two of us and then back to the empty spot.

Amanda sighed and curled herself around my left arm and our hands intertwined. Everything about it felt right—like she was meant to be next to me.

"The bed's big enough for three, Reed. Either get in or take the couch. Your choice."

Her eyes fluttered closed, but Reed clambered into bed, making it a point not to look in my direction.

Each of his movements was hesitant, but the pull of Amanda was stronger. He spooned her from behind and wrapped a hand around her waist, careful not to touch me. He buried his face into the hair floating around her neck and breathed deeply.

Once again, Amanda sighed, although that time, it was a content and happy sound. Her arms tightened around mine and squeezed my hand. I squeezed it back once, twice and a third time.

# THIRTY-ONE

Reed

SLEEP EVADED ME.

I'd tried what I could to slip into a blissful slumber, but the standard counting—sheep, numbers, breaths, swirl textures on Amanda's ceiling—was far from working. Even Amanda, who'd turned over an hour and a half ago and wrapped herself around me, wasn't able to pull me under. And I fucking loved cuddling.

If it were any other night with sex that good, I would have been out like a light the moment my head hit the pillow. But last night was different.

The sex was mind blowing, and our chemistry was intense. Josh and I moved around and inside of Amanda as if we were one person. It was one glance over her shoulder, and we both knew what the other was thinking. Whether we wanted to go faster or slow it down and draw out her pleasure, it was all communicated without a word.

And it wasn't a surprise that it was as good as it was. All of us—Amanda included—had been craving it since that night at the lake. We'd all admitted in one way or another that it was a connection we'd not found since. Something with such intensity that nothing else seemed to compare. And it was despite the possibility of it changing everything that we decided to do it anyway. That we'd decided to give in to the pure energy between us.

Although it didn't feel like much of a decision when the pull to each other was so immense. There was no longer a chance we'd fight it. I think we'd all lost the war that night at the lake; we'd already been defeated without knowing it.

And that was one of the reasons sleep evaded me. For me, there was no going back. I'd tasted perfection, and I was too selfish a man to give it up.

But there were three parts to our perfect triangle. And that was the thought I'd tried to fight from entering the front of my mind all night.

Carefully, I pried Amanda's small hand from where she clung to my chest and rolled from the bed. She stirred for a moment but didn't wake, and I let out a breath. I needed a second to myself and with my cluttered thoughts.

I stared down at the two forms. Amanda promptly rolled over to find Josh's warm body. The sheets tangled around her waist and bared the smooth skin of her back to the moonlight streaming between the blinds. One of her arms slung over his back, and Josh was sprawled out on his stomach, snoring softly. The white sheets also hugged around his hips since he'd kicked off the comforter almost immediately after falling asleep.

Just as I'd done with Amanda, my eyes traced the lines of his exposed back. Compared to Amanda, his skin was slightly more tan, and the hours he'd spent in the gym recently were apparent in the contoured muscles.

Therein was the problem. My hands fisted at my sides, and I escaped the bedroom, shutting the door behind me.

With nothing better to do and nowhere else to go, I paced into the living room. Catching a glimpse of the snow rapidly collecting on the ground outside through the tall windows and past the balcony, I took a moment to stare outside.

It was relatively uncommon in the southern part of Texas to experience snow. And for it to stick to the ground was another miracle altogether. Sleet and flurries were one thing, but actual flakes that stayed around for more than an hour or two were a strange phenomenon.

There was a peacefulness in the snow. Maybe because it was quiet as it collected on the cold, hard ground. And it was the exact opposite of my racing mind.

I wished my thoughts were as peaceful as the snow.

I was jealous of fucking snow. What the fuck was wrong with me?

I walked into the kitchen and grabbed a glass from the cabinet. The filter in her fridge needed to be replaced, so the water was barely trickling out. As I not so patiently waited for my glass to fill, I glanced over the supplies we'd brought.

Thankfully the power was still on, but we'd brought candles and flashlights that I was sure Amanda didn't have. We'd also thrown into bags some canned goods from our pantry and an extra case of water.

Over the past several days, Josh and I hadn't agreed on much. Actually, we hadn't spoken enough to agree or disagree on anything, but we did agree that Amanda was likely underprepared for the impending storm. We were both concerned enough to pack bags and plan to hunker down in her apartment with her.

In the truck on the way to her place, we'd barely said two words to each other, so it was obvious our stay would be tenuous. But we'd arrived, and as she always did, Amanda dissipated the tension between us.

But I'd undone it all.

All of her smiles and jokes and her overall infectious, happy demeanor were no match for my knack for complicating everything.

I had to go and make shit more difficult, complicate it more than it already was. A memory, or several, flashed through my mind. All of the times when my dad, the hard-ass he was, claimed I made things more difficult. There was the time in high school when I decided a college football career wasn't for me. And then when I majored in kinesiology and only minored in business. Or when I wouldn't let him invest his own money, riddled with stipulations, in the gym. One he claimed was likely to fail from the outset.

But as he always liked to say, I was a pro at making my very cushy life hard. And I'd done it yet again.

I'd made an already difficult situation a million times worse.

I'd kissed him. I kissed Josh in the spur of the moment. With Amanda pinned between us, pushing her ass back and welcoming my hard thrusts, I noticed Josh's legs first. The position we were in meant we were bound to brush against each other, and I could feel the brush of his legs against mine. And then I noticed his lips. They were plump and swollen from kissing Amanda and I'd suddenly wondered what they'd feel like on my own. And before I knew it, it was happening.

And it was mind blowing. The kind of kiss I'd only felt once before with our girl. A kiss that altered time and the course of your entire life.

A terrifying kiss.

Water trickling over my hand pulled me from my thoughts. The glass was completely overfilled and water spilled down the refrigerator and collected on the floor.

Hoping not to make a bigger mess, I carefully walked the full glass to the sink and set it down before grabbing a handful of paper towels to clean it up. Swallowing my self-pity, I stooped down and wiped up the small puddle that had formed and cleaned up the front of the fridge.

It wasn't healthy the way the two people I'd left in bed occupied my thoughts.

I stood and looked at the clock on the microwave. It was half past two in the morning, meaning I had a few hours to figure my shit out before they woke up. Figure out how to uncomplicate the situation.

I threw away the sopping wet towels and braced my hands against the sink, staring down at my full glass.

"I can hear you thinking from over here."

I jumped at her voice, my heart beating frantically, trying to propel itself out of my chest. But after taking a deep breath, I managed a small yet forced smile. She was still drenched in a post-orgasm glow and the smile that pulled at her lips didn't seem as difficult as mine.

She strode over to me with her long blonde hair in loose waves around her face. She only wore the T-shirt I'd discarded before I'd joined her and Josh on the bed. It was several sizes too big and hung loosely right above her knees.

"I could get used to seeing you in my clothes," I said, my smile mostly genuine when she wrapped her arms around my waist and rested her head on my chest.

"I like it because it smells like you."

My heart stuttered, and I hugged her harder.

"You like the way I smell?"

She chuckled against my chest and sighed. "Honestly, there's not much I don't like about you."

"I find that hard to believe; I thought you knew me better than anyone. But especially after the shit I've caused..." My words trailed off as I ground my teeth together. The fact that Amanda was in my arms and not screaming at me in frustration was more than surprising. I expected her to question everything and be furious with my actions.

"Why? Because you kissed him?" She pulled back and peered up at me with wide, deep-blue eyes. Again to my surprise, there wasn't an ounce of judgment in her eyes or in her voice. For a second, I waited to see the condemnation or a flicker of pain or anger. But it didn't come.

Reaching up, I brushed all of her hair behind her shoulders and gripped her neck. My thumbs traced the line of her jaw. She was so relaxed compared to me. I could feel the weight of every-thing bearing down on me.

When I went to respond, to say yes that I'd fucked it all up, the words wouldn't come. So instead, I settled with a slow nod, hoping she could read the apology on my face instead of in my voice.

"What are you worried about?" Her expression didn't change much, which could have been good or bad.

But it was a question I had to actually use words to answer. A shrug wouldn't have conveyed anything at all and probably just frustrated the shit out of her.

I cleared my throat and chose my words carefully. "What I'm *not* worried about would probably be easier to list. The list of shit I'm worried about is never ending."

Slowly she nodded and worried her lower lip between her teeth. "I'm not sure if this helps at all, but I had an idea that something was going on. Or that somewhere along the way your friendship had changed. I'm not quite sure when I realized it was a possibility, but when I did, all the arguing and lingering looks and overall change in attitudes seemed to make more sense. It's why I did what I did with pulling Josh away and... making sure you found us together. I knew you wouldn't be able to resist."

Her confession stunned me, and again, I couldn't find the words to clearly communicate my thoughts. She'd known? How had she known when I'd only realized *I* was feeling more than friendship feelings a few hours before?

My mind spun at the idea that I'd unknowingly given signals to the woman I was pursuing that I fucking *liked* my friend. Or was at least attracted to him.

"I can't tell if you're going to faint or puke. Either way, do you want to sit down? Maybe head into the bathroom?" She began to pull away, but I tightened my hold on her neck.

"No, I'm okay. This just... I wasn't expecting you to say that.

I'm still trying to come to terms and figure out how I'm feeling. But it seems like you already know."

She laughed and the sound was pure delight. "I don't have it all figured out, but I've had a suspicion for a while."

"That's crazy. And you're not mad?"

"It was one of the hottest things I've ever witnessed. And I can't imagine what it would be like to witness you two go even further."

A bolt of nervous energy shot through me. Going further with Josh simultaneously sounded amazing and terrifying. I'd never been with a man before—or even looked twice at a guy—so how the fuck was I supposed to know how it all happened or what to do?

"Okay, no, no. That's if you want to," Amanda said soothingly, gripping my face in her palms and forcing me to look back into her eyes. "I'm down for whatever, and I'm not going to push anything on you. Either of you, but I also can't deny that the thought of the two of you together is a serious turn-on."

For several seconds, we stood there silently. Each of us held on to the other as I attempted to get my head around the gravity of the situation.

Amanda wasn't mad. She was not only okay with it but she was aroused by seeing us together and the potential for more.

"But what if... what if... outside of the bedroom... we—"

Sensing my struggle, Amanda said, "What if it's more than sexual chemistry and attraction? What if you care about him more than a friend? Maybe similar to how you care about me?"

I nodded, and she smiled. Never before had I found myself attracted to a man the way I was attracted to Josh. Liking the same sex was a foreign concept until recently—until him. I hadn't once noticed the way another guy's throat bobbed when he drank or the way his hands and strong fingers flexed.

I couldn't remember a time that I craved the sound of another man's laugh or company the way I did Josh's.

And although I still struggled to reconcile each new feeling with what I'd experienced before, I knew without a doubt that it wasn't just sexual attraction.

"Then I'd be even happier."

"But you know that this doesn't change anything about the way I feel about you. *God*, this is so fucked. I still want you more than I've wanted almost anything. Ever. I—I don't want to push you away."

Her smile was soft and illuminated her entire face. "I never for a second worried about that, but thanks for telling me. Both of you are pretty clear with your intentions."

"Okay, but what does this mean? What happens from here?" Even if I could wrap my head around the fact that Amanda was excited about the prospect of something more between me and Josh, I still couldn't fathom a world in which I was permitted to pursue both of them.

All of this also bet on the idea that Josh also felt some type of way. "And I don't even know if Josh feels remotely the same. For all we know, he could be in there getting his beauty rest so he can wake up in the morning and beat the shit out of me."

Amanda's face fell, and she dramatically rolled her eyes. "If you think for one second that he doesn't reciprocate at least most of the feelings you have for him, then you're blind."

I opened my mouth to argue, but Amanda pressed her finger over my lips. "I can only tell you what I've witnessed, and based on the way he kissed you back, I'd bet my left tit on it. And that's my favorite one."

My brows drew together, and she sighed. "My left boob is my favorite, so I wouldn't bet it on anything I didn't absolutely, without a shadow of a doubt, expect to win. Now, my right is reserved for things I'm only fifty to seventy-five percent sure of."

"There's a difference between your tits?" I asked, amused and confused by her explanation.

"Yes. The left one is slightly bigger and more well-rounded compared to the right. But that's all beside the point," she said, placing her hands on my chest and imploring me with her eyes.

"You should talk to Josh and hear it from him, but I truly believe you are not alone in your feelings. And as for what this all means for the future, I think that's a conversation better suited for when the sun is also awake."

"How are you so perfect?" I was bemused, completely enthralled with the woman in front of me. I'd been on the precipice of a panic attack and she'd carefully, yet easily, talked me off the ledge.

She laughed. "I'm not perfect, but I guess I am pretty close."

And unable to control myself any longer, I slanted my mouth over hers. Quickly she relaxed into me and when I licked at the seam of her mouth, she eagerly let me in. She made sweet little sounds of pleasure, and I swallowed each moan and gasp. Each stoked the desire building inside of me.

"So, you want to watch me and Josh together?"

"Yes," she breathed as I backed her up against the granite counter.

Gripping her thighs, right under the curve of her ass, I picked her up and deposited her on the cold counter. She gasped at the temperature of the hard surface and squirmed against it. But I squeezed her thighs and held her down.

Resuming our kiss, she quickly forgot all about the counter, twisting her hands in my hair.

"Are you sore?" I asked.

She immediately shook her head. "Yes, but please keep going. I want this."

"What would you want to see?" I growled against her lips, and her eyes widened when my fingers climbed higher. I forced her legs farther apart and continued closer to what I hoped was her bare pussy beneath the hem of my T-shirt.

"I want…" she began, but her words trailed off the higher my fingers climbed.

"Keep going, or I stop."

"I want to see you suck his cock like I suck yours. I could teach you how." My hands stilled as the mental image overwhelmed me. After years of friendship and recent events with Amanda, I'd seen plenty of Josh's cock. But never before had I contemplated what he'd feel like in my hand or pressed against my tongue. I imagined he'd be heavy—he was well-endowed and thick. The skin of his shaft would probably be soft against my calloused fingers.

"You're imagining it, aren't you?" Amanda purred, her hands finding their way up my chest and then back down, scraping at each muscled ridge on my stomach. "I can tell because your eyes got darker, and you zoned out. Like you were in the middle of a really good daydream."

Quickly I yanked the T-shirt up over her head and exposed her entirely to me. Immediately my hand tightened around her slim, pretty little throat, and her hands flew back behind her to catch her weight before she toppled back on the counter.

I groaned at how her eyes flared with uninhibited lust when I was rough, when I gripped her throat and squeezed just enough to restrict her airway. And I nearly lost it when my eyes ran the length of her body, pausing over her chest, rising and falling rapidly, and her nipples peaked and waiting to be sucked. Her stomach was taut with the strain of keeping herself up.

Lower, I finally saw what I'd suspected, her bare pussy glistening with her arousal.

"Keep going. What else do you want to see?"

Her breath hitched and blush colored her cheeks when I wetted my thumb and pressed it against her clit. Small, light circles had her writhing and seeking more pressure.

And when I didn't hear what I wanted—another fantasy or desire—I stopped.

A needy groan tore up her throat, and I squeezed until it was cut off at the source. "Talk, tell me what you want to see, or I stop."

"I want to watch you jack each other off," she rushed out. And I picked up where I left off, circling her pulsing clit and enjoying the way she bucked against my hand. "Your hand around his cock and his hand around yours."

"You're doing so good. You want me to wrap my hand around his cock?"

"*God, yes,*" she groaned and I rewarded her by spearing a finger inside her tight, wet heat. Like she was starving for it, she sucked my finger deeper. "Then I want to watch you press your cocks together as you jack yourselves off."

My dick was so hard that just the little friction of my briefs was brutal.

My hand wrapped around Amanda's throat and my fingers buried inside her pussy while she described her desire to see me with a man, our best friend. It was mind numbing. It fed a soul-deep desire to take and have them both, to manifest our every want and need without restriction.

"And then I want to watch you fuck each other. You fuck me while Josh fucks you, and vice *versa.*" Her words cut off in a throaty moan as I freed my aching cock, yanked her to the edge of the counter, and thrust deep inside of her in one long stroke.

Unable to hold herself up any longer, her arms gave out, but I caught her around the waist. Pounding into her, I didn't let up as I pressed her against my chest, our bodies already slick with sweat. I buried my nose into her neck, inhaling her sweet and warm floral scent, letting its calming effects overwhelm me.

She was okay with it, my feelings for Josh and whatever came next.

"Cielo," I murmured into her ear.

"Cielo," she repeated breathlessly. "What does that mean?"

I smiled. "Heaven. You are my heaven."

Her eyes widened. "Fuck, Reed. *More,*" she begged, and I wasn't going to deny our beautiful girl anything she wanted. Ever.

I released my arm from around her and guided her back onto the counter with my hand collared around her throat. Her legs fastened around me, and she held on as I relentlessly fucked her.

My free hand fell to her hip, keeping her at the edge of the counter. The wet and carnal sounds of our fucking echoed through the kitchen.

"Yes, yes, *yes*," she cried, her hands gripped around my forearm, and her tits bounced with each thrust. "Fuck me and think about him. Think of all of us together."

And as I thought about all of us touching, tasting, and fucking, I closed my eyes and let my head fall back between my shoulder blades. The night before was only a taste of what it could be; I knew we could be so much more.

Amanda clamped down around me, growing wetter as my thumb found her clit. My eyes still closed, I relished the feel of her around me, letting it consume every part of me.

"Holy shit, Reed." Amanda's voice was strained, and my attention snapped back to her. Her blonde hair was fanned out around her in a golden halo and the sweat glistening on her skin made me want to run my tongue over every inch of her.

But she wasn't looking at me, her head was tilted to the side, staring back into the living room.

I followed her line of sight, and there, next to the couch, was Josh, fists clenching and unclenching at his sides. He was only wearing his black boxer briefs, and it was easy to make out the thick erection pressing against the material. My mouth watered at the same time my stomach clenched with a wave of nerves thinking about getting him in my mouth.

Josh's eyes were laser-focused on where Amanda and I were joined, my cock sliding in and out of her with ease. Like a statue, he stood, frozen to the spot, watching me pound into our girl.

# THIRTY-TWO

Reed

HE WAS RIGHT THERE.

"Josh," I said, my voice a mix of pain and lust. Saying his name was like I'd given up the fight. It was a losing battle anyway, trying to fight anything I was feeling for either of them.

In only a few strides, Josh ate up the distance between us and only hesitated beside me for a second before his hands were on me. One hand covered mine as I continued playing with Amanda's clit and the other gripped the hair at the back of my neck. His eyes met mine, and I could read it all there—everything I was feeling was reflected back to me. And then he slammed his mouth over mine.

There was nothing sweet about it. It was a desperate kiss meant to release the tension that had been building. And for once, I let someone else lead. He pushed his tongue into my mouth and devoured me whole. His lips were firm and unyielding against mine. Even the scrape of his scruff against mine made me desperate.

And God, he smelled so fucking good, like the ocean and a storm mixed together. It was a heady scent I needed more of.

Against Amanda's clit, his fingers shoved mine away, replaced by his own. Although the last thing I wanted to do was break away from our kiss, I needed to watch Josh help me get Amanda off. And the sight of his fingers, pleasuring our girl and so close to my cock, was well worth it.

His hand in my hair tightened, drawing my eyes back to him. "Fuck her hard," he demanded. "Make her come for us."

He made his intentions clear by leaning over where we were joined and spitting directly onto Amanda's clit. Her moan was instant, as were her inner walls tightening around my cock.

His spit slid down her cunt, and mixed with her arousal, coating my dick as his fingers resumed their motion. "Come around Reed's cock. We want to watch you fall apart." I could feel his fingers brush against my cock every time I bottomed out inside of her, straining to keep her from traveling across the counter.

It was no more than a few seconds before Amanda's entire body rocked with pleasure. Her orgasm ripped through her as she cried both of our names, and her release coated my cock. She choked me, tightening to the point it was hard to move.

"Your turn," Josh murmured in a lower voice. "Come inside our girl." His hand wrapped around the base of me, guiding me in and out of Amanda as aftershocks barreled through her.

The feeling of his large fingers wrapped around me was beyond words. He squeezed and pumped as he fed my cock into her. I couldn't hold out any longer. My balls seized the moment his grip tightened. Like a tidal wave, my own orgasm hit me. My vision blurring, I reached for the counter and Josh to keep me standing while I shot deep into Amanda.

Fully drained—of both energy and cum—Josh let me stumble aside before he took my place, kneeling in front of Amanda's spread legs. He was eye level with her cunt and got a front-row seat to my cum spilling out of her.

I found the counter behind me and leaned against it, my breathing slowly evening out. I watched Josh run his finger through my release and push it back into Amanda, who bucked and gasped against his fingers. When he pulled them back out, he reached up and offered them to Amanda. She took them eagerly into her mouth, twirling her tongue around them, sucking any remnants off, and leaving nothing behind.

Still between her legs, Josh dove in, licking her pussy and spearing his tongue inside of her. He cleaned her up and moaned into her cunt.

I wondered if he liked the way I tasted. And I imagined it was even better mixed with the tangy sweetness of Amanda we both craved.

He licked and sucked every inch of her, and I was transfixed by it until I caught the motion between Josh's thighs. As he devoured Amanda, Josh pumped his cock with long, hard pulls. He fisted the base and pulled at the tip, and I wanted it to be my hand, my mouth getting him off. The urge to feel him was over-whelming, and I stepped forward with the intention of doing just that.

But halfway into my first step, Josh sucked hard on Aman-da's clit, speared two fingers into her, and threw her into a second orgasm. Watching Amanda come was my favorite thing, and the only thing that could have made it better happened. Because Amanda's earth-shattering orgasm spurred Josh's, too.

And with a groan, he spilled into his hand. The muscles in his back tensed as the pleasure crashed through him.

They both stayed where they were—Josh kneeling between Amanda's thighs and Amanda sprawled out on the counter, breathing heavily. Josh came to first, standing on shaky legs and running his clean hand up her stomach and between her breasts. Amanda pulled herself up, and they kissed. It was nothing more than a brush of their lips, but it conveyed so much in a brief moment.

Josh turned around and hesitantly looked up at me as he stepped up to the sink. After everything that just happened, I was surprised to see any ounce of hesitation in his expression. I figured it all had signified the beginning of something. He'd kissed me, strode right up to me, and slanted his mouth over mine. Then he'd wrapped his hand around my cock and jacked me off as I fucked Amanda. And once I finally came, he'd cleaned my release from Amanda's cunt, giving her another orgasm in the process. It was the taste of my cum and Amanda's on his lips when he'd pumped into his hand.

There was no place for hesitation or uncertainty between us. At least not sexually—all evidence pointed to us being on the same page there. And it would be a matter of a conversation to see if he wanted more.

But I didn't want him to feel uncertain about anything between the three of us.

With his clean hand, he flicked on the faucet and moved to put his other hand under the steady stream of water before I caught it. He still hadn't really looked at me, and I didn't know what he'd heard of me and Amanda's conversation, but I had to make sure he knew.

I was fucking terrified, but I wasn't uncertain. My feelings were steady and remained unchanged even after finally admitting them out loud.

My fingers gripped around his wrist, and I looked down at his creamy white cum decorating his hand. My mouth watered and I licked my lips, imagining the taste. I guided his pointer finger to my mouth.

Our eyes locked as I wrapped my lips around it. His taste exploded on my tongue—tangy and salty and all Josh. The texture was as creamy as it looked, and I knew I'd want to taste him again and again.

Josh's eyes dilated, his jaw going slack as I licked the rest of his hand clean, flattening my tongue against his palm and sucking each individual finger into my mouth.

Finally, I released his pinkie and glanced down at his clean hand. "It was only fair," I muttered, and I was rewarded with a lopsided grin.

Any signs of doubt were gone from his expression.

"Holy fuck, please, tell me I get a round two," Amanda mused, still propped atop the counter.

Both Josh and I looked over at her. Her hair had spilled forward again and fell down her chest, hiding her nipples behind her locks. And her skin had that magnificent blush she always wore after several orgasms.

We stepped forward at the same time, a smile splitting Amanda's face, and I zoned in on her pussy, still slick and wet.

In the same breath that we reached for her, the power surged and the apartment was plunged into further darkness. The streetlights and small analog clocks above the oven and on the microwave were the only light illuminating the apartment. Simultaneously they all turned off. The ceiling fan in the living room ceased, and it was like the world inside was as quiet as the snow outside. The faint whirring of energy that was always in the background was suddenly gone.

"Can't believe it took this long for the power to go out," Josh said, tucking himself back into his boxer briefs. The fat tip of his erection was pressing against the thick band of his briefs like it was going to attempt escape at any moment.

"What do you mean? The weather isn't even—oh, damn!" Amanda scooted herself off the counter and padded on bare feet, arms wrapped around her naked chest, to the patio door in the living room.

"You didn't stop to look out the window as you were sneaking into the kitchen to come find me?" I tugged on my own boxer briefs and found my discarded T-shirt Amanda was wearing on the floor near the island.

Although I was fine with her never wearing clothes until we eventually had to leave her apartment, it was already cold in her place. And it was only going to get worse with the power out.

"No, I didn't even think about it. Especially when I saw you standing in the dark looking kinda… broken."

I held out the shirt but stiffened at her words. Swallowing

around thick emotion suddenly clogging my throat, I tried to school my features. Thirty minutes earlier, I absolutely had felt broken and torn. So broken that I wasn't sure it could be fixed.

So, I wasn't surprised that she'd noticed it. I just didn't want her to have to see it.

Amanda ran a hand down the length of my arm, and she gave me a reassuring smile like she knew exactly what I was thinking.

The three of us stood at the window, Josh at Amanda's other side, and watched the snow furiously fall from the sky. It obstructed most of our view of the parking lot; we could barely make out the tops of the trees just below her windows.

"Did we wake you up?" Amanda asked, turning to Josh.

"Actually, I woke up to take a piss, but then I heard moaning. And I couldn't *not* investigate."

"Hmm," Amanda hummed and glanced at me over her shoulder, wearing a look that accurately depicted the mischievous thoughts I knew were running through her head.

"And," she continued, "did you like what you found?"

Josh turned to us, looking at Amanda first and then up at me as he licked his lips. Lips that were on mine only a few minutes before and that I now knew the taste and feel of.

His eyes held mine for a beat until a lopsided grin pulled at his mouth, flashing a hint of his shallow dimple beneath his blond scruff. Then he looked back at Amanda.

"'Like' doesn't begin to describe how I felt about it. I walked in on one of my biggest fantasies playing out in front of me. I had to pinch myself because I thought I was dreaming."

"Walking in on us together?" Amanda clarified, reaching out and grasping one of Josh's hands in her free one.

He nodded. "And then joining in."

"What are some of your other fantasies?"

He chuckled and lifted their joined hands to his mouth, pressing a kiss to their interlaced fingers. "Babe, I don't think we have enough time to go through all of them tonight, especially since our man behind you looks like he's about to fall over with exhaustion."

Amanda looked back at me, and I tried to straighten, but it was a lost cause. I'd been up nearly twenty-four hours and was beginning to feel the effects. My eyelids were heavy, and all of my muscles felt strained—like I'd spent hours working out with the heaviest weights.

"But I'm feeling pretty good about the prospect of us all acting them out. I think I heard you describe a few of them between moans."

I laughed, and somehow, through the exhaustion threatening, my skin heated. I wondered which fantasies he'd been more interested in or which ones he'd heard.

"Let's go." Josh tugged Amanda's hand, and she pulled me along, bringing up the end.

We all fell into bed in the same positions we were in before—Josh at the far side and Amanda squeezed between the two of us.

Only, when Amanda wrapped herself around Josh and waved me closer to her back, I didn't hesitate. I folded myself over her, fitting every contour of her body into me. My hand that I slung over her hips also brushed Josh's stomach. It was barely a touch, only grazing the skin of his lower stomach, brushing through the dirty-blond hair there. But there was an electric current I'd felt, and based on the way his eyes darted to mine, I was sure he felt it too.

We held each other's eyes, cocooned around our girl, until mine eventually closed.

# THIRTY-THREE

Amanda

WHEN I WOKE UP THE NEXT MORNING, THE FIRST THING I NOTICED was that I was entirely enveloped in warmth. The two hard bodies on either side of me, with their arms and legs slung everywhere, were like furnaces under the shelter of my comforter.

It was slightly stifling, especially since nearly every part of them was touching every part of me, but before I opened my eyes, I let myself enjoy it.

An instant replay began behind my eyes of the night before. Each touch and kiss and dirty word was cataloged in my mind. After the three of us had been together, there'd been an obvious shift, at least for me.

With both of them inside of me, in a moment more intimate than I ever could have comprehended, one that felt like it altered the very makeup of my soul, I knew I wasn't giving them up. The three of us felt too good together for it not to be right.

And when they kissed, I'd felt triumphant. Like I wasn't actually going crazy thinking there was sexual tension between the two and I hadn't made it all up in my head. Pressed between the two of them, I'd felt the power and uncertainty in the way their lips clashed and their bodies formed around mine.

But the entire scene was erotic—two strong men dueling for power over each other and their feelings.

That kiss—although I wasn't technically an active participant —felt like the culmination of years of repressed desires and feelings.

Feelings and desires that I hoped they would stop fighting.

Because if last night told me anything, it was that we needed each other.

Our early morning in the kitchen proved that to an extent, but the day ahead was going to make or break it. If we could all be on the same page and agree on what we wanted... the possibility made me smile.

How I'd managed to get to that point, I wasn't sure. But I wasn't going to fight it.

The possibility that something more was brewing between my guys was also a plus.

Someone—I think it was Josh—to the right of me stirred, and I opened my eyes only to be met with utter and complete darkness. I blinked a few times, then untangled my arm from Reed's to scrub at my eyes.

Still dark, I realized I'd shimmied my way completely under the blankets. Reaching up, I pulled them down and grunted as the light streaming from the windows and the freezing cold air assaulted me.

Hurriedly, I scurried back under the covers into the warmth and immediately felt an ache in every part of my body. Especially between my legs, but that one made me grin to myself like a fucking idiot.

"Stop moving, it's too early," Josh murmured in a low voice drenched in sleep as he reached out for me, wrapping an arm around my stomach and tucking me close against him. My back to his front, he buried his face in my neck, and I could feel the tickle of his warm breath as he breathed in deeply.

I probably smelled like sex and sweat. But if I did, he didn't seem to mind. He breathed me in a few more times, and when I attempted to find a more comfortable position, closer to the warmth emanating from his body, my ass brushed against something long and hard.

He groaned into my ear the same time I let out a tiny gasp, heat and desire instantly pooling between my legs, soreness be damned.

"Shhh," Josh shushed, pushing his thick erection against me as I rolled my hips back into him. I swallowed the moan threatening to break free of my lips.

"Don't want to wake sleepy over there." His hand slowly inched up my stomach under Reed's T-shirt I was still wearing from the night before, until he reached the bottom of my breast, running his thumb a centimeter below it.

"Too late," Reed said, his voice also gruff and laden with sleep. We were all three crowded under the blankets, and through the minimal amount of light seeping in through an opening at the top, I watched his eyes flutter open. He was on his stomach, turned our direction and before saying anything else, his hand darted out.

Wrapping his arm around me, he pried me from Josh's arms and pulled me to his chest.

"Good morning," he said and kissed my nose.

"Asshole," Josh muttered behind me but quickly scooted closer, resuming his position curled around me. I relaxed into him and hoped there wouldn't be any tension. In the morning light, I knew there was a possibility that everything could look different.

"Good morning to you, too, Sunshine."

Apparently my morning breath wasn't an issue because Reed's lips found mine in a gentle kiss I could feel down to my toes.

"Good morning," I replied.

"Guys, I'm feeling a little left out over here," Josh murmured into my hair.

I chuckled. "Your hand is currently making its way up my shirt. I'm not sure how you feel left out."

Reed pulled back and stared down at my exposed stomach and where Josh's hand disappeared higher up my shirt. His palm was firm and warm against my soft skin. It was a battle not to close my eyes against the closeness of them both, but I kept them open, closely observing Reed for any shift in his expression. Waiting for jealousy or anger to cloud the desire I'd seen a moment before, I realized I'd be waiting forever. There wasn't even a hint of either emotion.

He enjoyed watching his best friend touch me, and it turned me on wondering if it was me or Josh he wanted to trade places with more. Because there was a longing in his eyes I couldn't have missed.

Josh brushed one of my peaked nipples with his thumb, and my groan of pleasure quickly turned into one of annoyance when there was a knock at the door.

"Who the hell is at the door?" Josh asked from behind me, not pausing in his playful touches long enough for me to begin thinking about it. All I wanted and needed was in my bed, tucked safely under the covers with me.

"Ignore it," I whined, only to hear a second, louder knock. "Fucking hell."

I whipped the comforter back and was immediately accosted by the freezing air swirling through the room. "One second!" I yelled loud enough that, hopefully, the person on the other side of the door could hear.

"Are you really going to get up? I liked the 'ignoring it' plan," Josh quipped.

I gave him an unamused look over my shoulder and proceeded to grab the closest pair of pants I could find, which ended up being a pair of leggings I'd tossed to the side a few days earlier.

"Why is it so fucking cold in here?" I asked, my nipples no longer hard from lust but from the freezing air.

"Power's out, which means no heat," Reed answered, recoiling against the cold as he pulled the covers back and hopped from the bed only a second after Josh.

After I pulled on a sweatshirt, I headed to the door, hoping it wasn't one of my neighbors in trouble or something of the kind since I wasn't expecting anyone.

Quickly, I glanced through the peephole of the front door, my smile falling slightly as I opened it.

"CJ, hey." I waved him inside and shut the door as quickly as I'd opened it. The temperature inside my apartment should have been enough of an indicator—the weather outside felt like the arctic.

"Hey, Mandy. Sorry to just show up, but I just wanted to check on you."

My smile returned. CJ was bundled up in a thick khaki jacket, gloves, and a beanie that covered his longer blond mop.

Glancing down, I saw snow clung to the soles and sides of his work boots.

"That's really nice of you, thanks."

"Well, with Adam being gone and everything, I wanted to make sure you were okay. Felt weird not checking up on you."

He tucked his hands into his pockets and glanced around my apartment. I couldn't remember if I'd mentioned that Adam was going to be out of town, but it wouldn't have surprised me if he'd noticed or if I'd just forgotten that I did tell him. CJ made it a point to keep an eye on all the comings and goings in the complex as per the request of management and the leasing office. Since he was always walking the grounds and going into people's units, he was in the best position to make sure nothing shady was going on.

"I appreciate you checking up on me, but I'm good. Just really fucking cold." A shiver racked through my body with only the thought of it.

"You've got enough water? If you need anything, I can—"

"I think we're good," a deep voice from my left responded. I turned to find Reed and Josh striding toward us with purpose.

I internally groaned at the looks on both their faces. Reed looked like he was about ready to fuck CJ up, whereas Josh looked like he was ready to fuck around with him—maybe get under his skin like only Josh could manage.

CJ's expression was neutral, but I didn't miss the slight tic in his jaw.

"Didn't realize you had friends over, Mandy."

"Boyfriends, yes," Reed said, stepping around to my right.

My entire body went still, and my jaw dropped. My head swiveled, hoping to meet his eyes and implore him to shut up, but no one noticed my reaction to Reed's statement. They were all too busy having a stare down over my head. Like they were playing some silent game wherein whoever looked away first had the smallest dick.

What was this, the Wild West?

When I was about to start mimicking gun noises with my mouth, CJ finally glanced down at me. "Just let me know if you need anything, Mandy. You know where to find me."

He untucked his hand from his jeans like he was about to reach for me, but I felt the two men flanking me tense and move forward. Thankfully, CJ thought better of it and with a small smile, he was out the door.

"Cavemen," I said, spinning on my heels the moment the door clicked closed. "You are both fucking cavemen. He was just being nice."

They traded unimpressed looks and then looked back at me. Exasperated, I tossed my hands in the air and rolled my eyes.

Reed scoffed. "Still stick to my previous assessment: I'd bet my left nut that the guy wants to fuck you."

Unable to suppress my laughter, I shook my head.

Josh's utter abhorrence at Reed's statement made it all the

better. "What the actual fuck? Why are you betting your nuts? And why is it the left one?"

Reed shrugged. "That's my favorite one. That's how sure I am that the maintenance guy wants our girl."

For a moment, I thought Josh was going to vomit, but then he said, "Yeah, then I'd bet his left nut, too."

"You're not supposed to—" Reed tried to argue, but I cut him off.

"Seriously? Stop bickering. CJ does not *want* me. He's a nice guy, and he's always looked out for me since I moved here. So, don't go all caveman on him."

Reed stepped forward and cupped my face in both his hands. His hair was mussed from sleep, the dark-brown strands pointing in several directions and flopping over his forehead—a sign that he'd slept hard. Actually, we'd all slept hard the night before. Lots of sex would do that to a person.

"He's playing the long game—weaseling his way into your life with the intention of sticking around," he said, his thumb brushing over my cheek. "And we just got you, babe. We finally have you, so you're going to have to put up with some caveman behavior."

There was a moment when I thought my heart stopped beating altogether, but it quickly recovered and instead began pounding in my chest.

I knew Reed wasn't kidding—it was written all over his face how serious he was—but it all felt surreal. In the years I fought the pull to both of them, I never imagined it would end up that way. His collective "we" was purposeful.

Over Reed's shoulder, I glanced at Josh, who'd taken a step closer to us. The same conviction I saw on Reed's face was also in Josh's expression, except one side of his lips was tugging up in a smile. It was a small smug little grin like he knew I would never say no to them.

All at once, relief and concern washed over me. Relief that we'd finally gotten there. That there was no longer a decision to be made, no longer two men vying for a hold of my heart. There was no longer the possibility of making the wrong decision or refusing to make a decision at all. The weight of it all had dissipated.

But with that sweet relief came all new challenges.

"We should probably talk about all of this," I said softly with a small smile. Reed reluctantly dropped his hands and I headed into the kitchen. "Since you've both just proclaimed that you are my boyfriends before I've even had my..." I trailed off, stopping in the middle of the kitchen and staring at my coffee maker. "Ugh! Are you kidding me?"

Like a child throwing a tantrum, I stomped my feet and fisted my hands. "I can't even make coffee, can I? This is the worst."

"Look in the fridge," Josh said with a smug grin. I eyed him warily but looked anyway. And just when I thought all hope was lost, I spotted a container of cold brew coffee on the top shelf.

I contained my squeal and grabbed the drink along with a glass from the cabinet.

"Anybody else want some?"

They both shook their heads but began moving around the kitchen, grabbing things from the pantry.

"What's really unfortunate," Reed said, opening a box of healthy granola cereal and pushing the other toward Josh. "Is that you have an electric stove, so we won't be cooking anything while the power's out."

"I looked it up a second ago, and it looks like the energy company is expecting it to be out for at least another couple hours. But it could be up to twenty-four hours without power."

Slowly I sipped my iced coffee, which wasn't doing anything to help how cold I was and peered out the window. The snow was still steadily falling, but you could at least see the parking lot beyond, unlike the night before. Anything that wasn't covered in snow was covered in ice—the plants, the cars, the street. Never in my life had I seen so much ice in southern Texas.

Without the infrastructure to prepare for the weather, we

were stuck. They didn't salt the roads or have snowplows. The best we could do was hunker down and try not to fucking freeze.

"This is going to be miserable," I murmured more to myself than anyone else, but Reed heard me.

"I think we can find a few ways to pass the time and keep each other warm," he said with a wink.

He slid a bowl of cereal in front of me—the sugary kind Josh was also eating, not his healthy shit—and said something about drinking the milk before it went bad in the fridge.

Silently we ate our breakfast and watched the snow fall outside the window. At the island, I sat at the barstool between them and appreciated that neither of them broached the topic of *us* until after my bowl was empty and at least half of my coffee was gone.

I stood and took all three of our bowls to the sink, placing them there to worry about later.

Leaning against the counter, I crossed my arms in front of me and peered over at them. They were both still seated at the island. Josh had his elbows braced on the counter, his fingers interlaced and propping up his head, while Reed was reclined back on his barstool with his arms crossed over his chest.

They both stared at me expectantly.

"Why are you both looking at me like that?"

"Like what?" Reed asked.

"Like you're expecting me to start."

He shrugged, but it was Josh that said, "Because I think we're both on the same page about you. It's you that seemed confused by us calling ourselves your boyfriends."

I looked at Reed, but he was wearing the same unaffected expression. Taking a deep, steadying breath that did nothing to actually help me, I decided to lay it all out there as I usually did. Above all else, they were two of my best friends and that had to be worth something.

"I didn't think this was actually a possibility or that you would both agree to it."

"What is it that we're agreeing to exactly?" Reed asked, and I knew he wasn't just being dense, he wanted to hear me say it. To put a name, a label on us. To define it the way I wanted to, so we were all on the same page.

Whether I actually said the words didn't make them any less true. But either way, nervous nausea coiled in my stomach.

# THIRTY-FOUR

Amanda

COHERENT SENTENCES MEANT COHERENT THOUGHTS AND AS BOTH Josh and Reed stared at me, I had none.

Not believing that there was even the slightest possibility that they would agree to something like that meant I hadn't given it too much thought. And defining it or labeling it seemed more daunting than I thought it would be.

What were we? Polyamorous? A throuple? Did we have to label it?

Frustration was seeping out of my pores, and I scrubbed a hand through my hair that seriously needed to be washed.

Before I could attempt to clear my head, I stopped and looked at them both. Patiently they waited for me to think it all through, and I knew that the first question I needed to answer was if I wanted it. If the three of us together, in a relationship, was what I truly wanted, and the answer was an unequivocal yes.

There was no decision to be made because there was no choosing. Even with a gun to my head, I could not, and would not, choose between the two of them.

"You're agreeing to both being with me… at the same time. Because I'm not going to choose between the two of you. I can't."

My words hung around us like my confession altered the chemical makeup of the cold air.

Only a second elapsed, barely giving either of them time to respond, but I couldn't take it. "Right? Or am I going crazy? Because you used the plural boy*friends*. Not one, but more than that—in this case, it would be two. And if I'm totally off base, I need you to tell me now because—"

"Whoa there, babe," Josh said, hopping out of his seat and rounding the island to stop in front of me. Reed also slipped out of his barstool, but rather than crossing to me, he leaned against the counter with his arms and ankles crossed.

"You're not crazy and that's exactly what we want. Right, Reed?" Josh asked without tearing his eyes from mine.

"Abso-fucking-lutely," Reed responded, and I couldn't help but smile.

Josh's palms cupped my cheeks, and I blinked up at him, losing myself in his ocean eyes. "This—the three of us together—is too good for it to be anything but right."

"Wait a second. When did you have time to discuss this?"

"When you were greeting your maintenance guy at the door."

Quickly I did the mental math and turned back to them with an incredulous look. "I was gone for all of thirty seconds before the two of you barged in. There's no way that conversation happened in that small amount of time."

Reed shrugged. "There wasn't much to say when we both agreed that you're ours and neither of us is letting you go. The rest of it can be figured out as we go. What else is there to say?"

He stepped forward, the two of them crowding around me and inhibiting my ability to talk or think. Their presence was intoxicating and wasn't conducive to making clear, smart decisions.

Before either of them could stop me, I slipped under Josh's arm and hurried across the kitchen, putting the large island between us. The more space, the better.

"Both of you stay over there, and I'll stay over here."

They wore twin devilish grins, which did little for my ability to think straight. To what deity did they sacrifice to look so damn good?

"Guess not much has changed in the past few weeks, huh?" Josh remarked, and I rolled my eyes.

"I just want to talk it all out before we decide anything because what we're talking about—the three of us—isn't going to be easy or simple. It's going to become complicated and people are going to have their own opinions that we have to be prepared for."

Although I was confident in the three of us, I wasn't delusional to think that we weren't going to run into people who didn't understand it. People who would threaten to make our lives more difficult. The more prepared we were for the worst possible case scenario, the more likely we were to survive it.

The maintenance guy flirting with me, for instance, would be the least of our worries.

"I seriously don't give a fuck what anyone else thinks," Josh said with conviction. My eyes, though, immediately found Reed's.

"Reed?"

His deep breath was heavy as he scrubbed a hand across his jaw and then through his hair. "I want you. Fuck what everyone else thinks."

For a moment, I watched him, but there wasn't any part of him that made me think he wasn't telling the truth.

I nodded, and for the first time in a long time—maybe my entire life—my heart felt whole. "Like I said, choosing between the two of you was never going to happen. And when the three of us are together... if this is what you want, then I'm all in."

Their smiles were instant and both of them stepped forward like that's all we had to talk about, but I held up my hands, taking a step backward. "Uh-uh. We're not done. Stay right where you are."

They both began arguing, so I put on my teacher face—the one I used when my students were being unruly and weren't listening—and waited. After several seconds, their voices quieted, and they waited for me to speak.

Men and twelve-year-olds both had a lot in common.

"I'm really glad you both want to be with me, but there's something else going on... between the two of you. And we can't *not* address it."

Reed, with his hands braced on the counter in front of him, let his head fall forward between his shoulders while Josh straightened, stuffing his hands into the pockets of his sweats and looking to his left, away from me and Reed.

Silently I let them sit with their thoughts and tried my hardest not to feel dejected that they didn't immediately begin talking and recounting their feelings. I knew it weighed heavily on them both. I already had a hard time reconciling the fact that my feelings for two men were strong enough that I wanted them both. I couldn't imagine the weight of feeling something completely new—feelings for a friend that were no longer just friendly.

The new circumstances seemed to mean more questions than answers, and I knew they'd both be struggling.

But staying silent about it, brushing it under the rug and hoping that at some point it worked itself out would have been detrimental to our relationship. We would have never stood a chance.

"I'm not saying that I want you both to declare your feelings for one another like this is *The Notebook* or something. I just... I think you should at least acknowledge the fact that something's there."

"This is hard to talk about," Reed muttered under his breath. Out of the corner of his eye, Josh glanced in Reed's direction, which I took as silent confirmation that he agreed.

When he didn't say anything more, his knuckles white from where he gripped the counter, I searched for a solution—one that would get them talking, if possible.

"Look," I said, crossing to Reed and watching Josh out of my peripheral. "I'm not going to force you to talk, but if it makes it easier, then I can leave or—"

"No," Josh interrupted from behind me. Peering over my shoulder, I watched him glance back and forth nervously between me and Reed. "We should talk, but you shouldn't leave."

"Okay, well then pretend that you're just talking to me." Turning back to Reed, I continued, "We had a pretty good conversation last night when it was just the two of us."

Finally, Reed let go of the counter and turned to me, propping his hip against it. His fingers trailed down the back of my right arm and loosely gripped my fingers that were barely poking out of the sleeve of my sweatshirt. He was silent as he peered down at our joined hands. With his thumb, he rubbed back and forth against the smooth red nail polish on my middle finger.

I could feel the heat of Josh's stare burrowing through my clothes and into my back. Like me, I knew he was anxiously waiting for the next words out of Reed's mouth.

I was honestly slightly surprised that Josh hadn't already spoken up. Out of the two of them, Josh wore his feelings more on his sleeve. He'd told me before that it was a waste to hide your feelings.

But I figured that, like me, he was treading carefully, waiting to see what Reed had to say before adding his own thoughts.

"Last night wasn't planned," Reed murmured, still staring at our hands.

"You don't say?" I quipped sarcastically.

His eyes flashed to me, and I felt a slight pang of guilt. "Sorry. Sarcasm is my defense mechanism and my default during awkward situations." I squeezed his hand. "Please continue."

His lips quirked in the faintest of smiles, but it quickly passed. I couldn't remember the last time I'd seen Reed so nervous. There was even a small tremor in his hand, still idly playing with my fingers.

The last thing I wanted was for either of them to be nervous —I just wanted them to feel whatever they were feeling.

"It wasn't planned, and I can't believe it fucking happened," Reed rushed out in one long breath.

"Mm-hmm," I mused and was content to wait for him to expand, but he didn't. He eyed me expectantly and for one of the first times in my life, I was at a loss for words.

"And…" I started, and the first thing to come to mind came tumbling out of my mouth. "Do you want to do it again?"

Reed's eyes lifted from our hands, and the flare of heat behind them made my sex clench. No words were needed for me to know what he was thinking, but I waited as a smile lifted the corners of my mouth.

"Yes," he said hungrily in a low, husky voice.

"Okay, good," I said breathlessly. "Glad we got that out of the way. Now—" I began to turn to Josh when Reed cut me off midsentence.

"But I don't want to pressure anyone else into anything. Just because I want something doesn't mean that the two of you also have to want it. I understand that I've made things even more complicated, and I—" Reed was breathing heavily when Josh finally interrupted him.

"I know that you have this uncanny need to take the blame for everything, but I think we're past that. Not only did I kiss you back last night, but I also jacked you off into our girlfriend.

So, yeah, maybe you started it, but I really took it to another fucking level."

While he spoke, Josh crossed the kitchen to where Reed and I stood. The only thing separating them now was me, and I tried to slink away without being noticed. Josh's hand on my waist stopped me.

I peered over my shoulder at him, but his eyes didn't move from Reed's. His stare was intense yet steady, and I could see the wheels in his head turning like he was preparing for anything.

Quickly I glanced back at Reed, who, with his hands balled into fists at his sides, was returning the same look to Josh. I couldn't tell if they were about to fuck or fight.

Both seemed equally likely.

But finally, and so slowly that for several seconds I didn't actually notice it was happening, Reed relaxed. His hands unclenching and his shoulders dropping.

With a shake of his head, he turned back to the island and braced his hands on the countertop. Josh's hand around my waist finally loosened.

"How did this happen?" Reed murmured.

Behind me, Josh let out a sardonic chuckle. "Hell if I fucking know, but I don't think there's much we can do about it now."

"Would you want to do something about it?" There was a hesitance in Reed's voice, and he eyed Josh from the corner of his eye.

"No," Josh said, his voice lacking all the hesitation laced in Reed's.

Finally, Reed straightened and looked at Josh behind me. "Okay."

"Okay," Josh said.

I looked at Reed. Josh looked at Reed. I looked at Josh. Josh looked at me. But no one said anything.

Was that it?

"Is that it?" I asked while huddling deeper into my sweatshirt. It felt like the temperature was dropping by the minute as the snow continued to fall outside.

"What do you mean?" Reed questioned, finding his phone on the counter and shaking his head slowly.

"That's all you have to say to each other? I don't feel like anything was really resolved."

"We said all we needed to say," Josh added, looking at his own phone.

Quickly, I glanced back and forth between them, thoroughly confused. "I don't think anything was *really* said. So, are you together? What's happening?"

They looked at me like I was crazy, and for a moment, I thought I might be. That maybe they hadn't had the conversation I'd witnessed and heard. But I also knew that couldn't have been true.

"Sure."

"Yeah, sure."

I lifted my hands in mock surrender to their insane thought processes. It was like they had a silent conversation that only the two of them could hear.

Reed stepped forward, slid his hand around my neck, and kissed my forehead. "I promise we're good, babe."

"Yes," Josh said, moving behind me and kissing my temple. "We're good."

They shared a soft smile, and finally, I felt like I could agree with them. My heart pounded in my chest, but it wasn't nerves that made my heart rate accelerate—it was happiness.

"I have to call Collin and see how things are holding up at the gym."

"Yeah, I'm going to call Sam and try to talk to Zach."

"On that note," I said, turning on my heels toward my bedroom. "I'm going to take a much-needed shower." The ache between my legs was evidence of last night I didn't mind. Actually, I loved that they'd used me so thoroughly that I could feel them both hours later. However, I wasn't necessarily fond of the dried sweat and body odor.

They shared a look and then glanced at me. "Hopefully your complex uses gas to heat the water," Reed said before putting his phone to his ear.

"I guess I'm about to find out."

"Save some for me, babe." Josh winked.

I rolled my eyes, but I also couldn't contain my smile.

# THIRTY-FIVE

Josh

YELLING WAS THE FIRST THING I WAS GREETED BY WHEN I OPENED the back door to Murphy's.

I recognized Rhonda's drawl immediately but not the other voice that participated in the argument.

As I approached, it seemed like they were at the tail end of their little spat. "Just get it done as soon as possible. I need to be open tonight!"

She rounded the corner from the back bar the same moment I did, and we nearly collided. With hands on either of her shoulders, I steadied the tiny spitfire of a woman.

"Christ on a fucking cracker! You scared the shit out of me, Josh." She braced a hand over her heart and took shallow breaths.

"Sorry. Leak still isn't fixed yet?"

In a dramatic motion, she waved her hands out beside her and shook her head. "No, it's still not fucking fixed. He promised it'd be done earlier this week, but then there was an issue getting a certain part. Then yesterday, it was something about his kid, and today he made me the same promise he did before."

Compared to most businesses—and people in general—the bar escaped the freeze nearly untouched. The leak, although significant, was our only issue.

It still meant that the water was shut off and without running water, we couldn't open the bar. And without opening the bar, we couldn't make money. Every night the place was closed was another hit to our pockets.

I didn't envy Rhonda's position as the owner and making all of the difficult decisions.

"But anyway, I'm glad you're here. I've already chewed him a new one, so let's go chat for a second."

I could count on one hand the number of times I'd been at the bar before nine a.m. And most of them were not for anything pleasant. Rhonda—or the previous manager and one of my best friends, Blakely—would only call me in if there was something wrong or if I'd *done* something wrong. The possibility of either happening that morning was making my heart beat at a wild pace.

She'd called me the night before to tell me that she needed to speak to me the following morning and that it was urgent. I'd tried—and utterly failed—to get her to tell me over the phone and reluctantly agreed to meet her at the bar before my workout with Reed.

As glad as I was that the winter storm was over, I also wasn't at all. Being locked in an apartment with Reed and Amanda was the happiest I'd been in a while.

Rhonda led us to the front of the place and took a seat at a high-top table near the door. I joined her at the opposite wooden barstool and nervously bounced my leg.

"Look, you know me, and I'm not going to sugarcoat it. I'm getting old, and I've been doing this for way too damn long already. This place has been my baby, but I can't keep up anymore. I'm a grandma and every second I'm at the bar is another second away from my grandkids."

All of that I knew. I knew she had a third grandkid on the way. They lived out of state, and it was part of the reason she gave me the manager job—my son was here, and with Sam's and my joint custody agreement, it made me available every other weekend. She also trusted me to build a staff that could handle the place when I wasn't on the premises.

But there was something more. In the decade I'd known Rhonda, she appeared nervous. Her wide gray eyes were uncertain, and instinctually, I straightened, preparing for what was coming.

"I'm gonna sell the place."

*What?* My mouth opened and closed, but I couldn't form words. My bouncing leg and my racing heart had both stopped completely, and something like shock filtered through my limbs.

"Please understand that this is not an easy decision to make. I've thought about it for the last year, and I can't keep up anymore. And—"

As politely as I could manage in my shocked state, I held up a finger. I caught her nod out of the corner of my eye, but I wasn't all there.

Murphy's was like a second home to me. In college, I'd spent more nights playing pool or sitting at the bar than I did in my own fucking apartment. It was where most of my favorite memories took place.

And sadly, some of the worst moments were also contained within its walls.

Valerie using our bar as a place to hold Hazel hostage was always going to gnaw at me. The kick of the gun in my hand and the silence that followed the bang would continue to haunt me.

But all of the bad—from the occasional bar fight to the horrific—didn't outweigh the happiness the place had created in my life. The people I'd met. The good that was done.

The thought of it no longer being there was devastating.

Because I knew the likelihood of someone buying it and keeping it exactly as it was and running it exactly as Rhonda had for the past, however many decades, was slim to none.

My eyes fell to the table as I took a short trip down memory lane. "When?" I asked, not looking back up.

"I'd like to be out of here in the next few months. I'm hoping to find a buyer that doesn't want to change too much because the place has been here so long and we just did those renovations. But I know that's probably not possible, which is why I brought you here. I want to give you first dibs."

"Dibs?" I asked, my voice cracking over the word.

She nodded. "I understand this place holds a lot for you, too. Lots of it good and plenty bad, but it's been like yours for a while now, so I wanted to offer it to you. I mean, you'd still have to buy it, but I'd make you a good deal. Give you a nice little discount if it comes down to it."

My mind began racing, and I felt like my entire world was falling apart around me. The high I'd felt coming off my several days with Reed and Amanda was replaced by doubt and uncertainty.

I wasn't going to kid myself—I didn't know what my future held, but it wasn't that. I hadn't made any definitive plans, but I'd at least thought about how the next several years of my life would play out. In all of my plans about what could happen, Rhonda selling Murphy's hadn't appeared in my wildest scenarios.

And knowing it was going to happen suddenly changed everything.

"Rhonda, I appreciate the offer, but I don't have the cash for that. And I'm also not confident in the possibility of getting a loan."

I'd saved up enough to last me several months in case anything were to happen and had recently begun investing—at the urging of Reed. But I wasn't liquid enough to buy a business. It was nearly impossible. An unachievable dream.

"Well, you could find investors, and I wouldn't completely write off the loan idea. Just..." She trailed off and for only the second time since I'd worked for her, Rhonda softened. She reached out and placed one of her hands over my own. Lines around her eyes and mouth appeared when she smiled, showing that she'd lived a happy and full life.

"Just don't dismiss the possibility yet. There are a few people interested, but if you can come up with something, you're first in line. No matter what. I'll give you until the beginning of May. Until then, I don't need an answer. Okay?"

As gentle as her tone was, there was also no room for argument in her request. So, I nodded and she patted my hand before letting go.

"Good, now get the hell out of here. I'm going to go yell at the plumber some more and make sure we're open. I've got tonight covered, but I'll see you tomorrow."

# THIRTY-SIX

Reed

WE WERE IN THE MIDST OF THE LONGEST DRIVE TO AMANDA'S EVER. Josh was quiet and contemplative. And his muted demeanor had me on edge. Out of the corner of my eye, I noticed his jaw work. He was likely grinding the shit out of his molars in an attempt to tamp down whatever he was feeling.

His hands—ones I'd grown fond of over the past week with their large veins and thick fingers—gripped the door handle with unrelenting force while the other nervously tapped against his thigh.

I'd already asked him twice if he was okay, which was my usual quota—after that, I'd butt out of his business because it wasn't my place. But the new dynamic we'd established meant new rules. My gut reaction was the same one I'd had if Amanda was in Josh's seat—I would have reached over and halted the nervous tapping with my own hand. I would have weaved my fingers through hers and then demanded she tell me. Or threatened to pull over and fuck the truth out of her.

But my usual unwavering confidence had faltered when it came to Josh. How did a person act with their best friend turned boyfriend? After more than ten years of friendship, it was hard to know what behavior was acceptable.

I was terrified he was in a mood because of me. My first reaction when he'd walked into the gym that morning, his mouth set in a straight line and only a grunt for a greeting, was that he'd changed his mind. That he'd seen the insanity of it and decided I wasn't worth it or was too much trouble.

I knew it was ridiculous—we'd seen each other at home that morning and nothing had been "off," but I wasn't above the occasional intrusive thought. If something had changed, it wasn't likely to happen in such a short amount of time, but I was about to explode if he didn't speak up. I would have rather known if he'd had a change of heart.

He'd come out of his room dressed in a navy-blue suit and a light-blue collared shirt for dinner with my parents. His shirt magnified the blue in his eyes to a color that was almost neon. We hadn't had much alone time during the week—both of us working longer hours trying to get our respective businesses back open after the freeze. There hadn't even been a lingering touch or word spoken that was out of the ordinary for our friendship. But when he'd walked out, straightening his cuffs and stopping to glance in the mirror out in the living room to smooth his hair back down, emotion sat heavy in my stomach. And so did desire.

"Light's green," he said. Effectively startling me from my thoughts. And the sound of his voice in the silent car didn't do anything for my anxiety. It was like it was taking on a physical form, crawling over my skin and embedding itself behind my eyes.

And when I thought I truly could not take anymore, Josh sighed.

"Just ask."

I stopped at another red light and the last one before we turned into Amanda's apartment.

"What?" I asked, my voice sounding foreign and quiet to my own ears.

"Ask the question that's making you all jittery. I know it has to be something, so just ask it or say it."

"You seem upset, and I can't help but think it's because…" I took a deep breath and tried to dig deep for that confidence I usually had, yet it was nowhere to be found. "Because you've changed your mind or something… about us."

My hands threatened to break the damn steering wheel with the force I was gripping it.

But then he laughed. Turning, I gawked at him. It was the exact opposite reaction I was expecting.

He continued laughing, and I hated that I really enjoyed the sound. Finally, the light turned green.

With one final chuckle, he said, "You're a little conceited."

My jaw dropped once again. "What the hell does that mean? I'm trying to figure out what the fuck is wrong with you. How does that make me conceited?"

"Because, of course, you think it has to be about you. That you are the only thing in my life that would affect me so much that I was in a bad mood. But, just so we're clear, there are other things going on that don't have to do with you."

"You're a fucking dick, you know that?"

And he snickered, followed by a slow shake of his head. "Sure, you keep telling yourself that. At least I know you like my dick."

His statement was true, which meant heat warmed my neck and colored my cheeks. *What the fuck?* I couldn't remember the last time I'd blushed. But one mention of his cock and I was like a thirteen-year-old girl.

"Is that your roundabout and insulting way of telling me that it isn't me that's upset you and that we're totally fine?" I asked. And when he was about to answer, I added, "And that you like my dick, too?"

Slowly, his eyes closed. And he wanted to look annoyed, but his tongue darted out and licked his upper lip. He wasn't annoyed at all—he was likely thinking about what my dick would taste like or what it would feel like in his mouth. At least that's what I was telling myself. *God* did I want that to happen. And soon.

I'd had a taste of him while locked in Amanda's apartment—together, both he and Amanda had jerked me off while she rode my face. And I'd returned the favor a little while later. But that little taste wasn't nearly enough—I needed more.

"Yes, that's what I'm telling you."

A lightness filled me, and total relief was on the horizon until I realized there was still something else bothering him. "But you don't want to talk about what's really going on then?"

I pulled into a spot near Amanda's place but hesitated before hopping out of the car, giving Josh the opportunity to start talking.

"Sam called me this afternoon… she knows about the three of us. And she wasn't necessarily happy about it."

"How?" The three of us had only just decided that we were together—no one else knew.

He sighed and scrubbed a hand through his hair, messing up the perfectly placed strands. "Travis, her fiancé, works out at RG Fitness. Apparently, there's been a rumor going around for a while that there was something between us," he said, motioning between the two of us. "And I guess the rumor was strong enough to get back to him. She called me and asked about it. I didn't feel like I had another choice but to tell her the truth."

I nodded and made a mental note to try to keep up better with the rumor mill. Some of my employees were worse than teenagers.

"What'd she say?"

He sighed and shook his head, staring out the window on his side of the car. "She was concerned about what Zach might think or how it could make his life harder. That I hadn't taken him into consideration."

"That's bullshit," I muttered, and Josh made a sound of agreement in his throat.

"It is, but I'm not sure I did so well changing her mind."

"This isn't going to cause any problems for you, right?" The last thing we wanted—both me and Amanda—was to come between Josh and Zach. He was the most important person in Josh's life, and if our presence disrupted that...

"It's nothing I can't handle. She just doesn't want me to introduce either of you as my partners and doesn't really want Amanda around him more than necessary until we know, as she put it, '*that this is going to last.*'"

"Doesn't have much faith in us then..."

"She said our track records don't bode well for the future."

I choked out a humorless laugh and glanced at the clock on the dashboard. Unfortunately, we didn't have too much longer to talk, but I wanted to make one last point.

"Our lack of relationships has nothing to do with commitment issues. They were due to a lack of appropriate candidates. We weren't going to waste time on anything that wasn't going to last. We waited... for a reason."

His nod was slow, and I knew he understood the deeper meaning of my words. We'd waited for each other—we'd waited until it could be the three of us.

A faint smile tugged at his lips, but then he was back to looking out his window. I could feel there was more he wasn't saying.

"Anything else?" I asked

"Nope," he replied quickly and opened his door. "Now, let's go get our girl."

# THIRTY-SEVEN

Reed

MY PARENTS' HOUSE WAS ENTIRELY TOO BIG FOR THE TWO OF THEM, but they wouldn't sell it. The tan three-story brick-and-stone structure was where I grew up, so my mom refused to let my father put it on the market. She said the walls held all of the memories of my childhood.

They'd purchased the eight-bedroom house only a few years after they were married, with plans to fill each room with a child. But they'd only been able to have me.

I assumed when they realized I was the only biological child they'd get, they would have sold the house and found something a little more reasonable for our three-person family. But they didn't—my mom said the rooms that never became nurseries were reminders of how thankful we should be for what we did have.

The place still felt like home. It smelled like Mom's cooking and I could hear the laughter around Christmastime—the one time of year my entire family was together.

Memories like that made me grateful they'd never sold it.

"I always forget how much money your parents have until

we pull up to this damn house and it's like you're smacked in the face with it," Josh quipped as I pulled into the long, winding driveway.

Mature oak trees my mom and I planted when I was a kid lined the drive that opened to the main house. With impeccable timing, the outdoor lights illuminated the brick facade and the surrounding landscaping as the last of the sun faded behind the horizon.

"Yeah, it's pretty impressive," Amanda commented from the back seat. "But still homey."

I snorted a laugh. My mom made it homey, but we could only hope that my father's reception was welcoming. That was if he came out of his office at all until Mom pulled him out for dinner.

We piled out of the car, Josh helping Amanda down in her heels with an outstretched hand. I met them on their side of the car and stared up at the house. For the first time since my mom told me dinner was nonnegotiable, I felt a flicker of nervous energy.

"Hey," Amanda said. "Did you tell your parents that you were bringing both of us?"

"Umm... not necessarily," I said, and they both gave me wide-eyed, concerned looks. Quickly, I continued, "But Mom always tells me to bring whoever. I promise it'll be fine. She'll be more than excited to see y'all."

"She better be," Josh muttered, and we headed up the walkway.

Placing my hand on the small of Amanda's back, Josh took one of her hands, and we approached the door. I tentatively tried the door handle.

"Unless you want to tell your parents, I recommend that we stop touching each other," Amanda said, and like she was suddenly a thousand degrees Josh dropped her hand and I yanked mine from her back.

She laughed as we stepped into the foyer, immediately over-whelmed by the smell of spices—the smell of home.

"Finally! Come in, come in!" We heard her voice and the click of her heels on the dark, hardwood floors before she appeared from around the corner to our left. She smiled and waved us farther into the house.

"It's been too long!" she cried the second her hands wrapped around my neck.

"Hi, Mamá," I said, returning her hug and savoring the comfort only a hug from my mom could provide.

"How are you doing? Remember you're supposed to eat between working out." She stepped back and appraised me from head to toe and back again. With one eyebrow raised, and her hands propped on her hips, a corner of her mouth tugged upward.

She turned to Josh and Amanda.

"And two of my other favorite people. I'm so glad you're here." I could see some of their apprehension dissipate.

She sauntered to them, smoothing her hands over her apron. It was tied around her dark-green dress, and her black hair that cascaded down her back was twisted into a bun. They both smiled fondly at her and returned each embrace.

"I'm so glad Reed finally brought some of his friends. There's too much food, so the more, the better! Now, let's go into the living room. What would you like to drink?"

She led us into the living room, discussing what she was preparing in the kitchen, and stopped in front of the fully stocked wet bar.

"I can make the drinks, Mamá," I said, noticing her eyes constantly darting back to the adjoining kitchen.

"Okay, let me just finish up a few things, then I'll be right back." She hurried back into the kitchen without a glance back in our direction.

"Do you want help?" Amanda called after her, but my mom waved her off and told her to make herself at home.

From the wet bar, I chose three crystal tumblers and poured whiskey for me and Josh while I added gin to the third for Amanda. I turned to find the two of them standing in front of the fireplace, eyeing the framed photos on the mantel. The warm glow from the small fire bathed them in soft light and there was a feeling in my chest that seemed to mirror that glow. It was pleasant and happy watching the two of them together.

"This one has always been my favorite." Amanda laughed as I handed her her drink.

She was pointing to a photograph of me when I couldn't have been more than four or maybe five years old. I'd found an old football helmet and jersey of my dad's and immediately begged my parents to let me try them on. They conceded, but I looked like a little bobblehead doll with the massive helmet and my little body. The jersey was hanging off of me in every direction, but through the face guard, you could see the largest, toothless grin splitting my face.

Simpler times. When a few missing teeth and having to wait to grow into a football helmet were my biggest concerns. When my dad didn't act like everything I did had disappointed him so thoroughly.

"It's my mom's, too. That's why it is still on the mantel even though I ask her to take it down nearly every time I'm here."

"Wow," Josh said from a foot or two away, and I knew which photo had caught his eye. "That was the first Friendsgiving with Hazel. When Blakely was trying her damnedest to break them up. I thought for sure Hazel wasn't going to stick around through that."

The photograph was all of us seated around Luke's couch after dinner with our stomachs full and smiles on our faces. Blakely's smile was clearly forced, sad even, but the rest of us were happy.

The three of us stood and stared at the photo, a sadness swirling around us that wasn't there moments before. The photo was taken before everything happened and before Blakely disappeared completely.

"Oh, that's one of my favorites," my mom crooned as she stepped between us. We all collectively sighed in relief at her perfectly timed interruption.

She took Josh and Amanda through the rest of the pictures on the mantel, sharing embarrassing stories of my school days and anecdotes from family vacations. I hung back, lounging on one of the dark leather armchairs near the fireplace, and watched the three of them. Every so often, I would cringe at a more mortifying account from my childhood.

But Josh and Amanda were eating it up. Occasionally, they would glance back at me, and I would chime in with my own version of the story, to which my mom would chide and silence me with only one fierce look.

"Where is Dad?" I asked after my mom finished another story of my childish antics.

"Office," she tsked and replaced the frame in her hands on the mantel, not letting her annoyance show. "He'll be down for dinner. Oh, could you and Josh move something for me, please? There's a dresser in the hallway by your room that I need to put in the attic. It should only take a second for the two of you."

"Of course, Mama G," Josh answered for us both and set his nearly empty glass on a coaster on the side table. He hesitantly reached his hand out like he was searching for mine but quickly tucked it into his pocket and moved toward the stairs.

Behind us, I could hear Mom ushering Amanda into the kitchen, requesting that she taste the dinner she had prepared.

As we climbed the curved wooden staircase to the second floor, I did a shameful job not staring at Josh's ass. It wasn't my fault that the hours we'd spent in the gym meant his ass was perfectly sculpted and on display in his tight dress pants.

I didn't notice until I got to the top of the stairs that Josh was watching me, too, except he had a knowing grin tugging at the corners of his lips. Yeah, he'd caught me gawking, and honestly, I couldn't give a fuck. We were together, and I couldn't keep my eyes to myself. It was already going to be torturous getting through dinner without touching either of them, I couldn't be accountable for also keeping my eyes off of them.

Josh chuckled, shook his head, and with his hands tucked into his pockets, led the way down the dimly lit hall to our left. The house was split up into two separate wings. My parents' wing, as I liked to call it as a child, was to our right, and mine was to our left. I turned left behind Josh, and our steps were quieted by the plush off-white carpet running the length of the hallway. And like Mom said, there was a lone dresser sitting in the otherwise empty corridor.

"She wants it in the attic?" Josh asked, looking above us for any sign of an access point on the ceiling. But I chuckled and opened my old bedroom door. The past smacked me directly in the face.

Neither of my parents had changed my space since I'd graduated from high school and moved out for college. The same navy bedspread was thrown over the end of the bed, and the walls were still medium gray.

"I think the last time I was in here was... Mama G's birthday a few years ago. I still can't believe they haven't changed your room after all this time." From my old bedside table, he picked up a picture of me and a few of my high school football teammates after a homecoming game one year. He set it back down, then opened the top drawer and smiled broadly before barking out a laugh.

"These had to of expired a long fucking time ago." The box of condoms in his hand was one I likely bought my senior year for the summer before college.

"Yeah, Mom washes the sheets every couple of weeks. Then the housekeeper vacuums and dusts this room like she does every other room, but otherwise, no one steps foot in here."

"Don't parents usually turn their kids' rooms into craft rooms or a gym or something?" he asked, continuing his perusal of all of my old belongings and posters plastered to the walls.

Opening the closet door, I turned on the light and jimmied open the attic access door in the back corner. When I was a kid, the smaller access door in the closet was a hideout I used in the cooler months. It was too hot to use in the summer.

When my dad began to notice I spent more time in the attic than I did with him when my mom was gone, he strategically began filling it with anything and everything. Suddenly, his office needed to be redecorated, yet none of the old furniture could have been thrown away.

My little sanctuary—which, to his credit, I did use as an escape when my mom was gone—turned into a storage space. The complaints I threw in his direction afterward didn't go over so well. It felt like it was always something with him.

"I'm sure they would have changed it if they didn't already have six other rooms that they could use for whatever purpose their hearts desired," I finally responded and stepped back out into the room. He was enthusiastically flipping through a yearbook he'd found somewhere as I nudged him. "Help me with this."

"You call me Sunshine because of my long-ass hair in high school, yet your hair was just as long."

We both grunted under the weight of the solid wood dresser and hauled it into my room, through the closet, and wedged it into the attic between a tall mirror and an old desk.

In the nearly empty closet—because I did take my clothes with me to college—I closed the attic door and turned to Josh, who was watching me with his arms crossed over his chest. He'd tossed his navy-blue jacket next to where I'd discarded mine over a desk chair in my bedroom before we did any heavy lifting, which left him in his light-blue fitted shirt. The shirt was tight in all of the right places—over his broad chest and along his toned arms.

"I don't call you Sunshine just because of your hair." I

stepped forward, crowding into his space. His arms fell to his sides and I took the liberty of running my hands down them. The muscles under my palms tensed even with the faintest touch.

"I call you Sunshine," I continued, returning my attention to his ocean-colored eyes that were locked on my face, "because you *are* fucking sunshine."

# THIRTY-EIGHT

Reed

His breath caught, and it was a reaction I probably would've missed had we not been so close and everything around us so completely silent.

"Is that so?" he asked with a small quirk of his lips.

"Yes," I responded and let all my resistance snap at once. My hands fisted in his short hair, and I crashed my mouth over his. His trim facial hair scratched against mine as his fingers looped around my wrists, holding me steady to him.

I could feel the slip of our tongues and the mixing of our heated breaths throughout my entire body. It quieted the incessant, warring thoughts that came with being in my childhood bedroom and replaced them only with ideas of what we could get up to in the minutes we had to spare in my closet.

"*Fuck*, Sunshine," I muttered against his skin, letting my lips travel across his jaw and down his neck.

How we'd gone from being best friends only a week before to so much more was unreal. But I wasn't pumping the brakes—if anything, I wanted to move faster.

"Don't you find it funny that we're making out in a closet

while we really are *in the closet?*" My lips poised against his throat, and I could feel the vibrations of his chuckle. His hands pressed against my stomach, and I knew he could feel my responding laugh.

"It does feel a little ironic." I lifted my head and met his eyes, taking in a shaky breath. There was a playfulness in his eyes and in the slight tip of his mouth, but I was again buzzing with nervous energy.

Of course, he could tell. "Tell me what you're thinking," he requested with a tentative hand against my cheek.

"This... I've been thinking about this all week." He didn't need any clarification—Josh knew exactly what I meant by *this.*

"There's something I've been thinking about, too," he said, bumping his hips against mine and urging me backward. Stepping between my legs, the hard length of his cock brushed against my own straining erection, pressing against the seam of my suddenly too-tight dress pants. Josh greedily swallowed my groans and swept his tongue against mine.

"What have you been thinking about?" I prompted, hoping it would continue in the direction we were going.

The hand he had cradled against my face lowered, trailing down the buttons of my shirt and only pausing a moment above my belt. He stepped back enough to look down to where his hand tentatively cupped my growing erection. If I questioned his intention before, I didn't then.

His grip tightened, and I couldn't help my sharp intake of breath. It had felt like the longest week without them.

I closed my eyes against the pleasure pounding through me, whipping down my spine and quickly hardening my cock. Josh's lips moved along my jaw and down my neck. It wasn't often I found myself willingly giving up dominance, but I was eager to let Josh take the lead.

I was ready to experience everything he would give me.

There was a tug and then I heard my belt fall open. My whole body was alive with anticipation, and I opened my eyes just in time to see his thick fingers plunge into my pants and wrap around my shaft.

The slight hesitation I felt in his earlier movements was nowhere to be found. He confidently pumped my cock from base to tip with the perfect amount of pressure. I reveled in the scrape of his calluses against my skin, and in seconds, my impending orgasm was growing at the base of my cock.

It felt better than I could have ever imagined.

"I'm not going to last," I muttered as his lips found mine once again in a slow, taunting kiss.

*God*, his tongue was perfect, and I was suddenly overcome by the need to know what it would feel like against my cock. I was sure he'd lap at me with the same confidence his hand showed wrapped around me.

My dick jumped at the possibility, and he upped his pace. Fisting me without mercy, he brought me to the brink of release with each slip of his hand. And when I thought I'd explode all over his palm and the inside of my pants, I witnessed something I'd only seen in my craziest fantasies—ones I'd allowed myself to have after that night in Amanda's apartment.

In his dress pants and button-down shirt, Josh dropped to his knees in one swift motion and tugged my cock free of the confines of my boxer briefs. It bobbed in front of his face and was angrily hard. The veins running the length were thick, as was the darkened, nearly purple crown.

He bit his lower lip and he took me in with an intense stare—one that showed a little hesitance but still swam with hunger like he was prepared to devour me. He'd barely touched me, yet I was ready to explode like a horny teenager. But the moment he licked up the seam, tasting the precum leaking from my tip and letting out a small groan at the taste, my knees buckled.

Then he wrapped his lips around me and sucked until the crown of my cock prodded the back of his throat.

The world spun behind my eyelids. He kept a hand tight at the base while his mouth fought to take the rest of my length.

Slowly, I felt his throat relax, and then he began to move. He worked slowly at first, bobbing his mouth up and down and sliding my shaft in and out of his warm, wet mouth.

Against the trim hair at the base and every once in a while against my skin, I could feel his stubble scratch and pull. A little reminder that my best friend, who was very much a man, was on his knees for me. Worshiping my cock with unexpected reverence.

His hand followed his mouth, pumping in long, hard strokes that never ceased. He sucked, lapped, teased, and I was greedy for it all. I was completely enchanted by the sight before me and the way he worked me over so perfectly.

My fingers dug into his intentionally messy dirty-blond hair, and I was a prisoner to him. Shackled and chained to the pleasure he brought to my life. Pleasure and fucking sunshine.

His hair was soft against my fingers, and he groaned when I tugged softly. *Pain.* That's what Amanda said—Josh liked pain as much as she did. So, I dug my fingers in and wrenched at the root of his hair. I was rewarded with another deep moan that vibrated my cock.

His tongue was just as magical as I had hoped.

"*Holy shit.* Don't fucking stop." My grip on his hair was merciless and my words were pointless. He wasn't fucking stopping.

"You've created a monster, Sunshine. I'm going to need you on your knees all the time. *Fuck*, so gooooood."

And I watched my cock glistening with his spit disappear behind his swollen, pink lips. His hand, with its thick fingers and prominent veins, was lighter compared to my tanned skin, but I liked how easily it wrapped around and pumped my cock. His hand met his lips at the base, and he swallowed around me, his throat pulsing around the crown in subtle yet impactful movement.

Too soon, there was a tightening and tingle at the base of my cock and my balls were drawing up. But I needed his ocean eyes on me, too, to see what he was doing to me. How he was unwinding me—tearing me down and rebuilding me as his. *Theirs.*

"Look at me," I commanded and his eyes, brimming with unshed tears from deep-throating my cock, popped open. "So fucking good. I'm going to come if—"

My words were cut off. I wanted to tell him if he wanted to pop off, he could, but he left no room for argument. My words disappeared when his free hand cupped and pulled at my balls that were already drawing up. The motion sent my orgasm barreling through me.

Shooting my release deep down Josh's throat, he took it all, never once pulling back or looking away from me.

My brain short-circuited, unable to fully process everything that happened until Josh slowly released my cock. My fingers loosened in his hair as he pulled back, and I hoped I hadn't hurt him with how tight my grip had become in the throes of pleasure.

The million-watt smile splitting his face when he stood told me he'd enjoyed it nearly as much as I had. Eye to eye, there was glee and happiness radiating from him.

"How'd I do?" he asked, wiping his mouth with the back of his hand.

An amazed chuckle was my only response for several seconds while I fully came down from the high.

"That was your first time?" I asked, and he nodded. He knew what I was asking and shrugged.

"I did my research—watched a couple of videos." I chuckled. Of course he had.

"Everything I said in the moment is true. I'm going to need you on your knees all the time. Even better if you can loop Amanda in with you," I said with a groan at the thought of both of them sucking me down.

"That can be arranged. How much you want to bet Amanda is going to know exactly what we were doing right when we walk down there?" His eyes were alight with mischief, and I tucked myself back into my pants as we walked out into my bedroom.

Standing in the middle of my childhood bedroom, I kissed the lips that were seconds ago wrapped around my cock and fully appreciated the calmness that he created.

"I wish there was enough time for me to return the favor."

"Something to look forward to after we get through dinner," he promised while adjusting his own pants to hide the erection that was eagerly seeking some attention. Hand in hand, we grabbed our jackets before heading into the hallway.

Downstairs, you could faintly hear Amanda and my mom talking in the kitchen. Josh walked slightly in front of me, our hands still clasped until he reached the first step. His fingers slipped out of mine, but when he glanced backward, the smile on his face hadn't faltered.

But mine did.

Standing in the doorway to his office, just beyond the top of the stairs, was my father. His eyes were transfixed on my hand, which was still suspended in the air. The sensation of Josh's fingers still lingered against my skin.

I couldn't move. Even if I wanted to, it felt like my feet were lead. And I felt like I was in high school again, getting caught sneaking a girl out of my room—except I wasn't in high school, I was an adult and it was a guy that I'd been caught with.

How long had he been standing there? There was no way to know how much he'd seen. Or how much he'd heard. Fuck, *that* thought alone was enough to make me move.

I pivoted and was down the stairs in a second flat, trying to get as far away as I could from my father's knowing stare.

My pulse was pounding in my neck, and I was completely out of breath by the time I met Josh in the living room. He was retrieving his empty glass from where he'd set it earlier. He turned to say something but, noticing my stunned expression, stopped.

"What happened?" He stepped forward and reached out like he was going to touch me, comfort me.

The hurt that crossed his face when I stepped back and tucked the hand he was reaching for in my pocket was something I never wanted to see again.

I didn't know what to say, but when I opened my mouth to try to fix it, someone cleared their throat behind me.

"Dinner ready, boys?" my dad asked, stopping beside me and eyeing Josh, who forced another smile.

One that was deceptively hiding his hurt.

"Not sure," Josh said. "We were just heading in that direction. Nice to see you again, Mr. Gregory."

My father nodded, then waved us through the living room and into the dining room, noticeably trying to look anywhere but at me.

# THIRTY-NINE

### Amanda

BY THE END OF THE MEAL, NEITHER REED NOR HIS FATHER HAD spoken a word, but his mother was ecstatic about the number of people seated around her table.

Neither of the two men had eaten much and both had to fend off questions from Mama G about why their plates were still mostly full as we cleared the table.

Reed's mood always shifted when his dad was around or when someone brought him up, but even so, the shift was more obvious than I remembered. They'd barely looked up from their plates at all and when they did, they made sure they didn't look at one another.

A few times, I looked to Josh, trying to glean what had changed while they were upstairs by his facial expressions, but he wasn't giving anything away. If anything, he looked hurt or uncomfortable but was a better actor than the other two men.

I thought we'd make a speedy exit after the plates were clear, but then the two silent men had disappeared into the office where they'd been for at least half an hour. I was anxious to know what was being said. We hadn't heard yelling or raised voices from where we were gathered around the fireplace in the living room, but that hadn't made me feel much better.

We were sitting close enough on the small sofa that Josh's leg was pressed up against my own, and it was the only thing keeping me calm until Mama G pulled out old photo albums and he'd shifted to allow her between us.

After several pages and stories about little Reed, I quietly excused myself to go to the bathroom. But I bypassed the small half bath near the bottom of the stairs and quietly made my way to the second floor.

Through the partially opened office door, I could see only the outline of each man. They were seated in twin leather chairs near another fireplace, fresh drinks in their hands. Reed's father, Sebastian, leaned back in his chair, speaking quietly enough that I couldn't hear from my position several feet away. Reed, on the other hand, leaned forward with his elbows on his knees and his head hanging low.

The dim, flickering light of the fireplace cast ominous shadows across his face. He looked broken, and I longed to wrap my arms around him. To do something to lessen the weight of whatever it was.

That was until he suddenly looked up at his father. I crept forward slightly, hoping for a better look and to actually hear what was being said. The minimal light only allowed me to see part of his expression, but his eyes were wide and his jaw was slack like he was surprised. A million different versions of the conversations they could be having ran through my head.

"I... appreciate that... that means a lot." I was straining to hear and still couldn't make out each individual word, but the gist of it seemed positive.

Satisfied and knowing I had been standing there too long, I began to back away but was suddenly frozen in place when Reed's eyes snapped to mine. My stomach dropped at being caught eavesdropping, but a small smile tugged at his lips. Like he knew I was standing there the entire time.

"Okay, let's go rejoin—" Sebastian stood from his chair and Reed followed. And the last thing I wanted was for my boyfriend's father to catch me snooping. Quickly, I hurried back downstairs and into the living room. I slipped onto the couch once again.

Josh shot me a warning look that said he knew I hadn't gone to the bathroom.

"Oh, there you two are. We were starting to get worried." Mama G peered over our heads at Reed and his father. Her face displayed more than worry, though.

But the pair rounded the couch and there was little to no tension. Sebastian even had a hand resting on Reed's opposite shoulder, and I was eager to know what had been said. I'd never seen them so at ease around one another.

"We should probably head out," Reed suggested. And thus began the long process of trying to leave the Gregorys' house. Mama G insisted we each take leftovers and proceeded to make us individual containers of chicken, rice, and veggies. And before we made it out the door, we had to promise to return soon and I also had to agree to cooking lessons in the near future.

"I'm exhausted." Josh wrapped an arm around my waist and muttered into my hair before he opened the front passenger door for me. "It's been a long night of refraining from touching you."

I hopped in and was immediately greeted by Reed's hand on the back of my neck, effectively drawing my attention to his large frame in the driver's seat. My eyes roved over the dark hair along his sharp jawline and the slightly upturned set of his full lips. His eyes danced with mischief that spurred my entire body to life.

"Didn't your parents teach you it's not nice to eavesdrop?" he asked in a low voice.

"My parents honestly didn't teach me much." My own voice was breathy to my own ears and the way Reed's eyes flashed, he heard it too.

"Stay with us tonight." It wasn't a request, and I wasn't

going to argue—it had been a long week without them. It honestly scared me how much I wanted them. How much I *needed* them.

His grip on my neck tightened until I answered. "Okay."

And he kissed me in a brief meeting of lips that left me wanting so much more. "That's our good dirty girl. Then I can show you what happens to people who eavesdrop on conversations."

What would have sounded like a threat to most people sounded a whole lot like a promise I was going to enjoy. I only hoped it would involve a few of the things my imagination was creating.

"Eavesdropping, huh?" Josh chimed in from the back seat. "I knew that bathroom trip took too long."

"Yes," Reed said as he finally released me and started the car.

"Are you going to tell us what happened in there?"

Reed's hands gripped the wheel, twisting it in his grip like he was trying to pry it off. We idled in the driveway so long, Reed staring ahead and not at anything in particular, that I was worried one of his parents would come outside to make sure we were okay.

Finally, he said, "My dad caught us."

My breath caught in my throat, and I immediately suspected the worst.

"Caught who?" I prompted. Josh straightened in the back seat.

"Josh and I were holding hands on our way back downstairs—"

"You mean after one of you sucked the other's dick?" I guessed. They'd been gone for too long—moving one piece of furniture shouldn't have taken more than a few minutes, but they'd been gone for nearly twenty. I'd had to make several excuses for them to Mama G, including that they'd gotten caught up looking at Reed's old stuff and taken a trip down memory lane.

"So fucking observant," Josh muttered, which was all the confirmation I needed.

Reed cut his eyes to me, obviously not appreciative of my interruption, and continued, "He caught Josh and me holding hands. I thought he was pissed. He looked... disappointed or uncomfortable. And I wasn't going to explain it to him either until he said he wanted to talk."

He finally put the car in drive and made the circle, going back out the way we came in.

"I didn't even notice him. What did he say?" Josh asked, and I could feel the new nervous energy rolling off of him.

"He said that he was proud of me."

Josh and I shared a look in the rearview mirror, neither of us expecting that.

"He said that he understood he'd been hard on me my entire life but that he had the best intentions. And even though I'd made all of the decisions he'd told me not to, I'd still turned out alright. That I'm successful in spite of refusing his advice. And then he told me that if we were together..." He glanced at Josh. "That he would support us. That's when I told him that we're all three together."

I swallowed thickly and fiddled with the hem of my dress nervously as I waited for him to continue.

"And..." Josh prompted the longer the silence went on.

Reed chuckled, he actually fucking laughed before he shook his head. "He said he didn't really understand it but that I'd obviously done something right if I could keep two people happy. Most people can't even handle one."

"That's so good," I said. My smile grew by the second and so did Reed's. He reached over the center console and gripped my thigh with his strong palm. The anxiety and caution we'd all witnessed at dinner had completely evaporated. If I wasn't mistaken, we were all sitting a little taller and feeling a little lighter.

The person we thought would be one of the most difficult to

convince of the validity of our relationship turned out to be unabashedly accepting.

"What did y'all and my mom talk about?" Reed asked.

Josh reclined, arms resting along the back of the seat like a king. "We flipped through photo albums of little Reed. Your ass looked cute even when you were a kid."

Reed groaned, and Josh laughed as we turned out of the neighborhood. "I also heard about the time that you were scared something was wrong with you because... wait, I need to remember the exact wording your mom used. I think she said you were scared because, and I quote, 'my pee-pee shrinks when I get cold.' She said you were concerned for weeks about the size of your manhood."

Josh and I both erupted in a fit of laughter while Reed shook his head, fuming from his seat and casting annoyed glances between us.

"I was like four years old, *maybe*."

"Are you sure you don't still have some deep-seated concern about the size of your—"

"No," he said firmly, cutting me off.

"Man, I get it. This is a judgment-free zone if you would like to discuss any insecurities."

Reed growled and abruptly came to a stop at a red light. He took the opportunity to throw daggers at us both. "You both know firsthand that I do not have a complex about my dick. And when we get back to our place, I will gladly show you how confident I am and how well I can use it."

"Promises, promises," I chided.

"I'd be careful what you hope for, Cielo. What Josh and I are going to do to you when we get upstairs..."

"I have some ideas," Josh added darkly.

And a delightful shiver hurried down my spine.

# FORTY

Reed

"ON THE BED."

Josh and Amanda were lip-locked from the moment we stepped into the apartment. But they both had the wherewithal to move toward my bedroom.

"Who?" Amanda asked in a low, breathy voice that zapped straight to my cock. My hand encircled her throat, and as she always did, her breath skipped in excitement.

"Cielo," I purred into her ear. "You know exactly who I was talking to."

Eagerly, she sat her pretty little ass on my bed and scooted back to the pillows. Her little black dress rode higher the farther up my dark-green comforter she moved. One glance at Josh standing beside me and I knew his thoughts were the same as mine—we both wanted that dress off of her.

"Take off the dress."

She did, whipping it over her head and revealing matching black lace bra and panties.

"*Fuck,*" Josh muttered and pressed a hand down the impressive bulge forming below his belt. Between the two of them, I couldn't decide where to keep my attention. They were both so perfect.

"Take everything else off, too. I need you completely naked in my bed."

Lost in her orbit, Josh and I were laser-focused on each movement she made, frozen at the end of the bed. The dim moonlight streamed through the blinds and illuminated the tops of her breasts as she slowly freed them. Her pink nipples were already peaked, and instinctively, I licked my lips.

She cupped them in her hands, and my palms itched because I knew how perfectly full they were and I was eager to touch them. And when she shimmied her panties down her legs, I didn't think I was going to withstand her punishment. The one I was supposed to be doling out.

Beside me, Josh reached forward and nearly wrapped his fingers around Amanda's ankle before I stopped him. I dragged his hand back to me and placed it on my hip.

"No touching," I told him. "She gets to watch."

And I kissed his smile as I tried to suppress my own. On the bed, Amanda groaned and her legs dropped open. And in less than a second, her hand was blazing a path to her already wet cunt.

"Uh-uh. No touching meant for yourself as well. Not until I tell you to."

Her groan was resounding, and she immediately snapped her legs shut.

"Open," I demanded.

"You're fucking sadistic," she growled at the same time she did as I instructed.

Josh's hand on my hip tightened, and I gave Amanda a no-nonsense look, warning her to heed my request. Then I turned to the man to my left, who'd had my cock in his mouth only a few hours before and who I was dying to return the favor for.

One of my hands fisted in the lapel of his jacket while the

other gripped the back of his neck and slammed his mouth to mine. The three of us moaned simultaneously.

Fire and fire, we were going to burn each other alive. And I knew we'd enjoy every single second and each lick of the infernal flames.

Our lips melded together and began a teasing dance. His were firm against mine, and for a minute or two, I let him take the lead. His hands pressed against either side of my face, and he tilted my head to the side.

My body nearly shook from desire when he pressed against me. His hard cock was flush against mine and I groaned at the closeness. He swallowed each of my sounds like he was starving for them, and I suddenly wanted both of us naked. There was too much fabric, too many barriers for the many, *many* things I needed to do to him. Things I'd been thinking of for far longer than I would have ever let myself admit.

My hands found his belt at the same time he sucked my tongue into his mouth with a low chuckle. I could hear Amanda panting on the bed, and I was on the precipice of insanity.

"I need you naked. *Now*," I barked. My fumbling was slowing down the entire process, so he dutifully took over, removing his clothes. I did the same, quickly flinging my jacket and shirt across the room and yanking my pants and boxer briefs off in one swift movement.

Undressed, we both pressed back together like two opposite ends of a magnet.

Never did I believe that the feeling of another man's cock brushing and pressing against mine would ignite a fiery desire. And never did I imagine that I would love it so fucking much that I craved it. But there we were, and I couldn't stop touching him.

I palmed his ass, and I deftly moved my hands over every inch of his skin. I raked my fingers through his tousled blond hair and traced the muscles of his traps. The smooth planes of his back were soft to the touch, and I could do nothing more than grab his shapely ass.

I tugged him forward and ground against him, relishing how firm his cock was against my own. It was an effort to break our kiss, but I wanted to see what we looked like together, so I pulled back. Between our bodies, our cocks stood proudly, mine slightly darker and wider than his. But he was longer and still thick with an engorged pink head that made my mouth water.

My hand wrapped around the two of us, and slowly, I began to pump. Josh tossed his head back and grunted a throaty *"fuck"* as I found my rhythm. My hand wasn't large enough to fit around us both, but neither of us was complaining.

Amanda was still on the bed, large, blue eyes locked on our cocks as I jacked us both off together. Her wetness was glistening between her legs, and her breath was coming in short, sporadic gasps.

She might have been right—I could have been somewhat of a sadist because I knew we were fulfilling one of her fantasies, and the knowledge that she wouldn't touch herself because I told her not to only heightened my arousal. It made me pump our cocks faster and grind my hips against Josh until I nearly came all over our stomachs.

I watched her watch us and knew I could never be without them again. I needed them nearly as much as I needed my next breath and every one after.

Actually, I would've given up my next breath for them.

"Do you trust me?" I asked, turning my attention back to Josh, who was trying to divide his attention between watching me stroke our cocks and Amanda.

Without so much as a moment of hesitation, he choked out, "Yes."

"Cielo," I said to Amanda, effectively breaking the trance I'd put her in with the steady cadence of my hand. "Top drawer of my nightstand to your right. Grab the bottle."

She fumbled for the drawer and fished out the bottle of lube I knew was right on top.

She tossed it to the end of the bed and lay back on the pillows, her legs still spread.

"You're so perfect," I said, and she glowed in the wake of my praise.

I took Josh's hand in mine and led him to the dark leather chair next to my bed. Amanda's eyes never left us as we stalked to her left, and I pointed for Josh to sit. There was a slight concern on his face, but when I kneeled in front of him and urged his hips to the edge of the chair, it was completely erased.

His hands tightly gripped the arms of the chair, showing off the impressive veins running up his fingers and the length of his forearms. Staring down at me, he waited so patiently for what I had planned.

I placed a light kiss on the engorged head of his cock and licked the drop of precum. He tasted just as I remembered. And I couldn't resist. I wanted to go slow, and it was my intention to do so, but the moment the flavor exploded on my tongue, it wasn't a possibility.

I wrapped my lips around him and slid lower, trying to remember what I liked, what I noticed Josh liked while Amanda had him in her mouth. But I didn't need to remember like I thought I would. It was like second nature having Josh's cock against my tongue.

Each groan, moan and mumbled curse spurred me on, and I took him deeper. I set a pace that I would have thought was perfect to keep him on the edge. Right where I wanted him because there was so much more I had planned.

I pumped and sucked him hard, trying to swallow around his length. He was firm and long, and on my final pass, I bared my teeth just enough to scrape them against the smooth skin of his shaft. His hips bucked up into my mouth, searching for further relief, but I pulled off.

My hands continued working him, though. One swiveled up

and down around his shaft, and the other cupped his balls, hanging heavily between his thighs.

"I want to try something, okay?"

In a desire-drunk haze, he nodded, his eyes flitting between my hand around his shaft and my face. For several seconds, I held his gaze, looking for further consent. "Say it."

"Yes." It was clear and confident and all I needed.

I reached for the lube on the table and spread a small amount of the cold liquid over my fingers. My eyes found Amanda's, watching us intently and silently fuming. I couldn't imagine how frustrated she was to not partake.

A warm flush decorated her cheeks, and she squirmed on the bed. "You're so hot together. I want to watch you all the time, but this is torture."

"Something to think about next time you want to eavesdrop."

Her argument died on her tongue when I returned to my position between Josh's spread legs. I wasted no time running my left hand up his thigh, enjoying the tickle of his dark-blond hair against my palm, before wrapping his cock in a punishing grip. His eyes flared, and his jaw slackened. And I was eager to push him further.

My right hand slipped below his balls, but my eyes didn't leave his face. I watched his jaw slowly shut along with his eyes the moment I found his ass. In teasingly soft strokes, I circled the tight hole, never once changing the tempo of my strokes around his dick while I got him used to feeling me—or anything—at his entrance.

His breaths came out in short, panting gasps and between his teeth, he held his plump bottom lip hostage.

So slowly, I added pressure and tested the waters. Josh's features tightened, and I hesitated to continue until his legs widened even farther. I pressed harder and breached the first ring of muscles when he breathed a curse and popped his eyes open.

"*Fuck*," he muttered at the same time Amanda cursed behind me. "More."

"Fuck yes." My finger pulsed inside of him, his ass clenching around me and pulling me in deeper. He was warm and tight, and I couldn't fucking wait to feel him around my cock.

I pushed my finger farther until I was finally knuckle deep, and I groaned as it disappeared. His balls were heavy between his cock and my hand, and I intentionally pressed against his inner walls. The stretch was so good, and his eyes were locked on where my hand disappeared between his legs.

I intentionally flexed my finger and drug it against his upper wall. I knew the moment I hit that glorious spot because his hips flew off the chair in one swift motion.

My opposite arm banded around his waist and pressed him back down into the leather as I stroked the softer, firmer spot only a few inches inside of him.

"What the fuck? Holy shit. Holy *shit*," he breathed out and did his best to thrust himself down harder on my finger, even with my arm over his waist.

I added a second finger and repeated each step. Enjoying the stretch of his body around my digits, I eased in two fingers and fisted his cock once again. He was as hard as fucking stone, and I was right there with him.

My fingers pressed against that electrifying spot as my mouth lowered over the crown of his cock, proudly dripping with precum and aching for more.

"*Oh, fuck.* If you keep doing that, I'm going to come." Around him, my mouth didn't stutter at an unrelenting pace, licking the length of him and sucking him to the back of my mouth. And my fingers were still buried deep, pumping in and out of his ass and pressing deliciously into him.

But I still had more in store. "Not yet," I said, and I gave the tip of him, glistening with my spit, one final kiss.

I reached to my left and opened the second drawer of my nightstand as I peered over at Amanda. She'd tugged her hair free of the bun she'd worn all night. And with her blonde locks cascading over the pillows, she watched us intently as she anxiously palmed her thighs. Thighs both Josh and I would be between before the night was over.

"Almost there, Cielo."

Her glazed eyes quickly flicked to me and then immediately back to where my fingers were still buried in Josh's ass. She licked her lips, and I nearly asked her to suck my cock while I continued playing with Josh. The idea of her swollen, pink lips wrapped around me was nearly as mind bending as the thought of being buried deep inside Josh.

"I want to try something else." I turned back to Josh, and he was already nodding before I even told him what I wanted to do.

"Do whatever you want," he panted. And I set the black silicone butt plug on his thigh. Never once did my fingers stop moving inside of him, and never once did he again appear concerned or anxious. Even when he glanced down to see the medium-sized toy propped on his leg.

All he did was nod and mumble, "Fuck yesssss." The last word was drawn out when I pulled my fingers free and brushed that spot again.

With slightly shaking hands, I popped open the bottle of lube and slicked up the silicone toy.

In front of me, Josh's wide eyes took in my every movement. They were steadfast on me even when I poised the tip of the toy to his ass and expected him to jump or ask me to stop.

Suddenly, I was nervous. I was in unknown territory—I knew him as my best friend and knew how to read him as such. But throwing in sexual interactions and emotions hindered my ability to know what he wanted.

Josh knew, though. He knew I was nervous, so he nudged his hips farther off the chair and caught my wrist in his hand. Shock and excitement pulsed through me at even the smallest touch. The reassurance in his touch burned away my hesitation.

So slowly I couldn't believe it was happening, Josh guided

my hand forward, found his entrance, and pushed the toy inside. Centimeter by centimeter, I watched in awe as it disappeared inside of him. His ass stretched and accommodated every inch of it.

He pushed and moaned against the intrusion until the black silicone was gone.

I was ready to combust. I didn't know how much longer I could last, so I turned back to Amanda, who turned her big blue eyes from Josh to me. And finally, I didn't ignore the desperate pleading I saw within them.

On shaky legs, I stood and offered her my hand, which she eagerly took. On equally unsteady legs, she jumped from the bed and stepped into me. Each of her curves pressed against my heated skin, and I reveled in the feel of her.

My hands cupped her face, and I placed a small, lingering kiss on her slightly parted lips. "Go ride our man's cock. I want to see your tight little cunt stretching around him."

# FORTY-ONE

Reed

AMANDA NODDED, AND GOD, DID I LOVE THAT SHE WAS SO transparent. Amanda always knew exactly what she wanted and how to ask for it.

I spun around and guided her to Josh, who was lazily stroking his dick and observing us both.

Eagerly, she braced her hands on his shoulders and his immediately found the curve of her hips. Her legs fell open, and she straddled his legs, his cock proud and throbbing underneath her. And always the gentleman, Josh ran his fingers between her thighs. His head fell back onto the leather and, with an awe-filled expression, peered up at Amanda.

"She's so fucking wet—so ready."

No longer willing to wait and done being tortured by me, she reached down and gripped his long cock in her hand and positioned him at her entrance.

"Watching the two of you is the best foreplay," she muttered.

My ass hit the bed behind me and I easily fell onto it, immediately wrapping my hand around my own cock in a forceful grip. And from my spot on the edge of the bed, I was in the perfect position to watch Josh's cock disappear into Amanda.

Just watching the two of them, it was like I could feel each sensation Josh was experiencing in that moment. We all simultaneously groaned, and I swore it wasn't my hand tightening around my shaft, but Amanda's walls clenching around me and sucking me deeper. I knew she was warm and welcoming and so fucking addicting.

Fully seated, she rocked back and forth. Her hips slipped over him in easy, languid movements, and his hands palmed her ass, spreading her wide. Her puckered hole was begging for my fingers, too. Or maybe my tongue or my cock.

"This is the perfect view—watching your pussy take his cock so well. Watching your ass bounce and that little toy in Josh's ass peeking out."

Amanda's rhythm turned frantic the more I spoke, and I noticed Josh's grip tighten on her ass. He squeezed, introducing a bite of pain, and guided her up and down him.

"Don't be careful with her. You know she likes it rough." My own voice was foreign in my ears. It was gruff and laced with the desire vibrating through me. The same desire that made my hand pump around my cock faster and harder.

And he took me at my word, also knowing the reaction he'd receive from Amanda, and smacked her ass. The sound was like music to my ears and so was her immediate toe-curling moan.

And he did it again. And again. And again. Even in the dim light finding its way into the room from the hallway and the streetlights outside the window, I could see the tender red handprint on her ass.

She was giving as good as she was getting, too. Her nails dragged down his chest and then buried in the hair at the back of his neck. She tugged, and he threaded his fingers through her hair, pulling her down and fusing their mouths together.

They were so good together. They moved in such synchronicity that it was hard to believe they were just learning each other's bodies. That there was still so much we hadn't yet experienced together.

"*Reed,*" Amanda pleaded in a breathy gasp. Only removing her lips from Josh's long enough to call me over.

I was standing and striding back to them before the final drawn-out syllable of my name escaped her kiss-swollen lips. As much as I loved to watch, being a part of them was always better. Feeling them both at the same time... nothing would ever compare.

My fingers smoothed down the column of her spine. And over her skin, glistening in a light sheen of sweat, goose bumps erupted over every pale inch. With a smile playing on my lips, I wound my fingers through her long, blonde hair trailing down her back and pulled it away from her body. My lips found the base of her neck, and I licked at the salty, sweet taste of her skin.

I trailed a line with my tongue and lips across her neck and nipped at her earlobe. "Don't stop," I whispered and tightened my hold on her hair, yanking it and throwing her head back. Ripping her free from Josh's lips, I slanted my mouth over hers and tasted them both at the same time. Tasted Josh on her lips and her tongue, the whiskey on his tongue and mine a perfect pairing to her sweetness.

Doing as I told her to, Amanda continued to bounce and grind down on Josh's cock as he played with her tits. He palmed them both and licked and nipped at her peaked nipples. Each scrape of his teeth against her tender skin drew another moan from her lips that I immediately swallowed down.

And she swallowed down my own when her small fingers wrapped around my cock.

Against the cruel clutch I kept on her hair, and without missing a beat on top of Josh, she drew back.

"Kiss him."

She pumped me with her left hand and used her right to urge my head toward Josh. But I didn't need to be persuaded.

No sooner did our mouths connect than I felt the warmth of

Amanda's tongue running up the underside of my cock. She circled her lips around the tip as I lapped at Josh's tongue and nipped at his lips.

"Both of your mouths will be the death of me," I growled into his mouth, my hand wrapping around his throat. I tried to keep myself steady and standing, but Amanda's mouth sucked me deep. She bobbed at the same pace she ground down on Josh.

He attempted to respond, but I kissed away his words. "How does it feel—having something inside of you?"

"So good. Better than I expected. Every time she moves, it moves, and I'm so close. *Fuck.*"

"And soon, it's going to be my cock. I'm going to be buried inside of you, watching you come undone as I hit every spot you didn't even know you had. And I'm going to do it over and over and over again until you're begging to come... and I'm begging for you."

The warmth of Amanda's mouth disappeared from my cock as she threw her head back and moaned to the ceiling. She cried out and Josh slammed into her from below, his face contorting as her orgasm racked her body and she clenched around him.

"*Fuck yes!*" she cried. "Josh, *oh my...*"

"Holy fuck, Amanda. I'm going to come," Josh gritted out, and I ran a hand over his chest as I kissed his neck.

"Yes, come inside our dirty girl. Pump her full of your cum, and then I'm going to fuck her as it's spilling out of her pretty little cunt."

His hands were iron around her hips, and suddenly, his movements stilled as he pressed as deep as he could and filled her. Amanda's fingers circled my cock once more and her other wrapped around Josh's neck, pulling his lips to hers in another mouthwatering kiss.

He cried into her mouth, and I let my hands freely run over every inch of them while he came down from his explosive high. And like she knew exactly how to, Amanda extended his plea-

sure, drawing out every second of his orgasm with subtle movements of her hips and strokes of her tongue against his.

"My turn," I mumbled against Amanda's neck, unable to
contain myself any longer. With an arm around her waist, I
plucked her from Josh's lap and threw her to the bed. I didn't
want a single drop of his cum dripping out before I got a chance
to feel it inside of her.

She bounced off the mattress, and I caught her hips midair. In
one swift movement, she wrapped her legs around my waist,
and I slammed home. Her warmth enveloped me, and I shuddered a breath when my balls slapped her ass.

I could feel his release inside of her, mixed with her own
wetness, my cock slipping in and out easily. Slowing my pace, I
made sure to graze each of her nerve endings and every inch of
her walls as I enjoyed the depravity of the act.

Below me, Amanda's eyes were hazy with lust and her hands
were tangled in her hair. Her mouth was hanging open on a
silent moan, and I almost came each time her tits bounced when
I slammed deeper. She was the picture of sex and every man's
wet dream.

And I'd never stop worshiping her and telling her how lucky
I was she was mine. *Ours.*

"Don't take it easy on her, remember? She likes it rough,"
Josh whispered against my neck, just below my ear. His hands
appeared in front of me and greedily roamed the planes of my
chest and stomach. His front pressed against my back, and *fuck*,
he was already hard again. His cock was perfectly positioned
against my ass and resting so close to a place I'd fantasized
about him exploring.

Amanda's small hands joined Josh's in outlining every
muscular valley over my torso, and I leaned down, planting my
hands and then my forearms on either side of her head.

Our breaths mixed, and I licked at her open mouth before
driving into her harder and faster. They were my world. Every-

thing revolved around them, and I was lucky to have found myself caught between them.

The bed dipped beside us, and Josh weaved his arm beneath Amanda's head, keeping her from moving higher up the bed as I fucked her senseless.

He licked up her neck and littered open-mouthed kisses over her jaw. He kissed her with a longing I craved to feel, too, and as if he read my mind, he turned his lips to me. He kissed me with the same passion as I felt his hand travel between me and Amanda. With practiced ease, he found the sensitive bundle of nerves at the apex of her thighs and played it in effortless circles, in sync with each of my thrusts.

Amanda cried out and lifted her hips, searching for an angle that would drive me deeper. Josh broke our kiss to look down at her and kiss the flushed skin of her cheeks.

"We're never going to get enough of you," he whispered against her skin. "I can't believe we went without you for so long, and now we have to make up for lost time."

I could feel my release building at the base of my spine. And as my balls drew up, there was a definitive tightening in her walls as her breathing became even more shallow. Her chest heaved and her eyes were unfocused even when she tried to listen to Josh.

"And there are so many things we want to do to you. *Fuck*, I want to…" He brushed his nose over her cheekbone and ran his tongue along the shell of her ear. She shivered in response and gasped when he nipped at her collarbone and continued lower until he took her nipple into his mouth. He sucked until she gushed all over my cock and then he bit down, and I watched pure ecstasy sweep across her face.

In the same moment, her walls tightened around my cock, and she sucked me deeper. Every inch of her body shook as she barreled headfirst into an endless orgasm. I held deep inside of her, letting her use my entire length to wring every drop of pleasure she could.

"I want to fuck you," Josh finally continued, releasing her nipple and kissing her lips between her panting, labored breaths. "And while I fuck you, Reed is going to fuck me. My cock is going to be buried so deep in your sweet little pussy while Reed's cock is buried in my ass."

And the orgasm I knew was on the horizon was suddenly barreling down my spine until I was pumping my release deep into Amanda. The mental images of what Josh described were pure and utter torture and euphoria.

It was all I ever wanted—the three of us so inexplicably intertwined that we couldn't decipher where one ended and the other began.

It was seconds—possibly minutes—before I returned to my body and my breathing steadied.

It almost physically hurt to remove myself from Amanda, but I did—I pulled out and flopped on her other side.

I glanced down just in time to see a sated smile on her face, and my chest rose with the knowledge we'd put it there.

# FORTY-TWO

Amanda

THE WARM AIR GREETED ME WHEN I OPENED MY APARTMENT DOOR. Warm air and the sound of the shower running at a little past five a.m.

I turned and locked the door behind me, throwing both my heels and my bag under the entry table before I headed to the kitchen. Impatiently, I waited for my coffee to dispense and suspiciously eyed the closed bathroom door.

He was finally back. And up early. Or late.

I knew Adam was flying in the night before, and after he quickly refused my ride from the airport, I let him know that I wouldn't be home and I'd see him the following day. I just wasn't prepared for him to be awake at five in the morning when the guys—both of them—dropped me off on their way to the gym for a quick, early morning workout.

My coffee finished brewing, and I topped it with some creamer as the shower shut off. The bathroom door opened at the same time I closed the refrigerator door and pivoted toward my room.

"Morning, roomie!" I said in a faux-chipper voice. Adam stopped dead in his tracks like he'd just seen a ghost.

"Hey, sis. Long time, no see," he muttered and scrubbed a hand through his soaked hair.

"I know, I can't wait to hear all about California—" My words disappeared as I neared Adam and noticed the darkness underneath his left eye and the cut above his eyebrow and along his cheekbone. "What—what the hell happened?" I stuttered and reflexively reached out and brushed the dark blue, nearly black bruising. My fingers brushed the small bandage covering his nose, and I slowly scanned over the rest of his face and chest, looking for any other injuries.

My mind immediately went to the worst-case scenario, and I could feel the panic bubbling up.

"I uh... I..." he struggled. He chewed the inside of his cheek, then looked down and to the right.

He was lying. Adam had the same tell since we were kids, and I'd had years and *years* of practice with it.

"Don't fucking lie to me," I seethed, and thankfully, he actually looked a little scared.

For a second, I watched his face morph as he contemplated which story to tell, but I held my ground. His sigh was one of defeat.

He scrubbed a hand across his chin but winced when his fingers grazed another scratch below his lip. "I was out with some people one night, and these two guys jumped me. I was eventually able to get away, but not before they landed a few good hits."

"They jumped you?"

"Yeah, stole my wallet and took off."

Then the questions came faster than he could actually keep up. "Who were you with? Where were you? Did your friends not jump in to help? You're supposed to just give them your wallet if that's what they're after. Why didn't you tell me? Do Mom and Dad know? Why didn't they tell me?"

He raised his hands, and I finally took a breath. I was angry and irritated and, unfortunately, not surprised in the slightest. I hoped he was telling me the truth. Although if past actions were any indication of future actions, I was sincerely skeptical of anything that came out of his mouth.

"I was with some friends I know that live in Cali now, and they were inside a bar when it happened. I'd stepped outside for two seconds when it happened. Mom and Dad know and even lent me some money until I could get a new credit card. But none of it matters. I'm fine, and it looks worse than it actually is."

I scoffed and rolled my eyes. "You've got to be kidding me. Of course it matters. Did you at least file a police report?"

He gave me an unimpressed look, and I glared right back. If it was a power of the will, I was going to win.

"Yes, Amanda, I filed a police report, but there's not much they can do unless they use my cards. There weren't any cameras nearby or witnesses."

My skepticism morphed into full-on disbelief. He was being evasive—trying to downplay the entire incident and only providing partial details.

For a long moment, we stood in the hallway, staring at each other and waiting. And I realized I barely knew anything about my brother's life. I knew he worked at RG Fitness most weekday mornings and then Murphy's a few nights during the week. I also knew he spent most of his time outside of our apartment. It was just a place for him to sleep—occasionally—and grab a change of clothes.

If he was in trouble or up to his normal bullshit, I wouldn't have known about it.

"What aren't you telling me?" I questioned.

He didn't say anything, and based on the look on his face, I knew I wasn't going to get any other information out of him. But I couldn't believe it was a lost cause. He'd made real, tangible strides to do better, and I was going to give him the benefit of the doubt.

"Just…" I began and reconsidered my words several times before I continued. "If you need me, I'm here. I just don't want another 'Hey, sis, I'm in trouble' call if at all possible. I want to figure out whatever it is before it gets to that point. Can you please promise me that?"

He nodded quickly, probably just to appease me, but I took it anyway.

"I gotta go get changed," he said, hiking his thumb over his shoulder. "I'm supposed to be at the gym in an hour."

"That's a really early shift."

He shrugged. "They asked me to go in early, and I need the money."

Quickly, he pivoted and swung his door open, but I had another thought. "Can we hang out sometime soon? Maybe go get dinner or see a movie like we used to?"

His brow furrowed like he was confused by the suggestion, but he finally mumbled his agreement.

I nodded and tried to smile, but it was a struggle. There was something more going on with him, but I felt helpless. All I could do was hope that he let me in, let me help, before it was too late.

# FORTY-THREE

Josh

IT WAS EIGHTY-FIVE DEGREES, AND THE WARMTH OF THE SUN through the car window was enough to put a smile on my face. I couldn't wait to be on the boat.

Excitement hummed through me with increasing intensity the closer we got to the lake. Did I ever need a fucking vacation.

The lake held some of my fondest memories. Not only that first night with Reed and Amanda, but the time we spent at the lake when I was a kid was virtually my only good memory from back then.

We'd sit on the beach and my dad would drink until he passed out in the sun. Until then, my mom would read a book or two and then she'd join me and Luke in the water.

The rest of my childhood was mostly riddled with partial memories of my drunken father and my mother's black eyes.

The water was my happy place. It was time to reset and a reminder that life wasn't always hell.

It was very much needed, especially since I'd spent the better part of a month and a half trying to come up with a solution that meant I could buy Murphy's. I'd tried to find investors or get a loan. I'd even contemplated less than legal measures. But nothing had panned out.

And it felt like the harder I tried, the further away I was from my goal.

I'd told Rhonda before we left. We were spending spring break at Reed's lake house with all our friends, and I could feel the weight of the news hanging over me. I'd waited to tell anyone until I knew for sure I'd exhausted all of my options. Telling Rhonda that she could move forward with finding another buyer was the last nail in the coffin.

The last thing I wanted to do was start off our vacation on a bad note, but I didn't know if keeping the secret for a second longer was going to benefit anyone.

"You're awfully quiet back there, Sunshine," Amanda mused from the front seat. She stretched to see me in the rearview mirror, and I returned her cautious smile with a very small, very forced one of my own. Her expression dropped.

"What's wrong? And please, for the love of all things holy, do not tell me 'nothing' again or so help me God…" I chuckled, but her scathing look quickly quieted me.

They'd both sensed something was off the past month, but I hadn't had the heart to tell them. Not only would it break their hearts—Murphy's was special to all of us—I knew they'd also try to come up with solutions.

"Fine, fine," I muttered and scrubbed my hands through my hair and closed my eyes for a moment. With one last deep breath, I opened my eyes to find Amanda turned completely around in her seat and Reed watching me with concern through the rearview mirror.

"Rhonda is selling Murphy's. She told me a few months ago and gave me first dibs. She said if I could buy the place, then it'd be mine, no questions asked. So, I've spent the last month and a half trying to figure out how to buy it. I've applied for every type of loan and tried to find investors. You name it, I tried it, but nothing panned out. I told her just before we left today that it wasn't going to happen. She's meeting with realtors and planning on listing it in the next few days."

They both sat quietly until I was finished, but the moment I was done, Amanda asked, "Why didn't you tell us?"

"Because this was my thing. I was going to handle it."

Amanda shook her head and stared at me with an unbelieving expression. She turned around even farther in her seat. "We could've—we could've helped. Come up with other ideas... pitched in. I mean, I don't have a lot of money, but—"

"No," I said, hoping my voice rang with the finality I felt.

Her face dropped, and she glanced over at Reed, likely hoping for some backup. But Reed was stone-faced, staring out the windshield at the quickly passing landscape. Even from the back seat, I could see the definitive tic in his jaw, like he was grinding his teeth. He gripped the wheel with white-knuckle force and didn't so much as glance back at me.

Not receiving any help from our boyfriend, Amanda looked back at me. "There has to be a way. I'm sure we could talk to everyone about it and come up with some solution."

I was shaking my head before she finished. "I've considered every possibility and tried every possible option. It's not going to happen. And besides, none of us have the funds to buy the place." As soon as the words left my mouth, Amanda glanced at Reed and prepared for the argument. I hurried to continue. "None of us have the money, the time, or the *desire* to own and maintain Murphy's. This is just the way it is, okay? I just wanted to tell you both so that you know. I don't need help coming up with a solution or trying to find another way. I've made peace with the fact that I'll have to find another job or get used to working for someone else. So, I just want to move on. But I wanted to tell you so it's not hanging over my head all week. Everything is good now, I promise."

Her eyes narrowed, and I could see the desire to argue still shimmering in her eyes.

"You have nothing to add?" She turned to Reed, who still didn't look away from the road. He shifted lower into his seat and shrugged.

"Seems like Sunshine's made up his mind, Cielo. Maybe we should let him do what he wants to do."

Amanda's attention bounced between the two of us, but with a groan, she conceded. She sat back down in her seat, facing forward, and propped her knee on the center console.

The car was quiet. The only sounds were the music softly playing over the speakers and Reed nervously tapping on the steering wheel. As I suspected, it only took a few minutes before Amanda was shifting in her seat, uncomfortable with the lingering silence.

Like I knew she would, she turned in her seat once more. I couldn't risk the topic being brought up again, so before she had a chance to speak, I said, "How's Adam?"

She stilled in her seat and worried her lower lip between her teeth. "He's fine... I think."

It wasn't the nicest tactic, but I knew bringing up her brother would permanently shift the topic from me and Murphy's.

Much to both mine and Reed's surprise, Adam had been a decent employee after the one incident at the gym. But as good of an employee as he was, he was shit at being a brother. When he wasn't at the bar or the gym, he was who knows where. And he did whatever he could to avoid her, including coming home at odd hours of the night and making excuses to bail on any of their plans.

And it was affecting Amanda more than she let on.

"How about this," Amanda said. "This week we don't talk about Murphy's or Adam or work or anything stressful. This is supposed to be a vacation."

"Works for me," Reed muttered and closed his palm over Amanda's thigh.

"And I swear if the three of us don't get some alone time..."

"What, Cielo?" Reed smiled. He casually leaned back in the

driver's seat, one hand slung over the wheel, the other squeezed Amanda's thigh. "Please, tell us what you'll do unless you get us alone."

She huffed, and both Reed and I laughed. "I don't know what I'd do, but it's not going to be pretty."

"And we still don't want to tell everyone?" I asked. We hadn't discussed it in a while, the prospect of telling our friends about our relationship. We'd all just continued as we were— keeping our sleepovers secret and downplaying the amount of time we spent together to remove suspicion.

"I don't think I want to," Amanda said.

"Do you want to?" Reed asked, finally catching my eye in the rearview mirror. The Murphy's news had rocked him more than I expected.

I shrugged and leaned back into the black leather seat. "I kind of like that it's still our little secret. The sneaking around and stealing little touches here and there. The fact that no one knows that I had your cock in my mouth last night."

I winked at him, and he finally smiled.

"Ugh, you both owe me for that cruel and unusual torture last night."

What Amanda called torturous was us videoing me on my knees, sucking Reed's cock and slowly fitting a plug inside him. We'd known she'd be irritated but also thoroughly turned on.

"How many times did you have to charge your vibrator watching the video?" I teased, and she threw me a scathing look that was interrupted by her smile.

"I plead the fifth. All I'm saying is y'all have some serious making up to do."

Reed caught my eye again as I leaned forward and brushed the hair away from Amanda's neck and fitted my hand around her nape. She leaned into the touch as my thumb stroked soothingly up and down the skin between her ear and shoulder.

"We can manage that," I muttered, wondering what the odds

would be that we would get there before everyone else and be able to steal away for at least an hour.

"Don't worry, Cielo. I figured we could fulfill one of those fantasies you mentioned. One we haven't done yet."

"*Fuck,*" I breathed. "Drive faster."

# FORTY-FOUR

Amanda

It was everything I'd ever dreamed of. The wind whipped through my hair, the sun was warming my skin, and the beer in my hand was fresh.

Hazel was laid out on the bench to my right, and we were both soaking up as much sun time as we could while the boys played. We'd both taken turns on the large tube Reed pulled behind the boat, but after a gnarly smack against the water on my last go-round, I'd called it quits. Not to mention, Reed and Josh had both nearly blown our cover by acting overly concerned. Luckily, Luke, Devon, and James were so preoccupied with another passing boat that only Hazel caught the lingering looks and glances.

There was a chorus of whoops and laughter before the boat slowed to a crawl.

"You okay, bud?" Luke laughed in his boisterous way, and I opened my eyes to watch him help heave James out of the water. Devon was only a second behind him, both of them flinging their life vests off and grabbing beers from the cooler.

"That hurt like a motherfucker. Reed, man, you got it out for me or something?" James griped and plopped into the seat at my feet.

"What? Can't hang anymore, James?" Hazel added and sat up to make room for her husband and Devon. She climbed into Luke's lap, and a feeling washed over me. I was jealous, plain and simple.

I'd always loved their relationship—it was perfect enough to make you want to puke.

But my envy had little to do with them and more to do with the fact that there were two men in my life and on that boat, and I couldn't do that with them. I hated it—even if it was partially my decision to keep us quiet a little longer.

I had to settle for Josh squeezing in next to me and lazily throwing his arm onto the seat behind me. Out of the corner of my eye, I noticed his hand flex, like he was about to touch me or pull me closer, but he thought better of it at the last second.

It didn't help that all day I'd watched the two of them shirtless, their skin shining with sunscreen and water.

"I can hang just fine, thank you. Just a little warning next time would be nice," James huffed, and my eyebrows rose. Since we'd arrived at the house late that morning, James's attitude had been off. He snapped at the smallest things and overall seemed like he'd rather be anywhere else.

"Okay, what the hell is up with you? Because I didn't do anything different than usual. And you've had a pretty shitty attitude all day." Behind my sunglasses, I glared at Reed, whose approach was severely lacking even if we'd all been thinking the same thing based on everyone else's expressions.

Reed turned down the music a few notches and watched James expectantly, waiting for his answer.

James scoffed and took a long swig of his beer. "What the hell ever. I have not had a—"

"Yeah," Devon spoke up, tipping his own beer at James. "You

chewed my head off in the car for being ten minutes later than we planned. So, tell us what the hell is up with you."

He sighed and ran a frustrated hand through his hair. Hazel and I traded concerned looks as she pulled her own hair up into a bun at the top of her head.

"Nothing is wrong—"

"Nope," Devon interrupted. "Try again."

"I'm just having an off day. I swear that's—"

"Ha!" It was Luke that interrupted that time. His large, tattooed arms were banded around Hazel's waist, and he held her tight to him. "Two days ago, when I called you to talk about watching Sadie, you were short-tempered too. Don't give us some bullshit excuse, okay?"

Defeated, James's shoulders slumped, and he shook his head. "My mom was in a car accident during the winter storm. My mom's best friend, Catherine, hit a patch of ice and veered off the road. They're both fine, but Mom broke her leg in a few places. I'm just irritated because no one told me. No one called me when it happened. I had to find out when I went up there this past week."

"Why didn't they tell you?" Hazel asked.

James was from a small town just an hour or two north of Austin. The warm wind whipped around us as we all sat in thoughtful silence. James stared at a spot far across the lake, and I gently nudged him in the side in an effort to not only get him talking again but to also acknowledge that we were there for him. Hopefully my soft smile conveyed as much.

"They made it seem like I wouldn't have wanted to know. That it wasn't a big enough deal to *disturb me*. I mean, I can't blame them for it. I hardly go back or visit… But either way, it's whatever." And we all knew he'd said all there was to say on the topic. At least at that point. "Josh, I think you've got next go!"

He hopped from his seat and returned the music to full volume. Josh shook his head at our friend but rose from his seat, letting his fingers trail over my neck and shoulders as he stood.

It was eighty-five degrees outside, yet goose bumps erupted over my skin.

The coy smile he shot me from above was evidence enough that each of his movements was intentional. I raised my middle finger in response which he took with a smile and wink before turning to Reed.

"Take it easy on me, ba—man," Josh hollered at him. I didn't miss the near slip of the tongue—not that Josh calling Reed "babe" would be too out of the ordinary, but it was the kind of thing we didn't want to happen, no matter how casually it was said.

If he had heard it, Reed didn't seem to be too worried about the pet name slip. "No promises, Sunshine. I know you like it rough," he threw back.

Oh my gosh. Thankfully, no one thought it odd and chalked it up to their usual playful banter.

As Josh prepared to hop on the inner tube, Hazel and Luke got lost in their own little bubble while Devon and Reed chatted about something on the boat. At that moment, a realization hit me like a Mack truck.

"Wait," I said abruptly, putting together the few pieces I had based on small tidbits of information I'd collected over the years. I turned to James, who had reclined next to me once again. "Isn't Catherine's daughter…?"

"Yes," James confirmed before I could finish the sentence.

With that little connection, his reaction made infinitely more sense. "Did you see her when you went up there?"

He shook his head. "Nope."

There was a definitive tightening in his jaw that was always there when the woman who broke his heart was brought up. We didn't know much about their relationship besides that it ended when he moved to Austin for college. Not that any of us would tell James, but we all believed there were unresolved feelings, at least on his end. It probably would have been easier to know for sure if he'd told us more of the story, but getting him to open up about her was his version of the seventh circle of hell.

"Ivy, right?"

He gave me a side-eye that said I was nearing my quota of *Ivy* talk. "Yes," he said in a voice so low and strained that it was difficult to hear him over the music and commotion around us.

I let the subject drop as Josh jumped off the side of the boat.

# FORTY-FIVE

Amanda

Hours later, the fire Reed made after dinner had dwindled to a few glowing embers. We were all gathered around it, talking about nothing and everything all at the same time.

Our laughter surrounded us and having us all together was my happy place.

James was reclined in a deck chair to my left, and Devon was across from him. But it was the two men across from me I couldn't keep my eyes off of—Reed and Josh were close on the small bench. Every so often, their legs brushed, or I'd catch one glance longingly at the other from the other side of the flames. I enjoyed watching them struggle to not touch or stare too long.

A smile tugged at my lips when their eyes found mine, and a desire similar to the fire burning behind their eyes flared.

My head was tucked into Hazel's lap as she cuddled up to Luke. Her fingers idly brushed through my hair, and for a moment, my eyelids fluttered closed. A slight buzz of alcohol still evident in my limbs, the cooler night air, and the lullaby of laughter was enough to set any worry at ease. All of the topics we'd defined as off-limits in the car were, thankfully, far from my mind.

"Hazel, I think you're going to put Amanda to sleep."

"James beat her to it," Luke said with a low laugh. "Our conversation was enough for him."

"What time is it?" I asked groggily.

"Time for bed," Josh said, standing and stretching before making his way around the fire to me.

I was all too eager to take his hand in the hopes that he'd lead both me and Reed back to his room. I didn't forget their promise about time together. Suddenly, I was wide awake, knowing the time had possibly *finally* come.

Like he could read my thoughts, Josh smiled and ran a hand down my back. The gesture was one that was too familiar for friends, but everyone else was too busy putting out the fire and righting the furniture to notice us.

Reed appeared before me and leaned down, his breath hot against my ear. "You ready, Cielo?"

My breath caught in the back of my throat, but I nodded.

To make it look less suspicious, they urged me to walk into the house first with Luke and Hazel while they stayed back to put the fire out completely.

Devon and James weren't too far behind us, finally splitting off in different directions to go to their separate rooms at the end of a long hallway. In front of me, Luke swept Hazel up into his arms which elicited a breathy giggle from her.

"Y'all keep it down, okay?" I yelled after them as they neared the main bedroom. Reed had willingly given it up to the two of them, probably to deter suspicion.

"You, too!" Hazel peeked over Luke's shoulder and said back. My steps faltered, and my jaw dropped.

"What does that mean?" Luke asked, also stopping before he could get the door to their room completely open.

Hazel's eyes conveyed her apologies as her attention bounced between me and Luke in a panic.

"I'm just giving her shit, babe," she said loud enough that I could hear too, but then pressed her lips closer to his ear.

Whatever she said quickly stole his attention as he kicked the door open in front of him with a growl. He couldn't get inside quick enough, but Hazel shot me an apologetic smile and waved a second before the door shut behind them.

We hadn't discussed my predicament for a while, but apparently, she knew more or assumed she did. I expelled a breath I hadn't realized I'd been holding and slipped into the room Reed had designated as mine.

It was the same room from two summers before. Not much had changed, although my memory had altered some of the details. The bed was still perfectly placed between two larger windows on the back wall directly across from the door. The dark-blue tones used throughout the space were the same as was the layout of the rest of the furniture.

There was a small nightstand on each side of the bed and a larger dresser to my left, with a mirror above it. A small lamp in the corner bathed the room in a warm light.

Remembering back to that night and walking in to find Reed sitting on the edge of the bed, Josh right on my heels, my body was overcome with every sensation and emotion from that night. It was like it was only yesterday instead of almost two years before.

Behind me, the door quietly clicked open and closed before I felt the press of a body against my back. Without looking, and only based on the presence and smell of him, I knew it was Josh.

Relaxing, I let myself lean back into his embrace. My head landed on his chest, and I peered up into his face. His features were relaxed, and the humor constantly playing around his lips was beautifully paired with the desire flaming in his eyes. With the amount of stress he'd been under recently, it was nice to see the Josh I knew coming back to life.

"The last time we were in this room together, I couldn't imagine we'd be back again. I wanted it so bad, though. I wanted both of you…" he confessed as he ran his fingers down my neck, followed by his lips. "But I wouldn't let myself think about it. It hurt too much to know that it wouldn't happen again."

His light touch continued over my collarbone and down the center of my chest. Within me, he stirred a desire that was already clawing and fighting to be released, but the dance and the lead-up were nearly as satisfying as the end result. And his voice was a husky melody I wanted to be swept away in.

I felt his smile against my neck. "But here we are. I'm kissing you and touching you, and I'm going to claim every inch of your body because you're mine."

"*Ours.*" Reed appeared near the bathroom and growled.

Josh smiled again and corrected himself. "Ours." He sucked and probably marked the sun-kissed skin of my neck, but I couldn't care. His hands traveled over every inch of my body he could reach as he lavished my neck with attention. All the while, every inch of my skin was aware of where Reed's eyes lingered.

I was hypnotized by their attention and the sucking and stroking of Josh's tongue, but we weren't moving nearly as quickly as I wanted to.

"Reed," spilled from my lips like a plea, and my eyes opened to watch him take slow, measured steps across the room.

"Hold her," he commanded Josh behind me, and instantly, one of Josh's hands weaved through my hair and the other banded around my waist. Reed's mouth descended on mine in a hungry, consuming kiss. My legs gave out beneath me, and I willingly allowed his tongue between my lips. He tasted like whiskey and smelled faintly of fire and smoke.

It was a heady combination and my hands roamed up his chest with the intent to pull him closer to me. But just as quickly as the kiss began, it ended, and he was gone.

An angry groan fell from my lips, but it was swiftly silenced when his rough fingers slid under the fabric of my dress. Suddenly, the ground disappeared from beneath me, and each of my legs was propped on Reed's shoulders. He flipped up my dress and growled again.

The sound went straight to my clit like an electric shock.

"No panties? Fucking dirty girl."

Josh yanked my hair, exposing more of my neck and licking a long line up to the pulse point near my jaw. "*Our* dirty girl," he whispered against my skin.

A grateful cry escaped my lips when Reed's skillful and urgent tongue licked a path from my ass up to my clit. He circled with a perfect amount of pressure around the swollen point, and my entire body was limp with pleasure. He lapped and sucked and devoured me while Josh covered my mouth with one of his hands and held up my dress with the other.

"There's nothing like his tongue, is there? So perfect and firm, and he knows exactly how to use it. But you have to be quiet. We can't let everyone know that your best friend is licking your pussy so well. That your best friend—your boyfriend—is about to make you come."

There was nothing better than the two of them lathering me in attention, worshiping my body, and owning my pleasure.

I was already so wound up from the anticipation throughout the day that there was no staving off my orgasm. It was more imminent than the sun rising the next morning. My hand dove into Reed's dark hair as the other wrapped around Josh's neck behind me for extra support. And when Reed shifted enough to plunge two fingers inside of me while simultaneously kneading my clit between his teeth, there was little even Josh's hand could do to quiet my cries.

Quickly, he replaced his hand with his mouth and swallowed down each moan, drawing out my pleasure with his soft lips and perfect tongue. My body rocked against Reed's face, and it wasn't until I had stopped convulsing that I realized I was close to suffocating him between my thighs.

I loosened my grip around his head and untangled my fingers from his hair, but he didn't appear to care that I'd mercilessly squeezed him. For good measure, he licked me once and twice more before looking up at us with a satisfied smile on his lips.

"So fucking good."

Behind me, Josh's chest vibrated as he ground out, "Let me taste."

Carefully, they let me down onto wobbly legs but didn't let me go. They stepped toward each other, pinning me between their muscular bodies and the hard planes of their chests as their mouths collided in a hungry kiss above me.

Josh's tongue dove deep between Reed's lips, searching for every taste and drop of me on Reed's tongue. In awe, I watched them fight for dominance. I thought Josh had won when he sucked Reed's tongue into his mouth, but then Reed bit Josh's bottom lip in one rough movement.

"Get on the bed," Reed demanded, then looked down at me. "Both of you."

Neither of us hesitated. Josh spun me around and looped his arms under my thighs, lifting me off the ground and into his hold. His mouth continued a thorough exploration of my neck while he sat down on the edge of the bed with me in his lap. The moment my knees settled on either side of his wide thighs, I felt the pressure of his long erection beneath me.

My hips, of their own accord, slipped back and forth over his cock, likely dampening his shorts with my recent release. But no one cared—we were all beyond caring at that point. We were wanton to the desire and our connection.

Reed's hands slipped over my shoulders, bringing the small, thin straps of my dress with them. I pulled my arms free without parting from Josh, whose tongue was greedy against mine.

The fabric pooled at my waist and hands found my breasts—they kneaded and pulled at my peaked nipples. It sent a bolt of desire straight to my clit, which was already humming with need again.

I pulled away from Josh's mouth to see the hand on my left

breast was his while the hand on my right was Reed's, and in perfect tandem, they played me and worked me into another frenzy.

Reed's hand suddenly disappeared, but behind me, there was the distinct sound of his buckle and then his belt hitting the floor. There was more rustling of fabric, and like I never needed anything more, I needed them both naked.

My hands shifted beneath me, and I ripped at the button on Josh's shorts, unzipped the zipper, and then frantically worked the buttons of his shirt that matched the color of his eyes. The fabric was soft against my fingers, but it was nothing compared to the smooth skin of his chest, lightly dusted with dirty-blond hair and golden from the sun. He was warm and hard in all the right places, groaning into my mouth as my hands explored the planes and valleys of his body.

"You ready for another one of those fantasies, Cielo?" Reed whispered into my ear, and before he'd even finished speaking, I was nodding.

He gave a low chuckle and nipped at the shell of my ear. His strong arms wrapped around me once more and easily removed me from Josh's lap. My dress slipped the rest of the way down my legs and fell to the floor as he set me back down on the bed.

With one hand firmly encircling my throat, he guided me back to the mattress, his thumb brushing over my pulse point with delicate precision.

"Keep these legs open so we can see your pretty pussy. I need to witness how wet we make you—how wet you get for us."

Like they had a mind of their own, my legs fell open. Reed's smile was immediate, and his grip around my throat tightened— it verged on the edge of pain, and it became exponentially harder to breathe. Just how I wanted it.

The moment he loosened his grip, I asked, "Which fantasy?"

His smile only grew, and he glanced beside us where Josh had finished undressing and held his throbbing cock loosely in his fist. A bead of precum gathered at the tip, and my mouth watered to lick it up. Josh's hooded gaze flitted from me to Reed and back again, likely wondering the same thing I was: which fantasy did Reed have in mind?

Reed bent over me, his hands on either side of my head, and kissed me thoroughly. He swept his tongue through my mouth and nipped at my bottom lip. My nails clawed down his back, and I urged him to cover me with his weight. I wanted to feel him on top of me, owning me.

He was gone too soon but was thankfully replaced by Josh, who wasted no time lowering himself over and onto me.

The head of his cock was perfectly poised at my entrance, prodding and teasing me. He sucked one of my nipples between his lips—hard. And I cried out at the pleasure and pain twisting through me. Promptly, Josh's hand covered my mouth, but he wasn't quick enough to completely stifle them. The sound bounced around the room and would have likely been heard elsewhere.

"Be quiet, or you only get to watch again," Josh growled against my breast. His tone was one I was familiar with from Reed, but I hadn't heard it from Josh. It was a pleasant departure from his usually playful, positive cadence.

A shiver racked through me all the same. And a small whimper escaped my lips. But I knew—no matter what—I was going to keep quiet.

"Our girl wants to participate, don't you?" Reed chimed in, stepping back into my peripheral as Josh slowly pushed into me.

Josh's hand drifted from over my mouth to my throat, where he loosely gripped the base just above my collarbone. His eyes bored into mine with increasing intensity each inch he pushed deeper.

"Yes," I whispered on a breathy, low moan. In one fluid motion, Josh fully seated himself inside of me, and my eyes rolled back in my head. His long cock hit my deepest spot, and I felt myself clench around him immediately.

Like my body was urging me not to let him go.

"Our dirty girl. You look so good taking his cock. And Sunshine, *fuck*." Reed absentmindedly licked his bottom lip, his eyes trained to the point where Josh's cock disappeared into my cunt. "You look so good feeding it to her."

Josh paused deep inside me, allowing me a second to adjust to his size. My head fell to the side, and I finally caught a glimpse of what Reed held in his hand.

It was a generous bottle of lube, and I hoped I knew what fantasy he was talking about.

"Oh *fuck*," Josh groaned above me. "I love it when you tighten around me like that."

Not missing anything, Reed grinned and followed my eyes to the bottle in his hand. "She's eager to watch me fuck you," he said in a voice as smooth as butter.

Josh's cock twitched inside me, and I pressed my hips upward as his jaw went slack. Based on his expression, Josh hadn't known that was Reed's plan either.

Reed watched Josh with hopeful eyes, his grip tightening ever so slightly on the bottle he held. There was a second of silence which seemed to stretch infinitely longer. Josh pushed himself up from where he'd leaned over me on the bed but stayed buried inside of me.

Standing at his full height, he looked at Reed and whispered, "Yes."

Reed's relief was clear in the way his shoulders dropped. A faint smile returned to his lips before he crashed his mouth to Josh's.

The two of them together were erotic. And another wave of desire flooded my veins. The need I felt for them was carnal and uninhibited.

"Fuck me, *please*," I begged, clawing at Josh's chest. His toned abs flexed under the pain of my nails scraping against his skin.

Reed pulled away and looked down at me reverently. "You take care of her while I take care of you."

He stepped around Josh, who moved inside me with deep,

unhurried pumps of his hips. Reed ran a tender hand along Josh's shoulders and placed a kiss on his neck before pushing him down closer to me. Welcoming his heat and weight, I wrapped my arms around him. He buried his face in the crook of my neck, kissing softly behind my ear and down along my throat.

He reared back to look at me, and I cupped his face in my hands.

"You feel so good," I moaned.

Each pump of his hips was torturously sweet and perfectly satisfying.

"Relax," Reed murmured, and Josh did. I couldn't see what Reed was doing behind Josh, but I had a good idea. Josh's eyes fluttered and his mouth opened on a soft groan, so I knew it had to be something good.

Josh's hips stuttered, but he quickly picked the pace back up. His thrusts were punishingly long and hard; his cock caressed every tender part of me on the way in and on the way out.

His eyes closed again, and he mumbled another curse. His hips paused, and I knew Reed had added another finger. Reed's hand appeared wrapped around the back of Josh's neck, and I further enjoyed the position I was in. Poised beneath him, I witnessed a myriad of emotions cross Josh's face. Most of which was somewhere on the spectrum of surprise and desire.

Our rhythm continued—Reed would adjust, Josh would still inside of me to get used to the new sensation, and then he'd quickly pick back up right where he left off. Josh's eyes were steadfast on my own and he whispered the dirtiest words as Reed prepared him to take his cock.

"I'm ready," Josh croaked.

"*Fuck*. Yes, you are." Reed's voice was low and coated in lust. He positioned himself directly behind Josh, and I craved to see what was happening. I wanted to witness the first time Reed pushed inside Josh, but I wasn't going to pass up having Josh inside me and watching his face contorted in pleasure.

Josh took a deep breath. He pressed forward, and his eyes closed. A low, manly sound emanated from the back of his throat while Reed murmured a long, muffled curse behind him. His cock twitched inside of me.

My hands ran down Josh's sides, over the flexed muscles and soft skin, until I found the globes of his ass. My fingers brushed against Reed's that were poised against his cheeks. We tangled our fingers together, and I squeezed and helped him spread Josh apart.

My eyes finally connected with Reed's, and I watched his whiskey depths overflow with emotion and unhindered craving. A smile twitched at the corner of his mouth, and he threw his head back in ecstasy. The muscles in his neck flexed and his Adam's apple bobbed with what I knew was restraint. He was trying, just as Josh was, to keep quiet against the new, overwhelming sensations overcoming them both.

"Holy shit. *Move*," Josh groaned.

"Are you begging me to fuck you, Sunshine?"

Josh choked out a humorless laugh and lurched forward when Reed thrust into him. "I don't beg," Josh ground out.

"Oh, but I would love to hear it. Hear you beg for my cock, because you're so fucking tight. You feel so *good*."

# FORTY-SIX

Josh

My body was overcome with more sensations than I ever thought imaginable.

Being buried deep inside Amanda's tight, wet heat was always better than the time before, but it was only magnified by having Reed inside of me. There were a few minutes of uncomfortable pressure as I got used to his fingers, but the feeling quickly morphed into a craving for more.

Each of his movements was intentional—relaxing and preparing me for his cock. When I felt the slick crown breach my ass, there was a moment of fear that I couldn't suppress. All of my concerns that I wouldn't enjoy it weighed down on me, as did some of the world's views of what we were doing. The label we'd both carry with the relationship and every other thought that would pull me out of the moment.

I closed my eyes against them and tried to focus on the good because there was so much of it. I needed it to outweigh the confusion buzzing through me, otherwise I knew I'd find myself imploding and taking two of the most important people in my life with me.

That's when I felt Amanda's hands run down my torso and tangle with Reed's. Together they spread me wide to welcome his cock. My eyes snapped open, and in Amanda's ocean blues, all I saw was awe and unyielding hunger.

All of my anxiety vanished with that one look. Because the three of us were all that mattered. I wasn't completely ignorant to believe that it wouldn't happen again—when we announced to the world our relationship, I knew we would likely face hatred and ignorance.

But that wasn't what I was focused on at that moment. I was focused on the woman beneath me and the man behind me. And how together, they were everything I never knew I needed.

"Holy shit. *Move*," I groaned.

"Are you begging me to fuck you, Sunshine?"

I laughed and lurched forward when Reed thrust into me. *Fuck*, he was big. "I don't beg," I panted through clenched teeth. But even as I said it, I knew I likely would have. Had he not begun moving in slow, even thrusts, I would have likely begun pleading that he do so.

"Oh, but I would love to hear it. Hear you beg for my cock, because you're so fucking tight. You feel so *good*." Listening to Reed come undone by the pleasure he was taking from my body was a huge turn-on. As was the feel of his pointedly masculine hands running over the planes of my back and gripping my hips. I loved the sensation of his calloused palms and the hair of his legs brushing against mine as much as I did Amanda's smooth softness.

He picked up his pace, and I timed my thrusts with Reed's, pushing into Amanda as he did the same to me.

"How does it feel?" Amanda hesitantly asked, running a hand down my face as the other continued to grasp my ass. Reed's hands maintained a punishing grip on my hips, and each time he pushed in and out, the tip of him slid deliciously across that spot he'd found only weeks ago. With each pass, and as

Amanda tightened around me, I knew I was going to come embarrassingly quick.

"So fucking good. Better than I imagined." Each word was more difficult than the last to get out.

Amanda gasped, and I pounded into her harder, snaking my hand between us to find her swollen clit. Her wetness coated the inside of her thighs and mine, and I drew my thumb in quick circles until she bucked off the bed.

"Yes, fuck her good and hard. Make her come while I watch my cock disappear into your tight ass. Are you going to come for us, Cielo?"

She nodded frantically. A light sheen of sweat covered her skin, and I bent lower to lick at the salty sweetness. My tongue traveled between her breasts and up her neck.

We were trying to be quiet, but if anyone else was still awake, there was no doubt they'd likely hear us. Reed's hips snapped forward at a punishing pace, his cock slipping in and out of my ass with ease as I met his pace between Amanda's thighs.

The walls of her cunt tightened, and there was a flood of heat and wetness. My mouth suctioned over hers a split second before she cried out. I hungrily swallowed each of her sweet sounds, and I wished I could hear and bask in each of the noises she made from the pleasure we stripped from her body.

In that moment, everything else in the world disappeared. It was only us—the three of us together in that room again. And the soul-deep connection pulling us together, anchoring us to one another.

Behind me, Reed's fingers twisted in my hair while the other hand drifted to my shoulder, urging me back against him. Thrusting forward, I buried myself in our girl as she drenched my cock, and pulling out, I impaled myself on Reed.

The sounds he made behind me were labored and restrained, and I knew he was close. I was close.

"You sound so pretty when you come on his cock. Now, come inside of her. Fill her up as I come in your ass."

Like a lightning strike straight to my balls, my release barreled down my spine, and before I knew it, I was doing exactly as Reed instructed. My seed coated every inch of Amanda's cunt as I felt Reed's release—hot and wet and so fucking satisfying—pump into my ass.

There was nothing like it. Both of those things happening simultaneously was beyond anything I'd ever experienced.

And I wanted to do it again and again and again.

My arms nearly gave out at the same time Reed's chest met my back. We were covering Amanda with most of our weight, and I tried to pick myself up, but I was entirely spent.

"We're crushing her," I said. But Reed just breathed deeply.

"I don't mind it. If this is the way I go, know I went happily."

We all broke out into a fit of laughter. I was softening inside of Amanda, and I could feel Reed softening inside of me. But I didn't want to move and break our connection.

Our laughing finally stopped, and Reed moved off of me. But before he stood, he placed a lingering kiss at the base of my neck. Amanda's sated state gave way to a smile when she noticed the gesture and the corresponding shiver that racked through me.

The next morning it wasn't the sun, an alarm, or the sounds of others moving through the house that woke me up; it was a hand that wasn't my own, covering my face and hot breath tickling my neck.

It was also miserably hot. Reluctantly, I opened my eyes, but my view was partially skewed by the hand precariously placed over my eyes. I rolled to the side and away from the furnace beside me.

Reed was completely passed out—his mouth slightly open and his hair a disheveled mess—between me and Amanda. I remembered Amanda waking up in the middle of the night and shimmying down the bed, vacating her usual spot between us to use the restroom. While she was gone, I guess Reed took the opportunity—likely still fast asleep—to crawl to the middle.

I peered over him, and sure enough, Amanda flailed across the bed. With the way she starfished, her small frame took up more of the king-size bed than both Reed and I combined. They were both miserable to sleep with—between Amanda taking over the entire bed and Reed being the world's biggest and hottest cuddler, I was doomed. But I also wouldn't have traded it for the world.

Reed rolled over to face Amanda, still completely passed out, and I kicked the comforter off before tugging the sheet back around my waist. The cool air lulled me back to sleep.

The second time I woke up that morning, I was wrapped around the furnace. Thankfully, only the thin gray sheet covered us and the air conditioning had kicked on.

My arm was loosely draped over Reed's torso, and my face was buried in his hair at the back of his head. He smelled like the cedar and citrus body wash he used, and I swore I could still smell the sunshine clingy to his skin. For a second, I let myself breathe him in.

Although we lived together and it would have been the easiest thing in the world for me to slip in his room and in his bed when I got home from the bar in the early morning hours, I didn't. And when it was the three of us, it was Amanda wrapped around me.

So it was the first time I'd woken up with a man in my arms. Like everything else, the feeling was foreign but unexpectedly good. Actually, I was past anything between us surprising me. Having him inside of me broke down any of the flimsy walls I had left.

My palm flattened against his stomach, and my entire front pressed against him as I breathed deeply. The muscles in his toned abdomen twitched, and he grunted softly.

"It's too early," he whispered in a sleep-laced voice that was lower than his normal speaking voice. It was ragged in the early morning hours, and I couldn't help but chuckle.

"It is, so go back to sleep."

"It's hard to sleep when your dick is impaling me."

His hips twitched, and he scooted back an inch. Enough for me to realize that my dick was, in fact, pressed against his ass. The thought made more blood rush to my cock.

"Your cuddling has finally rubbed off on me," I whispered back.

He gave a slight chuckle and readjusted, rubbing his ass against me once more. I felt pretty certain that the second time was intentional as well. "I can think of something else that probably needs to rub one out."

My hand, still poised on his stomach, began to explore. I dipped my fingers between each abdominal muscle—memorizing the ridges and valleys until I tentatively fingered the planes of his chest. I crossed his collarbone and followed the path until I collared my hand around his throat. Then I retraced my steps back down his body.

My hand brushed his cock. "I don't think this is just morning wood. I don't think you actually mind that my dick is pressed against your ass right now."

I wrapped my fingers around his shaft. He was hard, and his skin was velvety soft. Slowly, I pumped once, then a second time and finally teased a quiet grunt from him. I smiled against his neck and nipped at his ear. I pulled his lobe between my teeth and bit down hard enough to be rewarded with another groan, only deeper and slightly louder.

Under the sheet, I jerked him. Every time I wrapped my hand —or my mouth—around him, I forgot how long and thick he was. It was impressive, and just the memories of having him against my tongue made my mouth water.

My thumb brushed over the crown of him and collected the bead of precum. Quickly, I tossed back the sheet and licked the salty remnants from my thumb before sucking my middle finger into my mouth.

"Would you let me fuck you right here, right now? Take your ass the way you did mine last night."

He was silent but for his heavy, uneven breathing. I sat still, my cock still bumping up against him, while I waited for his answer.

And finally, when the tension between us was nearly unbearable, he whispered, "Yes."

Excitement poured through me like a dam breaking. I peered over my shoulder and retrieved the bottle of lube I'd spotted on the nightstand. We were too spent the night before to put anything away or pick up at all. After we'd each come down from our orgasm highs, it'd all started again.

Reed had muttered something about needing Amanda's pussy while she reached over to me and suctioned her mouth around the head of my cock. It ended with Amanda riding Reed while I stood on the bed so I could fuck her face.

I was thankful for the easy access to the lube. I dotted a small-ish amount on my finger and fit my hand between our bodies. In the faint morning light, the sun streamed through the blinds and glowed against Reed's tanned skin. His body was a work of art, and I was lucky enough to get to experience it.

"You're so perfect," I muttered against the bare skin of his shoulder as my finger found his tight hole. I wanted to work him with my tongue first, lick around his ass and then suck his miserably hard cock into my mouth while I fingered him. But I was desperate for him. I needed him like I needed Amanda, like I needed air.

He pushed back, seeking out my finger as I pushed inside of him. And I knew he was growing as desperate as I was. I worked my finger into his ass and gasped at the tightness. I'd fingered him a few times and used a butt plug on him once, but I didn't think I'd ever get used to how he wrapped around my fingers. The sensation spurred a hunger inside of me.

My other arm snaked under his head and wrapped around him until my palm flattened on his chest, pressing him infinitely closer to me.

He welcomed my second finger and let out a contented growl from deep within his chest after only a minute or two. I dragged the pad of my digit against the tender spot a few inches inside of his ass and smiled when he bucked. My only hope was that I could replicate that reaction when it was my cock in his ass.

Our ragged breaths mixed, and my own cock was weeping. Precum smeared on Reed's back and I was hard enough to cut glass. I was light-headed from the amount of blood being pumped to my lower half.

"Get inside of me *now*," he growled.

"Always so fucking bossy. I have half a mind to make you beg," I said this while extracting my fingers and dutifully lubing up my cock. "I think the word please would sound so pretty rolling off of your lips. It would be all growly and demanding, but—"

"*Please.*" I didn't expect to hear the word from him, but it was exactly as I expected it. His plea was rough and his voice was gritty, but I appeased him. The crown of my cock, slick with lube, pressed against his tight hole. Slowly, with one hand gripped around my dick and the other drawing small circles around his peaked nipple, I pushed into him.

He was warm and tight, and his body clenched around my tip. I shook with the effort to hold back. But slowly, he opened for me, and inch by agonizing inch, I slid into him until I slipped past the resistance. My teeth dug into the skin at his neck to keep the growl building in my chest at bay.

"I really thought the first time you let me in your ass, you'd be on top, riding me. Because you so thoroughly despise giving up power. But this..." I pressed deeper, bottoming out so well that my hips were flush with his round, sculpted ass. "Having you like this feels like so much more."

The words didn't make sense, but my desire clouded every

other thought. The desire and the feeling of Reed's sweet ass tightening around my cock had overtaken all sense. And then I began to move. At first, it was a methodical pace—one that gave him time to overcome the less-than-comfortable feeling and tumble into the overwhelming pleasure that lay on the other side.

A delicious moan vibrated through him, and my entire body flushed like my skin was on fire.

"Better be quiet before you wake our girl up. You know she's not a morning person."

"She's already awake." Amanda's voice was temptingly low. The sound was made of velvet and silk. Her blue eyes were hazy with a lust that made her appear drunk, and her tongue wetted her full bottom lip. Her hair was splayed across the pillow, and her skin was slightly burned from our day in the sun.

Just the sight of her, and her eyes so intently on us, made my cock twitch desperately.

"Didn't mean to wake you," I panted, not pausing my thrusts which were perfectly timed to Reed's panted breaths.

"Keep going." Her voice, unlike Reed's, held a plea I knew well—one that was on the verge of insanity if it wasn't satisfied.

"Yes, keep going." Reed urged me on.

With Amanda awake and her eyes flitting between us, I didn't hold back. I gripped Reed's hip, the blunt edge of my nails digging into his skin, and I drove my cock deeper. My movements were greedy—I wanted to take all of him, needed to feel all of him. Every inch of him, inside and out, was ours.

Each stroke created a new sensation—they were deep and thorough, yet steady. Just like the pleasure curling around my spine and settling in my groin, it felt never ending.

Wrapped in my arms, Reed began to shudder, and I held him tighter, dragging my shaft against his prostate.

His fingers twitched, and I knew what he was about to do. But I batted his hand away before it could make it to his erection. His pleasure was just as much mine as his ass.

"You're going to come in my hand with my cock in your ass. This orgasm is *mine*," I growled, and I could barely recognize my own voice.

My hand encircled his shaft, but in the next second, another hand was there—a smaller, more feminine hand. Amanda had turned from voyeur to active participant, and the change made my eyes roll back in my head.

Reed reached out and pulled Amanda closer. With a gasp, her chest bumped his as he ground backward, fucking himself back onto me. Between the two of us, our motion never faltered. My fingers tangled into her hair, and Amanda kissed Reed's neck, sucking and biting him as he turned back to me.

Our eyes connected, emotion bouncing between us and burrowing itself deeper.

"More. It's so much more," he grunted, and my mouth slanted over his. Those words were too beautiful not to fully enjoy—I needed to hear them and taste them, let them consume me.

His tongue slipped past my lips, and I was gone. My orgasm spiraled through my body, leaving every inch of me tingling as I drove long and hard into Reed. In the same breath, he went stiff in my arms and, with a low moan, pumped his hot cum into our fists and all over Amanda's stomach.

I jerked inside of him for a long time. It felt like the orgasm would never end, but when it did, we all still lay there, wrapped in each other.

"Who knew I would love a cock in my ass so much," Reed said with a chuckle, and even through my exhaustion, I laughed, too.

"It is pretty great," Amanda added, and the two of us peered over at her. Her face and chest were flushed, and her eyes were alive with lust. One of her fingers, the nail painted a blue that closely matched her eyes, dipped down and swept through Reed's release, painting her stomach. Purposefully teasing us both, she lifted her finger and sucked it into her mouth.

I hadn't yet pulled out of Reed, but I knew we both felt my dick react to the move. Apparently my refractory period was nonexistent around the two of them.

She whimpered around her finger. What a crime it would have been to leave our girl unsatisfied or wanting.

"You need the bathroom first?" I asked Reed, who shook his head.

"Okay, I'm going to go clean up," I muttered to them. "And when I get back, I expect to see your face between her legs."

Amanda smiled, and Reed rolled his eyes but moved to obey. "I let him in my ass one time and now he thinks he's the boss. I'll have to teach him otherwise later."

And there went my cock again.

# FORTY-SEVEN

### Reed

BETWEEN AMANDA'S LEGS WAS MY FAVORITE PLACE TO BE. AND THE ache—the evidence that only minutes before Josh had been inside of me—made it even better.

I hadn't ever thought we would get there, but we did.

It was better than I imagined—holding Amanda against me and both of them jacking me off as Josh relentlessly fucked me. When all of it began, I was cautious of the attraction—the pull to a man was something I couldn't wrap my head around.

But letting my attraction lead me and not questioning what I wanted was the best thing I could have done for the three of us. Holding myself back from it based on what I had known my entire life—an attraction to only women—or what the world expected of me would not have yielded the relationship we found ourselves in.

Because I knew they were my endgame.

And I was going to do anything to protect it.

My hands cradled Amanda's ass as I nipped and licked the soft skin of her inner thigh. She was already dripping wet, and I could smell her fragrant arousal the closer I moved to her cunt.

But it was too fun to tease her. I loved the way she squirmed against my hold and whimpered when I would near her slit, only a breath away, and suddenly retreat back up her thigh.

"Reed," she panted, and my name on her lips sounded like a prayer. My heaven praying to me—it was a glorious sound.

A sound that was abruptly cut short by the incessant vibrating of a phone on the bedside table. But the distraction didn't keep me from repeating the same pattern—marking her pale skin with my teeth and soothing the sting with my tongue —down her other thigh. That was until the phone immediately began vibrating for the second time.

Amanda let out an annoyed groan and lifted her head. "What time is it?"

My eyes flitted to the analog clock in the corner. "Not even seven thirty."

"That means whoever is calling could be an emergency. Whose phone is it anyway?"

Reluctantly I raised my head higher and saw the photo of Amanda and Hazel on her wedding day fill the screen. "It's yours."

"I'm so sorry. If it's not important, then I won't—"

I cupped her cheek and kissed her softly. "Don't worry about it, Cielo. Check it."

Her smile was sweet. She immediately reached for her phone and it began ringing for a third time the moment she had it in her hand. Her eyebrows furrowed, and her mouth opened like she was going to say something, but she decided to answer the phone instead.

"I thought I made myself pretty clear about you being between—"

"Shh!" Josh, in all of his naked glory, strode into the room as Amanda answered the phone with a tentative "Hello?"

He crossed to the bed, wearing a similar expression of concern that deepened over Amanda's features.

"Who is it?" he whispered.

I shrugged. "Not sure, but they've called three times. Adam, maybe?"

Josh gave me a look that I knew too well—if it were Adam in trouble, we both knew we'd be cutting our trip short. Amanda's ability to tell him no, or let him figure his own shit out, was nonexistent.

"No, no, it's okay. What's going on?" Amanda murmured, throwing an even more worried glance in our direction. She worried her bottom lip between her teeth as she intently listened to the person on the other line. Suddenly, her jaw dropped, and she let out a string of curses.

"Is he there?" she asked as she began frantically looking across the floor, retrieving the summer dress we'd discarded last night. Josh and I both jumped into action the moment she did, searching for our own clothes and quickly dressing.

"Yeah, we're on our way now. No, I'll handle it. We should be there within an hour. Thanks for, umm… letting me know."

Before she even had a chance to explain, both Josh and I were asking who it was, what had happened, and where we were going.

Amanda's mouth opened and closed a few times, like she couldn't find the right words. She stared down at her phone, and I glanced at it, too, hoping it held some sort of answer.

"That was CJ, the maintenance guy at my apartment. He said that he heard some crashing sounds coming from the apartment and then saw the glass on the patio. He said he tried to get in to see what was going on, but the dead bolt was locked. I don't know, but I need to call Adam and see if he's there. He should be there right now. I just… I need… I need to go."

"Yeah, let's go," I agreed, and began straightening the room and covering the evidence of what had happened in there only hours and minutes before. It smelled like sex, but there was little I could do about that—my parents' cleaning service would be stopping by in a few days to do a more thorough cleaning anyway.

Josh was doing the same thing, tugging on the shoes he'd discarded last night and righting a lamp that had somehow fallen over in the midst of everything.

"Y'all don't have to come with me. I would just need to take your car, Reed. Or I guess I can Uber."

Josh laughed, and I shook my head. Did she know us at all? "Baby girl, if you think you're going anywhere without us, especially in a situation like this, then you are sorely mistaken."

He crossed the short distance between them and cupped her face in his massive hands. Tenderly he kissed her forehead, her nose, and then her lips. "We'll figure it out, okay? No freaking out until it's time to freak out."

She nodded, and we gathered our things. "What are we going to tell the others?"

"Devon's probably awake. We can tell him that you have an emergency and we're going to help. If not, then I'll send someone a text. Don't worry about it." Thankfully, Amanda agreed quickly, and we were in my car in less than five minutes.

Ten times. Amanda tried to call Adam ten times on our drive to her apartment. He didn't answer once. Each time it would ring out, eventually going to voice mail and eliciting a murderous groan that would have been sexy had she not been thoroughly frustrated and terrified.

The car ride passed in silence. Amanda called Adam every few minutes, her legs bouncing nervously as she chewed her nails. I drove fifteen over the speed limit while Josh sat silently in the back.

It was killing me not to be able to comfort her or help more than I could. I was doing my best to get us there quickly, but I still felt helpless against the unknown. Slowly, I placed my hand on her thigh, which was relentlessly bouncing up and down. She settled and gave me a sheepish smile.

I went a little faster.

The hour-long drive only took forty-five minutes. And by the time I put the car in park, Amanda was already pushing her door open and making a beeline for the stairs. Josh's eyes connected with mine for a split second through the rearview mirror before we both took off after her.

She'd lost her damn mind, running directly into a possibly dangerous situation. We took the stairs two at a time and made it to the top to find her pounding on her apartment door and fumbling with her keys.

"Adam Allan, I swear to God, if you are in there right now, open the damn door!" she yelled.

Her keys tumbled to the floor, bouncing off the concrete. Josh and I flanked her, and she promptly shrugged off the soothing touch Josh offered while I retrieved her keys. She continued pounding on the wood, and I was sure every single one of her neighbors was awake at that point.

Finally, the door swung open. A disheveled and exhausted Adam stood just past the threshold.

From around the corner, CJ, my least favorite maintenance guy, called out to Amanda.

"Everything okay?" he asked, mock concern plastered over his face. He wanted in her pants—that's the conclusion both Josh and I had come to. We both took up a similar defensive posture around her and stared the prick down. He didn't tear his eyes away from her, and I wanted to remove them from his face.

"Yes, thanks for the heads-up. I'll see you later." Her voice was steady, but an edge of anger bubbled just beneath the surface.

She didn't wait for the dude to respond, rather, she pushed past Adam and stomped into her apartment.

But CJ paced forward like he was going to insert himself into the situation. Josh and I held our position in front of her door. "We've got it from here," I warned. "And honestly, you should just leave her the fuck alone. I'd prefer not to see your face again."

The guy wasn't completely stupid and stopped his approach in the middle of the hallway. But he smirked and glanced back and forth between us.

"I understand your position, but that's not going to happen." His smirk turned into a smile as he turned and paced back down the hallway. Then he added over his shoulder, "You boys have fun cleaning that up."

We didn't move until he disappeared around the corner, and neither of us said a word about his cryptic bullshit. We headed into Amanda's apartment and nearly ran her over in the process.

She'd stopped only a few feet inside the door.

"What. The. Fuck," she mumbled, peering around the room and surveying the damage.

So much fucking damage.

The first thing I noticed was the patio window was smashed and glass covered the laminate floor in a white powder littered with larger shards of glass. Every inch of the apartment had been destroyed.

The barstools were overturned, and all of the cabinets flung open, their contents strewn across the space. In the living room, the couch cushions were misplaced, some ripped, and the TV was almost as shattered as the patio window.

"What happened?" Josh was the first of us to say anything more. Amanda and I continued to stare, gobsmacked at the state of the place.

"I… uh… this…" Adam stuttered. His eyes bounced between the three of us, and I threw him my best, most intimidating stare. His lack of panic was proof enough that he had something to do with the state of Amanda's apartment.

"I was going to handle it!" he tried to defend himself when he saw the threat in my eyes. "Y'all weren't supposed to be back for another few days. I would have had it cleaned up before then."

Amanda scoffed and crossed her arms over her chest. "How the fuck were you going to do that? Everything is destroyed,

Adam. You don't have enough money to buy me new plates, let alone replace the damn TV!" Her voice rose until she was yelling at him and waving her arms at her sides, motioning to the disaster.

Josh swallowed next to me, and I briefly brushed his fingers with my own. A fierce protectiveness swept over me.

"You were going to have it cleaned up? How do you think that's the best way to handle this? You should have already called the cops. This is a fucking crime scene," I seethed. There was a broom in the corner and the vacuum cleaner was in the middle of the room. It looked like he'd already attempted to clean up what he could but hadn't gotten far.

Adam made a face but didn't get a chance to say anything else because Amanda cut off all arguments he may have begun to make.

She stormed forward, stepping around a stray, broken lamp, and shoved him in the chest. He stumbled back a foot or two and righted himself only just before he fell into what was left of the TV. She was small and not necessarily powerful, but she had the element of surprise on her side. I'd never seen Amanda use physical force, and the look on her face was downright scary.

"Don't even fucking begin to lie to me. You have to tell me the truth. How else are we supposed to fucking fix anything if you keep lying to me? You promised it wouldn't come to this. We talked about this."

Something changed in Adam's demeanor. The defensive walls he'd raised the moment we walked into the door seemed to come crashing down as his sister spoke. The seriousness in her voice and the levity of her words did the trick.

I was glad because I thought Josh and I would have had to hold her back otherwise.

"Okay," Adam conceded, and we all cumulatively sighed in relief. Amanda stepped back over the broken lamp and dodged a stray couch cushion while Adam scrubbed his hands through his hair. She stopped in front of Josh but turned back to watch her brother. Josh cautiously ran his hands over her shoulders and down her arms. Thankfully, she didn't shake off his comfort for a second time. It was short-lived, but there was a second look of relief that washed over her features.

"I came home this morning to it like this. But... I know who did this," Adam began.

"Good, so we can tell the cops that—"

"No," he quickly cut me off, shaking his head vehemently. "We can't call the cops."

"And why the fuck not?" Josh asked, continuing to rub circles on Amanda's back.

Adam paused, eyes bouncing between us, and appeared to hesitate. Amanda wasn't going to allow that to happen.

"I swear to God, Adam. If you don't tell me right this second why my apartment looks like the set of *Twister*, I'm going to—"

"Calvin," he choked out, his eyes going wide.

Josh and I shared a look and then glanced at our girl. Not a hint of recognition passed over Amanda's face. Her hands balled into fists at her sides, and I noticed the first of frustrated tears clouding her eyes.

"Quit dragging it out—who the hell is Calvin?" There was a shaky defiance contorting his expression, but it quickly disappeared.

"He's my boss."

We all stood quietly, still waiting for further explanation.

"I told him that I was done," Adam said, speaking only to Amanda, who was barely containing the fury I knew was bubbling inside of her petite frame. I think we all understood where he was going with this. "And I am, or I was supposed to be. Calvin is the guy we all answer to—the big boss. And he—" Adam fidgeted where he stood, looking extraordinarily uncomfortable. "He told me that if I could get this sale done in California, then I'd be free. When I was there, everything went off without a hitch—I was pretty much just the middleman for the entire thing. But it hadn't actually been as quick and painless as I thought. The product had gone missing, and now they're blaming it on me. *This*," he said urgently, waving his arms around. "Was a message sent by him to me."

"You're dealing?" I asked, and all he could do was nod. Amanda's silence was so loud. "Guessing it's more than weed?" I didn't need him to nod to know I was right.

"Is it your fault?" Josh asked.

Adam scoffed and rolled his eyes. "I understand I've fucked a lot of things up—"

"Fucking understatement of the year," I mumbled under my breath, crossing my arms over my chest and surveying the damage once again.

"But I wanted out. It was supposed to be a temporary thing anyway, but I got caught up in all of it. I wouldn't have fucked it up. I did everything in my power to make sure it went right. I want out."

Amanda sighed loudly and rolled her shoulders back. Even with this new information, and the state of her apartment, she wore an eerily calm expression. "So, what does Calvin want you to do? Go back to California and make sure the shit gets to whoever?"

Adam shook his head slowly, and my entire body tensed in preparation for what I knew was coming next. "He wants me to pay for it. Since the guy didn't get what he was promised, he's refusing to pay Calvin. He said since I'm the one that fucked it up, I get to front the money for the shipment."

"How much?" Amanda asked in a quiet voice, and I instinctively took a step closer to her. The silence between the four of us hung like a dense fog.

"It was fifty grand, but each day I don't come up with the cash, he adds a grand. It's nearly ninety thousand now. And look, sis, I know—"

Amanda held up both of her hands, effectively cutting Adam off midsentence. Slowly, she closed her eyes and took a deep breath. Her chest expanded, air filling her lungs, and hopefully, a calm blanketing over her.

As she lowered her hands and opened her eyes, I caught the distinctive tremor in each of her fingers.

"How do you know it's him? How do you know it has anything to do with that?"

"They spray-painted a message on my bedroom wall."

Amanda's eyes nearly pop out of her head. "Spray-painted?!"

Then she began pacing around the apartment, muttering to herself as she closely inspected the damage.

Josh, Adam, and I shared a look. "You broke her," Josh muttered in a flat tone. "You finally fucked up bad enough that she's lost it."

"Guys, I didn't—"

Josh and I simultaneously leveled him with matching scowls that warned him from spewing the excuse we knew was poised to slip from his lips. For so long, we'd watched him take advantage of his sister's kindness and desire to help her little brother. But enough was enough.

"Honestly, we're not fucking surprised," Josh began. "I mean, this is a new low for you, but you can't seem to stay the fuck out of trouble for anything. Can you?"

Amanda turned down the hallway and headed to her bedroom.

"No, you can't. And this time, we're not going to let Amanda break her fucking back or drive herself into the damn ground trying to fix it for you. She's done it every other time, she's given you a million more chances than she should have, yet you continue to make more mistakes," I added.

Clearly Josh and I were on the same page. All we needed was to make sure Amanda was too.

"I'll fix it," he whispered. His shoulders slumped in defeat like I hoped they would. Maybe if he'd taken the plethora of chances he'd been granted before, I would have had more sympathy for him. But he hadn't, and I wasn't prepared to put anyone else in danger because of him.

"And how do you plan on doing that?" Amanda asked, strolling back into the room and appearing slightly calmer. "Because last time I checked, you didn't have nearly a hundred thousand dollars." Adam opened his mouth like he actually had a response, but Amanda added, "And the plan shouldn't consist of selling or doing anything fucking illegal. I think we've had enough of that, right, El Chapo?"

"I know, and it won't."

"But you don't have a plan yet," Josh said, scrubbing a hand over his jaw. I could feel the irritation rolling off of him in frustrated waves.

Adam couldn't even say it, but he gulped and shook his head.

"This is what needs to happen." I let unrestricted authority enter my voice. "You're going to go to the cops and tell them fucking everything. If we have to follow you there, we will, but you're going to handle this. I'll pay for an attorney, but that's what's going to happen. You're going to tell them what you know about your boss, and hopefully they'll cut you a deal in exchange for more useful information. In the meantime, I recommend finding somewhere else to stay. With a friend or something, because this guy obviously knows where you live and could likely come back again when he realizes you have no intention of paying him. Sound good?" I turned toward Amanda, who was staring at me with her jaw slack.

She shook her head. "Reed, you don't have to pay for an attorney. I can—"

"Let him help. And then move in with us."

In the ten-plus years I'd known Josh, he'd never not had my back. That time was no different, except there was a pointedly different feeling stirring in my chest when I looked at him. The old feelings of friendship were still there, but they'd been overwhelmed by something that was so much more.

"Yes, you can stay with us until we get everything sorted out. Or forever," I said with a shrug.

Josh cocked a half smile, one corner of his mouth pulling into a small grin easily as he glanced between me and Amanda. We'd briefly discussed moving out of our apartment, finding a house, and then asking Amanda to move in with us. Neither of us was too keen on taking things slow—we'd already wasted enough time.

Amanda's tremendous sigh broke through my daydreaming as she cut her attention to Adam.

"I'll give you a week, and then we can go from there. Forever is a long time to live with the two of you," she said like the idea was unbelievable, but I caught a hint of a smile before she turned once again to survey the damage.

"I'm going to call the criminal defense attorney I know and give him the rundown. Cielo, pack a bag. I don't want to be here longer than we have to."

"Okay, but don't you think—"

Again, Amanda cut off Adam's words with one look over her shoulder. "You don't get to think right now. You want out of this mess? Your best bet is to listen to them and me, by extension. So, shut the hell up, and go pack your own damn bag."

# FORTY-EIGHT

Amanda

THEIR SOFT, DEEP-GRAY COUCH FELT TREMENDOUS UNDER MY ACHING body. Only a few seconds behind me, the guys lumbered into their apartment, carrying a few bags filled with items I'd need over the next week, at least. I'd strode into the apartment with my own bag, dropped it just inside the door, and flung myself on the couch without a glance backward.

They'd been my rocks all day—two stone pillars at my sides throughout the chaos.

Reed spoke to his attorney friend, who immediately agreed to represent Adam for what I expected was a tidy sum. We'd argued over his monetary contributions in hushed, heated voices on the patio while Josh waited in the living room with Adam.

He was not budging, and I had to face the facts—if I wanted my brother out of the mess he'd wound up in once again, I needed help. We both needed help. And I knew Reed's intentions were pure. The pounding on my apartment door stopped us midconversation anyway.

Maybe after a full night's sleep I'd bring it up again, but until then, I was letting it go.

One of the most beautiful men I'd ever seen appeared in the doorway to my apartment. The attorney Reed had hired was likely in his midthirties. His eyes were a startling blue, and his wide smile was contagious.

Reed greeted him with a handshake while Adam awaited his introduction. Josh and I watched the entire scene play out before us, and I hadn't noticed I was staring until Josh brushed his fingers across the back of my exposed neck.

A slight shiver danced down my spine at the tender touch, and Josh's chuckle was bright.

"You're drooling," he murmured into my ear. My attention bounced up to Josh only to find him also openly staring at the gorgeous man in the middle of my disaster zone.

"Oh, actually, I think you got a little something right about there," I said, pressing up on my toes to swipe at the invisible drool on Josh's chin. He caught my thumb between his teeth, eliciting an inappropriate giggle.

Reed finally introduced me to the attorney, Will, who was not only easy on the eyes but also had a résumé and a laundry list of credentials that would have made anyone gawk. He assured me he'd do his best by Adam, and whether it was the sincerity in his eyes or the fucking dimples, I believed him.

Adam led Will into my room—the one room in the entire place that hadn't been ransacked to pieces—to discuss the details.

They were in the room for half an hour at least before Will stepped out to tell us to call the police.

From there, the chaos truly ensued. The police arrived, took record of the damage, and interviewed us all. There wasn't much Reed, Josh, or I could tell them, but they questioned us, nonetheless. They asked me to take inventory of my belongings to identify if anything had been stolen.

Surprisingly, it didn't appear that anything had been taken. Most of my belongings were destroyed, as was the very makeup of the apartment—windows, walls, and doors. The only two things that hadn't been touched were my room and the TV stand in the living room.

After hours of sitting in my apartment, Will drove Adam to the police station as they were followed by a cruiser. As much as I wanted to go with them and lend support to my idiotic little brother, Will advised against it. Under his recommendation, we stayed behind, made calls, and picked up what we could in the apartment.

When we left after spending another several hours cleaning and logging all my belongings while getting almost nowhere, exhaustion felt like an understatement.

"Do I want to drink, shower, or sleep first? All three sound too good." Josh placed my bags near the one I'd tossed haphazardly on the floor and plopped down at the other end of the couch near my feet. I'd kicked my sandals off the moment I entered the door, so Josh idly picked up one of my bare feet and began massaging the arch. I scooted farther down, making it easier for him to find each tender spot.

Reed, never one to be left out, shut and locked the door, then made his way over to the couch as well. He shimmied underneath my head, and I dutifully lay back down on his thigh. Immediately his strong, calloused fingers were in my hair. They were gentle against my scalp, massaging at the root before finger-combing through to the ends. It was a tangled mess, but that didn't stop him.

Between the two of them—Josh expertly rubbed my aching feet while Reed soothed my pounding head—sleep was going to be the only thing I could manage on my list of things to do.

But there were other more urgent things on my mind, and although I was peacefully blissed out, I couldn't stop the incessant thoughts.

From the moment we woke up, they'd both been there. They'd made excuses to our friends to get us out of the house quickly, stood by my side while I confronted my brother, called and paid for attorneys, and helped with all the cleanup afterward. Neither of them complained about cutting their vacations short by five days or even muttered the words "I told you so." Words I wouldn't have been a bigger person to keep to myself.

My friends were always the most important people in my life. They'd dropped everything a number of times to help me with whatever I needed. But it was something different that time. Our relationship changed, but their support hadn't.

"I really appreciate both of your help today, and I'm sorry—"

"Eh, not happening, Cielo," Reed cut me off midsentence, and his hand stilled in my hair.

"Yeah, baby girl, you can't continue apologizing for your brother's mistakes," Josh added, his own hands sliding higher over my ankle, across my calf, until his fingers rested on my knee where he squeezed softly.

My breath was dragged through my lungs. "I'm not trying to apologize for his mistakes, I understand that his mistakes are his own and have nothing to do with me. But what I was trying to apologize for was dragging the two of you into it."

Josh chuckled. "Same difference."

Then there was a sharper tug against the root of my hair, and Reed slowly forced my gaze to him. My head craned back. I stared into his amber-colored eyes that had taken on a softer quality since we'd walked in the door. The hardness he'd worn on his face most of the day—for everyone else's benefit—had slipped away, leaving my Reed.

"We knew going into this that your brother often found himself mixed up in more shit than he could handle. It wasn't a surprise to us that something like this finally happened."

"But it isn't your job to take care of him. He's my responsibility. And being with me shouldn't come with the caveat that you also have to deal with my punk of a little brother. I just wanted you both to know that I truly appreciate all your help today and what will probably continue for a while. But if at any moment you don't want that additional responsibility…"

All of the words I wanted to say felt like fire rolling in my lungs, in my stomach. The pain of letting them out likely wouldn't have been as severe as the pain of keeping them in. But my words trailed off anyway. I felt like a coward.

They were both quiet for a moment, caught in silent retrospection and probably wondering how, in fact, they did get caught with the psycho girl and her psycho brother.

Josh broke the silence first. He reached for my hand, intertwining my slightly shaking fingers with his, and pulled me up from Reed's lap. There weren't tears in his eyes, but they were glistening with emotion. The blues and greens twisted together.

His thumb stroked the back of my hand in simple, small circles, but my entire body was aware of the fondness and care in that little touch. The awareness glided over my skin and bathed me in comfort. Reed's hand found the back of my neck and squeezed.

"Amanda, I don't think you realize that there is literally nothing in this world we wouldn't do for you. Dealing with your brother isn't a big deal when we get *you*."

My breath caught in my throat, lodged against a ball of emotion that refused to break free.

Then Reed leaned forward and brushed my hair around my other shoulder, exposing my ear and neck. My skin was covered in goose bumps as he breathed against me.

"Amanda," he said my name like a prayer, and it sounded so good coming from his lips. "Cielo, you already let us worship every part of your body," he said in a low voice but one loud enough for Josh to also hear.

"And let us inside your beautifully chaotic head," Josh continued for him as his free hand, the one not holding mine, lifted and pressed firmly against my chest. Between my breasts, it was impossible he couldn't feel my heart attempting to escape.

"So." Reed's hand gripped my thigh—holding me down like he was worried I'd flee, and when he continued speaking, I understood why. "It's okay to let us take care of you. To love you."

Every ounce of tension filtered out of my body. It wasn't the reaction I'd expected from myself when that loaded word left his lips. It wasn't like any reaction I'd had before. Running, joking, and freaking the fuck out were all reactions I'd had when it had undoubtedly been said before. But not that time.

The realization that they wanted to love me, and I them, was equally freeing and debilitating. Mostly because I couldn't comprehend the words I needed to use to express the change they'd sparked within me.

So I nodded. It wasn't enough compared to their combined declaration, but that single nod was more than I'd ever given, or planned to give, to anyone else.

"No matter what happens to us, every day spent with you is the best day of my life." Josh's words didn't waver, and I was rocked by the honesty in his voice. It felt like a strong hand took hold of my heart and squeezed it within an inch of never beating again.

Until I realized I'd heard those exact words before. The emotions causing chaos inside of me must have slowed my reaction time because it never took me more than a few seconds to identify a line from one of my favorite movies. My understanding must have been written all over my face because the serious expression he wore immediately morphed into the megawatt smile we all knew and loved. It was confident, like he was proud of himself.

"Did you just—" I stuttered.

"Quote *The Notebook*?" Reed finished for me. I could feel his own smile against my neck, on the soft spot below my ear. "Yes, he did."

The giggle that bubbled out of me was sudden, and I quickly slapped my free hand over my mouth, trying to keep it in. "I told you there didn't need to be any *Notebook*-level declarations, but how is it possible that you both know that movie well enough to quote it?" I asked, already aware of the likely answer.

"It's the first movie you made us watch with you, and it was the main showing of several movie nights after. Had we known being forced to watch random movies with you was going to become at least a weekly occurrence..." Reed was again enthralled with kissing and licking up my neck, so he didn't finish his sentence.

"We would've found you sooner," Josh finished for him, and I let my hand that covered my mouth drop so he could see me smile. But something was gnawing at me—I'd wanted to know about it for a while but could never find the time to bring it up.

"Back then... was there ever anything. I mean, did either of you ever feel...?" My inability to form a proper sentence had less to do with nerves and more to do with Reed's hand slowly inching up my bare thigh and hiking up the short skirt of my dress. His lips were also blazing a trail across my skin that was making it hard to think of anything else.

"Did we have feelings for you? Yes." Reed said confidently, but I already knew that. They'd made it clear since the day I sat down in that biology class and started talking a mile a minute that they were goners.

"No, for each other."

Silence followed. Reed's journey up my skirt stalled, and he lifted his head to peer over my shoulder at Josh. I could see Josh swallow, Adam's apple bobbing with the force, but I couldn't see Reed behind me. I could only feel their connection gliding over me like I always could. Like I was part of their connection, too.

"Looking back, I think maybe there was a reason why we were always drawn together. But it wasn't until recently—until you—that I understood it was because there was something deeper than friendship," Reed explained.

"I've thought the same thing," Josh agreed. "But I also thought you were kind of a pretentious ass back then. Nothing would have happened when we were in college for that reason," Josh confessed. I barely suppressed another laugh while Josh smiled.

Reed seemed like he was prepared to argue, even acting

offended with a quick "Hey!" But he shook his head and laughed along with us. "I was kind of an ass, but I was also eighteen. And you were too laid back and free-spirited. You annoyed the shit out of me most of the time."

"Yet you still wanted to be my friend," Josh joked. "So strange."

"My frontal lobe wasn't fully developed back then."

"So what's your excuse now?"

"It's just fucking insanity now. I feel like I'm going crazy between the two of you," Reed quipped, but there was a fondness in his voice that made me smile. With them, I felt lighter. The gnawing in the back of my head, waiting for Adam to call or for news from Will, lessened when they monopolized my time and my thoughts.

"As much fun as it is to listen to you two bicker," I murmured, dropping my voice lower and shifting my weight until I was propped on my knees. They were quick on the uptake and immediately snapped their attention to me, following every movement with an undiluted lust and longing. Their fingers tangled on the couch in front of me, the small displays of affection had become more and more frequent between the two of them, and I enjoyed every moment of watching their relationship grow alongside ours.

I threaded my much smaller fingers between theirs. "I'd really prefer to go back to that thing you were talking about—worshiping my body. The food, drinks, and shower can wait until after that."

Josh licked his full lips, and I could feel my sex clench in response to his crooked smile. A noise from the back of Reed's throat, something akin to a growl, made my nipples harden beneath the thin fabric of my floral dress. If I didn't feel their hands on me soon, I was going to burst.

They worshipped me, cherished me, cared for me, and *loved* me. There were so many pent-up emotions inside of me that I needed somewhere for them to go—their confessions raced through me. And although I couldn't find the accurate words to describe my own feelings, I knew I could at least show them in the interim.

"Actually I think we could knock out three of these at once. Reed's shower is massive, and we haven't fucked there yet. And a shower beer sounds *perfect,*" Josh said, seemingly confident with his masterful plan.

Reed rolled his eyes, but I saw a hint of a smile behind his grumpy exterior. "Fine. You make the drinks while I go get our girl ready to take both of us."

Quicker than I could anticipate, Reed lunged for me. His arms wrapped around my waist, and he hoisted me off the couch. A very uncharacteristically girly giggle and startled shriek erupted from me. He lifted me off the ground and over his shoulder.

"Wait a fucking second." Josh rose from the couch and swiftly blocked Reed's path down the hallway leading to the bedrooms. I hung uselessly over his muscled shoulder.

"When have we ever settled things like that?"

I swear I could feel Reed's eye roll even though I couldn't see it. "Seriously? You want to do this right now?"

I didn't hear anything for a moment, with the blood rushing to my head, until Reed instructed, "Hold on while I beat this guy's ass in Rock, Paper, Scissors."

I took his direction literally and gripped onto his trim waist as his hands disappeared from around my waist. They counted down and when Josh lost the first round, he demanded the best two out of three. I wondered if Reed could feel my eye roll, too.

Josh won the second round, but Reed won the third with a hearty "Whoop!"

"I want whiskey. What do you want, Cielo?"

"Wine!" I called out as Reed took off down the hallway, leaving Josh shaking his head to make our drinks.

In the bathroom, sleek with black tiles and slate-gray countertops, Reed carefully placed me on the cool surface and proceeded to kiss me breathless.

"I swear to God, if there are any orgasms before I get in there, then there will be hell to pay!"

Glasses clinked loudly from the living room, and I hoped I could heed his request. But Reed's hands twisted in my hair, urging me inevitably closer, and I couldn't help but find the very edge of the counter. I let my touch trail down Reed's back, moaning at not only the perfect pressure of his tongue against mine but the refined contours of his muscled physique.

My hands grabbed his ass and tugged him closer until his clothed cock was rubbing against my aching center.

"Fucking hell. All of my wet dreams have come true," Josh cursed when he entered the room, seeing Reed and I fully engrossed in our making out.

Without removing my lips from Reed's, I reached out for Josh. Quickly, he dropped the glasses on the counter with several clinks and stepped forward at the same moment Reed carefully pulled me off the counter and set me tenderly on my feet.

The arousal pulsing through me made my entire body limp and my legs especially weak, but Josh pressed behind me. Reed called me their heaven but being cradled between the two of them was mine.

Together they lifted my dress over my head, and I turned my head for Josh to take my mouth while Reed's hands did as promised—*worshipped.*

By the time Josh released me from his bewitching lips, I was light-headed. He reached over, opened the shower door, and turned on the water but quickly returned to his place behind me.

Then Reed and Josh kissed above my head while I let my hands roam over each of them. One of their hands tangled in my hair while another one fondled my breast, circling my nipple with a nimble finger and then pinching just hard enough.

They began undressing each other, and then Reed kissed me again as he cupped Josh's cock. Josh's hand teased the top of my panties before I moaned a plea, and he took pity on me, circling my clit in slow, tight circles. The moment my hand wrapped around Reed's heavy shaft, Josh dipped two thick fingers inside of me, and I bucked against them.

We dissolved into a frenzy of hands and mouths and sounds. Where one of us began and the others ended felt irrelevant as we found our way into the shower under the warm spray. And when they both lifted me off the ground and plunged deep inside of me, I felt whole.

Chest to chest, Josh and I panted and gulped the same air, his arms steadfast on my thighs while Reed pressed against my back and showered us with praise and adoration.

How we'd managed to fight it for so long, I'd never know. Because I was at its mercy. Chained and coaxed into submission with easy promises of something I couldn't have explained before. Not until I experienced it for myself. And even then, it felt impossibly big, nearly infinite, and unforgettable.

# FORTY-NINE

Josh

Sam's white craftsman-style house could have been the seventh circle of hell for how much I wanted to be there.

She and Travis had taken Zach on a trip to Florida for Spring Break and had only arrived back in Texas that morning. It had been more than a week since I'd seen my son, and all I wanted to do was spend a few hours with him. It was technically supposed to be my weekend anyway.

But Sam was standing just on the inside of the open front door, her arms crossed over her chest and an unimpressed expression twisting her features. Like she was standing guard, she refused to let me step inside while Zach gathered his things.

"I know Amanda is living with you," were the first words out of her mouth.

I tried not to let my shock or anger play out over my face or in my body language, but her eyebrow lifted subtly when my eyes narrowed of their own volition. I stayed silent, trying to prepare for what I assumed would be a methodical onslaught of questions and accusations. After learning that the three of us were in a relationship and Murphy's was being sold, things had taken a turn.

"When were you planning on telling me?" she angrily whispered, hearing Zach yell he was almost ready from his room.

After the week I'd had, the last thing I wanted to do was argue with Sam.

Adam had been released from custody less than twenty-four hours after he and Will made it to the police station, but that didn't lessen Amanda's anxiety. She flipped between being angry with her brother or at herself for not doing more. And then she would become a ticking time bomb of anxiety and pent-up frustration.

It didn't help that her parents were ambivalent about the entire situation—there was one phone call at the beginning of the week when she told them what was happening. They told her to tell them if he ended up being arrested and promptly hung up because they were "late for their brunch plans."

Thankfully she didn't plan to keep the news from our friends. Back in the city from their vacation at the lake, they were all eager to lend a hand in whatever way they could. Hazel had even offered their guest bedroom, actually their entire second floor, to Amanda for as long as she needed it. Amanda's brilliant excuse was that her stuff was already at our place, which Hazel argued could easily be moved.

If Hazel didn't know before about our little trio, she knew after Amanda's subpar lie.

And then there was the bar. Rhonda had called me on my way to pick up Zach to let me know that she'd accepted an offer from someone else to buy Murphy's Law. She said the new owner had some new ideas and a fresh perspective she found intriguing. That I would like him.

Although I'd told her that I wasn't going to be able to come up with the money, my stomach still soured when she finally said out loud my worst fears.

So, I'd reached my limit. Actually, I was so fucking far past my limit that it was a tiny little speck of nothing in the distance.

"Amanda living with us is temporary and will have no impact on my relationship with Zach or my ability to be a good father. Which I am, you know, a good father. There's a situation with her brother and her apartment, and she feels more comfortable staying with us. If it really bothers you that much, she will stay with Luke and Hazel next weekend while Zach is with me, okay?"

By some miracle, I finished speaking just as I'd begun, with a level, calm voice that didn't convey the frustration boiling beneath the surface.

One of her blonde eyebrows lifted in defiance as she assessed me. She opened her mouth like she was preparing to lay into me, but thankfully, our blonde-haired, blue-eyed kid came racing around the corner, saving my ass for the millionth time.

"Daddy!" he yelled, and his sneakers squeaked along the tile entryway. His hands were tight on the straps of his backpack, trying to keep it on his shoulders as his little legs carried him to me as quickly as they could. I stooped down just in time to catch him midair when he launched himself toward me.

*Fuck*, it felt good to hug him again. Every day—I wished I could do that every day for the rest of his life. I wanted to hug him and keep him safe from anything and everything out there.

"I missed you, bud." My words were muffled with my lips against his hair, but he heard me all the same.

"I missed you more, Dad."

I laughed and set him down, his little shoes lighting up the moment they touched the brick.

"Where are you taking him?" Sam's sharp tone caused my smile to fall as it always did.

"Luke and Hazel's. They haven't seen him in a while and wanted a visit."

"Did they buy their pool yet? Aunt Hazel said she wants a pool so she can swim with Sadie!" The exact opposite of his mother, Zach was endlessly excited about the prospect of seeing his aunt and uncle.

"Have him home by six, okay? First day back from school is hard enough."

"I'll have him back." I nodded in her direction and told Zach to hop in the truck. He yanked open the back door and heaved himself up, throwing his backpack down next to him.

Unfortunately, when I climbed in the truck and was greeted by an onslaught of questions and stories, I was already dreading having to leave him again in only a few short hours.

For the second time that day, I pulled into the long driveway leading up to Luke and Hazel's house. Zach and I spent the day at their place, playing with Sadie and spending time with his aunt and uncle.

Hazel had wholeheartedly taken on the role of Aunt Hazel and enjoyed his company nearly as much as my brother did.

They bought an inflatable pool with the promise that it would only be temporary until they put one in the ground. He made Hazel promise that she would let him watch them put the pool in the ground.

The only thing that would have made the day better would have been having Reed and Amanda with us. The last thing I wanted was for the most important people in my life to be separated. Not being able to share moments with all of us was a new, cruel type of torture.

Like we'd timed it—although we hadn't—I pulled up as Reed opened the passenger door of his sleek, black SUV for Amanda.

Both of them took my breath away. I hadn't had time to do more than change out of my swim trunks and throw on dark-blue shorts and a white Henley that was slightly wrinkled from sitting in my bag all day. My hair was unruly from sweat and water and my nose and forehead were a little red.

Amanda's hair was swept up in a loose bun at the top of her head, and she was fucking glowing. She wore a short red sundress that flirted with the tops of her knees and her feet were clad in small sandals.

Reed's light-gray shorts hugged his muscled thighs and ass. And he wore a tight white T-shirt that cost more than probably mine and Amanda's outfits combined. But he looked damn good.

My headlights illuminated their figures and reflected off their twin smiles. I couldn't get out of the car quick enough. The door slammed behind me, and I found myself jogging up to meet them. Even if it shaved half a second off of my time apart from them, it was worth it.

"God, how do you always look like my surfer boy wet dream?" Amanda confessed with a heat in her voice and behind her eyes that raked unabashedly over me from head to toe.

"You're fucking telling me," Reed agreed and wrapped his hand around my neck to pull me close for a short yet consuming kiss. When he released me, he licked his lips like he was savoring the taste of me there.

Bending down, I slanted my mouth over Amanda's and couldn't help but tease her lips apart with my tongue, even just for a moment. Her resounding moan was a gracious reward.

Standing back at my full height, my fingers tangled in hers, Reed looked back and forth between us.

"So, we're really doing this?"

Without hesitating, Amanda said, "Yes," as I said, "Hell fucking yes."

She squeezed my hand, and although we were both confident in our decision to tell our friends about our relationship, I could feel and see Reed's anxiety.

"Do you want to do this?" I asked.

His shoulders straightened and his eyes hardened. A newfound strength summoned from some unknown place, and it replaced any hesitation in an instant.

"Yes," he said in a voice that left no room for questions. Then he turned and led the way to their front door.

Reed tried the door handle but surprisingly met resistance. They normally kept the door unlocked when we were all coming over—especially for Sunday dinners—so instead, he rang the bell and stepped back with us to wait.

Unable to keep my hands to myself, I ran my fingers down Amanda's side, enjoying the swell of her breast, the dip of her waist, and the way her hips flared out. Her body racked with shivers and goose bumps pebbled along her skin even on the eighty-degree night.

"I've been thinking about you all day. Thinking about your ass and my face between your legs."

Over his shoulder, Reed threw me his best *"shut the fuck up"* look. But I only responded with what I hoped was a tempting, good-natured smile.

"Don't worry, babe, I've been thinking about your ass, too."

"I think I have another fantasy to add to the list. What if you—"

Through the glass in the door, Hazel came rushing around the corner, Sadie hot on her heels. Behind both of them, Luke appeared, scrubbing a hand over his mouth and trying to suppress a smile.

"So sorry about that. Not sure why I locked it. But anyway, come in!" Hazel rushed out. She was out of breath and seemed frazzled as she waved us inside.

Sadie greeted all of us like she worried we'd never return, drenching us in kisses and covering us in a healthy layer of dog fur.

"Zach said he left his notebook here this afternoon. Do you know where it is? So I don't forget." My question was directed at Luke since he was the one coloring with Zach earlier that day, but he didn't hear a word I said. He and his wife were locked in a silent battle—their only form of communication was the slight widening of their eyes, shakes of their heads, and mouthed words.

Reed and Amanda completely missed the show in front of us as they continued rubbing Sadie's belly and her favorite spot behind her ears.

After several seconds, Hazel spotted me watching and quickly pasted on a smile. "I'm sorry—what?"

"Never mind. Y'all okay?"

"Yes, we're great. Everything's great. Just great. Let's get something to drink," she said with jittery enthusiasm. There was something else behind her smile that I couldn't quite identify, and Amanda and Reed finally caught on, too. They both looked in my direction like I'd have the answers, but I only shrugged and followed her and Luke into the kitchen.

James and Devon, both with a beer in their hands, were already digging into the chips and dip our hosts had laid out on the island. Sadie weaved between our legs and plopped herself on her bed tucked in the corner of the space near the long, wooden table where we usually ate.

"What the hell did y'all do to your dog?" James asked around a mouthful of dip.

"Yeah, I'm not sure I've ever seen her that tired," Devon added, settling into a barstool.

"That would be Zach's fault. He and Sadie played in the little blow-up pool in the back for hours today. He was so tired he fell asleep midsentence on the drive back to Sam's." A small pang hit my chest, and my hand, with a mind of its own, rose to rub right over my heart and where it hurt the most. In front of me appeared a beer of my own, and I looked up to see Amanda giving me an empathetic smile.

"How's he doing?" Devon asked, hugging Amanda as she sidled up beside him and sipped at her own beer.

"Amazing. He's so fucking smart and hilarious. I can't believe Sam and I made that great of a kid."

"Yeah, it's a wonder he doesn't have an affinity for streaking," James added, and I shook my head slowly, eyes closing against the memories. Or the ones I could remember.

"That was one semester, alright. And who goes through college without streaking at least once?" Everyone besides Devon raised their hands, and we all dissolved into laughter.

"It might have been one semester, but I think you streaked or wanted to go streaking every time you got drunk. Never in my life did I think I'd have to see my only brother's junk that many damn times." Luke clapped me on the shoulder before crossing the kitchen to help Hazel, who was pulling containers out of the fridge and a dish out of the oven.

"Anyway, enough about my dick. Devon, you got some new ink?"

He twisted his arm, the one not wrapped around Amanda's waist, and showed off the dark butterfly right above his elbow. Its wings curved over his bicep like it had landed there and was settled against his arm.

"Yeah, for my mom. Butterflies are her favorite."

Reed stepped up next to him and eyed the new, dark ink closely. "Your own work, right?"

"Yeah, sketched it out last time I was in Houston with her for a doctor's appointment and got it a few days ago."

"You're going to catch up to Luke here soon," Amanda commented, stealing a glance at my brother across the kitchen, who acted offended. Devon was covered in ink, but he had a ways to go. Luke barely had an inch of skin left unless he suddenly decided to tattoo his face.

Most of Devon's ink was by his own design as well. But between the both of them, they had enough ink for all of us.

"This one might be one of my favorites you've done, though," James said, then glanced down at his phone with a shake of his head. Whatever it was he'd read or seen was enough to make him turn his phone over on the counter and down the rest of his drink.

"I don't know," Hazel said. Her hands were braced on the

island, and Luke bracketed her against the counter with his own large arms. She fondly stroked the skin of his inner forearm, where the tattoo Devon designed for him was placed, and smiled. "I may be biased, but I like this one the best." It was an angel and was representative of his nickname for her.

"Yes, you're absolutely biased," Amanda agreed.

"Thanks. Anyway, dinner's ready! It's all on the table, so come on."

# FIFTY

Reed

"No, Reed, why don't you sit between Josh and Amanda? Yeah, right there." Luke pointed to the chair that was, sure enough, between Amanda and Josh.

I gave him an incredulous look but pulled the chair out all the same. His creepy-ass smile widened as I lowered myself into the seat, and when I scooted closer to the table, I thought he was going to break out into hysterical laughter. But Hazel slapped his forearm and motioned for him to sit down himself.

Conversations picked up around us as bowls and trays were passed. We discussed the end of their lake trip at my parents' house and anything else new in our lives.

Hazel was still hard at work on her second book, and Luke was planning on opening his own veterinary practice. James was, as always, focused on work while Devon was still commuting back and forth from Houston every other week to take care of his Mom while she underwent experimental cancer treatment.

Josh narrowly evaded the topic of Murphy's, and I knew by the way he readjusted in his seat, clenched his jaw, and darted his attention to Amanda and me that there was something else he wasn't telling us.

"So your brother's okay?" Hazel asked Amanda in a small voice, like she was hesitant to bring up the topic.

Amanda cleared her throat and set down her fork softly against her plate. Similar to Josh, she shifted on her seat, uncomfortable under the attention of everyone at the table. What I wouldn't have done to reach out and comfort her. My hand balled into a fist on the tabletop as I resisted the urge to thread my fingers through hers or grip her thigh under the table.

"Yeah, he's okay. Will, his attorney, is amazing. From what we know, they offered him a deal—he's going to lead the cops to his boss for a lesser punishment. They've been looking for this guy for a while, so he has that on his side. The only problem is that he has to do it—if they don't get his boss, he's going to... he's going to go down for all of it."

No one spoke for several long moments. Everyone simultaneously mulled over the consequences if the plan didn't pan out.

"But you're letting him do it on his own," Hazel supplied, and slowly Amanda nodded.

"Good for you," James said, and everyone else agreed.

"And you're staying with your boys until your apartment is put back together?"

A forkful of vegetables hovered above my plate as my hand stopped midair. Carefully, I watched Luke and the hint of a smile appeared.

He *fucking* knew. Or at least he thought he knew something, but *how* was the question. I thought we'd been so careful. And suddenly, I couldn't help but reassess every second we'd been around them. We'd barely touched and been careful about looking at each other for too long. Every action that had become innate—touching, teasing, kissing—had all ceased while in public or around anyone else for the past two months.

It didn't make sense, but it also didn't matter. We'd planned to tell them all that night anyway. But that didn't mean that the unknown didn't gnaw relentlessly at my gut.

"Yeah, I'm staying with Reed and Josh for now," Amanda said and then looked over to Josh and me.

"You could have stayed here, you know? Had the entire second floor to yourself and wouldn't have to share a bathroom with one of them," Luke continued, leaning back in his chair like he was lord of the manor.

I knew this game. He was going to keep talking in an attempt to pry the truth out of us.

"It's not a big deal." Amanda didn't look up from her plate as she spoke.

"And I'm sure Hazel would have loved to have you here, right, Angel?"

Hazel sipped her drink. Her only response was an eye roll and a quick, "Yes, sure."

If Luke knew, then Hazel probably knew as well. Amanda promised she hadn't told them, but now, I wasn't so sure. Josh seemed unfazed by the conversation while Amanda's leg was bouncing anxiously under the table.

"I mean, unless there's a reason why maybe you preferred to stay with them instead of with us in our big, spacious, homey house—"

"We're dating." And there it was. The words were out of my mouth before I had fully formed them in my mind or actually made the conscious decision to say them at all.

Around the table, everyone's eyes widened. James choked on his drink, and Luke's smug smile widened to a new level.

"You and Amanda?" Devon asked cautiously.

"Yes, but..."

"But?" Luke prompted, and my eye roll put Hazel's to shame. My head fell into my hands as I braced my elbows on the table. I didn't understand why it was so hard for me. They were my best friends, and I was least concerned about their judgment than anyone else's.

"Amanda and I are dating, but so…"

"So are we." From the other end of the table, Josh finally spoke. He said the words like he was commenting on the weather and didn't stop eating his second helping of chicken.

"You're both dating Amanda?" James asked. Uncertainty laced every word and his eyes curiously assessed the three of us.

"Yes, but…"

"But, what?" It was Luke that time. He sat forward in his seat and braced his elbows on the table. He looked as shocked at my second "but" as everyone else, so he obviously was not aware of the entire situation. For some reason, that made me feel slightly better.

"Wait," Hazel spoke up and narrowed her eyes at Amanda, who cringed away from her friend's glare. "You told me you were going to choose. I thought you hadn't said anything else about it because you were still trying to figure it out."

"Well, yeah, I was going to choose," Amanda said with a sigh and then straightened slightly like she was preparing for battle. "But then I didn't have to."

"You didn't have to?" Hazel said slowly, turning the words over in her head.

"You're going to choose between Reed and Josh?" James asked, and Devon smacked his arm.

"No, aren't you listening? She used the past tense. She was *going to* choose, but she *didn't have to*." James still seemed confused, and I didn't blame him—I was confused, yet I was in the damn relationship.

I suddenly had a headache.

"Do you guys mind if I just take it from here?" Josh asked, but he didn't wait for a response before continuing. "Reed and I both pursued Amanda. It started after y'all's wedding and continued from there. We both took her on dates and then it became very apparent that choosing between us would not be happening. She didn't want to choose, and we decided not to make her. We were going to be content with that until things changed. Not only did we *not* want Amanda to choose between the two of us, but we also didn't want to choose between her and each other."

He took a deep breath and with a shaking hand, he reached for mine that lay on the table between us. With our hands joined, he said, "We're all three dating. All of us. Together. At the same time."

I wanted to keep my head down, pretending that there was no one else in the room besides me and Amanda and Josh. But instead, I anxiously watched each of our friends' faces transform. Most of them battled with shock and confusion. And my heart attempted to pound out of my chest. My pulse quickened and a slick sweat appeared on my forehead. My fingers tightened around Josh's, although I was also tempted to jerk my hand free and flee the room. Flee the insistent stares in our direction and the pounding in my head.

"This is…" Hazel stuttered and then smiled. "Amazing!"

My relief was instant and then I could feel it on Amanda and Josh as well.

"So this has been going on for… months?" James asked, also smiling at the three of us. We each nodded, likely all too stunned to form words.

"Well, I'm happy for you guys. Are y'all happy?" Devon continued eating like he wasn't concerned with any part of the news we'd just dropped.

"So happy," Amanda answered for all of us.

"Girl, I have *so* many questions for you. I can't believe you've kept this from me for two entire months." Hazel's genuine shock was surprising, and then I glanced at Luke, whose gaze was skipping between the three of us like we'd all grown several heads.

"Wait, you didn't tell Hazel?" I asked Amanda, and she vehemently shook her head.

"Then how did you know something was up?" I asked Luke pointedly. My curiosity had gotten the best of me.

Luke chuckled and shook his head while Hazel sighed loudly and hung her head. "After catching y'all at the rehearsal dinner, I kind of figured something may be up, or you'd tell us eventually. But y'all also have this awful thing about getting caught on camera, did you know that?" Luke explained.

His laugh grew louder as his wife explained. "Remember the whole incident with the doggy camera?" She waited for our confirmation and then she continued. "When you walked up to the door earlier, it triggered the camera connected to the doorbell to start recording, and well…"

"Oh, shit," Josh said and then joined his brother in an uncontrollable laughing fit.

"So, Luke and I watched you." She pointed at Josh. "Grab Amanda's ass and say something about thinking about both of their asses all day?" She said it like a question, but she'd heard every word we'd said on her front porch.

"Fucking cameras," I muttered and leaned back, scrubbing my hands through my hair. The lingering tension was intense in my shoulders and down my back.

"You know we don't care, right?" Luke said. And I looked around the table. No one had stormed off or yelled. There was no cussing or attempts to flip the table.

"Yeah, we know that," Josh said.

"Good, we only care about your happiness. And it's pretty fucking cool, too." James grinned and leaned back in his chair, reaching down to scratch Sadie, who'd taken up a cool spot by his chair. "I do have a question, though. If you don't mind, and you can tell me if I'm being an asshole," he rushed out.

"Go ahead. I'm sure I know where you're going with this," I said.

"I didn't think either of you"—he motioned to me and Josh—"were interested in men."

Hazel began to chastise him, and for a second, he actually looked terrified he'd said something wrong. "It's okay, I promise," I confirmed before Hazel could get up, find a rolled-up newspaper, and smack him with it.

"I don't think either of us thought we were," Josh explained.

"Definitely not," I added.

Then Josh cleared his throat. "But I think I might be bi."

My head snapped up to him, and I tried not to seem too surprised. It hit me then that we hadn't really talked about it.

Past our own attraction to each other, we hadn't discussed if it changed the way either of us identified. I'd thought about it myself, but I hadn't voiced it.

"Makes sense." Amanda shrugged, and I reached out for her, linking our fingers together.

"But I don't necessarily plan on being with any other men or even women... ever."

Hazel sucked in a breath across the table, and I swore I could see tears forming in her eyes. Luke leaned over and scooted her chair closer to his and tucked her underneath his arm, planting a soft kiss on her temple.

Since I'd seen them together for the first time, I didn't feel a pang of longing for a relationship like theirs. I had it—I'd found what Luke had gone on and on about while drunk at his bachelor party.

He said it was like when you've been holding your breath for so long you forget what fresh air feels like. And when you finally breathe again, you'd do anything to make sure you continue doing so. Your lungs no longer felt like they were on fire or like you were about to pass out from lack of oxygen.

When he'd said it, we'd all taken it for what it was—drunken bullshit from a guy in love.

It wasn't until I found them—or better yet, opened myself up to them—that I realized it was so much more than that.

"Not sure I can confidently say I'm bi, but I do really like this guy," I said with a smile, feeling impossibly lighter. My hand wrapped around the back of his neck, and Josh returned my smile with his genuine, uninhibited one that I prayed I'd see every day for the rest of my life. "And his dick."

There was a chorus of groans around us while Amanda shook with laughter next to me.

"On that note, this calls for celebration and a toast!" James proclaimed. He raised his glass, and we all followed suit. "To the best fucking throuple."

"Do you know any other throuples?" Devon asked while we all clinked glasses and sipped our drinks.

"No, but I feel pretty confident that those three beat out anyone else."

I couldn't argue with him, no matter how unfounded the logic.

# FIFTY-ONE

Reed

Sweat dripped down my client's face, but it was the smile I noticed the most.

"Reed, I'm telling you, this place is fucking phenomenal. I've told all of my work colleagues about you and RG Fitness. Expect a large influx of new membership applications here in a week or two."

I shook his hand and hoped he was right. We were doing well even without a large influx of new members, but more wouldn't hurt.

"I really appreciate that, man. Word of mouth is the best type of marketing, especially since it doesn't cost me a damn thing."

He laughed and waved as he trotted out of the gym, stopping at the smoothie truck parked outside.

Rodney was my fourth and final training session of the day, and it was almost two. The rest of my day, I'd left clear, so I could catch up on paperwork that had been piling up over the week. I'd been more focused on helping Amanda than working on the gym's taxes.

The training part of my job, and hell, even the hiring, organizing, and actually running part of the business, was more enjoyable than the paperwork.

For the first time in over an hour, I glanced down at my phone that I'd left charging in my office. I had a few unread texts from Josh and Amanda—the usual nonsense that occurred in our group text. There was also one missed call from Amanda and three from Sam.

All three calls were within a few minutes of each other, the most recent only two minutes earlier. I couldn't remember the last time Samantha actually called me. The only reason I had her number was when I RSVP'd for one of Zach's birthday parties.

Three calls seemed excessive, and I planned to send her a text after I called Amanda back, only for her to call a fourth time a second later.

I answered with a hesitant, "Hello?"

"Oh, thank God you answered! No one answers their damn phones anymore." Two seconds into the call, and I was already irritated.

"Sure. Why are you calling me?"

Her sigh was dramatic, and there were several muffled voices in the background. "I need a favor."

I tried not to, but my laugh had a mind of its own. Leaning back in my desk chair, I kicked my feet up between two stacks of papers, each nearly half a foot in height.

"Yeah," I said with a chuckle. "Me doing you a favor is as likely as pigs flying or world peace or getting struck by a meteorite."

I was going to keep going, already contemplating what other insanely unlikely things I could come up with when she continued. "It's Zach."

That stopped me immediately. I straightened in my chair, my hand tensing around my phone. "What about Zach?"

She sighed again, and suddenly I was frustrated with her constant exhalations every time I asked a question. "What about Zach?" I asked again through gritted teeth.

"He's sick, and I'm over an hour and a half away at a work meeting. Travis is traveling, and I called Josh, but he's not answering either. My friends aren't able to get him, so I was hoping you'd be able to pick him up from school and take him back to your apartment until I can get there."

She sounded like the last thing in the world she wanted to do was ask for my help, and the last thing I wanted to do was help her. But it was Zach. That kid was the exception.

"Yeah, of course," I said with the sudden realization that I didn't know the first thing about actually taking care of a kid. "Is me picking him up going to be a problem?"

"No, just send me a picture of your driver's license, and I'm going to email a letter to the registrar saying they can let you in to pick him up. When can you get there?"

After some quick mental math, I said, "About twenty minutes."

"Okay, that's great." Then she was silent for so long I had to check my phone to make sure she hadn't hung up on me. When I realized she hadn't, I put the phone back to my ear in just enough time to hear her say, "Thank you."

It was muffled and strained, but she'd thanked me nonetheless. I was concerned that Zach was sick enough to warrant a frenzied phone call to me, of all people.

"Not a problem."

And then she actually hung up.


"Uncle Reed," Zach groaned from the back seat. He had a nasty stomach bug—one I hoped and prayed I didn't catch—and puked all over himself at recess. The nurse sent me away with a few puke bags, one of which he was clasping for dear life against his chest.

I felt so bad for the kid. Being sick *and* being little had to be a pain in the ass.

"What's up, bud?"

"Am I going to die?"

My first reaction was to laugh, but then I thought better of it —catastrophizing was part of being a sick kid.

"No, you're not going to die," I said matter-of-factly. "This stomach bug probably won't last much longer. I bet you'll be running around and ready to go back to school by tomorrow."

"So I don't have the plague?"

That question threw me. What six-year-old knew what the plague was?

"No, you don't. And how do you know what the plague is?"

He readjusted in his seat, his head lolling back onto the leather cushion. He seemed so tiny in the spacious back seat, and I wished I'd had a booster seat for him.

"A boy in my class said only people who have the plague puke like I did, and that meant I was going to die."

Kids were so damn mean. I wanted to turn the car around and haul ass back to the school just so I could give the kid a piece of my mind. Then call his parents and make sure they knew what kind of little shit they'd raised.

"Buddy, I've been in your exact shoes before. I had a stomach bug and look at me now. I'm good as new."

He exhaled heavily and proceeded to hurl into the bag. I cringed and looked away. At least he made it into the bag.

"We're almost there. I'm so sorry," I tried to console him, but I felt helpless. I didn't know how people did this all the time— being in charge of keeping another person alive. It was a daunting task that I didn't feel nearly prepared enough for. But I'd do anything for Josh and Zach.

And it felt an awful lot like something maybe a stepfather would do. It was an interesting realization—that if it all worked out the way I hoped it would, I'd be like a stepfather to Zach. I, of course, wouldn't be more than *like* a stepfather unless Josh and I decided to get married, but I couldn't see that happening unless laws changed suddenly and three people were allowed to be married to each other. But I would love to be *like* a stepfather to Zach.

Until we had children of our own.

And with that equally as daunting thought, Zach puked one more time as I pulled into my reserved spot.

With the puke bag still secure around his mouth, I carried him up the stairs and didn't stop until I set him fully clothed in the bathtub.

On the drive to the school, I'd called the one person I knew would have the expertise required to tell me how to take care of a sick child—my mom. She answered immediately and told me a warm bath always helped. Then she gave me about ten other things to do or try and offered to come by to assist.

I'd told her that it wasn't necessary, but I was regretting that decision when Zach puked in the bathwater only about ten minutes after he'd settled in.

Once I finally got the bathtub and him cleaned up, I laid him down on the couch with a trash can directly beside his head. At least he was resting, and when he was asleep, he was less likely to puke everywhere.

I was watching him intently, prepared for any sign that he was about to get sick again when my phone began vibrating. The caller ID said Josh, and I immediately smiled. My stomach did stupid little flips when I answered.

"Hey, babe."

"Hey, you still at the gym?"

I suppressed a half laugh, half groan and stepped into the kitchen where I could talk slightly above a whisper while still keeping an eye on Zach.

"That's actually a funny story. I picked up Zach from school."

Silence greeted me on the other end of the line, likely Josh processing my statement.

"You picked my son up from school?"

"Yes."

"Why? What happened?" It wasn't my intention to put panic in his voice.

"He's fine, I promise. He is sick, but he's doing... better. Sam was a few hours out for work, and you had your meeting with Rhonda. Apparently, I was the only one that picked up the phone."

In the background, there was the definitive sound of the car door slamming closed and then the rumble of his truck engine. "I saw Sam called, but she didn't tell me it was urgent. She didn't text me either. What's wrong with him? How sick is he? Does he have a fever?"

"Whoa, okay. Hang on there a second. I know you're concerned, but I swear, I have it under control now."

"Now? Like you didn't before?"

I grunted and fought back the urge to call him overprotective. "As much as I love Zach, I'm not his dad. And he's the only kid I've ever really been around, so it was a little... *messy* there at the beginning. He has a stomach bug or maybe the flu, I think. But I just cleaned him up, and he's finally asleep."

Josh sighed, and I couldn't tell if he was relieved or annoyed. "Thank you for picking him up."

"I'd do anything for that kid. It wasn't a problem."

Zach had one arm flung over the side of the couch, with his chin tilted to the ceiling and his mouth partially opened. It was bizarre to me how much he looked like Josh sometimes. It wasn't just the light-blond hair and tanned skin—it was everything.

"I'm on my way home now. I'll be there in fifteen—shit," he groaned.

"What's wrong?" I asked while pouring myself a well-earned drink. The slight burn at the back of my throat as I swallowed the two knuckles' worth of whiskey was followed by warmth in my stomach.

"I told Amanda I would help her with her classroom—something about moving a few things around. But I don't want to leave you by yourself with Zach."

I chuckled and replaced the bottle back in the liquor cabinet. "I've survived this long, I think I'll survive a little longer. Otherwise, we can trade off—you come take care of Zach and I'll help Amanda."

"Guess that makes sense now why she said you didn't answer when she called earlier. You were too busy taking care of my kid."

"Yeah." I shrugged. "This is the first free moment I've had for a while. I'll call her and let her know that she lucked out and got the better end of that deal. I'll take care of her, you take care of him."

Josh's laugh echoed over the line, and my own smile widened. Everything within me lightened.

"Okay, you keep telling yourself that. Just keep my kid alive for the next ten minutes and keep your big head to a moderate size."

"Too late."

# FIFTY-TWO

Amanda

THE SUN WAS NEARING THE HORIZON, AND WITH ALL OF THE aggressive overhead lights turned off, my classroom was cast in a dim, warm light. I actually preferred the few lamps I scattered around the room to the fluorescent ones mounted to the ceiling, but they were not conducive to lab safety.

Everyone else in the building had long since left. I was the only one that was crazy enough to try to change up their room the first day back from spring break. And as the minutes ticked by, I became more and more creeped out.

Every once in a while, I'd hear the custodians moving through the halls or a toilet flush. But eventually they moved to the other side of the school, and I really was alone.

When my phone finally vibrated on my desk across the room, I was in the midst of contemplating leaving for at least the twentieth time. It wasn't necessary at all—rearranging the tables and moving a few other odds and ends—but I'd been wanting to do it for a while, and it was something to keep my mind off the chaos that was my life.

I hadn't spoken to my brother in a week. All of the updates I received on his situation were through Reed, who got them from Will. And I'd told myself that I wouldn't reach out to Adam—that I was no longer responsible for his mistakes. I wasn't going to continue to try to fix his problems and insert myself into every situation in which he needed me. In the nearly twenty-two years he'd been alive, he hadn't once actually heeded my advice except to get him out of trouble in the moment.

But that mindset lasted all of a week before I couldn't take it anymore. Will's updates weren't cutting it, and I grew more and more worried. I spent much of the day before calling and texting him. All I wanted to know was that he was okay.

He hadn't responded to one of my texts or returned one of my calls.

Hurrying around the awkwardly angled tables and precariously placed chairs, I slid to a stop in front of my desk and grabbed my phone. It was the first time I'd felt disappointed at seeing Reed's name scroll across my phone.

"Hey, you here?"

"Yeah, I'm at the side door near your classroom. Come let me in."

My mood immediately lifted even as I muttered, "So demanding today," into the phone. Although Josh was supposed to help me, and I was bummed Zach was sick, I was just as excited to see Reed.

"Just demanding today, huh?" he said as I rounded the corner and spotted him leaning against the brick exterior. "Thought that was an everyday thing."

With a smile, I pushed the door open but didn't have a chance to say anything more before Reed's mouth was on mine. His kiss was automatically intense and all-consuming. Confidently, one hand slipped around my waist, pressing my lower back and flattening my front against his muscular stomach. The other hand fitted around the side of my neck while his fingers tangled in the hair at the back of my head.

All I could do was hang on for dear life as he took exactly what he wanted from me.

So lost in each brush of his lips, the press of his tongue in my open mouth, and the tender yet firmness of his hands against my body, I almost forgot we were in the middle of a school. Abruptly, I staggered backward, putting a few feet of space between us.

"Not here. There are cameras everywhere!" I whisper-yelled.

"I can't help that I've missed you all damn day," he muttered in a low voice as he stepped forward and returned his hand to my cheek. His thumb tugged at my bottom lip and brushed across it. His eyes narrowed to my mouth and watched his finger move. "I've been thinking about your mouth, these fucking lips, all day."

I had no control over my smile, but I couldn't get caught at school dry humping my boyfriend in the hallway. Instead, I grasped his hand and led him to my classroom.

We walked through the door, and Reed let out a low whistle. "Looks like you already got started. That or there was a tornado that touched down just in this one specific classroom."

I rolled my eyes and weaved back through the mess of chairs to my desk. From the top drawer, I retrieved the drawing I'd completed during my planning period. I'd used washable markers to sketch a simple layout of my classroom and where I imagined each piece of furniture.

"A tornado named Amanda," Reed said, stepping into my space. The look in his eye was one I'd seen so many times recently I'd lost count. And one I'd probably never tire of since it usually meant lots of amazingly dirty things. But we had a class-room to put back together.

"Yes, and I'm an F5, especially when provoked. So, please help me before things get even scarier here."

Reed chuckled but pushed up the sleeves of his T-shirt. "Tell me what to do, Teach."

. . .

Half an hour later, the room was nearly perfect. We'd rearranged the tables, reset the lab equipment I'd needed for class the next day, and Reed even fixed my personal single-serve coffee maker that had been broken for longer than I cared to admit.

"That didn't take too long. We did pretty well," I commented while opening a new pack of colorful pens and dumping them into my designated pen drawer.

I looked up to find Reed watching me with one eyebrow raised. "Okay, fine. *You* did pretty well. Better?"

He seemed content, but that look I'd been fending off for longer than I usually could, returned. In the faint light, the warmth of his amber-colored eyes glowed even brighter than usual. Like a sunset I'd beg to burn me alive.

"What's my reward for doing so well, Ms. Allan?" Slowly, he stalked toward me, speaking in a voice that made it clear what kind of reward he was after. My hands braced on the desk in front of me—because I suddenly couldn't keep myself standing—Reed stopped just on the other side.

I ran my tongue along my lower lip, and like I knew he would, Reed followed the movement with rapt attention. "I could think of a few things, Mr. Gregory. Unfortunately, none of them are school appropriate and would likely get you expelled and me fired."

A delighted smile tugged at the corners of his mouth as I played along with the little game he'd begun. Mimicking my stance, he also braced his hands on the table. His strong hands, with prominent veins, flexed against the faux wood surface, and the muscles in his forearms tensed as he leaned farther forward.

"All the best things are against the rules, Ms. Allan. That's why they're my favorite."

"Do you have a teacher-student fantasy I didn't know about?" I asked, gliding my hand across the cold desk and barely brushing the tips of his fingers with my own.

I blinked and before I fully opened my eyes again, Reed was on my side of the desk, wrapping his hands around my thighs and lifting me onto the desk. He stepped between my open legs, and the fabric of his shorts brushed against the bare skin of my inner thighs.

His head dipped, dark hair falling over his forehead as he brushed his nose against mine. His lips trailed a path along my cheek, my jaw, and I shivered in anticipation. There was a definitive pulsing between my legs when his lips brushed mine, and he whispered against my mouth, "I have a student-teacher fantasy when you're the teacher. Had you been my teacher, I couldn't imagine the trouble I would have gotten up to. I probably would have jerked off to your yearbook picture more times than I could have counted."

"So dirty," I whimpered. His tongue darted out and caressed my bottom lip before he sucked it into his mouth. Hard.

"You wouldn't like me as much if I were any other way. Means I'm really, *really* good at doing very dirty things to you."

"Really? In a school, of all places?" A voice to my right spoke into the silent classroom.

My heart leaped into my throat, and I gasped at the unexpected interruption. I straightened on top of my desk, and Reed angled his body between me and the unwelcome visitor.

My brain couldn't catch up with my mouth quick enough, and thinking it was a custodian having caught us in a compromising position, I stuttered out an excuse. Trying to come up with any explanation to de-escalate the situation, my mind finally considered the man standing in the doorway.

His arms crossed in front of his body and with a shoulder leaned against the metal doorframe, CJ stood casually just inside my classroom, wearing a less than enthusiastic expression.

"What the hell are you doing here?" Reed spit out, stepping farther in front of me and all but blocking my view.

The hard set to CJ's features didn't thaw. For several seconds, silence hung between us as we waited for some sort of explanation. I couldn't come up with a decent reason why he would be there, staring at us like he couldn't care less who we were.

"Just running a quick errand in the area."

"That's not an answer," Reed said, gripping the edge of the desk with one hand and white-knuckle force.

CJ shrugged and sauntered farther into the room, casually stuffing his hands into the front pockets of his jeans. Slowly, he started a path around the perimeter, eyeing each piece of lab equipment and poster on the wall.

His presence was wholly unsettling and was genuinely pissing me off.

"You've told me so much about this place, Mandy. I never thought I'd get to see it in person."

I swallowed, and Reed cut his attention to me, silently imploring me with widened eyes to either not respond or watch my words. Either way, I could only heed one of those warnings.

"Does it live up to your expectations?"

He chuckled without looking away from the poster of the human body he was inspecting on the opposite side of the room. "It does. It really showcases your personality—a little messy, yet very… enthusiastic. I like the colors."

"Yes, well, if I'm anything, it's messy and enthusiastic."

He made a sound of approval in his throat and continued his exploration. Reed and I exchanged another look—one of confusion, frustration, and worry. Since I'd known CJ, I'd never felt uncomfortable in his presence until that moment.

Reed reached out his hand, offering to help me off the desk. I slid off and stood next to him. Having Reed steadfastly by my side did wonders for my nerves. I wanted him to wrap me in his arms and bathe me in the calm he created. My mind was racing for a reason why CJ would be there and how he'd gotten inside the school without someone giving him access.

"Did you think you'd come by to catch her alone and off guard?" Reed spit.

CJ scoffed, then calmly muttered. "I have access to her apartment. If I wanted her alone, that would've been easier there."

I don't know if that made me feel better or worse, but it absolutely made Reed even angrier.

"I—" Reed began, but I spoke up.

"Errands, huh?" My question cut off their argument.

For the first time since he walked in, CJ glanced over at us. He wore an impassive expression and only nodded.

That wasn't good enough for me. "What kind of errands?"

He said nothing, and my frustration grew.

"Grocery store? Post office? Have to return a few things to the mall?"

More silence.

"That reminds me, I actually need to go run to the mall. Hazel's mom sent me this beautiful sweater she knitted, and I was going to send her something in return. You know, as a thank-you. But I think shopping online would be the best option. Do you think I could fit an entire—"

CJ's chuckle cut me off. He was almost to the front of my desk, and without realizing what I'd done, I stepped farther behind Reed, who once again angled his body in front of mine. I was trying to get CJ talking using any method possible, including humor and sarcasm, but there was still tension in the air that made it harder to breathe. Like we were all drowning in only an inch of water.

"You can talk about anything, can't you?" CJ asked, and suddenly, I was at a loss for words. So I nodded. "My errands didn't involve any of the things you mentioned. I was actually meeting with your brother."

Everything else around me stopped. My brother? *My* brother? There was no reason for CJ to be meeting Adam. He must have been mistaken, I was sure of it.

Until suddenly, each of my interactions with CJ, especially those that included Adam, were at the forefront of my mind, playing in quick succession. My memory felt faulty, though, in my state of duress.

I remember him taking an interest when he realized my

brother had moved in with me. And their little stare down in my apartment felt like a dick-measuring contest more than anything, at least at the time. But he'd seemed to be aware of my brother's movements even more than I was.

He was the one to call me, frantic and concerned that my apartment had been broken into. That my brother was in danger.

CJ's face split into a devilish, knowing smile. I was sure he saw the confusion and apprehension play out over my face. I felt tears threatening to spill as the strangest thought crossed my mind. But there was no use for tears. Everything in the moment I could feel later—fear was a useless emotion when you already knew what the danger was and where it lurked. Especially when it was standing right in front of you.

But suppressing the anger, frustration, and confusion powering through me was no easy task, and my next question came out choked.

"Meeting with my brother, huh?" I swallowed and glanced up at Reed, something I'd refrained from doing since CJ was staring directly at me, and it felt like a bad idea. He was gazing down at me, concern shining in his eyes as it should have been.

"Yes, meeting with your brother. We had business to discuss. Well, we actually had to discuss his lack of discretion and overall insubordination in conducting *my* business." CJ continued his perusal of my classroom with his hands tucked back into his pockets like he hadn't just admitted that he was the drug dealer my brother worked for. The one he owed nearly one hundred thousand dollars.

*Calvin.*

Understanding washed over Reed's features, and I nodded. He tensed beside me and scrubbed a frustrated hand over his dark stubble. Waves of intense anger rolled off him as CJ took silent, slow steps toward the middle of the room.

Everything we thought we knew was a lie.

Unable not to, I reached out and gently ran my fingers down

the inside of Reed's arm, hoping to soothe some of whatever he was feeling. If Reed was anything, he was fiercely protective.

"Did you know before he moved in that we were related?"

After my apartment was destroyed, Adam confessed that he'd been dealing for longer than any of us could've imagined. He'd worked for Calvin for years. The likelihood that CJ intentionally sought me out to find another way to my brother was completely plausible.

"No," he said with a sigh. "Meeting you was pure coincidence. I had no idea the two of you were related until I saw that photo in your living room. Before that, I really did consider us friends. Still kind of do. Adam talked about you—his big sister who'd always looked out for him. And I knew I could use it to my advantage if I needed to. You were his weak spot. That was reaffirmed at our little meeting tonight."

"Your meeting?"

"Yes, I guess you could say it was eye-opening. Your brother, Mandy, he's a lot of things—he's lazy, irresponsible, selfish, inconsiderate. He has a lot of traits most people would find unflattering. But I *will* say he usually is a good liar."

Knowing I wasn't going to like where he was going, I braced myself for him to continue.

"Had I not already known that he'd gone behind my back to the cops, I probably would have believed him when he lied to my face earlier."

All of the air was sucked out of the room. My panic was at an all-time high, and my mind immediately flashed to the worst-case scenario. Adam was a little shit on the best days, but if he was hurt, no one would compete with the vengeance of an older sister.

"I can see the panic all over your face, Mandy. Don't start to worry yet. He's fine for now, which is actually why I'm here."

Finally, he stopped pacing around the room and propped his hip against one of the tables. He stared at us with intense curiosity, not saying anything more.

Beside me, Reed was humming with energy, and his hands clenched by his sides. There was no doubt that we were both done with CJ's stupid cat-and-mouse games.

"Get to the fucking point," Reed growled.

CJ's chuckle was likely the most annoying response he could have mustered.

"Your brother still hasn't come up with the money he owes me, and I've run out of time. There are bigger players involved— players that expect your brother to pay for the goods he didn't deliver. One way or another, these guys are going to get their money. And… the last thing I wanted to do was involve you, Mandy. I knew I could, but I didn't want to."

"That's why you trashed the apartment," Reed supplied while his jaw ticced.

CJ winked, and the gesture was unsettling.

"I knew it would either scare him straight or, better yet, you would get involved. I knew you wouldn't let your brother take the fall for all of this. You wouldn't let him lose his life over some cash, so you'd find a way to help him, especially when you realized how close to home it all really was. But what I didn't account for was the other two men in your life. They're very good at getting you to do the exact opposite of what I was hoping. Instead of involving yourself, you walked away."

"Fucking leave and leave her out of this then. You said you didn't want to involve her in the first place."

CJ stopped as Reed's voice cut through the nonsense he was spewing. My mind was trying to catch up to everything CJ had said when Reed stepped closer to him. The threat of a physical fight was on the horizon, and I couldn't let it get to that. I hadn't seen a gun or any other weapon on CJ, but that didn't mean there wasn't one there. I didn't have time to think it all through, but I did know that I didn't have another option. Quickly I wrapped my hand around Reed's forearm, stopping him midstep.

Without outright saying it, CJ threatened the safety of my

brother if I didn't help him. He wanted me to bail Adam out and, in turn, bail him out, too.

But there was only one problem.

"I don't have the kind of money you're looking for. I'm a fucking *teacher*," I implored him.

Again, CJ laughed. And I promised to wipe the smug fucking look off his face after all was said and done. Unless Reed beat me to it.

"I know you don't. I've already gone over that option with Adam and even the option of your parents. But that was a lot of work—going to California, convincing them to help me, or better yet, help their son out. It was all too difficult, especially when I need a very quick turnaround."

I shook my head, still not understanding what he was expecting of me if he knew I didn't have the money.

"If you know I don't have the money, then—"

"You don't have the money," CJ said. But then his eyes shifted to my left, and he pointed at Reed like he was issuing a warning and a promise. "But he does."

# FIFTY-THREE

Josh

"He could have just stayed here," I told Sam for the twentieth time as I carried Zach to her car.

He'd finally stopped puking an hour before. I'd sat with him and rubbed his back while he dry heaved into the trash can. I'd made him drink small sips of water and placed a cold washcloth on the back of his neck.

When the sickness finally began to subside, he fell asleep cuddled in my arms—something he hadn't done in several years. I'd genuinely missed it. That's how Sam found us—cuddled on the couch, Zach asleep and me with my eyes only partially open yet still awake enough to grab for the trash can if he started heaving once again.

As carefully as I could manage, I placed Zach in his booster seat and buckled him in. He groaned softly but cradled the blanket he'd stolen from our couch closer to his chest.

I kissed his forehead and gently closed the door.

"I know he could have stayed, and... you would have taken good care of him," she said. "Both you and Reed would have taken care of him."

"We would have, yes."

She nodded thoughtfully and stared off into the distance. "I'm trying to be more open-minded. I'm... I'm sorry that I wasn't to begin with."

Shocked by her apology and unsure how to really take it, I stayed silent.

"I think I always knew you were too much for one person to handle. You always needed two."

And with nothing else to say, Sam patted my arm and climbed into her SUV.

I watched her drive off, thoroughly confused by her complete change of attitude and too exhausted to question it.

Trekking back up the stairs, I pulled my phone from my pocket and dialed Reed. He and Amanda had been at the school for a while, and I hadn't heard a peep from either of them. Although Amanda promised it wouldn't take too long to reorganize and reassemble her classroom, it was easy to imagine them getting distracted by each other.

As my phone rang and I stepped back into our apartment, my mind wandered to the two of them. Reed bending Amanda over a classroom table or laying her on top of it while he kneeled down on the tiled floor between her legs were all inspiring mental images.

But I pushed them all away—at least for a moment—and glanced down at my phone. My first thought when I saw Adam's name across the screen was that he was calling to get his job back. Not that he lost it necessarily—he'd just stopped showing up since the break-in.

Begrudgingly, I answered the phone. "Hello?"

"Are you at the—" Adam quickly whispered. The last part of the question was too rushed for me to make out.

"Am I where? Why are you whispering?"

"*Fuck.* Are you at the school? Amanda's school?" He whispered louder the second time, and my stomach dropped.

I opened my mouth and stuttered a response. But I couldn't

form even one word before the call ended, and I was left staring at the blank screen.

There were no coherent thoughts in my head as I immediately redialed Adam's number and searched for my keys. I spent the entire time it was ringing searching the kitchen until I finally found them under a pile of junk mail. The keys jingled in my hand the moment the call went to voice mail and the automated voice told me the mailbox was full.

I hit redial again. Locking the door behind me and wedging the phone between my shoulder and my ear, I checked my pocket for my wallet.

With all my belongings, I sprinted down the stairs and across the sidewalk to our covered parking spots. A heaviness fell over me when I saw Reed's empty spot right beside mine.

But I had a one-track mind—nothing was going to prevent me from getting to that school or them. Whatever was happening, I didn't care. Something was wrong, or something had happened, but why Adam was calling me, I didn't know.

Nothing made sense. And for every small piece of information I had, I had an infinite number of questions.

I whipped the truck into drive and squealed the tires, trying to speed out of the parking lot. A quick left and a right turn later, and I was dialing Reed's number. Chanting to myself and quietly praying for him to "pick up, pick up, pick up," I blew through an iffy yellow light and glanced in the rearview mirror for red-and-blue lights.

*"You have reached the voice mailbox of—"* the stupid fucking automated voice announced through the Bluetooth speakers.

"Fuck!" I yelled and hit Amanda's name. Each ring was a knife to my chest. Each second there wasn't an answer, I felt further away from them. This couldn't be happening again. Not again.

I wouldn't survive it for the third time.

And like it never existed in the first place, all my hope vanished when I pulled into the school parking lot.

# FIFTY-FOUR

Reed

"That's not happening," Amanda said in a threateningly low tone. She took a step forward like she was going to physically fight him on it, but I stuck my arm out.

"I realized you didn't have the money, no matter how well-off your parents are," CJ said, ignoring Amanda's immediate refusal on my behalf. "That you wouldn't have access to cash like that and also wouldn't be able to get it even if it was your brother's life on the line. But one of the annoying assholes you keep around has immediate access to even more than I need." CJ turned to me. "You were useful, after all."

"No," Amanda said again, but I continued to block her path.

Annoyed, she glanced down at my arm pressed against her stomach and then back up to me. There was an unwavering fight in her eyes I'd seen so many times before. But the longer we stood there and listened to CJ give half-truths and minimal information, the longer she was in danger.

She noticed the resolution and decision play out over my face.

"You can't be fucking serious? You're actually thinking about giving him the money? Reed, I can't let you get more involved than you already are. This is my brother, *my* family shit. *I* will handle it."

I shook my head and shifted her farther behind me once again. She tried to fight me off, but my hands were steadfast on her shoulders.

"It's okay to ask for help or at least accept it when it's offered," I said quietly, so hopefully only she would hear. But the room was eerily silent. Even the air conditioning in the school had shut off, so the mechanical hum couldn't be used to buffer the silence.

"And it's okay to let me fight my own battles," she tossed back through gritted teeth.

"This isn't your battle."

"Although listening to the two of you bicker is the highlight of my night, I'd really like to get a move on," CJ piped up from across the room, but my attention didn't waver from Amanda.

"You're impossible," she said. "Why can't you just let it go? Let me figure it out."

There was only one reason why I did anything for her, and I'd known it for so long that it'd ingrained itself into every part of me.

Without thinking much past her standing beside me, staring up at me with emotions warring across her features, I whispered, "Because this is part of letting me love you. That's why."

And I didn't wait to see her reaction or hear her response. I didn't expect her to say it back to me, especially in that moment with CJ almost close enough to hear our every word.

I turned back to CJ, who didn't show any signs of having heard my confession—I'd assumed if he had, he would have made a comment or a stupid remark. Instead, he impatiently glanced at his watch and then lifted his eye to me in an unimpressed glare.

"How much?" I asked, and I could feel Amanda behind me.

The heat of her body so close to mine, and her breath fanning over the back of my arm, kept me grounded.

CJ laughed. "I'm feeling generous today, so we'll make it an even hundred."

Amanda inhaled a sharp breath, but she kept quiet. I didn't know what number I was expecting, but one hundred thousand dollars felt steep.

"How much of that is your cut?"

Amanda's fingers laced through my own, and she squeezed in a sign I could only conclude was a warning. CJ didn't seem upset by my question, though. He chuckled and paced back up the aisle between the blacktop tables.

"Enough of it. I did have to deal with Adam, and I had to hold off my California contacts. They were ready to let Adam pay in... *other* ways last week. It's only thanks to me that her brother is still alive."

Before I had a chance to say anything, Amanda scoffed. "Excuse me if I have a hard time thanking you for anything. Honestly, if I'm going to do anything, it's going to be blaming you." I knew she was scared—I could feel the slight tremor in her hand that was still wrapped in mine. But her voice was steady.

"It would be misplaced if you did," CJ argued, walking back toward the classroom door. "Mandy, I understand you love your brother, but he's a fuckup. He can't hold down a job. Hell, he couldn't even make it a week in community college, and he's a shitty-ass drug dealer. He has nothing going for him. It's not my fault that he chose this. And it's also not my fault he's in this situation."

CJ stopped in the doorway and glanced around the room. "For someone so smart, you sure are really fucking stupid when it comes to him. Every decision he made to get himself into this situation was his own. He could've just walked away. He could've said no."

My patience was gone. With my pulse hammering in my

neck and the sound pounding in my ears, I stepped forward and eyed the scissors placed in a *"Best Teacher Ever!"* coffee mug on the corner of Amanda's desk. I wasn't sure what my plan was, but I knew I needed a backup option in case things went further south.

"Thank you for that, Nancy Reagan," Amanda chastised. And further south things went. "You can't say no when your life is being used as collateral. I love my brother, and I'm telling you right now that's not a weakness."

CJ's demeanor changed instantly. He rolled his shoulders back and cracked his neck. His stare was firm on Amanda, who stood confidently at my side. Her own stare was just as hard and unwavering.

"Let's go. *Now,*" he commanded in a voice that left little room for argument.

When neither of us made a move, CJ shifted, flashing the metal of a gun tucked into the waistband of his jeans and purposefully hidden beneath his jacket.

My skin pricked with awareness, and my breath faltered for a moment. Out of the corner of my eye, I noticed Amanda stiffen beside me, realizing she hadn't missed the intentional threat.

The scissors I kept in my sight weren't going to do shit against the Glock propped against his hip. Don't bring a knife to a gunfight and all...

But that didn't change my only goal—to keep Amanda safe. Protect her at all costs. The gun didn't make things easier, but it also didn't make things impossible. If she was okay, they would be okay—she and Josh would be okay without me.

My mind was scrambling for a plan while I tried to keep an eye on CJ's hands and watch his face. His sneer was cemented in place, but his fingers twitched at his sides, prepared to reach for the gun at a moment's notice. I knew he wouldn't shoot me—injuring me wouldn't help him get his money. However, I knew without a shadow of a doubt that he'd hurt Amanda to make me more amenable.

I noticed every small movement he made, and I was acutely aware of the way Amanda's breath had quickened.

"We're leaving, and at this point, I don't give a fuck if I have to use lesser methods of persuasion to make it happen, Mandy. Your brother owes me, and some very powerful people, a lot of money."

The tension around us was stifling. CJ's hands were shaking and his voice was uneven. The calm he exuded when he walked into the room was long gone, replaced by a man that was just on the right side of insanity. A man who'd lost himself to greed and chaos and was willing to take anyone—including us—down with him in his pursuit of what he wanted.

I'd lost count of the number of times I'd shifted to keep Amanda behind me, but I did it again. The more space between her and the man with the gun, the better.

My body was buzzing with the effort it took to stay calm.

"Walking out of this classroom is the best thing you can do for him. And when I have my money in my hand, the three of us can have a nice long conversation. I have a few things I want to say to him after this is over."

Patience long gone, CJ reached for the gun, and I shoved Amanda toward the wall behind us. I didn't even have a chance to tell him that I'd willingly go with him. Vibrating with anger, I took a step and then another but was stopped by the familiar click of someone racking a gun.

My first thought was that I was too late, and I waited for the impending shot. The pain. Maybe the sound of the shot if I lived long enough to hear it. But I'd kept my eyes laser-focused on CJ's hand, and he hadn't yet freed the gun from his waistband.

"If you have something to say, why don't you just tell me now?"

As still and steady as I'd ever seen him, Adam pressed the muzzle of a gun against CJ's temple.

"A-Adam?" Amanda stuttered and clambered up from where she fell into her desk chair after I'd forced her back into it.

Amanda stopped next to me, and Adam glanced in our direction before quickly turning back to CJ in the same second.

With a grin, he said, "Hey, sis. Kind of funny, right? I'm the one rescuing you for once."

# FIFTY-FIVE

Amanda

I STRUGGLED TO COMPREHEND WHAT WAS HAPPENING. IN A MATTER of minutes, I'd gone from being fearful for my brother's life and terrified for my boyfriend's to being relieved to see a gun pressed to CJ's cheek. My heart was pounding furiously, and I couldn't seem to take a full breath. Each was greedily stolen by my blind panic.

"What are you—" I couldn't even get the entire question out before CJ was fuming.

"What the *fuck* do you think you're doing? I thought you couldn't get any dumber." Even with Adam's gun pressed into his skin, CJ reached for his own. I flinched back, and Reed threw a protective arm in front of me.

Without hesitation, Adam wrapped his hand around CJ's gun before he had the opportunity to. Freeing it from his waistband, Adam kept his own gun trained on him while he set CJ's on the ground and kicked it back and away from us all.

"It's not smart to talk shit when you're not the one holding the gun."

Those were the last words I heard before the room burst into chaos. The first man that charged in, holding a gun of his own, ordered Adam to drop the weapon and get the fuck back. Thankfully, Adam did as he was told and handed the gun over to the officer. Several more men and women, all dressed in various uniforms, badges dangling from their necks and pinned to their shirts, hurried into the room and secured the scene.

I pressed my back into Reed's front, and he wrapped his arm around my chest.

The room descended into mayhem, and I almost missed CJ being slammed to the ground by two officers that were even larger than him. The snap of the cuffs could barely be heard over the chatter and movement but was nonetheless satisfying.

When they hauled him up, dirty-blond hair a mess and his jacket torn, his calm facade was back in place. Like it'd never slipped at all.

We all had our breaking points—I guess CJ's was figuring out that his extortion plan was falling apart.

While the men, and a few women, surveyed my classroom and hauled CJ out into the hall, Adam weaved through them all to me and Reed.

"Hey, guys. Glad that's over," he said with a smile that I nearly slapped off his damn face.

"What. The. Fuck. Is. Going. On?" I asked and crossed my arms over my chest, waiting impatiently for an answer. "I don't hear from you all week. You ignore me for the past twenty-four hours, and yet here you are, being fucking Superman, swooping in to save the day."

He gave an unimpressed look, squinting his eyes and tilting his head to the side slightly. "Superman, huh? I thought it was all a little more Batman even though neither of them uses guns, but—ouch!"

I slapped him, not in the face, but in the arm. Either way, I made sure it stung.

I appreciated a joke probably more than the next person, especially to cut the tension, but his humor felt like he was making light of the terrifying situation we were just in and his part in all of it. Because that was the real issue—his choices had affected the people around him. It wasn't just his life he was playing with anymore. And the consequences weren't just his own.

"Are you seriously sitting here cracking jokes when we could have died?" Angry tears threatened to fall, but my will was stronger than the flood of emotions. The relief was indescribable. Relief that no one was dead, that both my boyfriend and my brother were standing there with me, still breathing. And that relief felt so good, but the outrage was just as potent.

Adam swallowed and looked from me to Reed. If he thought Reed was going to be on his side or try to placate me, he was sorely mistaken. All he did was shift his hand up my back to my neck and give me a reassuring squeeze.

"I wasn't going to let you die. *No one* was going to let you die, and no one was going to let Reed give him any money," he sighed and glanced around the room. Only a few of the officers and what I recognized as DEA agents were left. "You know I made a deal, right? Help them nab Calvin and a few of the other top guys in exchange for a lesser punishment."

I nodded and leaned farther into Reed for the added support.

"That's what I've been doing for the past week. I knew CJ had reached his limit and he couldn't wait any longer to get the money. He took me to one of his safe houses and was prepared to hand me over to them when he got a better idea. The guy I was stuck in the safe house with was an undercover DEA agent. After Calvin left, he called our team up and we hauled ass to follow him. They were taking forever, standing in the parking lot talking about letting y'all come out before we barged in because they didn't want a hostage situation on their hands. But I was done waiting."

"How'd he know?" I seethed, and Adam looked confused. "How did he know to find Reed? That he would have enough money?"

He didn't answer—his terrified, dumbfounded expression gave him away.

"You told him," I supplied quietly. He told CJ that Reed was loaded. He told him that we were both at the school. In one of the rambling messages I'd left for Adam, I'd told him that we were probably going to be at the school for a while. My own brother had sold us out.

"It was—it was completely unintentional. I—"

"Allan!" one of the officers called from across the room, probably louder than necessary. Both Adam and I jerked our attention to him, and he clarified, "Adam, we gotta talk."

Adam closed his eyes and shook his head, turning back to me. "I couldn't be more sorry. I'm sorry to both of you. But I may or may not have stolen his gun when I decided to come in here. Not sure what that will mean for me, but..." He trailed off but peered down at me with a never-ending sadness in his eyes.

"I promise, sis, this is the last time I'm ever going to see that disappointed look on your face."

---

Reed and I stepped out of the school, but I was still on edge. The sun had been replaced by the moon, which was low in the sky. And the high temperatures had given way to the slightly cooler night air.

The officer and DEA agent in charge of the joint team approached us not long after Adam walked away. And as I was in the middle of stuttering another apology to Reed, who wouldn't hear it.

They explained only the details they could, which wasn't much since the investigation was still ongoing.

The older man and younger woman explained that they weren't aware CJ would come after us. The plan—which we were not privy to—didn't include him leaving the safe house. Apparently, CJ was the only one in on his own plan to find the money through other methods—namely, Reed through me. They said that Adam only mentioned Reed casually and not, in their opinion, enough for them to think he'd be in any danger.

But neither Reed nor I were satisfied with their answers. Especially Reed, who was brimming with rage and hung on to me tighter as he berated the officer and agent for their lack of planning and responsibility.

After several minutes of subtle threats from my irate boyfriend, I stepped in, trying to finish the conversation.

"Well, now we all know that we would've probably preferred the cast of *Criminal Minds* or *Law & Order* to the two of you. But not much we can do about your incompetence now. Either way, I'm gonna go home, fuck my boyfriends, and then take a hot-ass bath. I think that's how you celebrate surviving a near-death experience." I'd left the room without looking back.

"I shouldn't be surprised by anything you say anymore," Reed mumbled into my hair, carrying my bags and still keeping me close with an arm around my shoulders. The doors clicked softly closed behind us, and we both took long, deep breaths.

"You shouldn't, but we're going to have to figure out how to tell Josh about all of this."

The words had barely left my lips when someone began yelling to our left. And like my need to see him had summoned him from thin air, I lifted my head to find Josh running toward us across the parking lot.

"Josh, I—" My words were knocked away as he barreled into me. He cradled me to his chest with one hand while the other reached behind me and tugged Reed as close as possible. His warm, sunshine scent overwhelmed everything else around me, and I settled into it. Being cocooned by my two men was undoubtedly the safest place I'd ever been. The three of us were an impenetrable force, unwavering against anything and anyone.

"You two—fuck—" With his cheek pressed against the top of my head, his voice broke over a sob. He stroked his hand down my back and then stepped back, lifting it shakily to my face.

His eyes were glassy and rimmed with red. And my heart shattered at the sight. He opened his mouth to speak again, but his jaw quivered. Quietly, he stuttered a shaking breath, his eyes stormy and pleading.

From behind me, Reed's hand appeared against Josh's cheek and then wrapped around the back of his neck. Their eyes met over my head.

"Told you I'd take care of her," he said quietly, snaking his other arm around my hip and pulling us all even closer.

"Adam called me. He was only on the phone long enough to ask me if I was there. He… umm… he hung up before I could ask any other questions, but I drove straight here either way. When I pulled up and saw the cop cars and vans, it was like the beginning of my worst nightmare. Like it was all going to happen again. Knowing that both of you were in there, and I had no idea—"

His voice shook, and I cupped his other cheek in my hand. His scruff scraped against my palm, and I urged his eyes to meet mine with a soft squeeze.

"We're here. We're fine."

"You could have just as easily not been fine," he argued. "I can't," he continued in a softer tone. "I can't lose anyone else."

One single tear spilled down my cheek. My broken, sunshine man wasn't ever going to lose anyone else. Not if I had a say in it. "Luckily, it didn't go that way, okay?" My voice wavered slightly, and at first, he wasn't convinced. But the longer we stood there together, the more he relaxed. The fear slowly dissipated and was replaced with the same relief finally beginning to flow through me.

"I'm going to kill your brother," he muttered.

"Not unless you beat me to it."

"Me three."

"And fucking CJ?" he added and then scrubbed a hand through his hair, making each strand stick up in several directions. "I never liked him. Mostly because I thought he wanted you, not Reed's money or leverage, but still, I can't believe it."

"How do you know about that?"

"I've been pestering everyone out here since I got here. They finally gave me some sort of information. The rest of it I overheard."

"Doesn't seem like he's going to be going anywhere soon, though," Reed murmured, and we all watched CJ get loaded into the back of one of the DEA vans. The van door slamming was music to my ears.

"Let's go home," Josh muttered, and I smiled.

"Yes," Reed chimed in with a decadent smile. "Amanda's already decided what exactly is happening when we get there, too."

Josh's eyes darted between us then his lips lifted in a similarly devilish grin. One that made awareness dance over my skin and excitement buzz through me.

"It involves a hot bath and both of you inside of me... at the same time."

His smile grew, and Reed chuckled behind me. Suddenly the ground disappeared from beneath me as Josh swept me into his arms. My laughter was genuine when he spun us around and started for the few cars still in the lot.

Still carrying my bags, Reed kept pace behind us. I watched him over Josh's shoulder, and his attention bounced between my face and Josh's very shapely ass, hugged in light denim jeans.

I realized we were heading toward Josh's waiting truck.

"Wait, I drove my car. Reed drove his car. We're both in the other lot." Josh's steps didn't falter. Instead, he sat me down next to his truck and pinned me against it with one hand on the window next to my head and the other wrapped around my neck.

His thumb stroked my jaw, and I couldn't seem to catch my breath. Not too far away, people were still packing up and leaving the school, and somewhere I heard Reed open the truck door and promptly close it. But I was too utterly consumed by the man in front of me to comprehend much else.

"I'm not letting you, *either* of you, out of my sight for a good long while. I need you both in my bed where I know you're safe. I'm not going to lose another person I care about. And I'm done with the close calls, too."

If my heart wasn't already broken, it was then. Hearing him say again that he couldn't lose someone else was my undoing. Between losing his mother to his abusive father and nearly losing his brother and sister-in-law to Valerie, Josh had seen situations go the other way. It was a heavy burden he carried with him every day, and no matter how much I wanted to help, it was impossible for me to carry enough to make it much lighter.

But damn it, if I didn't try.

"Okay," I said, and the seriousness of the moment dwindled with his smile. "How are you so perfect?" I asked and immediately made a face. "*God*, that was cheesy. I sound like you two. What have you done to me?"

He tossed his head back and laughed his intoxicating laugh. "I'm not perfect. I'm just really fucking in love with you."

Any thought I had in my head immediately disappeared. I knew my face had to display my shock, but Josh's smile didn't falter. Both of his hands cupped my cheeks, and he pressed a soft, chaste kiss to my parted lips.

The thing was, I had felt the same feelings for so long. I was more surprised that either of them felt it and was willing to vocalize it, too. Which was absolutely insane since they'd shown me in every other way possible that they loved me.

So, I wasn't going to question it. I wasn't going to analyze their feelings and deconstruct every little minute action leading up to this moment. I wasn't going to consider all the possible ways our carefully constructed relationship could shatter around us.

For us to work, I knew I couldn't hold back.

"Well," I said when he pulled back. "That's good because I'm just really fucking in love with you, too."

His smile widened, larger than I ever thought imaginable. My entire body flooded with happiness, and his mouth was on mine again. It was a quick kiss but was filled with all of the other emotions he hadn't vocalized.

"Okay, get in the truck," he said, kissed me one last time, and then reached to open the door behind me.

I slid onto the black leather seat and across to Reed, who leaned against the other door. He opened his arm, and I tucked myself into his side.

"He told you he loves you, didn't he?" He pressed a kiss against my temple, and suddenly, I was apprehensive. There wasn't a hint of jealousy in Reed's tone, nor was there a stiffness in the way he wrapped his arm around me. But the possibility of that one little word changing everything was there. We'd come so far, so I hoped that wasn't the case.

"Yes," I said hesitantly. An officer that was leaving the school stopped Josh as he rounded the front of the truck, giving Reed and me a few seconds alone.

"I'm not surprised. I can't believe it took him this long actually."

A little surprised, I leaned back and surveyed his expression. "Why?"

He chuckled and reached forward, taking a strand of my hair that had fallen from my clip between his fingers. "Cielo, we've both been in love with you since you walked into that damn classroom freshman year. We've been in love with you for over a decade, and it's been nearly impossible keeping it to ourselves."

It was a strange feeling—the lightness in my heart and the warmth collecting in my chest.

Unable to help myself, I twisted and swung my leg over Reed, straddling his lap with ease. My palms pressed against his dark scruff, and I enjoyed the scratch of it against my skin. His large hands gripped my hips and urged me to settle farther down against him. I could already feel him hardening beneath me as I scanned his features.

I loved the few lines around his eyes and mouth. They were the same ones Josh had and were evidence of laughter and happiness. And *God*, I loved his lips. They were plump and pouty and the perfect pink. I ran my thumb over his bottom lip as I got lost in his eyes.

He had the longest, dark lashes and amber eyes. Sitting so close, it was easy to see the various brown shades, lighter yellows, and oranges with a hint of green.

"I love you, too," I whispered against his mouth, and his smile prevented me from kissing him properly.

"Stop smiling so I can kiss you," I mumbled, and he dragged one of his hands up my side until his fingers were tangled in my hair. The other pressed against my lower back, and I willingly moved where he wanted me.

"I can't help it. I've been dying to hear those words come out of your mouth. Talk about heaven."

And then he finally did kiss me. And like Josh's kiss, Reed's kiss filled all the parts of me that I didn't realize were empty.

Behind me, the driver's side door opened and quickly closed. "How did I know this is exactly how I'd find the two of you?"

I glanced backward and, in the rearview mirror, noticed the smile in Josh's eyes.

Reed slid me off his lap and handed me the seat belt. "Let's get our girl home so we can both participate," he said with a wink.

# FIFTY-SIX

Josh

STANDING IN THE MIDDLE OF MURPHY'S, WAITING TO MEET THE NEW owner, I felt just as shitty as I did when Rhonda told me she was selling the place. My stomach was in knots, and I couldn't stand still, let alone sit. I needed a way to burn off the nervous energy, and pacing seemed like the easiest way to do so.

Rhonda giving me first dibs was a kind gesture, but I knew I'd never come up with the money. I'd only told her a few months ago that I wasn't going to be able to swing it and it would be better to start searching for an actual buyer.

I didn't realize that meant I'd be standing in the bar the first weekend of May, waiting to meet my new boss.

It was several hours until open, and the smell of the disinfectant from the night before was still in the air.

Amanda and Reed had invited themselves along, and the entire ride to the bar consisted of Amanda trying to lighten my mood one way or another. She'd almost been successful, but the moment we pulled into the parking lot, it soured once again.

Everything was going to change. Whether Rhonda believed it or not, nothing would be the same. She swore up and down that the new owner—one with decently deep pockets and a personal tie to the area—had no intention of changing much. He'd even promised to keep most of the staff the same.

He wanted to keep me on as the manager, but with my shitty-ass mood, I wasn't sure I was going to make the best impression.

For all that had happened in Murphy's Law—the good, the bad, and the horribly ugly—it was more of a home to me than anywhere else had been. Reed's apartment had become a close second, especially since Amanda practically moved in with us after her apartment was destroyed and CJ was arrested. But nothing would change the comfort the four walls around me provided.

"Babe, why don't you sit down? You're making me dizzy just watching you," Amanda said.

I'd been pacing next to the main bar for at least ten minutes, lost in my own thoughts, while we waited for Rhonda and the new guy.

"I can't sit."

"You're going to make yourself crazy. It's going to be okay," Reed chimed in. He was the epitome of calm, seated on a barstool and leaning back against the bar top. He was extra tan after our recent trip to the lake, and if I wasn't in the middle of an existential crisis, I'd want to make sure my lips touched every part of him.

"Easy for you to say," I snapped. "You haven't been working here for the past ten years, working your way up from barback. This place holds so much of my life—the good and the fucking bad."

Amanda slid from her stool only a few feet away and was about to cross to me when Rhonda finally appeared from down the hallway leading to the office upstairs.

"Oh, great, you're both here. I thought I'd be a little more sad, but honestly, I'm just excited to turn this place over. My oldest granddaughter is going to be ten next month, and I promised her I'd be there for her birthday."

In her hands was a manila folder and what I assumed were the keys to the bar. And in the years I'd known Rhonda, she'd never looked more at ease or relaxed. If anything, I knew selling the place was the best move for her.

"In this envelope is everything that wasn't in the closing documents. We've got the information for the security system, the cleaning service we use, and a couple of the handymen that haven't tried to price gouge me. Anything that's not in here is on my computer that I'm leaving."

Reed stood from his seat at the bar as Rhonda crossed to him. He willingly took the manila folder she offered. "Otherwise, here are the keys, and Murphy's Law is officially yours."

She dropped the keys to the bar in Reed's outstretched hand. Then they hugged, which was awkward since he was nearly a foot taller than her.

"Couldn't imagine leaving her in better hands." Rhonda patted Reed's arm and turned to me.

The world stopped for a moment. My attention darted between Reed and Rhonda—Rhonda was excited and hopeful, while Reed appeared apprehensive and maybe apologetic? To my right, Amanda stood with her mouth agape and her eyes wide.

Reed bought the bar. He'd purchased Murphy's Law. He was my new boss, and I'd had no idea.

Once I fully comprehended what was happening, the first thing I felt was betrayal and confusion.

"Okay, well, I'm going to get the hell out of here. Josh, hon, I'll come see ya before I head out of town," Rhonda said as she patted my arm and hurried out the front door.

"You…" I started but couldn't say anything else before I cleared my throat. "You bought… the bar?"

Reed sighed and set the manila folder and keys on the bar. He turned to me and, in a resolute tone, said, "Yes."

I scoffed. "What the fuck, Reed? When? Why?"

"I approached Rhonda about it right after you told us…" He

motioned between himself and Amanda. "I called her while we were at the lake. She said that since you couldn't buy it, it was mine."

I'd begun pacing again. My entire body was filled with unexpended frustration and energy. It felt like the only way to expel it was by walking a hole into the laminate floor.

"What the fuck? Didn't I tell you that I didn't want this—that I didn't want you to buy it?"

"I mean..." he began, preparing to argue before finally he sighed and agreed. "Yes."

Whether I'd said it explicitly or not, he knew what I meant. He knew I didn't want this.

"But you did it anyway?"

Calmly he ran a hand through his hair. "I did, but—"

"No. Don't try to give me some bullshit to try to get out of this. This is the last thing I wanted. Now you're what, my boss? I understand you have money, Reed. We all know that you've got a bunch of fucking money, so it's not necessary to go around flaunting it and buying random shit. I can't believe you bought this place!"

By the time I was done, I was yelling, and Amanda was at my side.

"Josh," she pleaded.

"Did you know?" I looked down at her. My jaw was sore from grinding my teeth together, but all attempts to relax were futile. She'd appeared just as shocked as I was when Rhonda handed over the keys to my home to Reed, but I wasn't so sure anymore. I didn't know what to believe.

"No," she implored me. "I didn't know."

There wasn't an ounce of deceit on her face or in her voice, but it was little help since our other partner had deceived us both.

"Do you really think I did this to flaunt my money?"

I knew he hadn't. Reed had never been one to show off, but

the hurt I felt won out, and I found myself saying, "I don't know what to think anymore."

The hurt I felt was reflected in his eyes, and if I had been in a better headspace, I would've taken my words back.

"That's bullshit. You know me better than that. Is it so hard to believe that I was trying to do a nice thing?"

I stopped pacing for a moment and laughed. "How was this nice? You bought it so someone else wouldn't? Sure, that's great, but now you're my boss. We already have so much stacked against us and our relationship, Reed. Do we really want to add that to it? An employee-boss relationship that is sure to blow up in our fucking faces?"

He turned to the bar and braced his hands against the dark wood surface. He let his head hang down between his shoulders, and there was a small pang in my chest. I wasn't trying to hurt him, but I couldn't understand his motives. I felt like he'd been plotting behind my back for months with the intention of pulling the rug out from under me. We'd already been through so much, I didn't understand how he could do this to us.

"We're a company."

Amanda and I looked at each other, both of us confused about what he'd just said.

"What do you mean?" Amanda asked.

Reed straightened and gave us both his full attention as he stepped forward. "I started a company. You'll both need to sign a few things, but all three of us are equal owners. I purchased the bar with the intention of transferring the ownership to our company if you both agree to it. My dad—" His voice broke over the word, and Amanda closed the distance between them. I was frozen to my spot.

Amanda linked their hands together and then stood between us. Reed gave her a soft smile before he continued, "After I talked to my dad about us, he suggested it. It's the only way to make sure it's all equal. Anything owned by the company will belong to the three of us. If we one day decided to buy a house, we would use the company for that as well."

"But you didn't buy it under the company," I clarified. *"You* bought it."

He nodded. "I did, but only because it all happened faster than I could get the paperwork in order." He noticed the disbelief on my face and took another step forward. "You told Rhonda that you wouldn't be buying this place back in March. I had to jump on it immediately, otherwise she was going to list it, and we'd all be fucked. What would you have done if, at the beginning of March, I approached you with this idea?"

I was silent because he was right. I probably would've told him he was insane and it was too soon to be making life-altering decisions like those.

"Exactly," he said, again reading my expression perfectly.

"Stop fucking reading me like that," I ground out, which made him smile.

"I can't help it." He wrapped an arm around Amanda's shoulders, leaned down, and kissed the top of her head. I don't think anything warmed my heart more than watching the two of them together.

"This still doesn't make sense," I argued, and Reed sighed loudly.

"What else do you want me to tell you, Sunshine? I bought the bar. I want the three of us to own the bar together and decide how we want to go about everything else involved *together.*"

"That doesn't explain why the fuck you did it, though. Especially when I specifically told you not to do it!"

"Because I fucking love you!" Reed yelled back.

I stepped backward, initially caught off guard by his confession. But of all his reasons and arguments, that one actually made the most sense.

I'd whispered the same words to him—without the profanity —one night after I knew he'd fallen asleep. I just wanted to know how it would feel to say them to a man. But Reed wasn't just any man or any person to me. He was one half of the loves of my life.

And I knew love made you do impulsive, crazy things.

"I fucking love you, too," I said simply. And he nodded at me. I nodded back, and Amanda cheered and fist-pumped.

"Fucking finally! I've been waiting forever for the two of you to get over yourselves and just say it. No more awkward pauses when we're saying goodbye or going to bed."

"So glad I could help," Reed muttered, and I gave up my argument. Although I didn't want him to buy the bar just for me, I knew he hadn't meant it as anything more than a kind gesture. A way to show his love.

I stepped up to them, pulled Amanda into my side where she fit perfectly, and weaved my fingers through the soft hair at the base of Reed's neck.

"Just because I love you doesn't mean you're off the hook. This was a lot of money."

His honey-brown eyes sparkled with mischief and a lopsided grin pulled at one side of his lips.

"Well, then I'm going to have a lot of fun figuring out ways for you to pay me back."

He didn't give me a chance to respond, instead pulling me in for a long, lingering kiss. I licked against his lips and was immediately rewarded with a deep groan that rumbled through his chest.

One of his large hands fisted in the front of my shirt as we both deepened the kiss. I responded with a groan of my own.

Reluctantly, I pulled away to find Amanda staring up at us with a hungry desire in her eyes.

"Let's christen it," she offered with a grin, and without a word between us, Reed and I both moved to lift Amanda onto the bar. Every inch of the place would have to be disinfected again by the time we were done, but that was the last thing on my mind. Staring at Amanda in her little sundress propped up on the bar, I knew she didn't have anything on underneath it.

And Reed knew it too when his hand began gliding up the inside of her thigh.

I'd never been so sure of something before, but that was exactly where I wanted to be for the rest of my life—with the two of them.

Reed reached Amanda's bare pussy, ran his tongue over his lower lip, and smiled at me.

"Our dirty girl."

# EPILOGUE

Amanda

*Two Months Later*

"ARE WE READY?" I ASKED MY TWO MEN AS WE STEPPED OUT OF Reed's SUV. Josh smiled and nodded while Reed grunted before reluctantly nodding.

It had been a long two months of learning all we could about the bar business and readying Murphy's Law for its grand reopening under new management.

We'd made minor, mostly cosmetic changes and had to close the bar for the previous two months until the work was complete. There were also a few of the staff that weren't keen on the change, so we began a hiring spree a few weeks ago.

Of the three of us, I was the most hands-off. Thankfully it was July and I was still on summer break, but the end of the school year was not the time for me to take on a new venture. With everything going on, I didn't have the capacity to be too active. Besides, Reed and Josh had it more than under control. The two of them worked so well together, they really didn't need my input, and I was happy to mostly observe. I didn't plan to stop teaching, and neither of them expected me to.

I'd finished out the school year, but being in my classroom the first few weeks after the incident was panic inducing. Which meant I immediately put in for a transfer to a new classroom for the beginning of the new school year.

Maybe at that point, my brother and I would be speaking. But I wasn't holding my breath.

Whether intentional or not, he'd mentioned Reed's name to CJ. He'd told him in no uncertain terms that Reed was wealthy and where he could find us. His stupidity had nearly killed us both in the process.

But after CJ was arrested and Adam realized we weren't immediately going to forgive and forget everything that happened, he flew directly to California with his probation officer's approval. He'd returned a week later and took that job at the auto body shop, cleaning and doing a few administrative tasks. Keeping a steady job and completing regular, yet unannounced, drug tests were both requirements of his probation.

Five years of probation and no jail time for his part in capturing CJ, who turned out to be only one midlevel criminal in a well-organized drug trafficking organization. With the investigation still ongoing, details were limited. But we knew they were selling some new and highly-addictive drug. And everything CJ'd told me and Reed seemed to be true—he'd decided the moment Adam moved in with me that I would be easy collateral. If ever he needed it, he'd use me to keep Adam in line or, eventually, use me to force Reed to pay Adam's debts when he realized I had no money of my own.

Attorney Will, as I liked to refer to him, was the only reason I knew anything. He'd kept us apprised of the investigation until Adam's part was complete. That was until the trial started—if there even was one.

But luckily, we all had plenty to keep our minds off of my brother. The guys had worked so hard, and we'd all decided that once the bar was back open, it would be Josh's business. We would only be as active as he wanted us to be. Otherwise, Reed would focus on the gym, and I would focus on teaching.

Outside the bar above the door hung a sign that read, *"Grand Reopening!"* Other than that one detail, the place looked mostly the same. We'd repainted and refinished the exterior and updated a few fixtures, but we'd kept the original character of the building and what made Murphy's, Murphy's.

Before heading inside, I reached for Reed, who, even when he was feeling left out, couldn't deny me. I pressed onto my toes, gripped his broad shoulders, and kissed him. The kiss was not work appropriate, but neither of us cared. Especially when I opened my mouth for him and allowed his tongue to taste the remnants of Josh's release still fresh on my tongue.

As he tasted me and Josh mixed together, I could feel him relax beneath my hands.

"You play dirty," he whispered against my lips.

"That's because I'm your dirty girl."

All of us took a combined breath and headed toward the door. The first thing that greeted us when we walked in was the glorious air conditioning we'd replaced and the upgraded sound system we'd installed throughout the rooms.

Behind the bar, the bartenders were busy setting up for the party while others ran around wiping down tables and finishing the few decorations I'd insisted on.

"It's my turn on the way home," Reed whispered as he kissed my forehead and walked off to make sure everything was running without a hitch. Josh kissed me, too and told me to relax before he jogged after our boyfriend. The two of them were immediately in deep conversation about what was happening behind the bar.

"Your face may get stuck if you keep smiling like that." I hadn't even realized I was staring at Josh and Reed and smiling like a lunatic.

"Thanks for the unsolicited advice," I said, turning to Hazel, who already had a margarita in her hand. Her chestnut-brown hair fell around her face in loose waves and her black dress flowed around her knees. "How do you always look so effortlessly perfect?"

She rolled her eyes, tried to suppress her smile, and handed me her drink. "Here. I think you need it more than I do."

She was right. For myself, I wasn't so worried about this venture. I was more worried for the two men who were diligently reorganizing coolers behind the bar. For them, the success of the bar meant so much more. I needed it to be a success for them.

"I'm sorry I can't provide more stress relief—all I've got is alcohol. I'm a great listener, though."

I laughed and then sighed. She was the best kind of friend—supportive in all the right ways. "It's okay. I kind of gave Josh a blow job in the back of the car on the way here. That did a little for both of our nerves."

Hazel closed her eyes and shook her head while she laughed quietly to herself. We made our way to the bar, grabbing two stools right in the center while she told me about the book she was currently writing.

"Oh, and I think I've convinced Luke that Sadie needs a sister. My mother keeps bothering me about grandchildren, so I'm sure she's going to be less than enthusiastic about us getting another dog instead."

One of the new bartenders we hired—whose name completely escaped me—acknowledged us and mouthed "one minute" while she finished talking to Grady, who waved and hollered, "How's it goin', boss?"

"I told you not to call me that," I yelled back, but all he did was laugh. Turning back to Hazel, I asked, "Y'all have been married less than a year. She's really expecting them *now?*"

Hazel shrugged. "Yes, and it doesn't help that if it were up to Luke, I'd be pregnant already."

"Yes, she would be," Luke added, coming up behind her.

"She's going to be fucking beautiful pregnant and such a good mom. I can't wait."

I gawked at them as Hazel rolled her eyes at his compliments but smiled nonetheless. "If you hadn't already written a book about the two of you, I would tell you to. I'm sure this man gives you more than enough material."

They kissed, and Luke headed to help Josh and Reed carry supplies to the back bar.

"Wait, did you talk to your parents?" Hazel quickly changed the topic and leaned forward in her seat. Her eyes were wide with anticipation.

"Yes, and they reacted exactly as I knew they would—with grunts and groans and other sounds of disapproval. Then they told me that they believed it was a phase, that no person could sustainably live in a *'ménage à trois.'*"

I'd expected the response when I decided to tell them that Reed, Josh, and I were not only in a relationship but also living together. I'd held off telling them because I really didn't want their opinion to rain on my parade. But having the truth hanging over my head was beginning to frustrate me. I wanted it all out in the open and I truly did not care what they thought.

Their disapproval meant I was doing something right.

But Hazel's face flamed with anger. "I'm sorry, but your parents are absolute assholes."

"Don't be sorry, it's the truth." I didn't mention them questioning my intentions. They wholeheartedly believed that I was dating Reed and Josh for attention since I'd always had a knack for the dramatic.

"Everyone knows now, right?"

I couldn't help the smile that crossed my face thinking about when we'd told Mama G. She'd invited us back over for dinner at their house, and in the middle of the meal, Reed had announced it to his parents.

Of course his father already knew which Mama G was not happy about—she wasn't keen on being left out. But her initial reaction was one of shock and then pure joy. There were so many tears and hugs all around. Their support was unwavering and unconditional.

That's the kind of reaction I would remember rather than my conversation with my parents.

"Yes, everyone knows."

"Hey, ladies. How are y'all?" The bartender approached us with a smile. The first thing I noticed about her besides her strawberry-blonde hair was her small-town Southern accent. I immediately remembered her interview and how I was impressed not only by her résumé but also by her demeanor and smile.

"We're good. I'm—"

"Amanda," she finished for me with a smile. "I remember. You're one of the owners—one of my bosses."

I nodded as she grabbed the tequila. "Two margaritas, right? Do we want them spicy?"

Hazel shrugged. "Why not?"

"How's everything going?" I asked while she grabbed two jalapeños and muddled them.

"It's going well, I think. Everyone's nice and laid back." She skillfully poured the tequila into the shaker and reached for the lime juice like she'd been behind the bar for years.

"Where are you from?" Hazel asked while she shook our drinks.

"This small town north of here. It's kind of a drive-through city, like a flyover state, but... on the ground." She laughed nervously and filled two glasses with ice before straining the drink into each.

"And you just moved here?"

"Yes," she said, not concerned about our inquisition and more focused on the drinks in her hands. "Decided it was time for a... change." There was a hint of apprehension in her voice, but she quickly continued, "I'm coaching the girls' varsity volleyball team at one of the schools around here, and I'll be doing this a few nights a week."

She smiled when she set the drinks in front of us and garnished each with another jalapeño.

"Well, we're happy to have—"

"Two of my favorite girls!" I hadn't finished welcoming our new bartender, whose name I still couldn't remember when a familiar voice called out behind us. Large tattooed arms encircled me and Hazel, and a tall form stepped between us.

"Nice to see you, too, Devon." Hazel laughed. He kissed the top of her head and then mine and glanced at our drinks.

"Spicy margs? We really are celebrating."

"Want one?" our gorgeous new bartender asked him. Devon, always slightly quiet around new people, gave her a small smile but shook his head.

Maybe I was making it up, but I thought I saw a little bit of interest in both of their eyes as each quickly observed the other. I'd gone crazy, but all I could imagine was the two of them—the strawberry-blonde bartender and our redheaded friend—and how fucking cute their babies would be.

Out of the corner of my eye, I watched Hazel cut her eyes to me, raise her eyebrows and her attention bounce between the two of them. Maybe I hadn't made up the chemistry between them.

"Just a beer." He specified which one, and she spun to retrieve it.

I opened my mouth to ask what he thought of her but was yet again cut off by a boisterously booming voice.

"Dev, you trying to steal our women?" It was Josh that time. He, Reed, and Luke were all three rounding the bar, smiling at the three of us.

"I would definitely be an upgrade," he joked and they all greeted each other with handshakes and manly hugs. Reed squeezed into the barstool next to me, his hand reflexively gripping my thigh, while Josh saddled up behind me, a hand settling on the back of my neck.

"Everything good to go?"

"We're all set," Reed confirmed with confidence. It was the first time in two months I'd seen the two of them even close to relaxed.

Josh wrapped his arms around my shoulders and leaned down to speak low so only Reed and I could hear him. "I think this is going to work."

Reed smiled. "It's absolutely going to work."

If Josh hadn't leaned forward and kissed him, then I absolutely would have.

"Ugh, get a room, you three," Luke said with mock disgust from the other side of Hazel.

We all three simultaneously gave him the finger.

"You're one to talk. I'd bet my third of the bar that you couldn't stop touching Hazel for more than five minutes."

Luke looked like he was contemplating the bet. But when he looked at his wife, he smiled, clasped his hands against her cheeks, and kissed the shit out of her. We all broke out into laughter.

"Exactly." Reed chuckled. In front of us appeared two whiskeys for my men and another beer for Luke down at the end.

"Shit, guys, sorry I'm late." Without looking, I knew the exasperated voice belonged to James.

"Were you working on a fucking Saturday?" Luke questioned.

Devon chuckled beside me. "Why are you acting surprised? Let me guess." I glanced over my shoulder in time to see Devon point to James's suit sans tie and disheveled blond hair. "You fell asleep in your office again."

James scrubbed a hand over his stubble which was also evidence of his office stay. He was almost always clean-shaven unless he hadn't had access to a razor.

"Anybody need anything else?" the bartender asked. And I was finally annoyed enough with myself for not remembering her name that I leaned forward and grabbed her attention.

"I'm so sorry. I feel awful. But could you remind me of your name?"

She smiled and opened her mouth to respond, but it was James behind me who said, "I-Ivy?"

At the sound of her name, the bartender—Ivy's—face dropped slightly. Devon stepped aside to allow James through. The moment he stepped forward to the bar, Ivy stepped back and her face became unrecognizable. Her bright-green eyes nearly darkened and any sign of a smile had completely vanished.

"What—what are you—" James stuttered over his words—something else I'd never heard him do.

And then it all clicked.

"Oh!" I exclaimed. "This is *your* Ivy from back home."

Neither of them looked at me, but I could feel everyone else's understanding around me.

"Not his Ivy," Ivy said in a low voice. "Not anymore."

My face flushed with my mistake and the obvious tension I'd intensified with an inadvertent slip of the tongue.

"What are you doing here?" James finally asked.

"I work here," she gritted out like it was painful to do so.

"Since when?"

"Yesterday."

"Why?"

She sighed and threw her arms out. "What does it matter to you?"

James laughed and braced his hands against the bar. "My friends own the place. I've been coming here since college. I still come here often. You take your pick."

She shook her head, opening her mouth to respond but quickly snapped it shut. She glanced at Josh. "Can I take a break?"

Josh nodded behind me, and Ivy quickly left the bar and headed to the back hallway, which led upstairs to Josh's office, the supply rooms, and our newly finished break room.

"What the hell was that all about?" I asked, but James didn't respond.

"I'm going to go talk to her," he proclaimed.

Hazel shook her head. "I'm not sure that's a good idea."

James ignored her, though. Shaking his head, he said, "No, nothing good can come from leaving it be. I'll be back."

And without another word, he was striding after her, also disappearing down the hallway.

"Anyone want to go play referee?" I joked, and there were a few small laughs around me.

"I'm sure they'll figure it out," Reed provided, and Devon nodded.

"Well," Josh piped up. "Since she's on a break, I'll jump back there." He rounded the bar and grabbed a clean towel, throwing it over his shoulder.

"You did always look good behind the bar. Confident," I said with a smile. I leaned forward, propping my elbows on the shiny wood surface and pressing my cleavage together. Josh licked his lower lip in response. There was a thud from above us, and for a split second, I was concerned about James and Ivy upstairs. But my attention was, once again, quickly stolen by Josh.

He leaned over the bar between us and whispered so only Reed and I could hear, "If you keep doing that, I'm not going to be able to stay back here for long."

"Stop flirting. You should be working," Reed supplied.

"You say that while your hand is sliding up my thigh and under my dress."

Reed's smile matched Josh's—dirty and full of promises that would leave me a puddle on the floor.

"When we get home tonight, we're actually celebrating," he whispered into my ear. His hand against my thigh disappeared as our new barback called his name.

"Music to my fucking ears," Josh said before he walked to the other side of the bar and began cleaning more glasses and reorganizing the same bottles for the third time.

It was just Hazel and me again, and she scooted closer to me. "You look happy."

My smile never faltered around the two of them. Happiness wasn't a descriptive enough word for what I felt with them. Even when we weren't together, I could feel them all around me.

Sometimes I got caught up in how we began and where life had already taken us. It seemed completely unbelievable that we'd made it work. But my outlook had changed. I'd gone from thinking the worst would always happen to believing that whatever was supposed to happen would.

Mostly I'd become one of those gross people walking around with hearts in their eyes all the time and making everyone else around them feel uncomfortable. And I was loving every fucking second of it.

If anyone else could feel what I did, they would understand. It was impossibly big, nearly infinite, and unforgettable.

"Yeah," I said, resting my head on Hazel's shoulder. "I'm really, *really* fucking happy."

THE END

# ACKNOWLEDGMENTS

This book was so much fun to write. I know I told so many people during the writing process how much I loved these characters and their stories. I even annoyed myself with how giddy I became when talking about it.

But Reed, Josh, and Amanda's dynamic is exactly what I hoped for when I set out to write their story—one is not more important than the other in their relationship. And they all play an integral part in how they work. Their banter and chemistry is exactly what I hoped for.

I knew from the moment I mentioned their hot night at the lake in *Unexpected* that their story was far from over. I loved the three of them together so much that it couldn't have worked out any other way.

As always, thank you so much to my Beta readers for your patience and feedback. And thank you to my amazing editor at My Brother's Editor for everything you do.

And the cover is absolutely perfect thanks to Mayhem Cover Creations.

Finally, thanks to my husband for always supporting my long hours in front of the computer. And for only raising his eyebrows slightly when I told him I was writing an MMF romance. After a short explanation of what that meant, his support, as always, was unwavering.

I really hoped you loved this book! Now, who's ready for James and Ivy…

# ALSO BY GRACE TURNER

If you haven't already, check out *Unexpected,* book one in the Murphy's Law series.

And to stay up to date on the rest of the Murphy's Law series and everything else Grace has to come, make sure to check out:

instagram.com/graceturnerauthor

facebook.com/graceturnerauthor

tiktok.com/@graceturnerauthor

amazon.com/author/graceturner

goodreads.com/graceturner

# ABOUT THE AUTHOR

Grace Turner lives in Houston, Texas with her husband and two rambunctious pups and has a revolving door full of friends and family always visiting. By day, she works as a lowly paralegal, and by night she reads, writes, and breathes contemporary romance.

Printed in Great Britain
by Amazon

29436574R00324